ART OF FRIENDSHIP

Erin Kaye was born in 1966 in Larne, Co. Antrim to a Polish-American father and an Anglo-Irish mother. She pursued a successful career in finance before becoming a writer. Her previous bestselling novels include *Mothers and Daughters*, *Choices*, *Second Chances*, *Closer to Home* and *My Husband's Lover*. She lives in North Berwick on the east coast of Scotland with her husband Mervyn, two young sons and Murphy the dog.

D1147418

ERIN KAYE

Art of Friendship

AVON

This novel is entirely a work of fiction.
The names, characters and incidents portrayed in it are the work of the author's imagination. Any resemblance to actual persons, living or dead, events or localities is entirely coincidental.

AVON

A division of HarperCollins*Publishers*
77–85 Fulham Palace Road,
London W6 8JB

www.harpercollins.co.uk

A Paperback original 2010
4

Copyright © Erin Kaye 2010

Erin Kaye asserts the moral right to be identified as the author of this work

A catalogue record for this book is available from the British Library

ISBN-13: 978-0-00-734036-1

Set in Minion by Palimpsest Book Production Limited,
Grangemouth, Stirlingshire

Printed and bound in Great Britain by
Clays Ltd, St Ives plc

FSC is a non-profit international organisation established to promote the responsible management of the world's forests. Products carrying the FSC label are independently certified to assure consumers that they come from forests that are managed to meet the social, economic and ecological needs of present and future generations.

Find out more about HarperCollins and the environment at
www.harpercollins.co.uk/green

All rights reserved. No part of this publication may be reproduced, stored in a retrieval system, or transmitted, in any form or by any means, electronic, mechanical, photocopying, recording or otherwise, without the prior permission of the publishers.

For the ‘Fabulous Four’ who inspired this story.

Chapter One

People said that time heals all wounds. But Janice Kirkpatrick knew that wasn't true. She could remember every minute of that New Year's Eve – the one just after she'd turned eleven – as though it were yesterday. She bit her lip, closed her eyes and, by sheer force of will, made the memories disappear. Just as she had done for the last twenty-seven years.

She opened her eyes and tried to focus on the present. It was the thirty-first of December and she was locked in the en-suite bathroom with her dearest friends – Patsy, Clare and Kirsty. Downstairs, the party was in full swing, the thud of a glam rock hit from the seventies reverberating through the thick walls of the house in Ballyfergus.

'Okay. Who's going to make their New Year's resolution first?' asked Patsy, a buxom, petite blonde perched on the lid of the closed bidet, her satin peep-toes the colour of bubble-gum. She hiccupped and slapped her hand over her mouth. Janice and the other two women giggled, the sudden exhalation of their breath causing the flames of nearby candles to flicker.

Janice, who was lying in the empty claw-foot bathtub, a champagne flute held aloft, felt suddenly uneasy. She wasn't in the habit of making resolutions, not public ones anyway.

'Aren't you supposed to keep them a secret?' asked Clare,

at thirty-five, the youngest woman in the room. She had one of those faces that could, with the right grooming, look striking. But in spite of all Janice's encouragement and advice over the years, Clare just wasn't cut out to be a glamour-puss. Tonight, enthroned on the closed toilet seat, she wore a plain black dress and sensible low heels, her long brown hair tied back severely in a diamanté clasp – her only apparent concession to the festive season.

'No,' said Patsy, waving the objection away with her hand and coming perilously close to spilling champagne on her black pencil skirt. 'Sure, if we can't tell each other,' she said, stopping to suppress another hiccup, 'who can we tell?'

Janice didn't like New Year's Eve and the retrospection and sentimentality that accompanied it. And the alcohol she'd consumed wasn't quite enough, yet, to obliterate all the dark thoughts. The idea of hosting the party – which she did every year – was to fill the house with noise and laughter in an effort to displace the depressing nostalgia she always associated with this night. However, she was well aware that her three closest friends had a more optimistic take on life and resolved to humour them.

'How about you, Kirsty?' said Janice, addressing the woman seated cross-legged on the laundry bin, a solid teak chest specially imported from Thailand. It suited the oriental theme of the black-and-grey tiled room – Janice's serene retreat from the world beyond. But before Kirsty had time to answer, Janice added, 'I know what *your* resolution should be.'

'You do? Oh, don't tell me. Let me guess. Time for me to get myself a man,' said Kirsty, rolling her pretty grass-coloured eyes. Unlike Clare, Kirsty's natural beauty did not require much in the way of enhancement. Tonight she wore little more than mascara and lip gloss and she looked gorgeous in a green halter-neck dress that matched the colour of her eyes and complemented the autumnal reddish tone of her shoulder-length hair. She could do with being a tiny little bit thinner – if she was a size eight, like Janice, and a tad taller, she would be model material.

'Not exactly,' laughed Janice. 'But it is time for you to have some fun. Time to get out and about and start dating. You need to remind yourself that you're a *woman*.'

'I know I'm a woman,' tutted Kirsty good-naturedly, swiping her hand in Janice's direction. 'I don't need a man to find that out.'

'Janice's right enough, though,' said Patsy, who was the oldest of the group, a full decade older than Kirsty and fancied herself a bit of an agony aunt. 'It might do you good to get out and meet *new* people,' she said euphemistically, though what she really meant by 'people' was men. She pulled herself up to her full seated height, the buttons of her grey satin blouse, the colour of Janice's eyes, straining against her large bosom. Patsy's eyes, the grey-green colour of the sea on a dull day, twinkled with mischief.

Kirsty let out a soft sigh and smiled, her eyes moist in the candlelight. 'I suppose you're right,' she said and immediately Janice regretted any pain she might have inadvertently caused. But before she could speak, Kirsty cleared her throat, raised her champagne glass and said gamely, 'My New Year's resolution is to . . . to get out more and date.'

'Too vague,' said Clare.

Kirsty's hand dropped to her side in frustration and she looked imploringly at Janice and Patsy. 'What should I say then?'

Janice spoke first. 'Clare's right. You need to be more specific. How about saying that this year you will date at least ten men?'

'Ten?' gasped Kirsty incredulously.

'Steady on, Janice!' said Patsy, almost choking on a mouthful of champagne. She pointed at Kirsty. 'Where in the name of God is she going to meet ten decent men? Have you seen what passes for eligible bachelors in Ballyfergus?'

'Point taken,' said Janice with a giggle. 'How about five, then?' Patsy raised her right eyebrow just a fraction and Janice rolled her eyes.

'Okay. Four. Come on! That's only one a quarter. Surely you could manage that? Unless of course the first one turns out to be The One and then you don't have to date any more!'

'Chance would be a fine thing,' said Kirsty with a wry smile and then, more upbeat, she added, 'Okay then. This year I will date at least four eligible bachelors.'

'Great. Well done, Kirsty,' said Patsy, sounding like a proud mum.

'Okay, someone else now,' said Kirsty, looking pleased to have her turn, like a visit to the dentist, over and done with.

'Kirsty, darling, do the honours,' said Janice, presenting an empty crystal glass to Kirsty who reached into the ice-filled sink and pulled out a bottle of Bollinger. Using a fluffy hand-towel to capture the beads of water that ran off the bottle like perspiration, she refilled Janice's glass.

'Thank you, sweetheart.'

'Anyone else for a top-up?' asked Kirsty and, in response to the murmurs of assent, she proceeded to dispense the effervescent straw-coloured liquid in the over-careful manner of the mildly inebriated. When everyone's glass was filled to the brim, she put the empty bottle back in the sink, alongside the one they'd finished earlier.

'So, what about you, Patsy?' said Kirsty. 'What's your resolution going to be?'

'Well, you know I've always wanted to go to Africa and on safari?'

'Yes!' said Clare. 'I remember you talking about it the very first time we all met at that art class. How long ago was that?'

'Fifteen years this September,' said Janice, quick as a flash. She'd signed up for the art class within weeks of moving to Ballyfergus, a busy port on the East Antrim coast, in the hope of finding new friends.

'God, you've an amazing memory,' said Clare. Janice smiled and wished this wasn't true – she wished she could edit her memories like digital photographs, ruthlessly choosing which ones to keep and which to discard.

'We should celebrate,' went on Clare, earnestly. 'It's quite special, isn't it, staying friends, the four of us, all this time?'

'I know! How about a girlie weekend in London?' said Patsy. She slapped her thigh like Doris Day in *Calamity Jane*.

'New York!' cried Janice. 'Think about the shopping.'

'Steady on,' said Clare, with a nervous laugh. 'We haven't all got platinum credit cards.' She flushed slightly and chewed the skin on the side of her thumb. Janice silently chided herself for being thoughtless. Clare was a stay-at-home mum to two small children and she and her accountant husband Liam had limited means.

'Mmm, Clare's got a point,' said Patsy. Her forehead creased into a frown, she rested her chin on one hand and pouted her red lips. Then she sat up suddenly and cried, 'I know. We could use my brother-in-law's place in London for free. Eamonn only uses the flat during the week. He's always on at me and Martin to go there.'

'He wouldn't mind us lot pitching up?' said Kirsty cautiously.

'Hell, no!' laughed Patsy.

'We could get a cheap flight,' said Clare thoughtfully, now chewing the nail on her little finger.

'Okay then. Let's do it,' said Janice decisively.

'Brilliant! No time like the present,' said Patsy, rising unsteadily on her heels. She tugged at her skirt, bunched up around her shapely hips. 'I'll go and ask Eamonn right now. He's here tonight.'

'But what about your New Year's resolution? I'm the only one who's made one so far,' said Kirsty, sounding peeved about the fact.

'Whoops!' Patsy sat down again abruptly, and grinned lazily. 'Forgot about that.'

'You were talking earlier about the African safari,' prompted Clare, who appeared the most clear-headed, though it was hard to tell. She could drink copious amounts and still appear relatively sober.

'Oh, yeah,' enthused Patsy. 'It's something I've always dreamt about. Ever since I was a little girl. It's our twenty-fifth wedding anniversary this September. And this'll be our second honeymoon. The one we never had first time round.' She stared at the wall, an enigmatic smile on her lips.

'What did you do for your first?' asked Kirsty.

'A week boating on the lakes of Fermanagh.'

'Sounds romantic.'

'It was,' said Patsy and she gave Kirsty a suggestive wink that made her friend blush. 'We never had the money back then to go abroad or do anything fancy. Martin had just got promoted to Assistant Manager in Bangor and he wasn't earning much. And neither was I. We spent the first four years of marriage saving up to buy our first house. Then I fell pregnant and there was never the money to go off and do something so indulgent. With kids there's always something more important to be spending your money on, isn't there?'

'You can say that again,' agreed Kirsty with a vigorous nod.

'But this – this'll be special,' went on Patsy dreamily. 'I know it'll be expensive but I've been stashing a bit away here and there from the gallery's profits. It's going to be fantastic!'

'Does Martin know?' said Janice, thrilled by Patsy's infectious enthusiasm.

'That's the best bit! It's going to be a complete surprise. I'm going to book it all and then only tell him at the last minute.'

'He'll need his jabs though,' cautioned Janice, a seasoned traveller. 'He'll know something's up then.'

'Okay, so I'll keep where we're going a secret. I've been looking at Botswana and September seems to be a good time to go – it's between rainy seasons.'

'We'll have to do our London trip after then,' observed Janice. 'Maybe October.'

Kirsty looked at Clare. 'And what's your resolution?'

'I'm going to take up painting again,' Clare said quickly, as though she had been waiting to be asked. 'Seriously this time, no amateur stuff. That's my resolution.'

There was a short pause while everyone took in this unexpected news.

'Jesus, you're a dark horse, Clare McCormack,' said Patsy, sounding surprised. 'You never said a thing before.'

'I've been thinking about it for a while,' said Clare, staring at the empty glass in her hands. She sounded like she was making a confession. 'I've done the mummy thing and, well, it's about time I got back into the real world, I think. That's why I'm thinking of painting.'

'Commercially?' said Patsy, and she sat up straight, her interest as art connoisseur and gallery-owner stimulated despite her lack of sobriety.

'Don't you think I'm good enough?' asked Clare, too quickly, her glance bouncing between Patsy and the glass in her hand like a ping-pong ball. Then, as though it was too much of a distraction, she set the flute on a shelf behind the loo and folded her arms. She blushed, her insecurity laid bare.

'Hell's bells. You're more than good enough,' enthused Patsy. 'Sure, before you had the children, your pictures sold like hot cakes at the annual art show,' she added, referring to Clare's striking watercolours of local scenes. Janice nodded in agreement.

'Yes, but that was all very . . . very amateur,' said Clare. 'I'm thinking of trying to make a career out of it.'

'And you will, Clare. Won't she, girls?' said Kirsty, looking round the room for support.

Everyone nodded. 'Just think, you could be the new Sam McLarnon,' Janice said, referring to a highly regarded local artist who, like Clare, specialised in watercolours of the East Antrim coast.

'If I was half as good as Sam, I'd be delighted,' said Clare.

The conversation turned to the going rate for a McLarnon watercolour and Janice tuned out. It was her turn next to make a resolution but she had no idea what to say. Clare's clear-headed ambition served only to underline the inherent futility of her own existence. She didn't make resolutions as a rule, past experience having taught her that what happens, happens. You just have to ride the wave of life, deal with it, cope. Just as she had always done. Fate dealt you a hand and it was foolishness, almost bordering on arrogance, to think that you could actually influence it.

Just as she hated looking back, Janice abhorred the notion of planning ahead. She'd discovered long ago that the best way to deal with life was to live, like a child, in the moment.

The making of resolutions implied that you had control over your life. And Janice knew that this was not the case.

Still, she had more sense than to share these deterministic views with her friends. She didn't want them to think her depressing on this of all nights, when as well as looking back, everyone wanted to look forward with hope and optimism. And most of all she didn't want to disappoint them.

'Your turn, Janice,' said Clare, right on cue.

'Well,' said Janice, clearing her throat. 'I've decided that this year I'm going to . . . to start a new project.'

There was silence, the others waiting for her to go on, assuming she had some further clarification to share with them. Patsy nodded her head encouragingly.

A loud rap on the door saved her. 'Janice, are you in there?' said her husband's voice.

'Yes, Keith!' she shouted in response. The women collapsed into a spate of girlish sniggering, like they'd been caught smoking behind the bike sheds at school.

'Who's in there with you?' said Keith, not waiting for her to answer and sounding slightly peeved. 'You've been gone ages. People are wondering where you are.'

Janice peered at the gold Rolex on her arm and said, in a stage whisper, 'Shit! Is that the time?' She pulled herself to her feet, hoisted her long black velvet dress to her knees and stepped gingerly out of the bath. 'It's just me and the girls in here, Keith,' she shouted. 'We're coming.'

And then to the other women she added in what she thought was a whisper, 'Come on, girls. It's gone eleven.'

They filed sheepishly out of the bathroom into the bedroom, where Keith stood with a smile on his face, but not in his eyes. At fifty-two, he was fourteen years older than Janice but he still had the build of a rugby player – stocky legs, broad shoulders and muscled arms. He wore smart dark blue jeans with a brown belt and soft chocolate suede shoes. His white shirt sleeves were rolled up to the elbow. His greying hair suited his tanned face – by anyone's standards, he was a handsome man.

'What were you doing in there?' he whispered, as he took Janice proprietarily by the elbow and steered her along the landing after the others.

'Not so fast, Keith,' she protested, shaking off his hand. 'I can't walk in these heels.'

'You can't just go off in the middle of a party and leave me like that,' he persisted.

She stopped to face him at the top of the stairs. Down below in the hallway, people milled about, the sound of their chatter rising like a chorus, and the rhythmic beat of too-loud music filling the air. In heels she and Keith were on a level, nose to nose. She could see from the softness in his hazel eyes that he wasn't really angry with her. Just a little annoyed. 'I'm sorry,' she said. 'I didn't realise we were in there so long.'

'But you're neglecting the other guests.'

The truth was Janice didn't really care about the other guests. She wanted to spend time with her best friends. Most of the people downstairs were business contacts of Keith's. Though she would never admit this to her husband, she found them intimidating. They were lawyers, barristers, doctors and the like – all the well-heeled of Ballyfergus. She felt intellectually inferior to them.

'Aren't the staff doing their job?' she said, referring to the caterers they'd hired in for the night to serve food and drinks.

'Yes. But that's not the point, Janice. You're the hostess and it's rude to abandon your guests.'

Janice opened her mouth to speak, then closed it. He was right of course. And then she remembered, as she had done every single day for the last fifteen years, what she owed him. This knowledge didn't loom large over their marriage – and no doubt rarely crossed Keith's mind, if at all. But it was never far from Janice's, and it moderated all her thoughts and actions. She did not resent Keith because of the debt she owed him, far from it. She was inordinately grateful. But it was there nonetheless.

'Janice?' said Keith.

'Huh?'

'What are you thinking?'

'Nothing,' she said brightly and smiled. 'I'm sorry. I didn't . . . think. It was rude of me. Come on, let's go down.'

'Just a moment,' he said, reaching out to flick a lock of dark chestnut hair off her shoulder. 'Have I told you that you look gorgeous tonight?'

'Thank you,' she replied automatically and returned a frozen smile, self-conscious and awkward. Keith's frequent compliments had her spoiled. So often had he told her he loved her and that she was beautiful, that she had become immune to his praise. It wasn't that she doubted the sincerity of his words. They just did not penetrate the surface of her, as though they were arrows meant for some other target, someone more worthy.

'There you are, Janice! Keith!' came the sound of Patsy's voice from the bottom of the stairs, demanding their attention. 'You've got to come and see this. Hurry up!'

'We'd better go down,' said Janice, without looking back, and she picked her way down the steps. At the bottom, Patsy grabbed her by the hand and pulled her in the direction of the large drawing room. When she glanced over her shoulder Keith, swallowed up by the crowd, was nowhere to be seen.

Chapter Two

Patsy led her into what used to be the playroom. Now that Pete was nearly eighteen, it served as a second, more informal, lounge. Someone had pulled both of the black leather sofas into the centre of the room facing each other, thereby switching the focus from the big flat-screen TV in the corner to the coffee table between the sofas. There were a dozen or so people in the room.

Patsy let go of Janice's hand and, sauntering her way across the cream shag-pile carpet, called out, 'Don't start without us!'

Janice spotted Martin sitting on the edge of the sofa fiddling with his mobile phone, his huge feet like plates on the floor. His legs were so long his bony knees jutted up awkwardly, like he had been badly folded. Skinny as the lamp in the corner, he had a tousled mop of brown curly hair and a long, thin face. Physically he was not Janice's cup of tea, but he was a great guy. And, in spite of the physical differences between him and his curvy wife, they were a perfect match for each other. Patsy hopped onto the arm of the sofa, put her arm round Martin's shoulder and kissed the top of his head. He looked up and winked, beaming.

'Come over here, Janice,' said Patsy, waving her across the room with an urgent flapping of her right arm. Janice went and stood behind Martin so that the coffee table was in clear view.

'This'll never work,' said Martin.

'Give it a chance,' said Liam, Clare's husband, who sat opposite him.

Liam's slight build and boyish face made him seem younger than a man in his late thirties. This impression was reinforced by his bright periwinkle eyes and, when he became very animated, the peculiar and entirely unconscious habit of raising the pitch of his voice. Clare and Kirsty, who were almost the same age and great friends, had gravitated towards each other and now stood talking behind the sofa. They each held a fresh glass of white wine in their hands and paid no attention to what was going on around them. Even though Janice was only a few years older than them, she had more in common with Patsy – perhaps because, unlike Clare and Kirsty, they both had grown-up children.

Liam spotted Janice and said, 'Great party, Janice. Come here and see this.' He pointed to the table where three mobile phones were laid out in an arc.

'What are you doing?' asked Janice, perplexed.

'A party trick! Just watch,' declared Liam with gusto. 'Ah, there you are. Thanks, Pete.'

At the mention of her son's name, Janice looked up, surprised. Under his choppy highlighted hairstyle his face was lightly freckled and his delicate frame was bony under a t-shirt and low-slung jeans. He dropped a handful of caramel-coloured kernels into Liam's hand, a half-smile on his face. Or smirk, depending how you looked at it.

'Right. We're ready to rock,' said Liam. 'Just need one more mobile phone.'

Another phone hastily appeared. Liam placed it on the table with the others so that they formed an even-armed cross shape, with a space in the middle. The top of each phone was six inches from the one opposite. Liam said, 'Now call each mobile on my signal.'

Janice was sure Pete caught her glance but, if he did, he chose to ignore her. She fixed her gaze on the mobile phones. Pete wasn't supposed to be here – he had said he was going out. He must've changed his plans, she thought, and tried not to allow his presence disturb her. Pete folded his arms and watched Liam with a bemused expression on his face.

'Okay, key in the phone numbers now,' said Liam and he scattered a few of the kernels on the table, in the space at the centre of the cross.

'Popcorn!' exclaimed Patsy.

'Hit dial now!' ordered Liam and, after a few seconds' delay, Martin's phone began to ring followed quickly by the others.

The room fell silent, everyone fixated on the vibrating phones. Even Clare and Kirsty suspended their conversation to watch.

'What's supposed to happen?' said Janice, but no-one replied. The phones continued to trill. After several rings, they stopped, presumably as they tripped to voice mail. Janice looked around at a roomful of puzzled faces. Pete had his hand up to his mouth. He seemed to be trying not to laugh. Janice looked away.

'I don't understand. I saw it on YouTube just the other day,' said Liam, and he glanced at Martin who raised his eyebrows and shook his head. 'The energy in the mobile phones cooks the popcorn.'

Suddenly Pete emitted a loud burst of laughter and everyone looked at him. 'Oh man!' he cried and slapped his thighs theatrically, his wiry frame bent double with hysteria. Then he straightened up and composed himself enough to say, 'I can't believe you actually did that. Everyone knows that YouTube video was a hoax. It's, like, *months* old.' The left side of his lip curled up in an Elvis-style sneer. 'How could you think a few phones would emit enough energy to pop corn? You're a total dork, Liam.'

Janice closed her eyes briefly, her face already aflame with embarrassment. Liam bit his bottom lip, grabbed his mobile off the table, and stuffed it in his pocket. Clare shot Pete an angry look and Janice opened her mouth to speak, then closed it.

Pete was nearly a grown man. He should know better. More to the point, she and Keith should've taught him better and she, and everybody in that room, knew it. She put a hand over her eyes in shame.

'Any more drinks?' called a cheerful voice and Janice looked up, grateful to see a young man, one of the waiters, holding out a tray of glasses – red and white wine and champagne. The tension in the room was dispelled immediately as several people made a dive for the drinks and a chorus of good-humoured ribbing went up from the men in the room.

'Well, Liam, boy,' said someone. 'It looks like you'll have to get a microwave to make your popcorn, like everyone else.'

'It'd be a lot cheaper than four mobile phones,' said someone else while Pete slipped from the room.

'And you can do more than four kernels at a time,' added another and Patsy, in a fit of giggles, nearly fell off the end of the sofa.

'Okay, okay. Point taken,' said Liam, permitting himself a glimmer of a smile and raising his hands, palms outwards, above his head, surrender fashion. He added, through gritted teeth, 'Bet I wasn't the only one duped, though.'

'I thought it would work too,' said Clare, in defence of

her husband. 'And you don't know till you try, do you?' She placed her right hand on Liam's shoulder and gave it a little squeeze. Fleetingly, he touched her hand with his own.

'Phew!' said Patsy. 'It's only clever people with degrees in science and physics and . . . and whatever would know it wouldn't work.'

'Hey, are you saying we're not clever?' said Martin good-naturedly, as Janice walked quickly over to the door just in time to watch Pete sauntering up the hallway. All merriment had evaporated – she was suddenly and completely sober. She felt a hard, cold knot in her stomach like a stone. She snatched a glass of champagne from the tray, knocked it back in one, replaced the glass and followed him, keeping her eyes fixed determinedly on the place between his jutting shoulder blades.

'Janice!' called Keith's voice. 'Over here.'

'I'll be there in a minute,' called Janice, her voice like iron. She did not move her eyes from Pete.

He stopped to talk to two of his friends in the doorway to the kitchen – what were they doing here? Free drink of course, she realised, noting the beer can in Al's hand and the crystal tumbler full of amber-coloured liquid in Ben's. From the glazed expression on Ben's face it looked like he was already well-acquainted with the contents of the spirit cabinet. But that was the least of her concerns right now.

For just then a young waitress, not more than sixteen, with her blonde hair scraped back in a severe ponytail and not a scrap of make-up on her fresh face, turned sideways to navigate her way past the boys, who were blocking her way into the kitchen. Not one of them made any attempt to move. She raised the tray above her head, facing Pete and smiled at him in an embarrassed sort of way. In one swift movement, so quick Janice almost missed it, he put his hands up, grabbed the girl's breasts and squeezed them hard. The girl let out a yelp like an injured puppy, pulled the tray down like a shield across her chest and stumbled past him into the kitchen.

Seconds later Janice reached him. Ignoring Al and Ben, she grabbed Pete by the arm and dug her nails in hard enough for him to flinch. Pete didn't appear surprised to see her. In fact when he turned to face her with that knowing smile on his face, it was almost as though he was expecting her. She put her palm on the handle of the cloakroom door and hissed, 'In here. Now.' His friends had the grace to stop laughing and look at the floor.

Pete flicked his long black eyelashes at her, looked away, looked back, sighed audibly. When he returned his gaze to her, it was full of insolence.

'Now,' she repeated through gritted teeth.

'Whatever,' he said, looking away again. She released her grip and he followed her into the cloakroom, slowly, making her wait. Janice flicked on the light and closed the door behind them. The room smelt of rugby boots and wet wool.

Janice folded her arms. 'I saw what you just did.'

He stared at her insolently.

'Are you drunk?'

'Nope,' he said and she knew from his clear-headed gaze that he was telling the truth. She wished he wasn't – she wished that he was pissed out of his head. At least that would partly explain what she had just seen – and his unspeakable rudeness to Liam.

She exploded with rage. 'How dare you touch that girl! How dare you! She's an employee in this house and she should be treated with respect. She doesn't look a day over sixteen, poor thing.'

When this failed to make any impression on Pete she

added, 'You could be charged with sexual assault, you do know that, don't you?'

'I never touched her. She just bumped against me on her way past. Big deal.'

'Liar.'

He shrugged, looked away.

'And how dare you talk to Liam McCormack like that?' she said, her voice more controlled now, the rage simmering underneath. Her heart pounded against her ribcage, the adrenaline, released by fury, coursing through her veins. It felt like she was looking at him through a tunnel.

Again, Pete shrugged his shoulders, sharp at the edges like a hanger. 'He deserved it. Anyway, I was only having a laugh. Don't be so uptight, Janice.' He'd stopped calling her Mum when he was nine, much to her irritation and hurt.

'I didn't see anyone laughing,' said Janice. 'Apart from you. You were unforgivably rude and what's worse, you encouraged him, knowing the trick would never work.' In spite of her best efforts, her speech became more rapid and high-pitched as she went on. 'You set him up. You *deliberately* set him up.'

Pete rolled backwards on the heels of his Hush Puppies, the middle-aged man's shoes now inexplicably hip among his age group. His face was expressionless.

'Why didn't you tell him it was a hoax as soon as you realised what he was doing?'

'You gotta admit it was funny,' he said.

'It wasn't funny. It was horrible.'

'That's a matter of opinion. Al and Ben thought it was fly when I told them.'

'What are they doing here anyway?' said Janice. 'I thought you were going out?'

'We are. Later.'

'If you leave it much later it'll be tomorrow. And Ben's had enough to drink. It's time he and Al left.'

Pete turned and Janice said, 'Where do you think you're going?'

'I'm leaving,' he said, opening the door. The sound of the party, a wall of noise, came crashing through the door. 'Isn't that what you want, Mummy dearest?'

Janice resisted the urge to smack him like she had sometimes done, to her shame, when he was younger. Pete had always pushed the boundaries in a way she was quite sure other kids did not do. She lunged at the door and pushed it closed with the flat of her hand, muffling the noise.

'You'll go and apologise to that girl first. And then Liam.'

He snorted derisively. He furrowed his brow in an exaggerated fashion, pretending to give grave consideration to her demand. 'Nah,' he said at last, bringing his lazy gaze back to Janice. 'That ain't gonna happen.'

'You bloody well will,' said Janice, putting on a brave face but knowing already, from previous form, that it was a battle lost. How could she make Pete apologise? She had long ago lost the ability to influence him, let alone control him.

Pete folded his arms and said, 'And who's going to make me?'

'We'll see what your father has to say about this,' said Janice. Deferring to Keith was her last resort and an ineffectual one at that. She was defeated, and both she and Pete knew it. Angered by her powerlessness, she flung the door open and marched into the hall.

'There you are, Janice!' cried Keith, over a sea of heads, his face flushed with beer and excitement. He side-stepped a circle of people engrossed in conversation, and, when he reached her, thrust a glass of champagne into her hand. 'Here, quick, you need a drink! This way.'

Never more pleased to see him, she followed him into the hot and noisy drawing room. A temporary bar had been set up against one wall, behind a table covered in a now-drinkstained white cloth. The table was littered with beer-bottle tops and dirty glasses and underneath the table there were great plastic bins of ice containing bottles of white wine and champagne and cans of beer. A thin, pale-skinned young woman brushed past proffering a tray of full champagne flutes. She held the tray in both hands, biting her bottom lip in concentration.

'Did everyone get a glass of champagne, now?' Keith asked her.

'I think so, Mr Kirkpatrick. Emma's been round the rest of the house already,' she said, referring to the other waitress. The one, Janice assumed, Pete had just molested.

'Good, good. You're doing a grand job,' he said and the girl smiled, showing uneven teeth. She visibly stood up a little straighter. Keith had the special knack of making everyone that came into contact with him feel that little bit better about themselves.

'Can we talk, Keith?' said Janice. Her anger had started to subside, replaced by the onset of distress. She felt a pricking sensation at the back of her eyes – if she wasn't careful she would break down in tears. And she was determined not to cry. If she did, Pete would've won – again. 'About Pete. You've no idea . . .'

'Not now, Janice. Later,' said Keith. 'It's nearly twelve! Lads!' he called to a group of men from work. 'It's nearly time for the bells.'

The countdown chant arose from the playroom, where someone must've switched on the TV, and it rolled out like a wave through the rest of the house.

'But . . .' began Janice.

'. . . five, four,' shouted Keith, as the chorus grew around them. He threw his arm around Janice's slim waist and squeezed her until it hurt. He raised his glass into the air like a trophy.

'Three, two, one,' she joined in. She forced a smile, determined not to spoil this moment for Keith, furious that Pete had spoilt it for her. But he wouldn't get away with it, she'd make sure of that.

'Happy New Year!' cried Keith and he clinked his glass against Janice's so hard she thought the crystal might crack. Then he pulled her to him until they were chest to chest.

'Careful!' she cried, teetering precariously on her stilettos, the glass in her hand tilting dangerously. 'You'll spill the champagne.'

Keith loosened his grip and placed a soppy kiss on her lips.

'Happy New Year, darling,' she said, returning the kiss, and he beamed happily. How she envied his contented nature, his ability to always look on the bright side, to see the good in everyone and everything. She loved him for it. Indeed, it was one of the reasons she had married him.

She had hoped, mistakenly, that some of Keith's magic would rub off on her, that she would become a happier person just by being around him. But it hadn't worked that way – in fact she worried that, if she wasn't careful, the opposite might be true. She thought that if he knew the full extent of her pessimism, she would destroy him. Worse, he would stop loving her. For these reasons she did not share with him her darkest thoughts. Like how she really felt about Pete. Tonight, however, she thought determinedly, the issue of Pete's behaviour could not be ignored.

'Keith?'

'Yes, darling?'

'I know now's maybe not the time,' said Janice. 'But we need to talk about . . .'

'There you are,' shrieked Patsy, appearing from nowhere. She threw her arms around Janice and cried 'Happy New Year!' into her left ear.

'Happy New Year, darling,' said Janice, embracing Patsy. Her soft, maternal body was comforting – Patsy's perfume enveloped her like a blanket. She didn't want to let go.

Soon Janice was surrounded by well-wishers, and, when she looked over at him, so was Keith, his head thrown back in laughter, radiating bonhomie. Janice glanced through the door to the place in the hall where Pete and his friends had been only moments before. They had disappeared. It looked like the topic of Pete would have to wait.

Clare and Liam appeared suddenly, Liam with his navy sports jacket on and Clare carrying a black wool coat over her arm.

'You're not leaving already, are you?' she said, disappointed.

''Fraid so,' said Clare. 'We need to get back for the babysitter.'

'Our taxi'll be here any minute,' confirmed Liam. The people around them peeled away like onion skins until only the three of them were left.

'Well, thanks for a great party, Janice,' said Liam.

'Yeah, thanks a million. It was fab,' said Clare.

If Pete wouldn't apologise to them, thought Janice grimly, then she would have to . . .

'We'd better get going, Liam,' said Clare, ever the worrier. 'We don't want the taxi driving off without us. They're like hen's teeth on New Year's Eve,' she added, trying to be light-hearted.

'Liam. Clare,' began Janice.

They stared at her, waiting.

'I must apologise to you about Pete's behaviour earlier.'

'No, no, no. There's no need,' mumbled Liam, stuffing his hands in his trouser pockets and finding sudden fascination with his shoes.

'None at all,' said Clare, shaking her head and avoiding eye contact with Janice.

'Just high spirits,' said Liam, looking at his wife. 'A few drinks too many, that's all.'

'We've all been there,' said Clare, nodding her head at Liam. 'Haven't we?'

'Oh yes,' he agreed. 'I insult people on a regular basis, don't I, pet?' he said and laughed. Then he added hastily, his face colouring, 'Not that I was insulted, you understand. No, not in the least. I just meant . . . I . . .'

His voice tailed off and there was an awkward pause. Their efforts to mitigate Pete's crime only served to embarrass Janice further. They were too nice to be honest. Janice took a deep breath.

'He was unforgivably rude to you and for that I must apologise,' said Janice. 'And I wish I could put it down to drink but I can't. He was completely sober. I asked him to apologise but he simply refused,' she said blankly, laying out the bare facts. The temptation to invent excuses for him was great. But she would not spare herself the censure that was rightly hers.

'Taxi for McCormack,' hollered a rough male voice from the hallway and the relief on the couple's faces was obvious.

'Come on, Clare,' said Liam. 'We need to go.'

'God, yeah!' said Clare, suddenly flustered. Her bag slipped and she juggled it and the coat until she had secured them both safely in her arms again. 'Well, Janice. It was a fabulous party. Thank you so much,' she said with a broad smile, placed a kiss on Janice's cheek and then they were gone.

Janice, grim-faced, headed for the kitchen, looking for Emma, only to find out that she had gone home early, ostensibly with a headache.

Later Janice sat alone in the drawing room as Keith saw the last guests to the door. She nursed a glass of water, her shoes at her feet. The room had been cleared of glasses and bottles and the bar dismantled. The furniture needed to be put back in place, ornaments reinstated where they had been removed for safe keeping, and the room given a good clean. But there was little real damage, bar a few spillages on one of the rugs. Nothing that couldn't easily be rectified.

She wished the same could be said of Pete. That the blots on his character could be shampooed out like the stains on a carpet. But she feared his nature was too ingrained now. This realisation shocked Janice for, up until now, she had always held out hope that Pete would somehow be redeemed. She had been doing so all his life.

From the very early days when, as a toddler, he bit other children so hard he left bruises, right up until tonight, she had told herself it was a 'stage' he would grow out of. And Keith was happy to buy into that fallacy too. They mistook Pete's maliciousness for mischievousness, cunning for cleverness and deviousness for precocious development. They shut their eyes to the fact that his behaviour didn't improve with the years. It just became more covert as he gradually began to understand what he could get away with, and what would get him into deep trouble.

And, when the hoped-for brothers and sisters for Pete failed to arrive, they, Keith especially, indulged him. If they had been able to have children together Janice wondered if it would've made any difference to the way Pete turned out. He wouldn't have been so spoilt, but somehow she doubted if his character would've been fundamentally different. So much of character was down to genes, wasn't it? Janice bit her lip and blinked back the tears. At one time she had convinced herself that good parenting would be enough to overcome the curse of Pete's legacy. And she had been proved wrong.

Keith came into the room, let out a long, weary sigh and collapsed onto the elegant green sofa opposite Janice. He rested his elbow on the arm of the couch and rubbed his brow with forefinger and thumb, as if smoothing out wrinkles.

'I'm knackered,' he yawned. He kicked his shoes off and put his feet on the coffee table.

'Me too,' said Janice, exhausted by the emotional roller-coaster of the last few hours. She rubbed the tender red welts across the arches of her feet – the painful price of fashion.

'Do you think everyone enjoyed themselves?' asked Keith, resting his head on the back of the sofa.

'Everyone except Clare and Liam. And Emma, the waitress,' said Janice, her anger reignited.

'What are you talking about, Janice?'

Janice, feeling suddenly chilled, pulled a beaded beige cashmere throw off the back of the sofa and draped it across her shoulders. 'Pete.'

Keith sighed loudly. 'What's he done now?' The uninterested tone of his delivery irritated Janice. Her husband was always quick to jump to Pete's defence.

Janice rolled her shoulders to ease the tension across her upper back and took a deep breath. She told Keith what had happened and tried not to colour the story with her opinions and prejudices.

'Oh, Janice. Is that what had you storming out of the cloakroom with a face like thunder?' he said when she had finished. Janice felt herself bristle with indignation. 'It sounds like nothing more than a case of high jinks to me. And that's hardly a crime on New Year's Eve, is it?'

Janice took a deep breath and counted to five. Getting Keith to understand that there was something wrong with Pete was an uphill battle. 'He assaulted that girl right in front of my eyes. And it isn't so much *what* he did to Liam. Yes, I can see how it might sound like a harmless prank. And handled the right way, perhaps it might've been funny. But it was the way he did it. He wasn't joining *in* the fun, he was poking ridicule at one of our dearest friends.'

'It doesn't mean anything.'

'I'm sorry, Keith,' said Janice stiffly, 'but you weren't there. There was this awful silence and people didn't know where to look. Everybody was embarrassed. And Liam was furious.'

'You're imagining things.'

'I'm not,' she said patiently.

'Well. Look,' said Keith. He removed his feet from the table, leant forwards and held his hands out wide, palms upwards as though weighing the truth in them. 'Did Clare and Liam say anything to you about it? I saw you talking to them just before they left.'

'No,' said Janice and shrugged her shoulders. 'Of course not. They're far too polite to criticise their host's son. I apologised to them though.'

'And what did they say?' said Keith.

'They made out like it was nothing,' she was forced to admit.

'There you go then,' said Keith, dropping his hands and relaxing back into the seat again, barely managing to keep the smile off his face.

Janice was reminded yet again of the pitfalls of arguing with a barrister. Keith had a way of rounding an argument into a corner, like a sheepdog. And once he had you cornered, you felt just as stupid as a sheep. She gripped the edges of the wrap and pulled it tighter, like a swaddling blanket.

'I always said you let him wind you up too easily, Janice. The trick with Pete is not to let him know he's got to you.'

Ignoring this comment she said, 'And what about him molesting that waitress? You're not going to shrug that off too, are you?'

He said, 'Again, I think you're over-reacting. Maybe they were just messing about – both of them. I don't know. But a quick grope in the hallway hardly constitutes sexual assault.'

'She didn't ask for it, if that's what you mean, Keith. It wasn't like that. It was totally inappropriate. She was horrified and when I went looking for her later on, I was told she'd gone home.'

'Her going home may have had nothing to do with Pete.'

'You're not taking me seriously, are you?' she said, balling her fists in frustration. 'You never believe me when it comes to Pete.'

'I never believe you,' he repeated, nodding his head slowly. 'Hmm.' This was one of his favourite devices in a debate. By drawing attention to her inaccurate generalisation, he was attempting to divert the argument into a siding. She knew what was coming next. 'Do you think it's fair to say that "I never believe you when it comes to Pete"?'

'That may be an exaggeration,' said Janice quickly, determined not to let him deflect her. 'But you persistently fail to accept that Pete isn't . . . isn't . . .' She floundered, searching for the right word. 'He isn't *right*.'

Keith rubbed his hand through his hair until it stood up on end. 'He's a normal seventeen year old, Janice. And, yes, I acknowledge that his social skills aren't as refined as we might like. But that'll come with experience. You know sometimes you talk about him as though you don't even like him.'

'Don't be ridiculous. He's my son,' protested Janice.

Keith sighed. 'Look, if it makes you any happier, I'll get him to phone Liam tomorrow.'

'Thank you,' she said ungraciously, pleased to have made some ground but frustrated that she had had to fight so hard for it.

'Though I'm sure he'll wonder what on earth Pete's calling him for . . .'

'No he won't,' said Janice.

'I've said I'll get him to apologise, Janice. What more do you want?'

'And what about the waitress?'

'I'll talk to him about that. It wouldn't be . . . wise,' he said, placing careful emphasis on the last word, 'for him to contact the girl about that. Just in case she decided to take it further. But I'll make sure,' he added firmly, 'that he understands his actions were unacceptable.'

Janice sighed. That was something. 'Okay,' she said quietly, mollified but not entirely content.

'Right. Let's just leave it at that, shall we?' he said.

She nodded.

'Let's go to bed,' he said and came over to her and held out his hand. She took it, stood up and he kissed her on the forehead – without heels, she was three inches shorter than him. 'I know you worry about Pete, Janice. But he just needs to find his own way a bit. And he's going to be alright. I know it. Let's forget about him for now.'

Janice rested her head on his shoulder and swallowed the lump in her throat. She had a terrible sense of foreboding. Something bad was about to happen; no, more specifically, Pete was about to do something bad. And yet when she tried to articulate this thought, it sounded ridiculous. She closed her eyes and tried very hard to believe Keith's optimistic words.

'Oh Keith,' she said, 'I do love you.'

'I know you do,' he replied, with the unerring confidence of someone who believes that good things are their due.

Chapter Three

It was Saturday afternoon, a fortnight after the party at Janice's, when Kirsty stood by the bedroom window in her unnervingly quiet house, facing up to the reality of making good on her New Year's Eve resolution. Janice had talked her into her first blind date – her first date of any kind – in over fifteen years. And while Janice and Keith would be there to support her at the meal in a local restaurant – and she was sure Janice would not pair her up with someone horrible – she was absolutely petrified. She puffed up her cheeks, then blew out slowly, trying to calm her shaky nerves.

Her instinct was to cancel, but that would be the coward's way out. She would be letting Janice and Keith down and insulting Keith's colleague, Robert. She told herself that there was nothing to be afraid of. She was sure Robert would be perfectly charming. But it wasn't him Kirsty was worried about.

She had no idea how to act on a date. Not any more. She was so out of touch with everything. She had only the vaguest handle on current affairs. She had no idea what was hip in the music world. The only movies she went to see were rom-coms with her girlfriends. All she had to talk about, really, when she thought of it, was her two sons and re-runs of *CSI*, *House* and *Numbers* – her favourite TV shows. Not for the first time, she told herself, she should get a job – at least then she would have something interesting to talk about and, God knows, she could use the money. But this time she really meant it. She should've made *that* her New Year's resolution, forget about men, and save herself all this emotional angst.

But focusing on work wasn't the answer. She was lonely and the only remedy was male company. She had not been with a man since her husband, Scott, died three years ago. He'd been killed while out cycling early one crisp Sunday morning in November, by an old man driving his battered Peugeot 107 to church. Scott's helmet had not been secured properly, it had flown off in the impact and he died instantly. The first Kirsty knew about it was the call from the police.

Looking back, it comforted her to know that Scott was not alone when he died – that members of his cycling club, people who cared for him, were there. She prayed that he hadn't endured even a second of consciousness in which to remember her and his little boys – or to realise that he was never going to see them again. She prayed that he died still believing that she loved him.

Three years was a long time to be alone. Since the accident, everything had revolved around looking after the children and helping Scott's devastated parents, Harry and Dorothy, come to terms with their loss. More and more Kirsty found herself dissatisfied with the narrowness of her life. And, increasingly, she found herself ready to face the world again. Not only did she need a job – Scott's insurance money had almost run out – she wanted a job so that she could meet people, laugh with colleagues and feel part of something. But above all, she wanted to be loved.

Instinctively Janice understood this. Kirsty had allowed herself to be coaxed into tonight because, in spite of her fears and excruciating shyness, she did really want to meet someone and fall in love. And Janice was right – she wasn't going to meet him sitting at home every night watching TV, or going out with her married girlfriends.

Kirsty turned and stared at the long panelled skirt which lay on the bed. It was made from black-and-grey tartan wool fabric, with decorative pouches at the hem, each one embellished with ivory embroidery. The tartan reminded Kirsty of her Scottish roots, and the bohemian design of her days at the Glasgow School of Art where she had met Scott.

She smiled, remembering, and lovingly touched the fabric of the garment as if it could transport her back to that world. Scott Elliott had been a second-year student studying Product Design when she met him. She was a first year, specialising in ceramics and textiles. He was full of infectious enthusiasm about all the ergonomic products he was going to design which would make the world a better place. And which would make his fortune.

She was swept off her feet. Their affair was intense and sustained over the next two years and, when Scott graduated with no prospect of a job and was persuaded to go back home to Ballyfergus to work in his father's paper mill, their romance survived the separation. When she graduated the following year, she followed him there.

The phone made Kirsty jump.

'I was just ringing to see how you were?' Patsy said when she picked up. 'Janice hasn't rail-roaded you into tonight, has she?'

Kirsty laughed. 'Well, just a bit.'

'You don't have to go, you know,' said Patsy quickly. 'Just tell her you're not feeling well.'

'It's alright. I'm nervous as hell but Janice is right. I do need to start putting myself about a bit.'

'I certainly hope not, Kirsty,' said Patsy with a snigger.

'That wasn't a very good turn of phrase, was it?' Kirsty giggled, then said, serious again, 'Janice is doing me a favour. She's giving me the push I need. I would like to meet someone and I'm not going to do that unless I start going out on dates, am I?' She pressed on. 'Actually, I'm just trying to work out what to wear. It's blooming freezing out there tonight.' She wrapped her free arm around her waist and glanced out at the grey sky.

'What are you thinking of?' said Patsy.

Kirsty looked at the skirt as she described it and Patsy said, 'Nice. What are you going to wear with it?'

'I was thinking of that black and lace top with the satin trim and . . .'

'Mmm, a bit fussy,' said Patsy, doubtfully, stopping Kirsty dead in her tracks.

'What?' she said, her heart sinking. She sat down abruptly on the bed beside the skirt. Never mind knowing how to behave on a date, she wasn't even capable of dressing herself for one.

'Do you want to know what I think?' said Patsy and ploughed on, without waiting for an answer. 'I think it would look fabulous with a plain black polo neck. You know the ribbed, cotton type. Have you got one?'

'Yes . . .' said Kirsty, cheering a little in the face of Patsy's enthusiasm. She got up and opened the wardrobe door. Thankfully the polo neck was there and not in the laundry basket.

'Now imagine it with one of your big funky necklaces, a big black belt and your black suede boots. The ones with the wedge heels. And that grey fur gilet of yours. Better still wrap the belt round the gilet – that's very now.'

Kirsty hastily assembled a mental picture of the ensemble

and breathed a sigh of relief. It was chic without being old-fashioned and she knew exactly which handcrafted necklace she would wear. Along with a chunky belt (the one with the big silver buckle, designed by one of her old pals from college), she would be true to her bohemian instincts. 'Patsy,' she said, 'you're so right. The last thing I need is a fashion disaster on top of my nerves.'

'You'd look great whatever you wore, Kirsty. You're so pretty. But in that you'll be absolutely knock-out.' Kirsty smiled into the phone, grateful for the blessing of her wonderful friend. There was a short pause and then Patsy spoke again. 'Where are the boys?'

'Dorothy and Harry have them for a sleepover. They collected them just after lunch. They were planning to take them to the pictures in Ballymena and then for a McDonald's.'

'The boys will love that,' chuckled Patsy. 'Harry and Dorothy are fabulous, aren't they?'

'The best,' said Kirsty. She held her in-laws in the highest regard. The only complaint she had about them was that, in their generosity and love, they could sometimes be a bit suffocating. But that was a small price to pay for the unstinting affection they lavished on the boys, and the practical help they had selflessly given Kirsty over the last three years – and continued to give, without thought of return.

'What do they think of you going on a date?' said Patsy.

Kirsty paused. She worked at an old splat of white paint on the window with her fingernail. It wouldn't budge. 'I haven't told them. They think I'm just going round to Janice's.'

'Oh,' said Patsy, and there was an awkward silence which Kirsty felt obliged to fill.

'I don't know why I didn't tell them the truth. I just feel a bit awkward about it. I know it's ridiculous.' She sank down on the bed again, careful not to sit on the skirt.

'You're not being unfaithful to Scott, you know, if that's what you're thinking,' said Patsy.

'It's not that . . .'

'And Scott would want you to be happy, Kirsty.'

'I know,' agreed Kirsty, with a long sigh. She wrapped her legs around each other until she was all tied up in a knot. 'But it's his parents . . . Oh, I don't know. I suppose I just don't want to hurt them.'

'You should tell them. They're going to have to face up to the fact that you're only thirty-six, for heaven's sake. Wish I was thirty-six again,' she said wistfully and then went on, 'it's only natural for you to want a life of your own. Sooner or later you're going to meet someone and everything will change.'

'I think that's what they're afraid of. I think they like things the way they are. And part of me likes it too. I've got used to living this celibate life within my comfort zone.'

'You deserve more than that, Kirsty,' said Patsy. 'Don't sell yourself short.'

'I won't. And that's why I've agreed to this date tonight. Much as I'm dreading it.'

'It'll be fine,' reassured Patsy. 'Just try to relax and be yourself.' And then, 'Oh, gotta go. Someone's come into the gallery. Now you go out and have a blast! And don't forget we're meeting at No.11 on Wednesday night. You can tell us all about it then. Bye.'

Kirsty threw the phone on the bed and dropped her chin onto her chest, rubbing her forehead with the heels of her hands. Patsy was right – she ought to tell Harry and Dorothy. Ballyfergus was a small place and it would be unfair if they heard it from someone else. She reminded herself that she was perfectly entitled to go out with whoever she liked. As a widow for three years, she was a free woman, for heaven's sake. So why did she feel so uncomfortable with the whole idea? And why so very guilty?

She sighed and stood up. Dusk was already starting to fall, bringing to an end the short winter day. The rest of the afternoon and early evening lay ahead of her, long and empty with nothing to do but get ready. As a single mother, Kirsty wasn't used to luxurious stretches of time to herself. Other women might have revelled in the opportunity for some serious pampering; Kirsty was at a loss what to do with herself.

She went over to the window, put her palms on the cold glass and stared out at the deadened garden, prettily shrouded in a blanket of hard frost. The street-lamps came on, illuminating a circle of tarmac at the side of Kirsty's property, which glistened with frost. The garden was plunged into darkness. Little whorls of ice began to form on the outside of the window. She shivered, flicked on the bedside lamp and closed the curtains.

She thought of Janice's luxurious en-suite bathroom and the rows of exquisite glass bottles that lined the shelves above the bath. Janice knew how to pamper herself. Kirsty could learn a thing or two from her.

'Right,' she said and clapped her hands together. 'Let's do this properly, girl.'

She ran a scented bath, lit some candles and put on a Mariah Carey CD. She removed her flaking nail polish and, when the bath was ready, peeled off her clothes and got into it. She eased herself in slowly. The water was hot – just at that exquisite point between pleasure and pain. The sensation when her shoulders submerged was like a lover's caress. She closed her eyes, concentrated on the music and tried to cultivate a positive frame of mind.

At the very worst her date could be a complete bore but

she would still have a good time with Janice and Keith – they were always good fun. However, first she would have to get off this guilt trip she was on. Easier said than done. Because her guilt about dating stemmed not from concern for Harry and Dorothy, or for her children, or because she felt that she was betraying Scott's memory.

It arose from the fact that, for the last three years, Kirsty had been living a lie. Cast in the role of heartbroken, grieving widow, it was a mantle she wore uncomfortably, especially around Harry and Dorothy, who were so clearly devastated by the death of their beloved only son. When Scott died Kirsty had been traumatised, there was no doubt about that. She'd ended up on tranquillisers for a full six months after the accident.

But the crucial difference between her and Scott's parents was that, at the time of Scott's death, she no longer loved him. For a while after he died, she tried to convince herself that she had – it would've made all that well-meaning sympathy easier to bear. She tried so hard that she almost came to believe her own fantasy that they had just been going through a bad patch. Witnesses to her anguish at the time put it down to grief – she wore herself out trying to re-write the past.

But, with the passage of time, she was forced to concede that she was kidding herself. She had loved Scott once, with a passion. But, at the time of his death, their relationship was on the brink of falling apart. There were no histrionics or arguments. No violence, door slamming or walking out. Just insidious bickering between two people who had drifted apart and no longer had anything to say to each other. They had not slept together for six months before Scott's death. The only thing that had kept them together was the children.

Falling out of love with Scott hadn't been her fault, she told herself regularly, even though she felt guilty about it every day. Scott had changed. Not in any dramatic way, not so that other people would notice. He wasn't a monster – he provided for his family and he'd never laid a hand on her or the children in anger. But he'd come to hate working in the family business and, in his frustration, he'd hinted more than once that if it weren't for the responsibilities of marriage and children, he'd be long gone. He never made it clear if he meant long gone from Ballyfergus, or long gone from her and the kids. He was grumpy and irritable at home – and nothing she did seemed to make it better.

Instead of finding release in talking to her, he found it in cycling, and increasingly he took to going off on long weekends. She'd tried to get him to do more family-oriented things instead but he was never interested. She was truly shocked the time she took the kids to Belfast Zoo, on her own again, and realised that she hadn't thought about him all day. It was then that she realised she no longer loved him.

Harry and Dorothy heaped constant praise on her for her courage and strength, for supporting them and the children when she herself was mourning the loss of her husband. And she was torn between the desire to tell them the truth about her and Scott so that she could assuage her terrible guilt and the need not to. Clearly, more harm would come from telling them than good. They were heartbroken enough as it was. It would've been pure selfishness to add to their misery.

And so she told no-one, not even her closest friends. Because to do so would've meant disparaging Scott's character. It would've meant saying, directly or indirectly, that he was flawed. And Kirsty was simply not prepared to do that – she would not tarnish his memory. It was all she had of him now. She would not talk ill of the dead. Plus it wasn't all Scott's fault; she must bear some of the responsibility too. Or perhaps no-one was to blame. Sometimes these things just happened.

Luckily, she had only spoken in the vaguest terms about her marriage difficulties to her closest friends. But if they had ever suspected all was not well, as soon as Scott died, no-one asked her about the state of her marriage again.

Kirsty slid her head under the water and tried to block out these thoughts. She was beating herself up over something which she could not change. And much as she would've loved to offload her guilt so that she could feel better, doing so would mean hurting Harry or Dorothy, both of whom she loved. She would not do that. Painful and lonely as it was, she would keep her own counsel.

The bath water was getting cool – it was time to get out and have a shower. From experience, Kirsty knew she could not wash her hair in the bath. The bath milk would leave a residue on her hair, which would result in lank, dull locks. Pampering, Kirsty concluded, was hard work.

Three hours later Kirsty was buffed and polished, painted and combed, fragrant with perfume, her shabby nails transformed into dark red talons. She stood in front of the mirror in the outfit Patsy had advised and felt pleased with the result. Her shoulder-length auburn hair was smooth and shiny, her face well made-up, her clothes immaculate. Her wedge boots added an extra two inches to her height making her look slimmer than she was, though she had never been bothered by her weight. She was a size twelve and the same weight, more or less, that she had been in her early twenties. She smiled at her reflection. Patsy would be proud of her.

And she was proud of herself for getting this far. Here

she was, about to go on a date and, though it was unlikely, there was a chance that this man might be The One. The possibility made Kirsty feel alive again. The doorbell went.

'Wish me luck,' she said to her reflection, and smiled.

Izzy sat at Clare's kitchen table. A High School Musical lever arch file was propped against the glass fruit bowl, opened to a page of notes untidily scrawled in blue ink. On the table lay a jotter, the virgin pages as yet unsoiled by Izzy's hand. Alongside the jotter was a Hannah Montana pencil case – Izzy chewed on the end of a matching pencil. Everything of Izzy's had to be themed. When Clare was her age – God, was that really twenty-three years ago? – she didn't have a branded item in her battered denim satchel. How times had changed.

Simultaneously, with her right elbow resting on the table, Izzy twirled a lock of blonde hair between her forefinger and thumb, the tiny earpieces of an iPod jammed in her ears. Izzy insisted that music helped her concentrate. But, as far as Clare could see, the expression on her pretty face was more vacant than inspired. This, ostensibly, was Izzy doing her homework. Clare bit her lip. Izzy was Liam's twelve-year-old daughter by his first marriage and, much as she wanted to, it wasn't Clare's place to tell the child what to do.

Clare rolled her eyes at her daughter Rachel, just four months shy of her second birthday. She was seated happily on her booster seat eating beans and toast from a blue bowl with her fingers, a yellow plastic spoon discarded on the floor. Rachel grinned back joyfully, her face and hands smeared with tomato sauce. Four-year-old Josh had already wandered off to watch *Space Pirates* on CBeebies, his half-eaten meal abandoned. She really ought to wrestle him back to the table, thought Clare, but tonight she just didn't have the energy. She cleared away his plate.

Clare bent down to load Josh's plate and cutlery into the dishwasher and shook her head, torn between the urge to smile at Izzy's idleness and the urge to intervene.

But, as far as Izzy was concerned, any interference by Clare was a violation of her human rights. As she frequently pointed out, Clare was *not* her mother and had no right to tell her what to do. Which made life very awkward, for she was sometimes in Clare's sole care. Like now, on a dark Wednesday evening, with Liam not yet home from work.

Clare glanced at the clock. She bit her lip, stole a sideways peek at Izzy, and wished Liam would hurry up and get there. And not just because of Izzy. She wanted him to take over from her so that she could get ready to go out with her friends. He had been late almost every night these last two weeks. Clare shook her head and let out a long sigh – so much for the New Year's resolution. What a joke that was, she thought. So far her attempts to paint had been laughable. She'd managed a few hours here and there but, without more support from Liam, she really couldn't see how on earth she was going to realise her dream.

Izzy drummed her pencil on the jotter in time to whatever music she was listening to, the page still blank. Clare certainly wasn't going to say anything and risk getting her head bitten off. Well, if she didn't get down to it, thought Clare a touch spitefully, Zoe, Izzy's mother, would just have to supervise her homework when she got home.

Clare thought Zoe got off lightly. Liam had Izzy three weekends out of four, plus every Wednesday night. Izzy usually stayed over on Wednesdays, but not tonight. Liam had to be in Londonderry for nine the next morning so he wouldn't be able to take her to school. Wistfully, Clare wondered what Zoe did with all that spare time on her hands.

'Rachel!' squealed Izzy all of a sudden. In one fluid

movement, she leapt from her place at the table like a scalded cat and flattened herself against the fridge door.

At the same time, out of the corner of her eye, Clare saw Rachel send her bowl flying off the table.

'Shit!' she cried and instinctively lunged from sink to table, her right hand outstretched in an attempt to thwart disaster. Amazingly, she made contact with the bowl but, slippery with sauce, it slid out of her grip, flew upwards into the air and then descended, disgorging its contents over her. It continued its descent to the floor where the melamine dish made a satisfying crack on a ceramic floor tile. Rachel clapped her hands in delight.

Stunned, Clare looked down at her just-clean-on blue polka-dot apron, now splattered with baked beans. Sauce dripped from her hand. It was everywhere – sprayed across the table, over Izzy's jotter and pencil case, up the cream wall and on the skirting board. It was splashed across the floor like blood – splattered up the chair legs and on her beautiful cream Shaker-style kitchen units. It was amazing just how much coverage you could get from half a cup of Heinz tomato sauce. Miraculously, Izzy had escaped unmarked.

Izzy stood shoeless, both hands clasped over her mouth, her eyes wide with horror. She looked from Rachel to Clare and back again. Skinny legs, encased in opaque black tights, emerged from beneath her minuscule black skirt. She wore an Argyle multi-coloured knitted tank-top over an open-necked white shirt, this rag-tag ensemble passing for a school uniform.

Suddenly Izzy began to laugh, her delicate hands still covering her mouth, her slight frame bending with mirth like a sapling in strong wind.

'Oh, Rachel,' she cried, removing her hands, her face now

red with hilarity. 'You are a naughty girl.' And she laughed again, holding her right side this time, a child once more, her usual attitude forgotten in the heat of the moment.

Josh appeared in the hall doorway, drawn by the commotion. He pointed at Clare's head and smiled. Just then a cold baked bean slid down her nose. She caught it with her tongue and ate it. Josh squealed with delight. Rachel battered her small fists on the table and shrieked with joy. Their high-pitched voices filled the room like Christmas bells.

Clare looked at the mess all around her and smiled. Then she started to laugh. What else was there to do? Sometimes things were just so bad, you had to see the funny side.

'I'm supposed to be going out in two hours' time,' she said, shaking her head. She removed a cold baked bean from her hair and examined it. She gave Izzy a wry smile.

'I'm sorry,' gasped Izzy. 'That is just soooo funny, Clare.'

'Oh dear. I'm going to have to wash my hair now,' Clare said, which sent Izzy into more peals of laughter.

It wasn't often that she and Izzy shared a moment like this when they were both just themselves, their defences disarmed. Clare grasped it, almost giddy with pleasure, not wanting the intimacy to end. She gave her stepdaughter a wide grin and for once it was returned by one of Izzy's less guarded smiles. Not a completely open, warm smile; that wasn't in Izzy's nature. Not now, anyway.

Clare had not known Izzy before her parents' divorce, but there was no doubt in her mind that the girl had been damaged by it and by the ongoing hostility Zoe bore towards Clare and Liam. Not that Zoe had any rightful cause to bear a grudge against Clare. She wasn't a marriage breaker. Liam was already separated, and in the process of divorce, when they'd first met.

Izzy, a clever child with a high level of emotional

intelligence, had learned to navigate her way through the minefield that was family life. Her main objective, as far as Clare could determine, was to stay 'on side' with her mother. She had very quickly worked out that the best way to achieve this was not to be too friendly towards Clare. By keeping a frosty distance from her stepmother, Izzy could successfully walk the tightrope that was her life. It wasn't fair on her, thought Clare – no child should have to walk on eggshells all the time.

And it meant that, try as she might, Clare found it well-nigh impossible to integrate Izzy into her own little family unit. Instead she hovered on the margins, cautious, watchful, reserved. It wasn't for want of trying on Clare's part. She felt genuinely sorry for Izzy and for Liam's sake she tried very hard with her stepdaughter. So an unguarded moment like this with Izzy felt like a breakthrough.

Now that the drama was over, Josh ran out of the room, cackling with laughter. Rachel slid off her booster seat and made to follow him.

'Not so fast, young lady,' said Clare, her laughter ebbing but a smile still on her lips. She caught Rachel in her arms as she scooted past, carried her over to the sink and rubbed her face and hands vigorously with a wet flannel.

'There, that's better,' she said, releasing the wriggling child. As soon as she set her daughter on the floor, she padded out of the room.

Izzy's hysterical laughter had subsided. She wiped tears from beneath her eyes and sighed.

'Here, you'll need one of these,' said Clare, proffering the big box of Kleenex she kept in the kitchen for such domestic disasters. 'Your mascara's all run.'

'Has it?' said Izzy, plucking a tissue from the box.

'Uh huh.'

Izzy dabbed at the black stains under her eyes and asked, 'That better?'

Clare nodded and there was a pause. Izzy looked away and fiddled with her hair. Feeling the moment slipping away, Clare sought to retain it. 'How'd you get on with your homework?' she began, and regretted it as soon as she said it.

'Fine,' said Izzy indifferently, pulling the shutters instantaneously down. She took a step away from Clare.

'Here's a cloth to wipe your things,' said Clare cheerfully, acting as though she had not noticed the return of Izzy's habitual coolness. She threw a damp dishcloth onto the table. A knot of sadness formed in her stomach like indigestion. 'I don't think you'll get the tomato sauce off that jotter, though,' she chattered on nervously. 'You'll need to rip those pages out.'

Izzy said nothing, picked up the cloth and wiped the table, her pencil case, file and jotter, smudging the pages with ugly orange smears. She did not remove any of the damaged pages and settled down at the table again.

'Aren't you going to tear out those dirty pages?' said Clare, unable to let the fact that Izzy had ignored her pass unremarked. She forced a laugh, trying to sound lighthearted. 'You can't submit homework on *that*, now can you?'

As soon as she'd said it, Clare bit her tongue. She'd broken the cardinal rule about interfering. And Izzy wasn't slow to react.

'Aren't you going to get on with cleaning up?' she said, throwing a careless glance over her shoulder at the messy room.

'I would get on better if I had a bit of help,' snapped Clare, her balled fists on her hips.

Izzy snorted. 'It's not my job to do the cleaning. That's what you stay-at-home mums are for, isn't it? Cleaning up everybody's . . . sh . . .' She stopped, thought better of it, and finished the sentence with, 'mess.'

Clare closed her eyes and counted to ten while bright flashes of colour throbbed behind her eyelids. She would not rise to Izzy's bait. The child was no doubt repeating her mother's sentiments, but that knowledge did not make the remarks any less offensive.

Clare opened her eyes and, determined to ignore Izzy's last remark, glanced at the clock. A wave of panic washed over her. She had to clean up the mess in the kitchen, bath both children and put them to bed, plus get herself ready to go out. Of all nights, why did Liam have to be late tonight? He simply had no idea how stressful home life could be, especially when complicated by the addition of Izzy with her attitude and raging hormones in tow.

How was she ever going to carve out the time to paint?

'Do you fancy giving me a hand with Rachel and Josh tonight, Izzy?' asked Clare, knowing how much Izzy loved to play with the children, especially when Clare wasn't around. 'If you could get them washed, it'd give me a chance to clean up down here. You know how they love it when you bath them.'

'Sorry, I have to do my homework,' said Izzy with a sly sideways glance, the end of the pencil back in her mouth. Clare could've swung for her. She'd sat at the table for a full forty minutes and not written a thing. Now that Clare was under pressure she was refusing to help, and cutting her nose off to spite her face, simply to get at her stepmother.

'Right,' said Clare. She picked up the melamine bowl and threw it forcefully in the stainless steel sink. 'You do that then.' Her voice came out cold and brittle like thin ice. She found a cloth under the sink and started to wipe down the wall.

'Where's Dad?' said Izzy sharply, after a few minutes had passed. Her voice was accusing. As though it were Clare's fault that Liam wasn't here.

'You know he's been held up at work, Izzy,' said Clare irritably from a crouched position under the table, panting with the exertion of wiping the chair legs. 'You know he would be here if he could.'

'What's the point of me coming on a Wednesday if he can't even be bothered to be here? The whole point is so that we can spend some time together.'

'And see your brother and sister.'

'They're *not* my brother and sister.'

'Alright, *step*brother and -sister then,' said Clare, seething. She added sharply, 'I thought you said you had homework to do?'

Izzy did not reply. Instead she smiled to herself, inserted the iPod earpieces in her ears and, miraculously, started to write in her jotter. Clare glared at her, but Izzy was now entirely engaged in scribbling furiously away. She had allowed Izzy to rattle her cage and Izzy knew it. One–nil to Izzy.

By the time Zoe rang the doorbell at eight o'clock, Clare was standing in the bedroom in her underwear – bra, pants and pair of black knee-socks. Both Rachel and Josh were settled in bed and Clare had managed to shower, wash and dry her hair and apply make-up. She heard the front door open and close and then Zoe's sharp voice drifted up the stairs. 'What? He's not home yet? Have you been sitting down here all on your own?'

Clare came out of the bedroom and stood on the landing, out of sight, listening.

'Yes,' said Izzy, sounding sorry for herself. 'Clare took Rachel and Josh upstairs just after six and she hasn't come down yet. I was left downstairs on my own watching TV.'

'Get your coat. I'm taking you home.'

Clare wasn't going to let Izzy get away with that. She ran back into the bedroom, grabbed the first dressing gown that came to hand and pulled it on. The belt was missing but there was no time to change. She wrapped the gown around her body, held it in place with her hands and marched down the stairs.

Zoe stood at the bottom, scowling, her lips pursed up like a prune. When she saw Clare coming, she folded her arms aggressively. She was dressed entirely in designer black with polished high-heeled boots and a bold silver necklace resting on a fine cashmere polo. Her long blonde hair flowed over an open black leather jacket. As usual, she looked skinny and stunning and successful. Which she was – Zoe owned three boutiques in as many towns. Izzy, looking sheepish, pulled a coat on over her slight shoulders.

'Izzy decided not to help with bathtime tonight,' said Clare by way of greeting, pulling herself up to her full height in what she hoped was an assertive manner. And then, giving her stepdaughter a hard stare, she added, 'She had homework to do. Didn't you, Izzy?'

Izzy looked at the floor and, though she said nothing, at least she had the grace to blush. Not that Zoe was watching. She was too busy staring at Clare – her cold, critical gaze took in the entire length of her body from head to toe and back again in three seconds flat.

'And hello to you too, Clare,' she said pointedly.

'I'm getting ready to go out,' said Clare, suddenly feeling at a disadvantage. She pulled the gown closer to her body and, looking down at herself, realised what a sight she was. A white toe sporting an unpainted yellow nail poked through a hole in the sock on her right foot. She curled her toes in embarrassment. The dressing gown was an old grey flannel one of Liam's. She remembered now that Josh had ripped the belt off by swinging on it. Clare kept meaning to sew it back on but had somehow never got round to it. She pulled the gown closer and felt her face go red.

'Somewhere nice?' said Zoe.

'Just No.11 with some girlfriends.'

'Well.' Zoe's pale blue eyes narrowed. 'I hope you're not relying on Liam to babysit. God knows when he'll be home. Used to do it to me all the time.'

Clare's anger was now directed at Liam as much as Zoe and Izzy. Not only had he left her with both of the little ones to put to bed when he knew she was due to go out, but he had placed her in this mortifying situation with Zoe. He should be here to deal with his ex-wife and he should've been here for Izzy.

Just then the front door opened, letting in an icy blast of dry air, and Zoe said, clearly enjoying herself, 'Speak of the devil.'

Liam stepped into the hallway, his overcoat opened to reveal a top shirt button undone and his tie askew. His brief-case hit the floor with a heavy thud and he slammed the door closed. He rubbed his hands together, blew into them and looked at the faces of the three females in the hall, each one, for different reasons, glowering at him.

'Oh, Izzy,' he said and went to put his arms around her. She stiffened and pulled back.

'Where were you, Dad?' she said, sounding pained.

'I'm so sorry, babes,' said Liam, and his arms dropped to his sides. His boyish face was lined and tired-looking. He shrugged his shoulders helplessly and gave Izzy a crooked smile. Clare was torn between being angry with him and wanting to hug him. 'You'll never believe what happened,' he said animatedly. 'I was in the car park just about to get in the car when this spaceship landed right next to me and guess who stepped out?'

'Dad . . .' said Izzy warningly, without a hint of a smile.

'Okay,' he said with a sigh. 'I couldn't get away. I tried, but this thing in work blew up and . . . well, I just couldn't leave.'

'Couldn't you?' said Zoe, her voice laden with scorn. 'You only have Izzy one night a week, Liam. Is it too much to ask that you organise your diary around that?'

'It's not always that simple, Zoe,' Liam muttered. 'Sometimes it's complicated. You know that.'

'It's not rocket science either,' snapped Zoe.

Clare had to bite her lip. How dare Zoe speak to him like that! And why did he take it from her? She treated him like dirt and he let her.

'Let's not bicker about it,' said Liam, with a glance at Izzy. He was always the one to back down, always the one placating Zoe.

Zoe turned her attention to Izzy and said brightly, 'We really need to be getting home now.' She placed a proprietorial hand on the small of her daughter's back and said in a wheedling tone, 'Did you get something to eat, pet?'

'Beans on toast,' mumbled Izzy.

'That was what she said she . . .' began Clare, but Zoe talked over her.

'Never mind, darling,' she tutted. 'We'll get you something decent to eat when we get you home. Excuse me,' she said, this last icy comment directed at Liam. He stepped out of her way and she opened the front door. Izzy ducked her head against the wall of cold and pulled her coat tighter around her.

'I'm so sorry, Izzy,' said Liam as Zoe propelled their daughter through the door. 'I'll make it up to you,' he called out, but Zoe had already slammed the door in his face. Liam sighed again and traced around his eye sockets with the middle finger of both hands.

'I'm sorry, love,' he said.

Clare was angry about so many things she didn't know where to start.

'Did you hear her?' she demanded. 'Implying that I didn't feed Izzy properly. She refused to eat the casserole I made. She *asked* for baked beans on toast.'

Liam shrugged. 'All she did was ask Izzy what she had to eat. I don't see what's wrong with that.'

'You never see, do you, Liam?' said Clare. 'You take everything Zoe says at face value. That was a pointed remark aimed at me.'

'It's not worth getting worked up about, Clare.' Liam hung his coat on the hat stand. 'You shouldn't let her come between us.'

'*You* let her come between us. I don't know why you ever divorced Zoe and married me. All she does is insult me and all you do is defend her.'

'Hey,' he said, raising his hands in the air, palms facing outwards towards Clare. His usually mild demeanour was gone, and an angry look flashed across his features. 'That's really not fair.'

Clare blushed, knowing that she had gone a step too far but, now on a roll, she could not stop. 'You're intimidated by her, aren't you?'

'I'm not intimidated by Zoe. I just prefer not to be confrontational with her.'

'But you let her walk all over you. And in front of Izzy.'

'That's the way you see it.'

'That's the way it is.'

Liam sighed again. 'I prefer not to argue with Zoe in front of Izzy. Listen, Clare, Zoe has problems. She's on her own and life's not easy for her. She doesn't have many friends and I still feel guilty about leaving her. I guess I feel sorry for her. I wish you would show a bit of compassion too.'

'Compassion?' Clare nearly choked on the word. 'You want me to show compassion to Zoe? Liam, in case you hadn't noticed, she's a . . . a first-class bitch.' The last words sounded common, harsh, unkind.

'That's enough now,' he said sharply and Clare bit her lip, annoyed with herself. She'd lost the moral high ground and deflected the argument away from her main gripe – that Liam did not do enough to defend her against Zoe's persistent, insidious put-downs. 'Look,' he added, in a conciliatory tone, 'I'm just trying to keep the peace, Clare. I've had a rotten day.'

'Well, so have I thanks to you. And don't you ever do this to me again,' said Clare, remembering just in time that wagging a finger at Liam would necessitate letting go of the dressing gown, making her look even more ridiculous than she already did. Instead, she folded her arms tightly across her chest.

'What?' said Liam.

'Come home at this time when you know I'm supposed to be going out. How often do I go out with the girls, Liam? Once or twice a month? Is it too much to ask you to be home on time just this once?'

'Clare, that's unreasonable. If I could've been here earlier, I would've been. You know that.' He ran his hand over his face. 'I've had a hellish day.'

'And to leave me with Izzy as well.'

'Sure, Izzy's no bother,' said Liam.

'She's a little madam, Liam,' snapped Clare. 'When you're about she's all sweetness and light and when you're not she's a complete pain. Like tonight.'

'What did she do that was so awful?'

'She . . . she refused to help bath the kids.'

'Well, to be fair, that's not really her job, Clare.' Liam raised his eyebrows, and cocked his head to one side the way he did when he thought she was being unreasonable. This infuriated Clare even more.

'You don't understand. The kitchen was a mess – Rachel had spilt baked beans everywhere,' said Clare, waving her hands about in an agitated fashion. The dressing gown gaped open. She snatched it shut, gripping the collar of the gown under her chin. 'I asked for her help and she refused just out of spite. And then she was making out to Zoe just now that I'd left her downstairs all on her own when it was her choice.'

Liam shook his head, not really listening. 'Clare, I'm sorry but I just don't have time for this right now. I'm only just through the door,' he said, consulting his watch, 'and you were supposed to be at No.11 ten minutes ago. Look, why don't you go and finish getting ready and we can finish this conversation another time?'

'I suppose so,' said Clare flatly, torn between the desire to pursue the argument, and the desire to meet her friends before the evening was ruined. She suddenly noticed that Liam looked exhausted and guilt diluted her anger. 'Why don't you go and get something to eat?' she suggested, softening. 'There's a casserole in the oven and a crusty loaf in the bread bin.'

'I will, thanks, love.'

'What was so awful about your day?' said Clare.

'Oh, the usual. Office politics. You don't want to know.'

He was right – she didn't. And she conveniently interpreted this as meaning that he didn't want to talk about it. 'I'm sorry for going on about Zoe.'

'It's alright. I know what she's like. Believe me, I'd rather battle Boadicea than Zoe any day.'

Clare giggled. Liam looked at her from under a cocked eyebrow and the corners of his mouth turned up in one of his irresistible smiles. 'But have I told you that you look very fetching in that ensemble?' he said. He put his arms around her waist and pulled her to him. 'I always think a woman looks very sexy in her man's clothes,' he breathed into her ear.

'Not in this old thing!' said Clare, looking down at the dressing gown and smiling. 'I'm buying you a new one and this one's going straight in the bin!'

'Go on, then,' he said, patting her bottom. 'You'd better get yourself ready before I ravish you!'

Clare ran up the stairs, giggling, and remembered that Liam's ability to make her laugh was the reason she had fallen in love with him in the first place.

Chapter Four

By the time she finally made it to No.11, Clare was half an hour late. No.11 was a small bistro housed in the front of a former hotel on Quality Street. The rest of the hotel had long since been turned into apartments. The original sash windows had been replaced by concertina floor-to-ceiling ones that were pulled back in the summer months and tables placed on the sunlit pavement outside, continental style.

Tonight, though, the windows were firmly shut against the bitter January night. The room was warmly decorated in stylish shades of brown and strategically placed lamps cast pools of warm yellow light on the artfully worn wooden floor. Clare headed over to the table by the window occupied by Janice, Kirsty and Patsy. They were all cosily dressed in trousers, warm jumpers and boots, in marked contrast to their party-wear of a few weeks ago.

'Come and sit down, Clare,' said Patsy, patting the seat of the remaining unoccupied brown-leather chair. 'We wondered where you'd got to.'

Clare greeted everyone with a kiss, sat down and apologised for being late.

Janice, who was, as always, immaculately dressed in a pink cashmere v-neck with grey check trousers, said, 'What're you drinking?'

'White, please.'

'I'm having soda water and lime,' said Patsy rather proudly, raising her glass up for inspection. 'I'm on a detox.'

Janice tutted and said, 'Yeah, we'll see how long that lasts. Last year you managed five whole days.'

'Cheeky cow!' exclaimed Patsy, and lifted her nose in the air in mock indignation.

The others laughed and Clare said, 'Well, I could certainly do with a glass of wine. Especially after the day I've had.'

'Sounds ominous,' said Janice and she floated off to the small bar at the far end of the room. The only member of staff on duty was Danny – all five foot seven inches of him. With his short, spiky blond hair and cherubic face he looked like a boy trying to be a man, even though he was well into his twenties.

'Well,' said Janice once she had returned from the bar, set two very large glasses of white wine in front of herself and Clare, and settled down in the chair opposite. 'Tell us all about it, darling.'

'Just a minute,' said Clare, took a long slug of wine and immediately felt herself relax. She set the glass on a coaster. 'It all started at teatime,' she began, and the women listened attentively as she related the day's events.

'You poor thing,' said Kirsty when Clare had finished. She put her hand on Clare's knee and left it there – an act of solidarity. Kirsty's propensity to touch still caught Clare off-guard sometimes. Like now. She sat there feeling slightly uncomfortable and sorry for herself, fighting back tears, feeling both foolish and annoyed for letting Zoe wind her up so much.

'That Zoe Campbell,' said Janice, 'is a right cow. You shouldn't have to put up with her.'

'I don't have any choice,' said Clare miserably. 'Because of

Izzy. Sometimes she drives me up the wall but she is only a kid after all. I don't really blame her.'

'No, I blame Zoe,' said Patsy firmly, folding her arms across her motherly bosom. 'She's poisoned Izzy's mind against you. And I bet the wee thing's too scared to go against that witch of a mother.'

'Mmm,' said Clare, thinking that her friends had a point. Zoe *had* forced Izzy to take sides. 'It's just so disappointing,' she went on. 'I so wanted Izzy and I to have a good relationship – for my own sake as much as Liam's. I didn't realise how hard it would be to make this family work.'

'It's not your fault, Clare,' said Kirsty in her thoughtful, measured way. 'Stepfamilies are never plain sailing. You just have to accept that you can't make it perfect.'

Perceptively, Kirsty had pinpointed the primary cause of Clare's grief – her desire to have the perfect family. She'd come to Ballyfergus to escape her hometown of Omagh where she'd been raised, an only child, by parents who fought all the time, mainly over money. Clare had not forgiven them for her lonely, miserable childhood and, even now, she rarely saw them or spoke to them on the phone. Clare felt the tears threaten to sting again. For, try as she might, she could not 'fix' Zoe, or Izzy, and she found that failure hard to accept.

'We've been married five and a half years now. I've known Izzy since she was seven and, if anything, things between us are worse than ever.' She plucked at a loose thread on her black wool slacks.

'She's at a difficult age, Clare,' said Patsy, nodding her head vigorously. 'All twelve-year-old girls are a nightmare. It will get better. Honestly.' Patsy was an authority on the subject, having raised two daughters of her own, but Clare remained unconvinced. She hid her scepticism by putting the glass to her lips and taking another long, welcome drink of wine.

She believed that Izzy had resented her from the day they met and would never forgive her for marrying Liam. She suspected Izzy still harboured dreams of her parents getting back together. Zoe was still single and, from what Clare could gather, hadn't had a serious relationship since splitting up with Liam. Perhaps if she met someone who made her happy, it would assuage some of her anger towards Clare – and Liam . . .

'At the end of the day, Clare,' said Janice, holding out her upturned hand as if offering Clare the gift of her wisdom, 'it's Zoe who has the problem, not you.'

'If it was just Zoe, I could cope with that,' said Clare. She realised she was picking at the hangnail on her left index finger. She squeezed her hands together in an effort to stop. 'I don't have to see her. But Izzy spends a lot of time at our house.'

'Have you tried talking to Liam, sweetheart?' asked Patsy. She leant forwards, her hands clasped together between her knees, unconsciously pushing her breasts together. The low cowl neck of her grey mohair jumper revealed a handsome cleavage.

Clare put a hand on her own chest and gave a hollow laugh. 'He thinks I'm being paranoid. When she's around Liam, Izzy's perfectly pleasant. But when she's with me she's quite different. Rude and uncooperative. Like tonight.'

'And what does Liam have to say about all this?' said Kirsty. 'She's his daughter, after all.'

Clare shrugged. 'I don't think he really understands. When I report the things Izzy's said, or done, he argues that she's just being a normal teenager. I don't know. Maybe he's right,' she said and Patsy nodded.

'It's just a stage. It'll pass,' she agreed confidently. 'You'll see.'

There was a long pause and then Kirsty brought a welcome change of subject. 'What about your plan to get back to painting, Clare? How's it going?'

Clare let out a long breath. 'It's not.'

There was a collective sigh of empathy from her friends.

'Why not?' said Patsy.

'I tried a few times but the problem is that I don't have anywhere to paint. Not somewhere dedicated anyway. I set my easel up in the study but it's just not working out. There's not enough space and Liam needs to be in there to work, so I have to clear my stuff away every time I finish. I'm only able to paint in snatches – an hour here and there because of the children – so it's completely impractical to keep tidying the room. And the floor's carpeted so I'm paranoid about staining it. It's very frustrating.'

'I'm sorry to hear that,' said Patsy and she frowned, thinking. 'If I can come up with anywhere . . .'

'I know!' cried Janice, interrupting. 'What about Keith's study?'

'Keith's study?' said Clare.

'Yes. You know the way he got that old garage in the garden converted a few years ago. He had this idea that he would work from home a couple of days a week. Of course that didn't work out as planned.'

'Yes, I remember,' said Clare, her hopes rising. Janice had shown her the study a couple of years ago, just after the conversion. It was a large, north-facing room with floor-to-ceiling windows installed in place of the old garage doors. It sat in the grounds of Janice's house, fifty yards or so from the back door. Clare set her drink on the table and sat on the edge of the chair.

'Why don't you use that? The floor's stone so you wouldn't need to worry about carpet stains.' Janice became more animated as she went on. 'There's heating and light and even a toilet. And do you remember the tiny kitchen in the back with a sink and a kettle?'

Clare nodded excitedly. It could almost have been designed as an artist's studio.

'It's got everything you need. In fact,' said Janice, with a childlike clap of her manicured hands, 'it's absolutely perfect. Why didn't I think of it before?'

'Oh, Janice. It sounds wonderful,' said Clare. It was the answer to her prayers – but one that was beyond her reach. 'But I don't think I could afford to rent just now.'

'Who said anything about rent?' cried Janice, her eyes ablaze with excitement. 'I don't want anything for it. Sure, it's lying there empty. And we're paying for the heating anyway so that it doesn't get damp.'

'But won't Keith want to use it?'

'No. I can't remember the last time he was even in there,' said Janice. 'If he ever does the odd bit of work from home, he uses the study in the house. There's nothing in the office but a dusty desk and an old office chair. To be honest, Clare, I'd rather see it used than lying empty.'

'Why, Janice,' said Clare, and she paused for a moment, lost for words. 'I don't know what to say.' She put the cool flat of her palms against her hot cheeks. The pessimist in her found it hard to believe what she was hearing.

'All you have to say is "yes",' said Janice.

'I can't believe it,' said Clare, searching in the faces of the others for affirmation that she wasn't imagining things. Patsy and Kirsty were all smiles.

'My own studio. It's a dream come true. I can't thank you enough,' said Clare, 'I really can't.' She fought to hold back tears of gratitude brought on by Janice's largesse.

'I've always fancied being a patron of the arts,' said Janice.

'And now you can help me become one. I have high hopes for you, Clare McCormack!'

'I hope I don't let you down,' said Clare. Her stomach made a sound and she placed a hand on her solid belly, tight with excitement and nerves.

'You won't,' said Janice firmly. 'Now come round first thing in the morning and I'll give you the keys.'

Clare swallowed. 'I really don't know what to say. You don't realise what this means to me.'

'I think I've a fair idea,' laughed Janice.

'I am so very blessed in you,' said Clare, holding her right hand over her heart. She closed her eyes momentarily, opened them, and looked at each of the three women in turn. 'So very blessed to have you as my friends. All of you.'

The women exchanged happy glances and there was a long, not entirely comfortable, silence. Kirsty's high cheekbones went red and Clare wondered if any of them realised just how much their friendship meant to her. In spite of the differences between them, they were the sisters – the family – she had never had growing up.

A little later, Clare, realising that they had talked about nothing but her for the last half hour, said, 'What about everyone else's New Year's resolutions? How are you getting on?'

'Kirsty's got something to report,' said Janice, with a mischievous smile and a glance at Kirsty. 'She's been on a date.'

Immediately Kirsty felt her cheeks burn even brighter. She did not like to be the centre of attention, preferring to be an observer. Even among her dearest friends she was quiet and reserved.

'Of course! How did it go?' demanded Patsy, crossing her legs and settling into the chair to listen, her glass balanced on her knee.

'Do I have to?' pleaded Kirsty, recalling the evening with discomfort. It had been a disaster but not one that she was ready to laugh at just yet.

'Yes!' the others chorused.

'Oh, okay then. Well, you all know we went to Alloro.' Alloro was a posh Italian restaurant on the High Street Kirsty had never been to. 'The food was very good,' she said. 'I had . . .'

'For God's sake, we don't want to hear about the food,' tutted Patsy, waving her hand dismissively in the air. 'What about the date?'

'Well, he was a lawyer friend of Keith's.'

'Oh, a *lawyer* no less,' said Patsy playfully, pretending to be impressed.

'So. What was he like?' said Clare gently, ignoring Patsy's teasing.

Kirsty thought back to the moment she'd first seen Robert and the pool of disappointment that had settled in her stomach. His dishwater-grey eyes had stared out at her from behind thick glasses – strangely, he'd hardly blinked, reminding her of a goldfish. His dark hair was thinning slightly on top and his smile was reserved, as though he was holding something of himself back. It had the unfortunate effect of making him appear as though he felt himself superior.

'Average really. Average height, well built,' said Kirsty, picking her words with care, not wanting to be unkind and reminding herself that she couldn't afford to be choosy at her age. The pool of available men clearly had its limitations.

'You mean heavy,' corrected Clare.

'No, he wasn't heavy. Just, you know, solid.' He had, in fact, one of those stocky, thick-necked builds that could so easily go to fat. Kirsty preferred men who were fit and lean.

Clare looked at Patsy, put her hand up to her mouth and said in a loud, theatrical aside, 'Fat.'

Patsy grinned and said, 'Nothing wrong with a bit of beef on a man. But more to the point, did you like him?'

'Mmm, not really,' admitted Kirsty. 'He ignored me most of the night.'

Janice nodded in agreement and Clare said, with a cross frown, 'What do you mean?'

'Exactly that,' said Kirsty, the annoyance she had felt that night rekindled. She put her arms around herself and gave herself a hug. 'He spent more time talking to Keith than me and Janice put together. He wasn't interested in a date. Not with me anyway. At one point I turned to speak to him and Robert actually put his elbow on the table, like this,' she demonstrated, 'so that I was totally excluded from the conversation he was having with Keith. And then he cut me dead when I was telling him why I didn't like lamb. Isn't that right, Janice?'

Patsy and Clare looked at Janice.

'She's right,' nodded Janice. 'Turns out Robert's looking for promotion to partner. I think he thought it was a great opportunity to get the ear of Keith. Maybe he was hoping he would put in a good word for him. I'm sorry, Kirsty. If I'd known I never would've suggested the night out.'

Kirsty shrugged, pretending that it was water under the bridge, that the rejection hadn't hurt as much as it had. Her first date in fifteen years and the guy had hardly even looked at her. Even Keith, out of politeness or, more likely, because Janice had primed him, had commented on her appearance. Robert hadn't given her a second glance, let alone a compliment all night.

'Well, screw him!' declared Patsy crossly. 'There's plenty more fish in the sea. And you can do far better than a toad like him. Can't she, girls?'

'Mind you, you might have to kiss a few more frogs before you meet your Prince Charming,' teased Janice.

'Oh, God,' said Kirsty, putting a hand to her throat and pulling a face. 'Don't even talk about kissing him. It makes me feel quite queasy.'

The others roared with laughter and Kirsty felt marginally better. She reminded herself that there was nothing wrong with her. Rather it was her date who had the problem.

She tried to brush it off lightly, but it was a blow to her confidence. All that getting ready – what a waste of time. She could've been sitting at home with a tub of Häagen-Dazs watching re-runs of *House*. She sighed and took a very long slug of wine.

After a few moments, when the hilarity had died down, Kirsty said, 'What about everyone else? What about your resolution, Janice? You never did say what your project was going to be.'

'I'm going to get some new equipment for the gym and get this tummy back in shape,' said Janice, patting her enviable, almost-flat, abdomen. Kirsty instinctively tightened her stomach muscles and sat up straighter. And tried not to glance at Clare, who at a size fourteen was the biggest of them all.

'Sure, there's not a pick on you,' said Patsy. 'You don't need to be worrying about losing weight. Not like me.' She looked down at her boobs, which appeared even bigger than usual under the fluffy jumper, and frowned.

And for a fleeting moment Kirsty thought that Janice's resolution seemed a little vacuous. With all the money and time Janice had at her disposal, surely she could do something more worthwhile, more rewarding? Like charity work, for example. Then she blushed, ashamed of her tendency to judge others.

'I have to exercise or I would get fat,' argued Janice and

then added quickly, changing the subject, 'Now, Patsy, tell us all about the safari . . .'

Liam was still awake, reading a set of company accounts, when Clare got home. She threw herself on the mink-coloured bedspread beside him, fully clothed, her high-heeled boots still on her feet. The smile on Clare's face had been fixed there for the last hour and a half. Her facial muscles ached with the effort and yet she could not stop grinning.

Liam looked up and smiled. His chest was bare; he never wore anything in bed, even now in the depths of winter. 'Good night?'

'The best! You will not believe what happened.'

Liam laid his papers to rest on the bedside table. 'Tell me.' Unusually, for a man, Liam took vicarious pleasure in the gossip she invariably brought back from a night out.

Clare threw herself onto her back, stared at the ceiling, and marvelled at her good fortune. 'Something wonderful, Liam. Something absolutely wonderful.' There was a pause. Clare turned her head to look at him. 'Janice has just gone and offered me a studio to paint in. And – wait 'til you hear the best bit – it's completely rent-free.'

Liam frowned and said, 'Really?'

'I know, it's amazing, isn't it?' She went on to explain all about Keith's old office.

When she'd finished, Liam said, 'That's certainly a very generous offer.'

'It is, isn't it?'

'You didn't accept, of course.'

Immediately Clare felt her hackles rise. It was a win-win arrangement between friends. What on earth could go wrong? And what possible objection could Liam have to the proposal? She raised herself up on one elbow, facing him, and said, 'Of course I accepted.'

Liam whistled air through his teeth and said, 'I'm not sure we should, Clare.'

'What do you mean, "we"?' snapped Clare. 'She offered the studio to me.'

'But Keith doesn't know a thing about it, does he? He might not agree.'

'Janice wouldn't have made the offer if she wasn't sure he'd be okay about it.'

'All the same, I don't feel comfortable accepting it gratis.'

'Well, I do. I can't afford to pay for it and Janice knows that.' Clare rolled onto her back and stared at the ceiling again, her body hard with tension, her hands balled into fists at her sides. 'Janice doesn't want money, Liam. She certainly doesn't need it. She wants to be part of what I'm doing. You should've seen her face. She was so pleased to be able to help me. It would've been downright churlish to say no.'

'What exactly *are* you doing, Clare?'

Clare turned her head to look at him again, annoyed by his line of questioning. How many times had she talked about her dream? 'I've told you,' she said, narrowing her eyes. 'I'm trying to establish myself as a painter.'

'You mean more than a hobby, then?'

'If all goes to plan, yes,' said Clare patiently. 'Patsy said my work's as good as Sam MacLarnon, you know. But I can't sell paintings unless I'm producing them, and I can't produce them without a decent place to work.' Clare paused for a moment and said, 'Why are you asking me these questions, Liam, when you know the answers already?'

'Don't take this the wrong way, Clare.' Liam paused, lowering his voice. 'But how are you planning to find the time to do this? With Rachel and Josh to look after, and the house to run as well, you're run off your feet as it is. I can't see how you'll have the time to paint.'

'Mmm . . .' said Clare and she wrinkled her nose in the face of this rather unpalatable truth and stared at the headboard. 'I guess I'll have to work evenings and put the kids into nursery a few mornings a week. Or with a childminder.'

'Expensive,' said Liam, ever the accountant.

'I know. And it would be a leap of faith. But we'd have to look at it as an investment. Once my paintings start selling I'll recoup the costs.'

'It's not only the expense,' said Liam, in not much more than a whisper.

'You don't want me to do it because of the effect it'll have on your life, do you?'

'It's not my life I'm worried about, Clare. It's the kids.'

Clare turned her gaze on him again, her anger now abating to be replaced with anxiety. 'What d'you mean?'

'I don't want strangers looking after my children,' he said and gave her a hard stare. His right eyelid twitched involuntarily. 'I thought we agreed this when you gave up work. That you would stay at home with the children at least until they were both at school.'

Clare bit her lip and looked away. He was right. That was what they had agreed. But he wasn't the one who'd given up a good job as Arts Officer for the local council to stay at home and play earth mother. And if truth be told, had she known what was involved in being a full-time mother to two under fives, she never would've agreed to it. She would've kept on working, at least part-time. And she would've definitely kept on painting.

'Izzy was practically raised by childminders,' went on Liam, in the face of her silence. 'I don't want that for Rachel and Josh.'

'Neither do I. But I'm only talking about a few sessions a week. And things change, Liam. It's time for me to be thinking about going back to work. And, if you think about it, painting is perfect. I can be my own boss and I can fit it round the family. This is my big break and I don't want to fluff it.'

'You're talking it up, Clare. All that's happened is that Janice has offered you an old office to work in rent-free. That same offer would probably still be there three years from now. At least by then Josh and Rachel would both be in school.'

'I can't wait that long.'

'Why not?'

'I just can't.'

'You mean you won't. You're not prepared to.'

Clare sighed and said, 'You don't understand what it's like being at home with young children all day, Liam. It's absolutely mind-numbing.'

'And I think you've forgotten what the pressures of corporate life are like, Clare.' He picked up the sheaf of papers he had been reading, scowled at them, threw them down again. 'Do you think I like sitting in bed at night reading this crap?'

'No,' lied Clare. He had surprised her. She had come to believe that Liam was wedded to his job. It suited her to believe that he enjoyed working long hours, that he was passionate about what he did for a living.

'Are you unhappy at work?' she asked, considering this possibility for the first time.

Liam rubbed his chin. The stubble rasped against his palm. He sighed. 'No, not really. It's just that sometimes . . . sometimes I'd rather be doing other things. Like spending more time with the kids.'

A mixed blessing, thought Clare, but also a point well made.

'I know I'm fortunate to be able to spend time at home,' said Clare, choosing her words like she was walking through a minefield. 'But I resent it too.' She ignored Liam's sharp intake of breath, and addressed the flimsy paper lampshade hanging above them. She'd meant to replace it when they'd moved in four years ago but, like everything else in her life, such tasks had played second fiddle to the all-consuming activity of child-rearing. 'I know that sounds like I'm contradicting myself. But it is possible to feel both. I know *I* do. Maybe other women don't. Maybe there are women who can give themselves wholly and completely to mothering without a sense of loss of self. Do you know what I mean?' she asked and looked at him.

It was clear from the blank expression on Liam's face that he did not. She felt a pressing desire to connect with him, to make him understand what painting meant to her sanity.

Clare touched the space between her breasts, pressing down on her ribcage with the pads of her fingers until it hurt. She closed her eyes and said, 'There's this need inside me to express myself. I haven't painted since the day Josh was born and every day it feels as though a little of me . . . sort of disappears. And I'm afraid that if I don't do something about it soon, I'm going to lose my identity altogether.'

'That is sad,' said Liam, but without a hint of compassion. 'Having two healthy children and the inability to enjoy them.'

Her disappointment stung like a fresh burn. She had opened her soul to him only to be met with cruel cynicism. She wanted to cry then but would not give him the satisfaction. It took her a few moments to compose herself before she could bring herself to speak again.

'You're wrong, Liam. I do enjoy my children,' she said in a steely voice. 'I love them and I treasure every precious moment with them. But is it wrong to ask for precious moments away from them too? Is it wrong to desire more from life? If we don't have our dreams, Liam, then what do we have?' A tear, cold as glass, slid out of the corner of her left eye and dropped onto the pillow.

'Reality, Clare.' He sounded sour, like milk gone off.

'You used to have dreams once, Liam.'

'I still do. I'm just a bit more realistic about achieving them than you are, Clare.'

'I'm not asking for the earth, Liam. I'm asking for a few hours a week so I can go somewhere on my own and paint. It will cost little and harm no-one. And I might just make some money out of it.'

Liam reached out an arm, switched off the bedside lamp, pulled the covers up to his chin and faced the wall.

'If that's what you want to do, Clare, then don't let me stop you.'

And Clare lay there for a full half hour until Liam went to sleep, thinking. Then she undressed, got into bed and lay awake, Liam's opposition radiating from him like heat from a fire. After a while, her thoughts took flight and she pictured herself in the studio, working in the quiet solitude of the ghostly winter months and later, in the spring, the garden bursting with new growth and the light flooding in through those big windows. She heard the rushing silence, felt the brush in her hand and saw a picture of the Black Arch, near Ballyfergus, take form under her hand. She smiled.

And by the time she drifted off to sleep, she knew that this was something she had to do, with or without Liam's support. Painting was essential to her existence, as necessary as breathing. She wished she could make him understand that.

Chapter Five

All things considered, thought Patsy, trying to ignore the sound of her two daughters bickering upstairs, she and Martin had made a pretty good job of rearing their family. Both were well-rounded, kind, loving. Not like some she could think of – like Pete Kirkpatrick. She'd known him from the age of two and had never warmed to him.

Patsy drained the rice, turned the oven off and went and called up the stairs, 'Will you two stop that this minute? You're not kids any more.' Silence. Good. She sweetened her tone and added, 'Dinner's almost ready. Hurry up and come down.'

Back in the kitchen, Patsy lifted a sizzling chicken and broccoli bake from the oven and set it on a trivet on the table, along with a dish of rice and one of sweetcorn.

Sometimes the girls irritated her no end, like just now, but she wouldn't be without them. Her life was full, what with working at the gallery, running the home and making time for her circle of loyal friends. She particularly enjoyed running the gallery and she was justly proud of her success which had been achieved through sheer hard work. She'd started the gallery seven years ago, after a break from work to raise the girls, with a small business loan from the bank. She'd built it from nothing, ending up with an enviable clientele of loyal customers and a rounded portfolio of artists. She was proud of the fact that she'd repaid the bank loan within three years.

But it was her family which gave purpose to Patsy's day. It was Martin and the girls that made her want to get out of bed in the morning. She would do anything for them.

Patsy filled a plate for Martin, who'd just phoned to say he would be late. She covered the food with metal foil and placed it in a low oven to stay warm.

As well as making a significant contribution to the family income, the gallery was her insurance against empty-nest syndrome, the idea being that it would keep her too busy to miss the girls when they eventually left home. But her nest was far from empty and it looked like staying that way for the foreseeable future. She and Martin might never be rid of the girls! At least that was what she joked over a glass of wine in company. Truth was, she didn't want them to leave home. She wanted them to stay right where they were.

Not that she would ever admit this, not even to Martin. She didn't want to be seen to be holding the girls back in any way. But at the end of the day, all that really mattered to Patsy was family. And with her parents both dead, and her siblings living overseas, family meant Martin and the girls.

Sarah had gone off to do nursing at Queen's in Belfast three years ago but, after graduation last summer, she'd been driven back home by low wages and the high cost of living. By the time she'd paid for her car (essential to commute to Antrim Hospital where she worked), clothes, entertainment and the rest of it – she paid no board at home – there was nothing left at the end of the month.

Patsy encouraged Sarah to spend, told her she deserved 'treats' and plugged the holes in her daughter's shaky finances.

In short, Patsy made sure life at home was very comfortable for Sarah. No girl in her right mind would give it all up to go and live in some grotty bedsit in Antrim where she would struggle to make ends meet.

So, just as Laura prepared to embark on a life outside the family home at the University of Ulster, Coleraine, Sarah had come back to fill her shoes. Patsy knew she couldn't hold onto the girls for ever, and she truly wanted the best for them – good careers, happy marriages and healthy children. But she made no apologies for trying to keep them with her just as long as she could.

The door overhead slammed shut and Patsy sat down at the table, calmly filled her plate and began to eat.

Sarah padded noiselessly into the room, wearing black tracksuit bottoms and a pair of battered, sand-coloured shearling boots on her feet. Her long auburn hair hung loose, framing a perfect oval face, delicate mouth and green almond-shaped eyes. She pulled at the sleeves of her hoodie, stretching them down her long arms to the knuckles, as though the backs of her hands were cold. At five foot ten Sarah towered over her mother and her figure was lithe like a cat. Nothing like Patsy at all, who had always struggled with her weight. She thanked God that both girls had inherited their father's 'slim' genes. Sarah flopped into a seat and piled her plate with food.

Laura appeared soon after, dressed in tight jeans and a canary yellow angora sweater. She gave her sister a narrowed-eyed glare and sat down opposite her at the table. Laura was shorter and slimmer than her sister, blonde where Sarah was a red-head and her prettiness was of a different nature, emanating more from her vibrant personality than classical good looks. And while Laura hadn't inherited Patsy's frame she had inherited her mother's bosom, giving her the most amazing Barbie-doll figure, with an incredibly slim frame and disproportionately large breasts. That chest could turn heads – Patsy had seen it in action on Ballyfergus High Street.

Laura sighed softly at the sight of the food. 'This looks delish. Thanks, Mum.'

'Yeah, thanks Mum,' chimed Sarah.

'You're both welcome,' said Patsy. 'But I wish you two would stop fighting. It gives me indigestion.'

Immediately Laura, always the one to cave in first, addressed Sarah. 'Can I borrow your straighteners, *please*?'

'Course you can,' returned Sarah, fast as a tennis ball.

Laura stared at her sister, her clear hazel eyes wide like saucers. 'What was all the fuss about upstairs, then?'

'You didn't say please,' said Sarah quietly, a sly smile creeping onto her lips.

'You're a big kid, Sarah. Do you know that?' said Patsy, starting to giggle and soon the three of them were laughing uncontrollably. Patsy held her hand over her belly and, said, 'You two crack me up, you really do.'

When they'd quietened down, Laura helped herself to some food and asked, 'When's Dad coming home?'

Patsy glanced involuntarily at the clock. 'Don't know. He's going to be late again.'

'He's always late,' said Sarah, her mouth full of food. 'These days anyway.'

Patsy paused, considering this. Sarah was right. Martin had been getting in later and later, rarely making it home before eight. He blamed it on pressure at the bank in Belfast where he worked and the ever-worsening commuter traffic that clogged up the city's arteries like cholesterol.

'Is everything alright, Mum?' said Laura, helping herself to more chicken. 'I mean with Dad.'

'Of course it is. He's just busy, that's all,' she said, the maternal instinct to protect them springing forth. Some habits were hard to shake.

She pushed her plate away, the food like a balled fist in her stomach while the girls ate in silence. Since Christmas, Martin *had* been withdrawn, uncommunicative. She'd put it down to the January blues and, if truth be told, she'd been so busy she hadn't really paid too much attention. Was it just work, like he said? Or something more sinister? She glanced at the clock again. Could he be having an affair? Her heart stopped, started again. She shook the notion off energetically like water from an umbrella.

'Where are you off out tonight?' said Sarah to her younger sister, scraping her plate clean.

'A crowd of us are going round to Catherine's to watch a DVD.'

'Tell me something, Laura,' said Sarah. 'If you're just going to watch a DVD at Catherine's what d'you need to straighten your hair for?' Sarah winked at Patsy. 'Will Kyle Burke be there?'

Laura blushed, still young enough to be embarrassed by a crush on the best-looking boy at St Pat's. 'He might be,' she said casually, looking at her plate. 'I don't know.'

'Leave her alone, Sarah, will you?' said Patsy, standing up and carrying her plate over to the sink. 'Come on. Help me clear up.'

Laura collected the glasses from the table and Sarah stacked the plates. Patsy said, 'Aren't you going out tonight, Sarah?'

'No. I'm tired,' she said, punctuating her sentence with a yawn. 'I'm going to watch the telly and have an early night.' She carried the plates over to the dishwasher.

If she's tired at twenty-one, thought Patsy, what's she going to be like when she's my age? She rubbed the small of her back, achy from being on her feet all day. Sarah loaded the dishwasher and Patsy regarded her thoughtfully.

Her elder daughter was a self-contained, solitary girl who was a bit of an enigma. Patsy was proud of Sarah and she loved her, of course, but she did not easily identify with her. Laura she understood. Like Patsy she was fun-loving, gregarious, people-orientated, always in the thick of any social action. She hated even being in the house alone.

And Patsy had known, almost from the moment of her birth, that Laura was her favourite. She had accepted this realisation with equanimity; she didn't love Laura more than Sarah, she just enjoyed her more. And because she was acutely aware of this favouritism, she took great care to make sure she treated the girls equally.

'You can't stay in on a Friday night,' scoffed Laura, who had been out for the last three nights on the trot.

'Not everyone's like you, Laura,' said Sarah pointedly, picking a cherry from a bowl on the island unit and popping it in her mouth. 'Some of us are quite content with our own company.'

'Oh, my God! Look at the time,' cried Laura suddenly. 'I'd better get ready. Louise is coming for me at eight.' She dropped the glasses in her hands into the sink with a loud clink and ran out of the room.

Sarah opened the bin, spat the cherry stone into it, and let the lid slam shut. 'She goes out too much,' she observed. 'She should be studying.'

'Ach, sure she might as well have some fun while she can,' said Patsy indulgently.

'You'll not be saying that if she fails her exams,' said Sarah darkly.

'She'll knuckle down when she has to,' said Patsy. She hung her apron on a brass hook on the back of the kitchen door and wondered how two siblings, raised the same way, could be so very different in nature and temperament. 'So what's on telly?'

'*NCIS* and *Numbers*,' said Sarah, moving towards the door into the hall. 'Fancy watching them with me?'

'No, thanks, love. I've got some work to do,' said Patsy. 'I might as well get it done before your dad gets in.'

Half an hour later, Patsy was engrossed on the PC, looking at dates for the Irish art fairs. Perhaps Janice, Clare and Kirsty could be persuaded to join her at the Art Ireland spring fair at the end of March – the perfect time for an overnighter in Dublin, a warm-up for their more ambitious trip to London later in the year.

'Well, that's me off,' said Laura, bouncing into view at the door. She'd changed into another (even tighter) pair of jeans, with the over-priced and completely impractical grey knitted Ugg boots she'd so desperately wanted for Christmas. One good rain shower and they'd be ruined. Her face was shining with youth and vitality.

'Well, you have a great time, love. And be . . . safe,' said Patsy. 'Tell Louise to drive carefully.'

The doorbell went and Laura said, 'Gotta go.' She gave her mother a forceful hug and kissed her on the top of the head. 'Bye, Mumsy,' she said and Patsy laughed.

Laura bounded out of the room. Patsy got up immediately and followed her but only as far as the landing so that she could watch her daughter trip nimbly down the stairs, open the front door and slam it shut behind her. Coatless as usual. Patsy pulled her cardigan tighter and smiled, remembering the thrill of going out at that age. The feeling that the whole world was there to explore, that endless possibilities awaited you. The feeling of having your whole life ahead of you.

A few moments later a car pulled up outside. A door slammed and Martin came in, pushing the door to quietly. He did not see Patsy watching him. He put his keys in his jacket pocket, set his briefcase on the floor and then paused. He put both his big hands over his face and stood there for some moments, rocking back and forth, in a state of private grief. He might have been crying.

Patsy put her hand to her throat, shocked. Martin rarely showed emotion. She had never seen him cry. Not even when the girls were born or when his father died. Suddenly she felt like a peeping Tom, observing while herself unseen. She took a few steps back, so that she was out of Martin's sight line should he happen to look up, and waited.

'Patsy,' came his voice after a few moments, sounding just like normal. 'That's me home.'

She took a deep breath and stepped out onto the landing again.

'Hello, darling,' she said brightly and descended the stairs. 'Laura went out just now. Did you see her?'

'I saw her in the car. With Louise,' he said and attempted a smile. His face was tired, wretched even, but he acted as though nothing was wrong. 'Where's she off to, then?'

'Oh, just round to Catherine's.'

Patsy went over and put her arms around Martin's waist, still slim but thicker than it had once been – but then he'd been a beanpole when she'd first met him. She rested her head on his chest and asked, 'What's wrong?'

'Nothing. I'm tired,' he said, and he stiffened a little. He did not put his arms around her. 'And I'm starving.'

Was this how people kept secrets? Using half-truths as diversions? Acting as though everything was normal when clearly it wasn't?

Patsy swallowed the lump in her throat, broke away and said, 'I'll get your dinner. Do you want to change first?'

What on earth was he hiding from her?

'No,' he said, pulling roughly at the dark blue tie around his neck. It bore narrow green stripes and the bank's logo, a gold harp intertwined with shamrock. He discarded the tie on a nearby chair. 'I'll just eat like this.' He took off his suit jacket and threw it carelessly on the coat stand.

Patsy moved automatically to the kitchen followed by her husband. He went to the fridge, got himself a bottle of Becks, flipped the cap off and sat down at the table. He took a long swig as Patsy set his dinner in front of him.

'Watch, it's hot,' she said, letting the plate slip gently from her gloved hands onto a wicker place-mat and removing the metal foil she had used to cover it.

'Thanks, love,' he said. 'That looks great.'

'I'm just in the middle of something,' mumbled Patsy, laying the gloves and lid quietly on the granite worktop. She slipped from the room and left him there, eating at the table alone, because she could not bring herself to engage in meaningless chit-chat. Not when her heart was so heavy and Martin was lying to her.

She went into the snug and sat with Sarah, watching the television but seeing nothing, and thought of all the things he could be hiding. Drugs, alcohol, gambling debts – all the usual vices that people fell victim to, even people like Martin who were sensible and balanced. But none of them rang true. None of them seemed to fit the Martin that she knew. And neither did adultery. He must've received bad news of some sort. But, if so, why hide it from her? Was it his health?

At this thought she got up immediately and went back into the kitchen. Her timing was perfect: just as she walked through the door, Martin pushed his empty plate away.

'That was good,' he said with a smile and ran his hand over his face as though wiping away his worries. But whatever they were, they remained etched on his face.

Patsy sat down on the chair opposite him, rested her elbows on the table and clasped her hands together, as though she was about to pray. 'Martin, I know something's wrong. Are you going to tell me what it is? Or are you going to lie to me?'

Martin's pleasant expression, placed there by a square meal and the beer, fell away. He looked like he'd been caught out, taken unawares. The corners of his wide mouth turned down and he stared at her for some moments, long enough to make Patsy uncomfortable.

'Are you ill?' she asked softly and blinked. And when he did not answer immediately, she stretched her hand out and put it over his. 'Are you, Martin? Because whatever's wrong you know I'll face it with you, don't you?'

He laughed nervously and made a tutting sound. 'Of course I'm not ill. I'm perfectly well. Just tired, that's all.'

He slipped his hand out from under hers and went and got another beer. He prised the cap off and stood there drinking it, in front of the open fridge door. 'The share price fell again today.'

'Again?' said Patsy and she put a hand to her throat. Almost all of their hard-earned savings were in bank shares – they'd planned to sell shares to fund Laura through uni, just like they'd done with Sarah. But they'd had to watch helplessly these last few months as the markets fell and the value of their investment plummeted.

'They're now worth less than a pound, Patsy. From nearly six pounds just a few months ago.'

'The value of shares can go up as well as down.' Patsy reminded herself, as much as Martin, of this mantra. She removed her hand from her throat. 'All we have to do is hold onto them and they'll go up, won't they?' she said, optimistically. 'Maybe the worst is over.'

'It'll be years before they recover.' Martin shook his head and took another reckless swig of beer. 'I can't believe I've been so stupid, Patsy,' he said angrily and stared at her, his face tight and pinched. 'We shouldn't have put everything in the bank's shares. It's such a fundamental error – not to spread the risk. I don't know what I was thinking . . .'

'Please, Martin, don't beat yourself up about it. It was a . . . a joint decision,' said Patsy, limply. 'Who could have foreseen this happening to banks?'

'I should've.'

Patsy did not refute this. Martin *was* the financial expert – she'd always left these things up to him. What did she know of investments and shares and stock markets? But even she knew not to put all your eggs in one basket. She relied on him and he'd got it wrong. Her resentment took her by surprise – she bit her lip and tried to focus instead on what this meant in practical terms.

'Well, what's done is done,' she said, trying not to sound like she blamed him. 'There's no point fretting over it now. We'll still be able to put Laura through uni, Martin. That's the most important thing. We'll just have to cut back on luxuries for the time being. It'll be tight but we can do it out of our income. And, if worst comes to worst, she can take out a student loan.'

Thanks to careful management of their finances, Sarah had graduated unburdened by debt. And even if Laura had to take out a loan they would repay it for her – eventually. The situation was disappointing but not desperate.

'Hmm,' said Martin dully.

'Cheer up, love,' said Patsy. 'It's not the end of the world.

All we have to do is weather the storm and the shares will eventually recover their value. Other people are much worse off. Other people are losing their jobs.'

She took Martin's plate and cutlery over to the sink where she rinsed them. She hummed loudly and thought nervously of the deposit she'd laid out for the safari. She glanced at him. He was seated again, long legs splayed apart, with a third bottle of beer, already half-drunk, in his hand. He was staring at the black-and-white poster of the Eiffel Tower on the wall opposite. A place they'd visited with the girls when they were in their early teens.

Twenty-five years they'd been together and they'd never had a holiday like the one she'd planned, just the two of them. They'd no money in the early days and then, when the children came along, holidays were always family-focused – Disney, Eurocamping and, lately, packages to the Med where they'd all squeezed into too-small apartments so the girls could spend a fortnight topping up their tans. If ever they needed a holiday like this, it was now.

She thought of Martin's thinning hair, her own recurrent backache. They were getting older faster than she liked and they weren't as close as they used to be. She longed to rekindle their romance – she wanted to feel the way she did when she'd first met Martin and truly believed she could not live without him.

It probably wasn't prudent to take a luxury holiday in the midst of economic uncertainty but, if they didn't go this year, when would they go? It would never be the right time. There'd always be something else to spend money on – in a few years it would be weddings and grandchildren. She had saved hard for this holiday – her own, hard-earned money Martin knew nothing about – and it meant so much to her. It was now or never.

'You need a holiday, love,' she said, into the sink.

'The way things are looking at the moment, we might not be taking any holidays for a while,' said Martin glumly and took another swig of beer.

'Now, now,' scolded Patsy, coming over and sitting down in the chair beside him. She patted his bony knee and gave him a sparkly smile. 'I thought we'd agreed not to be pessimistic.'

'I'm not,' he said and the corners of his handsome mouth turned up in a laconic smile. 'I'm being realistic.'

'Well, you have to take some time off, don't you?' said Patsy.

'I guess so.' The corners of his mouth fell as he shrugged and looked away. Took another swig of beer.

'Well, look, why don't you book the last three weeks in September?'

'Why three weeks? Why September?' he said, sounding slightly irritated.

'Oh,' said Patsy. 'No particular reason. Just that Laura should be off to uni by then. It seemed like a good time.'

'It's the worst time if you ask me.'

'Maybe we could book a nice holiday, just the two of us,' she ploughed on, ignoring his last comment.

'I dunno,' he said, uninterested, and a little knot formed in her stomach. Did he not want to go on holiday with her? And had he completely forgotten it was their twenty-fifth wedding anniversary in September? She tried not to let his indifference hurt.

'Don't let's make any rash decisions just yet,' he said. 'Let's wait and see how . . . how things turn out with the economy.'

Patsy got up and busied herself with tidying away the supper things. She thought back to the image of Martin standing in the hallway earlier, wracked with grief. Sure, he'd made an error of judgment about the shares, but it wasn't that big a deal. They would adjust their finances, work round it. She couldn't imagine that was what was upsetting him so much. No, there was something else. Something he wasn't telling her.

When Martin got up to leave the room she went over to him and put her arms around him. She raised her face to his but, before she could speak, he stiffened and turned his face away. 'I need to get changed,' he said and simply walked out of the room.

Tears pricked Patsy's eyes. She put her hands to her face and blinked fiercely to prevent them flowing. Something was wrong, seriously wrong. She knew it in her heart. Was he lying about his health? Had he done something stupid he was trying to hide from her? But what? She wracked her brain. And then the cold hand of fear settled on her shoulders, causing her to sink into the nearest chair. Had her first instinct been right? She thought of all the nights he'd been late home from work. And much as her heart told her it couldn't be true, her head told her it could. Was he, after all these years, having an affair?

She thought of the vows they had taken all those years ago – vows she had believed in then and still did. The question was, did Martin? She'd hoped the safari might help them re-connect, inject romance back into their lives, help them find each other again. Now she needed it to do much more. She needed it to save her marriage.

Chapter Six

'Dorothy,' said Kirsty. 'It's really good of you to have David and Adam overnight. Again.'

'It's no trouble, love,' said Dorothy, a comfortably rounded woman, with jet-black hair from a bottle and bright red lipstick. She smelt of face powder and Chanel No.5 and was well-dressed in a smart black skirt, patterned blouse and scarlet cardigan. She wore a set of pearls round her neck and discreet diamonds twinkled in her fleshy earlobes.

They were standing in the hall of Harry and Dorothy's handsome Victorian three-storey home on The Roddens – the house in which Scott had grown up. The boys had been here since lunchtime – Kirsty had been grocery shopping and called in on her way home to deliver their overnight things.

A grandfather clock tick-tocked at the foot of the stairs. The bold floral wallpaper, now fashionable again, dated back to the first time Kirsty had visited this house nearly eighteen years ago, when Scott had brought her home to meet his parents. The collection of china plates, each one depicting an agricultural activity of a bygone age, which covered the walls and snaked up the stairwell, had been in its infancy back then. And Kirsty had gone back home to Scotland with the impression that Dorothy and Harry had not approved of her.

The wallpaper might be the same, but everything else had

moved on. Grief had a way of changing people. Now she felt accepted by her in-laws, loved even. And every birthday and Christmas since had seen a new addition to Dorothy's plate collection – it certainly simplified the task of buying presents for her – until every inch of wall space was covered.

David and Adam ran in from the garden where they'd been kicking a ball about and shouted, 'Hi Mum!' in unison. Then they threw off their coats, hat and gloves, kicked off their mud-coated shoes and left everything in a tangled heap by the front door.

David was well-built with ears like question marks, sandy-coloured hair, grey eyes that were a little too close together and highly coloured cheeks. His little brother had inherited more classically handsome looks – he had a pretty cupid's bow mouth, china-blue eyes, darker hair and a slighter build. Neither child looked much like their father but Dorothy was never done rooting out family resemblances on the Elliott side of the family.

Suddenly Kirsty noticed something different about them. 'Their hair!' she exclaimed.

'Yes, I gave them both a wee trim. Thought they needed it. You know, for school.'

Kirsty swallowed and tried to smile. Their haircuts, while not a complete disaster, had been crudely done. Adam's fringe was slightly crooked and David's thick hair was cut just a tad too short above his ears.

'But I always take them to Alison at Faith's,' said Kirsty faintly. 'I was going to take them next week.'

'Ach, no point wasting good money when you can do it for nothing at home. I always cut Scott's hair when he was a boy.'

Kirsty's heart sank. 'I really would rather you didn't do it in future,' she said quietly and felt her face redden.

The smile fell from Dorothy's face and she gave Kirsty a sharp glance. Then she gave her shoulders a quick shrug. 'As you wish,' she said shortly and she ruffled Adam's dark thatch. 'Your grandpa's on the top floor,' she said. 'Go and see what he's up to. I think he might have something for you.'

'SWEETS!' screamed Adam. 'It's sweets, isn't it, Gran?'

'Let's go and see,' said David, always the leader.

They scampered up the stairs on all fours, like monkeys, almost delirious with happiness. They were so loved in this house, so spoilt by their grandparents – like all children should be. Kirsty felt a lump in her throat and swallowed. She just wished Dorothy and Harry wouldn't overstep the mark.

Dorothy extended her hand to Kirsty and said, 'Sure, you know we love to have them. We'd do anything for those boys.' Her gaze drifted to the top of the stairs.

Kirsty stared at Dorothy's outstretched hand, and tilted her head to the right. It took her a few foolish moments to realise that Dorothy was waiting for her to hand over the boys' overnight bag. Not that they needed much – among other things, Dorothy kept pyjamas, dressing gowns and toothbrushes for them here. The bag contained only clean clothes for the next day.

'Are you sure it's not too much trouble? I could always get a sitter,' said Kirsty, clutching the bag to her breast.

The smile on Dorothy's face fell away as did her hand and she said, 'Now don't be silly, Kirsty. Where would you get a sitter so late in the day?' She paused, adjusted her tone, and went on, smiling brightly as though to reinforce the truth of her words. 'We're their grandparents, Kirsty. They belong here.'

No, they don't, thought a horrified Kirsty, they belong with me. She put her hand to her mouth as though she had uttered this realisation aloud. And in that instant her relationship with Dorothy altered for ever.

Scott's death had united them all in grief. Although they did not live in the same house, in many respects the family unit consisted of grandparents, Kirsty and the children. The parenting of David and Adam had become the business of Dorothy and Harry as much as Kirsty. They often collected the boys from school, fed them, helped them with their homework, played with them, took them places and regularly had them to stay. They had even taken them on holiday twice, both times for a week in Portrush, to give Kirsty a break. But now, the dynamic had unexpectedly shifted. More precisely, Kirsty had changed.

Her life these past three years had been meshed with Dorothy's and Harry's. Together, they had focused all their energies on coping with Scott's death – and the shared goal of minimising the effect of this disaster on the boys. And between them, they had made a very good job of it. The children seemed well-adjusted, happy, polite. And both were doing well at school. Kirsty couldn't have coped without her in-laws, and her gratitude knew no bounds. They were good people and she loved them.

But three years on, she longed for a more independent life for herself and the boys. That was selfish of her, for the boys' close relationship with Dorothy and Harry was entirely, and overwhelmingly, positive. Sadly, they did not know their maternal grandparents well – they were aged and suffered from ill health and did not like to leave Cumnock, on the east coast of Scotland where they lived.

And while Kirsty reminded herself of the importance of extended family, she couldn't help but feel increasingly uncomfortable with the level of Dorothy and Harry's involvement. It was time to put some distance between herself and her in-laws. At the back of her mind was the vague notion that her future happiness depended upon it. If she was to stand a chance of meeting a man – and making a new life for herself – she couldn't have her in-laws living in her pockets.

But how on earth was she to disentangle herself and the boys without hurting Dorothy and Harry? They lived for their grandchildren – they had made them the centre of their lives.

'Can I have the bag?' said Dorothy, startling Kirsty.

'Oh, yes. Of course,' said Kirsty. She pushed it into Dorothy's arms eagerly, to compensate for her earlier caginess. 'And thanks again.'

For the first time Kirsty felt under an obligation to her in-laws. Before it had all been easy and uncomplicated. Now, as if she were looking through a different lens, she saw every act of kindness as a further nail in the coffin of her independence.

'So, where are you off to tonight?' asked Dorothy. 'You mentioned Ballymena.'

'Yes, there's some art exhibition on that Patsy and Clare want to see. Me and Janice are just going along for the ride.'

'Hmm,' said Dorothy, her interest already beginning to wane. She had always struggled to understand Kirsty's fascination with all things arty. She placed little value on art, financial or otherwise – it was simply something to fill a space on the wall. Dorothy's interest extended only as far as her painted plate collection.

'Do you have time for a cup of tea?' said Dorothy, glancing at the ornate face of the grandfather clock.

'Please,' said Kirsty, and she paused before blurting out, 'There's something I want to talk to you and Harry about.'

'I see,' said Dorothy, and she gave Kirsty a searching glance.

'Ah, here she is,' came Harry's voice from the top of the stairs, providing a welcome distraction. He descended gingerly, holding onto the banister, dressed in rust-coloured cords, a green checked shirt and worn brown suede slippers. With his greying hair and moustache, he looked like a picture-book grandfather.

He came over to Kirsty and placed a warm kiss on her

cheek. His skin against hers felt thin and papery. 'My favourite daughter-in-law,' he said and looked at her for a few seconds, holding onto the forearms of her jacket. It was an old joke between them. They were no other daughters-in-law. Their surviving child, Sophie, was married to a doctor and lived in Dublin.

'Kirsty's going to stay for a cuppa,' said Dorothy and she led the way to the cosy kitchen at the back of the house.

Dorothy made tea, noisily, and Harry and Kirsty exchanged small talk. When they were all seated with thin china cups and saucers in front of them and a plate of Rich Tea biscuits on the table, Dorothy poured the tea and said, 'So what was it you wanted to talk to us about?'

Kirsty put her spoon in her cup and stirred the tea, even though she had added no sugar. She took a deep breath. 'I'm thinking about going out to work.'

'Oh, love. You don't need to be doing that,' said Harry with one of the tolerant smiles he usually reserved for the children when they said something silly. 'Sure, she doesn't, Dorothy? There's plenty of time for that when the boys are grown.'

'They are grown,' said Kirsty into her cup, unable to meet Harry's gaze. Her voice was little more than a whisper. 'Grown enough anyway. I'm in the house on my own most of the day. There's only so much cleaning and cooking and coffee mornings you can do.' The spoon clattered against the saucer when she set it down.

'What's brought this on all of a sudden, Kirsty?' said Dorothy, her brows knitted. Her gaze, when it met Kirsty's, was like a laser.

Kirsty took a biscuit and broke it in half. Pale golden crumbs littered the spotless table. 'It's something I've been thinking about for a while,' she said. 'Ever since Adam started school last year.'

'I see,' said Dorothy and she lifted her cup to her lips and took a sip of tea. She let the silence sit between them like a fog. Harry stroked his moustache, a nervous habit, and stared at his reflection in the window. He looked confused. Disappointed.

'I'm only talking about part-time,' said Kirsty, looking at their unresponsive faces.

Cocking her head to one side, Dorothy placed the foot of her teacup in the depression on the saucer, as though she were putting a jigsaw together. 'Do you have something in mind?' she said.

'There's a job advertised at the museum.'

Ballyfergus's small museum was housed in the old Carnegie Library on Victoria Road. The building, which dated from 1906, had been beautifully refurbished and now housed a bright modern museum dedicated to the history and heritage of Ballyfergus and the surrounding area.

'It's only twenty hours a week,' said Kirsty.

'What about school holidays and when the boys are sick?' said Dorothy.

'I'll arrange childcare.'

'But me and Dorothy would look after the kids,' said Harry, sounding slightly affronted.

'I . . . I . . . well, that's a very kind offer but I can't expect you to drop everything to look after the boys. You have your own lives,' Kirsty added, though she didn't really believe this to be true. Their lives revolved around their grandchildren.

'That's what we're here for, isn't it, Dorothy?' said Harry, sounding a bit annoyed.

Dorothy nodded and Harry went on, 'They're my grandsons and I don't want some stranger looking after them.'

'Well, okay then. If it's what you want . . .' said Kirsty, feeling yet again that she had been bulldozed into something she didn't want. But she couldn't very well deny them access to the boys. She would pay for it though, in an indirect way – book a holiday for them, or something.

Harry, suddenly warming to the idea, said, 'Maybe Kirsty's right, Dorothy. It might do her good to get out a bit.'

Kirsty's spirits lifted at finding an unlikely ally in Harry. Dorothy's eyebrows, as effective a means of communication as her speech, crept up her brow a fraction. She waited for Harry to go on.

'But don't you see? There's a much better way to go about it than this,' he said firmly, pleased with himself.

'There is?' said Dorothy, the space between her eyebrows puckering.

Harry grinned broadly at them both, revealing a set of perfect dentures. 'Kirsty's a highly educated girl with a lot to offer.'

Kirsty smiled at him, grateful and relieved. And surprised. Of the two of them, she had expected more resistance from Harry.

'I'll tell you what, Kirsty. You can come and work for me at the mill,' he said grandly, presenting his offer with all the flair of a generous gift.

Kirsty swallowed hard and tried to smile. She thought of the InverPapers mill, the relentless hum and thud of machinery and the sickly-sweet smell of the chemicals used in the manufacturing process – a nauseating stench that had permeated Scott's hair and clothes and which, no matter how many times he showered or how many times she washed his clothes, never completely went away.

'She could work in the office, Dorothy, like you used to do. Help with the accounting, payroll, bills, that sort of thing. You can use a computer, can't you?' Though supposedly semi-retired, Harry still played an active part in the business.

Kirsty pictured the stuffy office with its worn eighties furniture and single-glazed aluminium framed windows – and froze in horror.

She had never worked in an office in her life. She couldn't think of anything more depressing. The factory employed one hundred and fifty people and it produced toilet roll. Toilet roll! Millions of sheets of toilet roll a year. Bog roll, Scott used to call it. Harry wanted her to work in a bog-roll factory. She bit her lip and blinked to stop herself from crying.

'I don't think . . .' began Kirsty, faintly, when she could bring herself to speak.

'Mmm,' said Dorothy, as though Kirsty had not spoken, her eyebrows uplifted with possibility. 'Now that is a good idea. You could work the hours that suited you, Kirsty, and take all the time off you need.'

'Don't you see, love?' said Harry, laying a cool hand on Kirsty's sweating one. 'It's perfect. You can work whatever hours you like. And keep it in the family. I like that idea. I think Scott would've liked it, too. Don't you, Dorothy?'

At the invocation of her dead husband's name, Kirsty stared down at her lap. For all his faults, Scott would never have condemned her to work in the family business. He'd hated it himself.

Harry rubbed his hands together as though he'd just closed a deal and said, 'And I'd make sure you were handsomely remunerated, of course.'

There was a long silence and Dorothy said, 'What do you think, Kirsty?'

'I think . . . I'm not sure. It's not exactly what I had in mind.'

Harry frowned and looked from his wife to Kirsty.

'I really like the idea of working in the museum. I think it would be interesting.'

'The paper industry is interesting too,' said Harry.

'I'm sure it is, Harry. And I'm very appreciative of your generous offer. But I'm not sure I can accept it.'

'Sure you can,' he said. He folded his arms across his chest like a buffer.

'Harry,' said Dorothy, who had been quiet for some moments. 'I don't think it's a case of not being able to accept. I think it's a case of not wanting to. Is that right, Kirsty?'

In spite of her burning cheeks, Kirsty was determined to show them that she meant business. So often in the past she had been persuaded to go along with things that went against her better judgment. Little things, like how much TV the children were allowed to watch and what time they went to bed when they had sleepovers. But this time it was her life, her future, at stake.

She sat up straight and said, 'Yes. That's right.'

Harry let out a long sigh and visibly deflated. He rubbed his nose with the back of his right hand, sniffed, and refolded his arms. 'I was hoping the boys would take over the business one day, you know,' he said. 'I would've been retired by now if Scott . . .'

'Harry,' said Dorothy tenderly and she paused, then lowered her voice. 'That's got nothing to do with this discussion.'

Admonished, albeit gently, Harry shrugged and looked out the window, though there was little to see in the rapidly falling dusk. Kirsty reached out and touched his elbow. 'Harry?' she said. He glanced at her hand and looked out the window again. She had offended him and for that she was truly sorry. But the offence was inevitable. He would never see things from her point of view.

'You'd better watch your time, love,' said Dorothy with a glance at the clock on the wall. 'It's gone five.'

'Has it?' she said dimly, without taking her eyes off Harry. She did not want the conversation to end on this unpleasant, unresolved note. She realised that she wanted them to give her something they could not – their wholehearted support.

But, for now at least, she had been dismissed. Kirsty stood up and said goodbye to her in-laws, awkward in their company for the first time in over three years. Then she slipped upstairs to say goodbye to the boys and, when she came down again, Dorothy was waiting for her at the front door. 'Don't you pay too much attention to Harry, love. He's just . . .'

'Hurt?'

'Aye, that. And grieving. Still.'

Kirsty sighed and pulled on her coat. 'I didn't mean to offend him.'

'I know. But he doesn't think sometimes.'

Kirsty buttoned her coat and slipped on a pair of black leather gloves.

'You apply for that job at the museum, Kirsty. And we'll help you with the boys when you need it.'

'It's very good of you to offer,' said Kirsty, rather formally. She gave the older woman a brief hug, stepped outside into the cold, damp night and onto the gravel path.

'Just one thing though,' said Dorothy.

Kirsty turned around, the gravel screeching under the ball of her foot.

'Don't ever forget how much we love those boys,' said Dorothy.

'I won't,' said Kirsty brightly, understanding only too well the plea – or was it a warning? – behind this statement.

Kirsty marched purposefully down the path towards the car but stopped as soon as she heard the front door close behind her. Then she turned and stared at the house, the windows bright with yellow light, her two sons happily and safely ensconced inside. And separated from her, it seemed, by more than just a Victorian brick wall. A few flakes of snow began to fall, swirling in the wind. She shivered, pulled the collar of the coat around her neck and hurried to the car.

The exhibition was in Cornerstone Gallery on Mill Street, Ballymena – directly opposite the Town Hall. The gallery was spread over two floors and Paul Holmes' paintings were displayed on the ground floor. It was busy and noisy, people elbow-to-elbow with their complimentary drinks clutched like talismans in their hands. Kirsty did not have the means to splash out hundreds of pounds on original watercolours, however handsome. But she appreciated the high quality of the artwork, exchanged a few words with the artist himself and enjoyed the buzz. They didn't stay long, mindful of the falling snow outside and the treacherous drive home over Shaneshill which awaited them. Parts of the road were lonely and deserted and at a higher altitude than the surrounding countryside so that snow often lay where there was none in town.

By nine o'clock they were back in Ballyfergus and settled at their usual table in No.11. The bar was two-deep with the familiar faces of local businessmen, ties removed and top buttons undone, who had dropped by for their regular Friday pint, or two, on the way home.

'Good job you booked, Janice,' said Patsy, 'or we'd never have got our table.' She arranged the folds of her wool skirt round her knees and ran her fingers through her short, dyed hair. She'd worn it in the same spiky, youthful style all the time Kirsty had known her. It showed off her good bone structure, and suited her lively personality. When she moved her head large diamond earrings winked in each lobe.

Janice, urbane in a black cashmere roll-neck, figure-hugging black skirt and boots, handed round the menus. 'Let's order quickly, shall we? The kitchen closes in half an hour.'

Once the food was ordered and they all had a drink in

front of them Kirsty asked, 'So what did you think of the competition, Clare?'

Clare downed a third of a glass of white wine before answering. She was more casually dressed than the others in black jeans and a patterned shirt. Around her neck, on a green leather thong, she wore a piece of pink shell sculpted into the shape of a flower. As usual her face was bare of make-up, and her long brown hair was freshly washed and fell around her shoulders like a waterfall. Over the years Clare had put on the pounds and it did not suit her. She had been prettier when she was slimmer. 'Well, Paul Holmes's got talent, that's for sure.' Clare let out a long sigh. 'I'm not sure my work's up to that standard.'

'Oh, don't say that,' said Kirsty, loyally. 'You paint just as well. Better even.' If Clare had a fault it was that she fluctuated wildly between confidence and self-doubt – and more often the latter. She was always putting herself down. 'How's the studio?'

'The studio's fantastic,' said Clare, enthusiasm returning to her voice. 'Complete peace and no interruptions from screaming kids! So far I've managed a couple of evenings and a few hours on Sundays.'

Janice smiled broadly.

'And how's the painting coming on?' asked Patsy.

'The painting . . .' Clare's voice trailed off. She wrinkled her nose. 'Well, let's just say I'm a bit rusty.'

'We just need to get you oiled then!' cried Janice, laughing. 'Speaking of which,' she added, raised a glass and took a long drink. 'That's better.' Clare almost finished her wine.

Janice looked round at the others and said, 'Seriously though, Clare showed me and Patsy what she'd done and it was good. As good as what you were painting four years ago, Clare. Isn't that right, Patsy?'

Patsy shook her head distractedly. 'I'm sorry. What did you say?'

'I said, Clare's work is good, isn't it?'

'It is so,' said Patsy, nursing her glass and staring at Clare. 'Do you know what I think, Clare? I think you're too hard on yourself. Way too hard.'

Clare blushed, and looked at a spot on the floor which she rubbed with the toe of her brown boot.

'I know what we should do!' exclaimed Patsy and everyone said, 'What?' at the same time.

'I think we should plan an exhibition for you.'

'No,' said Clare with a gasp, and she put the tips of her fingers to her lips. Her nails were badly bitten and her hands work-worn – the scourge not only of mothers of young children but artists too.

Patsy cocked her head to one side. 'I'm thinking something pretty low-key, maybe in conjunction with another artist. Someone who works in a different medium. Mmm, let me think . . .' She sat back in the tub chair and was quiet for a few moments, then came to life again. 'I know. I was hoping to do a wee exhibition for Bronson in the spring.' She was referring to an old friend of hers, the unlikely-named Bronson Gaffney, a local artist who did traditional landscapes in oil. 'I could have a chat with him and see if he would be willing to do a joint exhibition. I'm sure it wouldn't be a problem. It would get you a bit of exposure, in a low-pressured way, and give you something to work towards. And Bronson's just lovely, so he is.'

Clare's fingers pressed against her lips until the colour leached from them but her eyes were alive with excitement. 'Do you really think I could do it?'

'Of course you could,' said Patsy. 'And what's more, I bet you I sell every one of your pictures!'

It took Clare only a few seconds to consider the offer. 'In

that case, okay then. You're on!' she cried and the others gave a little cheer.

'I'll give you a call tomorrow and we can talk about it some more,' said Patsy.

'I think that calls for another drink,' said Clare, flushed with excitement. She got up and went to the bar. Patsy, who was driving, declined the offer of another drink. When Clare returned, Kirsty asked, 'So, how's everyone else getting on with their resolutions?'

'I ordered a new treadmill for the gym,' said Janice.

'I thought you had one already?' Clare frowned in puzzlement.

'Oh, we did, but that's absolutely ancient,' said Janice with a dismissive wave of her hand. 'This one's state of the art.'

'Well, rather you than me,' said Patsy, unconsciously skimming her stomach with the flat of her palm. 'There's nothing of you as it is, Janice. If you exercise any more you'll disappear!'

'Always room for improvement, my dear,' retorted Janice good-naturedly.

Listening to this exchange, Kirsty wondered why Janice, poised and elegant, was so obsessed with continual self-improvement. There was nothing wrong with making the most of yourself – and Kirsty was as vain as the next woman – but Janice pursued physical perfection with religious fervour. For the first time it crossed Kirsty's mind that, perhaps, Janice wasn't as happy as she appeared. In exercising every pick of fat away, was she exercising away demons too? Kirsty might have known her for fifteen years, but did she know the real Janice?

'Have you been on any more dates recently?' asked Patsy, rousing Kirsty from her reverie.

She let out an audible sigh and smiled wryly. 'If you could

call the last time a date. I think I need a few weeks to recover from that experience and drum up the enthusiasm to give it another go. I should have made a different resolution,' she went on, seriously. She was sick already of the others asking her about dating. 'I should've made it something simple. Like getting a job.' Something, she thought, that she could realistically achieve.

'Are you thinking about going back to work, then?' said Janice, leaning forwards with interest.

'Yeah. I've seen a job advertised. At the museum,' she said.

'That's exciting. What does it involve?' asked Clare.

'The job title's "Museum Learning Assistant". I'd look after groups and schools coming in for visits, as well as welcome visitors. There'd be a bit of admin – answering email and telephone enquiries, that sort of thing. To be honest, the job description's very varied and a bit vague. Which is a good thing 'cos I think it'd be easy to make the job my own, if you know what I mean.'

'Yes, once you've got your feet under the table,' said Patsy, shrewdly.

'That's right,' said Kirsty, realising that the more she talked about this job, the more she wanted it. 'It's only part-time and Dorothy and Harry have offered to help with the boys. But they didn't hide the fact that they're not happy about it,' she added glumly. 'Well, Harry isn't.'

Patsy gave Kirsty a knowing look. 'Not that it's any of his business.'

Kirsty tilted her head in Patsy's direction, acknowledging the comment but giving it no credence. Patsy didn't understand how it was. Kirsty's existence was so bound up with her in-laws, she had difficulty separating her life from theirs, especially when what she chose to do impacted on them. 'He warmed to the idea after a bit,' she went on. 'But only because he had the bright idea that I would work in the factory office.'

'And that's not something you want to do?' said Janice.

'God, no!' exclaimed Kirsty, jerking with such sharpness that some wine slopped out of the glass in her hand onto the table. 'I couldn't think of anything worse. I think it would kill me. He suggested I do the books, pay the wages, that sort of thing. Apart from hating it, I don't have the background for office work.'

'I'm sure he meant well,' said Janice gently, patting the back of Kirsty's hand with her French-manicured one.

'He did. But he doesn't seem to understand that I need to build a life of my own. Neither of them do.'

'I take it you said "no"?' said Clare.

'I did and he took the huff. I think he was hurt.'

'He'll get over it,' said Patsy. 'I know it's hard for them. It's understandable that they want to be as close to their grandsons as possible. And that's great – you wouldn't want it any other way. But they mustn't expect you to be answerable to them. They have to respect your right to an independent life.'

'Hear! Hear!' said Clare and she gave a little round of applause.

Right Patsy may be, thought Kirsty, but it put her on a collision course with Dorothy and Harry.

'You're much more likely to meet an eligible man working in the museum than stuck in that factory all day,' mused Janice.

'That hadn't occurred to me,' said Kirsty, unable to contain the smile that sprang to her lips. Janice was far more interested in finding a man for Kirsty than she was herself. All the same, the observation helped to strengthen her resolve. 'But you're right, Janice.'

'Are you going to apply for it, then?' said Clare.

'I'll have my application in first thing, Monday morning. Wish me luck!'

'To Kirsty,' said Clare, always quick to raise her glass, and the others copied. Then the food arrived and everyone was absorbed in eating and exchanging chit-chat.

When Janice was finished – she'd eaten only half of what was on her plate – she leant forwards in the chair, and said conspiratorially, 'Now, what's the latest on your safari, Patsy?'

Patsy started and her napkin dropped to the floor. She bent down under the table to pick it up and reappeared somewhat flustered-looking. She shook the napkin in the air and laid it across her lap.

'Well, I've paid the deposit,' she said.

Everyone was silent, waiting for her to go on. It wasn't like Patsy to be so reticent. Kirsty was just beginning to wonder if something was wrong when Patsy's face broke into her more familiar smile. 'It hasn't been easy keeping it a secret from Martin, let me tell you,' she said brightly. 'I had to hide the holiday brochures under the bed and I'm terrified someone from the travel agency's going to call when he's there and spoil the whole thing!'

'What's the itinerary, then?' asked Janice. Patsy pulled a slim brochure out of her bag and passed it to Janice, who flicked through the pages and nodded approvingly while Patsy talked.

'We're going to the Central Kalahari Game Reserve – it's the second biggest in the world. And the Chobe National Park, which has sixty thousand elephants. Then there's the Makgadikgadi saltpans, which are supposed to be amazing.'

'Saltpans?' asked Kirsty, picking up the brochure from where Janice had discarded it on the table. It all sounded so incredibly exciting, so far removed from her dull, everyday existence.

'They're very remote, shallow basins containing salt deposits from an evaporated lake. They stretch for miles and you explore them on quad bikes.'

Kirsty nodded, her eyes coming to rest on a picture of a vast white plain, the edges disappearing in a shimmering heat-haze. In the photograph a rugged explorer sat astride a black quad bike, a pair of slender arms wrapped round his waist.

'I know it's just a holiday,' said Patsy, looking round at the others, her grey-green eyes misted. 'But for me it's a dream come true. A once-in-a-lifetime experience for me and Martin. I doubt if we'll ever do anything just as exciting, or expensive, as this again. It's going to be the proper honeymoon we never had. I've been thinking we could renew our marriage vows.'

'Ohhh,' the women chorused in unison and Kirsty said, 'That's so romantic.'

'It would be, wouldn't it?' said Patsy and paused. 'When you've been married a long time, well, you have to do things to . . . to re-connect every now and then. It's easy to lose each other in the everyday business of living, isn't it?'

'I know what you mean,' said Clare and Kirsty wondered if that had been part of her and Scott's problem. Had they allowed themselves to drift apart? Given up too easily? If he had lived would they have been able to re-connect? Would she have been able to save her marriage?

Kirsty eyes pricked with tears and she picked up the brochure and stared at the glossy pictures of majestic lions and leopards, a prehistoric-looking hippo, vast herds of antelope, and a great cloud of long-legged birds rising from a lake. It was a magical world, so remote from small-town Ireland, so exotic, primeval even.

Maybe one day she would go and see these things for

herself. She'd like to. But not on her own. It was an experience to share with someone – and not just anyone. Your soulmate. She threw the brochure down in the middle of the table as though it had suddenly become too hot to hold and pushed the remains of her spaghetti carbonara away. Her appetite had evaporated.

She had so much to be grateful for, but she was fed up being alone. Fed up standing on the sidelines of life watching other people, like Patsy, getting on with theirs. She was absolutely delighted for her friend but she couldn't help but wish it was her planning the holiday of a lifetime with the man she loved.

She would just have to try harder. She glanced at the men at the bar, almost all of whom she knew – or knew of. Ignoring the married ones, she studied the four available men in her age group, three divorced, one single. The fact that Vincent Agnew, plumber, was in his forties and had never, so local gossip went, been in a committed relationship didn't bode well, Kirsty thought. And not only did she know the ex-wives of the others – she even knew the names of their children. That was problem with Ballyfergus; you knew far too much about everybody and you never met anyone new. And try as she might she didn't find any of them in the least bit attractive.

She averted her gaze and looked out of the window instead. Outside an icy fog had settled and the crisp night air was punctuated only by the soft haze of the street-lamp and squares of yellow light in the low-rise block of flats opposite. The only males she liked spending time with these days were David, Adam and Harry – how sad was that? Things, she decided firmly, would have to change.

Chapter Seven

The letter from the council finally came on a wet and windy Friday morning in the last week of February. Kirsty, recognising what it was at once from the frank mark on the envelope, retrieved it from the doormat before the boys trod on it in their muddy shoes. She set the long white envelope carefully on the hall table, drove the boys to school and could think of nothing else 'til she was back home.

Candy the cat, with her ragged patchwork coat of brown, marmalade and white, was there to greet her on her return. When Kirsty opened the door, Candy slanted her eyes and screwed her nose up in distaste, recoiling from the foul weather.

Kirsty shook the rain off her coat vigorously and hung it up to dry. She carried the letter into the kitchen, put on the kettle and stood by the sink examining the envelope, front and back. It was thin – it probably contained only one sheet of paper. Was that good or bad? She set it down on the counter and regarded it from a distance, realising only now how much hope she had placed on this job application.

Already she could see herself, smartly dressed in black trousers and a white shirt, standing behind the reception desk at the museum, smiling, helpful, professional. She imagined the different people she would meet, how time would fly, how she would have something else to think and talk about other than the buy-one-get-one free offer on dishwasher tablets at the supermarket. And how useful the extra money would be.

The kettle came to the boil and switched itself off.

But then there was that panel interview. She sighed and put her hands over her face. It had taken place a fortnight earlier in the council offices on Victoria Street, the former cottage hospital. She'd been intimidated by the grey suits and felt out of her depth – she was sure she'd spewed out a load of old rubbish.

Kirsty made a pot of tea and put milk in a mug. In her basket, Candy circled three times, kneaded the fleece rug with her paws, extending and retracting her claws, and then curled up with her eyes closed.

No, Kirsty was quite sure she'd blown it at the interview. Best not to get her hopes up. She picked the envelope up, put it down again. This was her first job application in years – she couldn't expect it to be successful. The sensible thing would be to view it as a learning experience. She would be better prepared next time round. She told herself there were probably hundreds of people more suited to the job than she was. And there would be other jobs, other opportunities.

But, oh, how she wanted this one!

Unable to bear it any longer, she took a deep breath, snatched the envelope up and ripped it open. She unfolded the crisp sheet of white paper inside and skim-read the short typed letter. Her eyes came to rest on the phrase, 'successful in your application'.

'Yeessss!' she cried and danced around the empty room, waving the letter above her head. She stopped, and read the letter again, just to be sure. Then she continued her celebratory dance around the island unit.

'Oh, Candy! I got the job! I got the job! I got the job!' she chanted. Candy looked up impassively, shut her eyes and went to sleep again.

Kirsty threw her head back and laughed, feeling euphoric for the first time in years. Her life was so dull, so pedestrian, so focused on the needs of the boys. This job was something just for her, a bit of independence, a chance to live a little, earn some money, maybe even have some fun. Wait 'til she told the girls! She punched the air with delight.

It was then that she saw him through the rain-streaked window, watching her. A man in a green waterproof, the hood pulled up over his head. His face was partly hidden, but the lopsided smile was unmistakable. It was Chris, the gardener.

Her hands dropped to her sides and she froze. Her heart pounded in her chest – the effect of the shock she'd just had, she supposed. She took a moment to compose herself, then stuffed the letter in the rack on the wall. She opened the back door, stood on the threshold with her arms folded and called out, 'You'd better come in out of the rain. You'll get drenched.'

Chris ducked his head as he entered the kitchen, dripping wet, his workboots leaving a brown slick on the tiles. He pulled the hood of his jacket down and was still grinning when he said, 'Thanks. I didn't mean to startle you.' His eyes, deep-set in a tanned, craggy face, were the colour of the blue hydrangea that grew in the front garden.

Kirsty blushed. 'It's okay.'

Chris Carmichael was a tall, broad-shouldered man with a figure honed by years of hard outdoor work that belied the fact that he was well into his forties. His short, greying hair, wet with rain, stood up in spikes as if it had been thickly gelled – though Kirsty was certain Chris had never used a hair-styling product in his life.

He did not proceed into the room but stopped just over the threshold, so that they stood together in the tight space between the open door and the fridge. Kirsty was suddenly aware of his proximity, the smell of wet and diesel and manly things. Unsettling smells and sensations she wasn't used to. She pressed her back against the fridge door, trying to put a little space between them.

'So what's made you so happy?' he said, pinning her against the fridge with his eyes. One corner of his full mouth turned up, causing a deep crease in his right cheek. In his younger days it would've been a dimple. He must've been so handsome back then. She noticed for the first time that he still was, though his attractiveness wasn't so much in his looks but his character. He exuded a virile magnetism and charisma that made Kirsty feel flustered.

'I got some good news, that's all,' she said off-handedly, a little afraid that he might be laughing at her.

'Please,' he said and smiled again, this time a full-on hundred-watt grin. He put a hand, strong and sinewy, to his head and attempted to flatten down his hair. While he did so, he looked down at her from under a deeply furrowed brow, his features taking on a boyish character, and said, 'Whatever it was, don't let me spoil it. I haven't seen you laugh like that before.'

Kirsty glanced at the letter in the rack and slipped away into the middle of the room. 'It's nothing really,' she said shyly, though the smile that crept to her lips belied this. 'Only I got a letter this morning offering me a job at the museum.'

'Why, that's really great, so it is, Kirsty. Well done you!'

His obvious delight in her success pleased Kirsty more than it ought to have. She went over to the sink, filled the kettle, then realised she'd already made tea. She turned to face him with her hands behind her back, as though she was hiding something. She held onto the edge of the work surface and asked, 'What are you doing here, Chris?'

She hadn't meant her question to come out so abruptly. She looked at her stockinged feet, embarrassed by her rudeness.

'I'm going round all my customers just to check that they're wanting me to come back this season.'

'Of course,' she said quickly. 'Of course I want you back. How would I cope without you?'

And she meant it. The garden had been Scott's pride and joy. He had designed it, planted it, built the pond one summer with the help of his father and spent every spare minute from March to October (when he wasn't out cycling) working in it. Kirsty, on the other hand, had never so much as turned a sod of earth nor cut a blade of grass.

The following spring after Scott died, Harry attempted to take on the maintenance of the garden but, also with his own large plot to tend, it soon became clear it was too much for him. The final straw came when he ended up in bed for a week with a strained back. That night Kirsty chose Chris at random from the Gardening Services section in the Yellow Pages.

'That's good,' said Chris. 'I don't like to make assumptions. I reckon the grass'll need its first cut in a couple of weeks.' She stole a glance at him in profile. He was staring out of the window, his eyes narrowed slightly, his crow's feet deep like scars. The rain hit the window loudly in bursts, like handfuls of peppercorns. 'And a feed,' he went on, 'the season's starting earlier every year.'

'Good business for you, then,' said Kirsty.

'Aye, I suppose it is,' he said in his soft Glens of Antrim accent and brought his gaze back to her. He shifted his weight from one foot to the other and placed the flat of his hand on the adjacent work surface.

'Would you like a cup of tea?' asked Kirsty, opening a cupboard and lifting out a second mug before he could reply. 'I've just made a pot.'

'So long as I'm not holding you back.'

'No, you're not. Stay.' She poured the tea and listened to the sound of his boots on the floor, the squeak of the chair being pulled out, the creak as it took his weight. When she turned around he was seated at the head of the table, his elbows resting on the oilcloth.

She placed a steaming mug in front of him, took a small round tin out of the cupboard, removed the lid and placed it on the table. 'Help yourself,' she said. 'Homemade shortbread.'

'Thanks,' said Chris, taking a piece and examining the crumbly biscuit. 'You've been busy.'

Kirsty laughed at the notion of her baking – she rarely did – and sat down in the chair next to him. She relaxed, comfortable to have him here in her kitchen, sitting at the table the way she used to sit with Scott in earlier, happier times. She realised how much she missed having a man about. 'I can't take credit for that. Dorothy made it.'

Chris nodded, took a bite of the shortbread and said, 'Haven't seen Harry and Dorothy since last summer. How are they doing?'

'Just the same. They're both well,' Kirsty said and took a big gulp of tea.

'They're good people, your in-laws,' he observed.

'Yes. I don't know what I would've done without them.' She thought fleetingly of the weeks immediately following Scott's death and pushed the horrible memories from her mind. 'You know, in some ways the last three years have flown. I look at the boys sometimes and can't believe the size of them. David, especially, is getting very grown-up.'

Chris finished the shortbread, blew on his tea, took a noisy sip. 'Hard to imagine now but they'll be up and away faster than you think, Kirsty. In a blink of an eye, really. You've probably heard people say that a hundred times but it really is true. And suddenly you're on your own.' He paused, looked a little sheepish and added hastily, as though worried he might have upset her, 'Though I guess that's a long way off yet.'

'No, not really,' she said, keen to show him that she wasn't troubled by the prospect. 'In seven years David will be sitting his driving test. I imagine by the time they're fourteen or fifteen, they're not going to want to spend much time with me. That's one of the reasons I'm taking this job at the museum.'

He nodded approvingly, and she took it as encouragement to go on.

'Dorothy's been supportive but Harry's not very happy about it. He wanted me to take an office job at the mill. Can you imagine? I can't think of anything worse!'

Chris laughed and she went on, 'He doesn't understand that I need a bit of independence from them. I need to start getting out and meeting people, living a little. You know.'

Chris nodded once and said, 'Don't be too hard on him, Kirsty. It's just that he cares for you and the boys. And I . . .' He paused, then went on, ' . . . Well, it's understandable, isn't it? After what you've all been through, it's understandable that he's a bit protective. I would be too.'

A little ashamed, Kirsty stared at him for a few moments, taking in the detail of his profile – the weatherbeaten skin on his cheeks, the strong line of his jaw, an old scar she'd not noticed before that ran from his ear into the neck of his shirt. She liked the way every emotion played out across his craggy features and the stillness of the rest of him. He was, she thought, a man at peace with his world and his place in it. 'I know he's only thinking of what's best for us. He means well.'

'He'll come round, you'll see.'

Kirsty bit her lip and there was a short silence. Chris cleared his throat and frowned before addressing her. 'And I suppose you'll be starting to date,' he said, without taking his eyes off his motionless hands where they lay, palms down, on the table.

Kirsty started, a little shocked by such a personal question. She put her hands together and pressed them so hard her knuckles went white. Her pulse throbbed in her temple, filling her ears with noise. She managed to shrug and said, 'I have been on one or two dates, yes. My friends keep setting them up. In fact,' she added nervously, 'they seem more interested in pairing me off than I am!'

Too late, she wished she could retract what she'd just said. She didn't mean to give Chris the impression she wasn't in the market for a partner. 'It's just, well, I don't think I've met the right person yet,' she said and felt herself colouring.

'I hope you don't mind me saying this, Kirsty,' he said softly, tracing the harlequin pattern on the oilcloth with his right index finger. 'I know that it's really none of my business. And if you don't want me to say another word about it, I won't.'

'Say what?'

'It's just that, well, I saw you in No.11 the other week.' He drained the mug.

'You were in No.11?' asked Kirsty, incredulously. 'I didn't see you.'

'It's not a place I normally go. You know the way I live down at Glenarm?'

Kirsty nodded, though this was news to her. Glenarm, dating back to the twelfth century and lying ten miles north of Ballyfergus, was one of the prettiest villages in County Antrim. Named after one of the famous Nine Glens of Antrim, the village nestled at the bottom of the glen from which it took its name, where the wide river, rich in brown trout, met the sea.

'Well, I was down this way one night a couple of weeks ago, seeing about a bit of business,' said Chris, 'and popped in with a mate for a drink. And that's when I saw you.'

'Why didn't you come over?' said Kirsty, perplexed. Chris was usually so friendly.

'Well, you were with someone,' said Chris and shot her a meaningful glance. She felt her face colour. 'And,' he went on, looking away, 'I didn't like to interrupt.'

'Oh, that'll have been Vincent Agnew, the plumber,' she said airily, taking care to sound dismissive. 'Sandy-haired fella, tall like you, about six foot two?'

Silently Kirsty cursed Janice for persuading her to meet Vincent for a drink – and herself for going along with it, in spite of her misgivings about the man. The date had been a disaster. She should have known. When Vincent wasn't staring at her cleavage, he was eyeing up other women in the room. No wonder he was single.

'Aye, it was Vincent Agnew alright.'

She'd only done it to get Janice off her back. Now all she cared about was making it clear to Chris that she and Vincent weren't an item. 'I'm not seeing him, you know,' she said, far too quickly. It sounded like an apology.

'You're not?'

Kirsty shook her head almost violently and laughed. 'God no, I mean I just met him for a drink that once. All he talked about was golf and his Mercedes. I never saw him again. Why do you ask?'

Was it possible that Chris was jealous? She held her breath.

'Well, that's a relief,' he said, blew air out softly through his nose and placed his palms on his thighs. 'I don't usually go round slandering people, Kirsty. But Vincent Agnew is trouble. He's a reputation as a gambler and he likes the drink too. Let's just say that he's not the sort of bloke I'd be happy for my daughter to bring home.'

'You have a daughter,' echoed Kirsty faintly and she put her hand to her throat.

'Two actually. All grown up with kids of their own. I'm a grandfather now,' he said and chuckled. He picked up the empty cup and looked inside it. 'Can you believe it?'

'No,' she managed to say, forcing her lips into a smile that felt more like a grimace. Why should she be surprised by this news? Given Chris's age, it was only natural that he should have a family. And probably a wife too. She wondered what she was like. She'd known him for two and a half years, and yet she knew so very little about him.

'I hope I haven't spoken out of turn, Kirsty. But I just couldn't stand by and let you get involved with someone like that. Not without saying something.' He smiled then and added, 'I'm as bad as Harry in some ways, you know. I suppose it's because you're on your own. I hope you don't find that patronising. Or mind my interfering.'

'No, no, not at all,' said Kirsty, stumbling over the words.

'I haven't offended you, have I?' He reached out and patted her hands.

She coughed and said, 'No.' She cleared her throat and went on, 'No, not at all, Chris. I appreciate the concern. I really do. But you've no need to worry on that front. I won't be seeing Vincent Agnew again.'

'Good,' he said and gave the table a slap with the flat of his hand. 'You know what, Kirsty?' She thought she detected a catch in his voice. 'You're a lovely woman. I think you can do a whole lot better than the Vincent Agnews of this world.'

And with that he got up abruptly, went over to the sink, rinsed his cup and set it upside-down on the draining board. A simple gesture, yet one that spoke of thoughtfulness.

'Oh, there was one last thing I meant to ask you,' said Chris.

'Yes?'

'Would you like to pay me by direct debit now instead of cash? You can set up the payment with your bank and then you just cancel it in the autumn. Saves having to scrabble round every week finding cash. Most of my customers like the idea.'

'Oh,' said Kirsty and added instinctively, 'No. I don't think I'd like that.' Handing cash over was a good excuse for instigating a conversation and it meant that Chris had to come at a time when she was in. 'I like to see you.'

'You do?' he said and stood stock still.

'Yes. I like to talk to you,' she said, and added hastily, 'I mean it's important that . . . that we talk about what you're doing in the garden.'

'Yes, of course. Well, whatever suits you. I really don't mind.'

'Cash then. I'll give you cash like before.'

'Okay,' he said, zipped up his coat and put up the hood, ready to face the elements. 'I'll be off then,' he said as he made for the back door. 'See you in a few weeks. And good luck with the new job.'

After he'd gone, Kirsty went upstairs and energetically stripped both boys' beds. When the sheets, pillowcases and rocket-covered duvet covers were heaped on the floor in a tangle of dark blue cotton, she sat down on David's bed clutching the nearly-bald panda he clung to every night in bed, even though he was nearly ten.

She should've asked Chris about his wife when he mentioned his daughters. She could've slipped the question in quite naturally and it wouldn't have seemed like she was prying. Now the moment had passed and she was sure she wouldn't have the courage to raise it again.

But Ballyfergus was a small place and Chris must be relatively well-known. Someone would be able to tell her. His wife might be dead – God rest her soul – or he could be divorced. Or maybe never married in the first place. She would not give up hope just yet.

She carried the washing downstairs, knelt on the floor and stuffed it into the washing machine. Then she stood up, threw in a washing tablet, closed the door with her knee and paused momentarily. All she could think about was Chris. She put her fingertips to her lips and breathed in deeply. What was she thinking?

He was, she guessed, about ten years older than she. He was undeniably handsome and yet, though Kirsty had always liked him, she had not thought of him romantically before. Now she couldn't get him out of her mind.

She imagined what it would be like to be enveloped in his arms, to feel his rugged cheek pressed against her forehead. She shook her head and smiled. She was acting like a besotted teenager. But daft though it might be at her age, it also felt good. There was nothing wrong with a bit of fantasising, was there? For one thing it was harmless and for another, it restored her belief in love – a faith that she feared had been lost to her for ever.

The very next night Kirsty sat at the usual table in No.11 waiting for her friends.

'It's great to have something to celebrate!' said Patsy

brightly when she arrived with Janice. Though she was smart in a green wrap-dress and black boots, she looked a little jaded to Kirsty. 'Congratulations on your new job!'

Janice leant across the table and air-kissed the place beside either side of Kirsty's cheeks. Her lips were carefully glossed to match her thin red jumper, cinched at the waist with a plaited black leather belt. Although Kirsty had made an effort and changed into smart black jeans, a shirt and belted 'boyfriend' cardigan, she still managed to feel underdressed. But then she always felt underdressed around Janice.

'Well done, Kirsty. Though we always knew you'd get the job, didn't we, Patsy?' Patsy nodded. 'Now where's Clare?' Janice swivelled round to look at the door, a clutch of bangles on her wrist clinking against one another.

'She should be here any minute,' explained Kirsty. 'She came over with the kids today. They had an early tea together before I took Adam and David over to their grandparents'. She's probably running a bit late.'

It wasn't long before Clare arrived, casual in jeans and a grey t-shirt. She was followed shortly by Danny, dressed all in black save for a white bartender's apron that reached below his knees. In one hand he held a steel ice bucket, in the other the stems of four wine glasses were wedged between his fingers.

'A little bird told me you ladies have something to celebrate tonight.' He winked at Patsy and set the ice bucket, beaded with condensation, on the table. Then he placed the wine glasses, one by one, alongside it. 'This is for you and it's on the house,' he said pulling a bottle of white wine from the ice and presenting it to Kirsty with a flourish.

Kirsty put a hand on her breast. 'Oh, Danny. Thank you. That is such a lovely thing to do.'

'That's why No.11 is the best wee bar in Ballyfergus,' he said, gave her a cheeky wink and disappeared.

Janice filled the glasses and handed them round while they all remarked on Danny's thoughtfulness. 'Here's to Kirsty's success now and in the future,' she toasted, holding her glass aloft and momentarily drawing the attention of people seated nearby.

Kirsty reddened and ducked her head.

Everyone took a sip of wine and Janice said, 'You must be so excited.'

'Yes, I am,' said Kirsty, looking at Clare. 'I was telling Clare earlier that I'm really looking forward to getting started. And earning some money. I'm nervous too. It's been a long time since I went out to work.'

'You'll be absolutely fine, Kirsty. The museum is lucky to get someone of your calibre,' said Clare loyally, her plain features illuminated by a warm smile. The others murmured their agreement.

'That's sweet of you to say so,' said Kirsty, both a little embarrassed and heartened by their confidence in her. She twirled the glass in her hand and, staring at it, said, 'There's just one thing.'

'What's that?' said Clare.

'I haven't told Dorothy and Harry yet.'

'What job you take has got nothing to do with them,' said Patsy firmly.

Kirsty sighed and looked at her friend. She opened her mouth to explain that it had everything to do with them, then closed it again. Patsy would not understand. None of them would. It would be hard to take on any job without her in-laws' support. And she was certain that the best she could hope for on this particular occasion was resentful acceptance.

'They might surprise you,' said Clare quietly.

'I doubt it.'

'Well, there's only one way to find out,' said Patsy pragmatically.

There was a short silence while they all considered this. Kirsty let out a long sigh and then said flatly, 'I'll have to tell them tomorrow.'

Janice broke the sombre mood. 'I thought this was supposed to be a celebration?' she said brightly. 'Come on! Drink up, girls.' She lowered her voice then and a conspiratorial smile spread across her face. 'The wine's very nice but you can't have a proper celebration without champagne, now can you? And this time it's on me!'

Harry came out as soon as Kirsty pulled the car up outside his house the next morning, as though he had been watching for her. He hailed her with a raised hand in the air, not so much a wave as a salute.

'How are you, dear?' he greeted her heartily as she stepped out of the car. 'Did you have a good time with your friends last night?'

'Great,' said Kirsty, who was nursing a bit of a hangover. She gave Harry a brief kiss and patted him on the back. 'Thanks for having the boys.'

'Ach, we've had a great time with them,' said Harry, with an indulgent shake of the head. He slowed to a halt just outside the open door, even though it was cold and neither of them had on an outdoor coat. He put his hands in the pockets of his sharp-creased trousers and rolled back slightly on the heels of his brown leather brogues. 'I've been thinking, Kirsty, about what you said about going out to work. And I'm sorry I was a bit abrupt when we spoke about it before.'

'Oh, Harry,' said Kirsty, touched by his apology. 'You don't need to be worrying about that. It's all forgotten.'

'Well, I've given it some more thought and I should have

realised before.' He said this with an air of confidence that set off alarm bells in Kirsty's head.

'Realised what?' said Kirsty, raising her guard.

'What if I said that I would make sure you and the boys were alright for money?'

'I don't follow . . .' said Kirsty.

'You've never asked Dorothy and me for a penny, Kirsty, and I respect you for that. I know that there was an insurance payout but all the same, it can't have been easy. I don't want you to feel you have to work just to make ends meet. You don't have to. There's money there for David and Adam. You might as well have some of it now if it makes life a bit easier.'

Kirsty's heart sank. The last thing she wanted was to be having this conversation with Harry. She just wanted to get the boys and go home and daydream about Chris. She sighed. Poor Harry. He was right. She *was* going out to work to make ends meet – but taking this job was about much more than just money.

'I'm okay for money, Harry. Really,' she said firmly, and surprised herself by holding eye contact with Harry even though she was lying.

For the past three years she'd been living on the proceeds of the insurance policy. Of course, she'd always known that one day the money would run out and she would have to return to work. The mortgage had been repaid on Scott's death but there were still utilities to meet and the ever-increasing cost of food. The boys had only been three and six when their father died and for two years after Scott's death she had been petrified to let them out of her sight, entrusting them only to the care of her in-laws and Clare. She had put off returning to work as long as possible – but she could delay it no longer. And she no longer wanted to either. She was ready to face the world again.

A cloud passed over Harry's face and Kirsty, both touched and frustrated, said, 'Oh, Harry, it is sweet of you to offer and I really appreciate it. You keep the money for the boys – they'll need it when they're older for college and university and stuff.' She paused, softened her tone and added, 'One of the reasons I'm going out to work is because I need to move on from what's happened. I need to rebuild my life, Harry.'

'But what would Scott want?' he said and eyeballed her. 'For you and the boys.'

'Scott's not here any more,' she parried straight back, and immediately regretted it.

Harry winced as though from some physical pain and she could've kicked herself for her insensitivity. 'I'm sorry,' she said. 'I shouldn't have said that.'

Harry looked away, at the bird's-eye view of Ballyfergus which spread out below them, the red-brick houses so tiny they looked like they were made of Lego bricks.

'Scott loved this house,' he said. 'When he was a boy he used to say that it felt like being on top of the world.' He shook his head. 'I thought that you and he might live in it one day. After Dorothy and I were gone, I mean.' He smiled at her then, his eyes glazed with tears that he would never shed, not in her presence anyway.

'I'm so sorry, Harry.'

'Well, it wasn't to be.'

They stood side by side for a few moments, staring at the view of the town which Kirsty had come to love. She took a deep breath, exhaled and steeled herself for the delivery of unwelcome news.

'I've been offered the job at the museum,' she said quietly and glanced at Harry to gauge his reaction. He ground a toe into the gravel, thrust his hands deep in his trouser pockets. 'And I've decided to take it,' she said.

Harry nodded and a little of the ramrod straightness went out of his stance. His shoulders dropped a fraction and he nodded resignedly. There was something defeated about him that reached out to her.

'You do know that this doesn't change anything, Harry? Not for you and Dorothy and the boys. In fact, you'll probably see more of them, so much so you'll be sick of the sight of them!' she said, injecting a note of humour.

He forced a grim smile. 'Never.'

'Please be happy for me,' said Kirsty. 'It's only a part-time job, Harry. It won't interfere with my responsibilities towards the boys. It won't change things,' she added, and realised that this was not true.

Taking the job was the first step towards cutting the ties that bound her so closely to her in-laws. She knew it and so did Harry. For her it was a positive move towards a new sort of life. She was young enough to start over, to have a second chance at happiness.

But what of Dorothy and Harry? All they had were memories of a beloved son taken in his prime, a daughter they rarely saw and two grandchildren who were the centre of their world. No wonder they were terrified of a change in the status quo. For every step towards independence on Kirsty's part would, by necessity, undermine the intimacy of their relationship with her and the boys.

'Okay,' said Harry resignedly, and he had the good grace to summon up a pleasant smile. 'If it's what you want.' He put his arm around her shoulder then, heavy like a yoke, and steered her up the steps into the house. 'Come on, then. I suppose we'd better tell Dorothy the good news.'

Chapter Eight

Since taking up scrapbooking last year, Janice had commandeered one of the spare bedrooms on the third floor as her work room. The never-used single bed had been removed and replaced with an office chair on wheels and a large ash-coloured table, pushed up against the window to make the most of the natural light. A bookcase held all the things she needed in pretty cardboard boxes decorated with floral prints.

Neither Keith nor Pete ventured up here often and the work room had become something of a sanctuary for Janice. A place where she could escape and immerse herself in a hands-on practical activity that she had once derided – and now found addictive and strangely therapeutic. And, if truth be told, it helped to fill her long, purposeless days.

This particular wet and windy Friday afternoon at the end of March, finding herself with nothing to do, Janice had chosen a project that she knew she would find absorbing, though difficult. She wondered if it had escaped the notice of her new friends from the scrapbooking course, that she had never made an album of her only child. They probably thought it odd. And it was.

She'd made albums of her wedding, holidays they'd taken as a family both abroad and in Ireland. She'd given books as gifts and even made one of the house, The Rectory, to pass down to future generations, whom Keith imagined would inhabit the place long after they were gone. But, in almost a year of scrapbook-making, she had never made an album of Pete. Now she was about to rectify that.

In planning this album Janice had come to the realisation that it wouldn't be a baby album as she'd first envisaged, and there was a very good reason for that. She had only two dozen or so pictures of Pete under the age of two, all of them taken by other people. She hadn't owned a camera until Keith bought her one, two months after they met. So the album would be a childhood album instead, populated by photos of Pete in his Scout uniform, playing football, in his rugby kit, Christmases and birthdays – all the memorable events that formed the pillars of a happy childhood. Only the first few pages would be devoted to his babyhood.

It would be a special gift from her to him before he left home to go to university – her way of saying that she loved him, even though she hadn't always been able to show it. She would give it to him in April, on his eighteenth birthday. After he'd left home, she doubted he would ever come back home again to live. He was so incredibly self-sufficient, so determinedly self-contained. He had told her once that he did not need anyone for anything and she believed him. She did not know if this fierce independence was an asset or a flaw.

Standing on tiptoe and reaching, just, with the tips of her fingers, she teased a brown cardboard box from its place on the top shelf of the bookcase. There was a thin film of grime on the top; she ran her index finger lightly across the lid then examined the soft pad of flesh on the tip. It was, as she knew it would be of course, charcoal with dust. She wiped her finger on her jeans.

Once seated at the table, she removed the lid, set it on

the floor and lifted out a handful of the mostly six-by-four inch photos that lay at the bottom of the box. She spread them out and sifted through them until she came across the ones she was looking for – the earlier photos of Pete. She found twenty or so photos in all, half of them taken with her in the picture too, either holding him in her arms or on her knee. They were of varying quality from very poor to okay.

Blond-haired and delicate, Pete looked like someone else's baby, staring out from the photos with those pinched blue eyes and that hostile expression. In only one photo was he laughing, revealing shiny gums and four brand-new front teeth. In every picture he was dressed in bright primary colours – his clothes, she remembered, had come mainly from charity shops. Janice hardly recognised the young woman in the photographs. It pained her to look at herself as she was then, knowing the misery and the pain behind that sunny smile and pretty face. For she *had* been pretty, beautiful even, though it had taken Keith to make her realise it.

She had met him when Pete was two, after she had dropped out of a degree course in physiotherapy at Jordanstown. Falling pregnant with Pete, her one and only child, in her second year had put paid to any dreams of obtaining a degree. It was just too damned hard. She had raised Pete alone with no practical or financial support from anyone but the state – until Keith came along. She had sacrificed her ambitions and hopes to give her child the very opportunities his birth had so cruelly taken from her.

Not even their closest friends knew that Keith was not Pete's real father. She'd gone against Keith's wishes in not telling Pete he was adopted. But that had been a mistake, Janice could see now, and one that, as Keith repeatedly pointed out, they would have to rectify soon. Pete would find out anyway when he eventually saw his birth certificate – he'd need it to enrol at university. They couldn't put it off much longer. He was almost an adult, careering towards the day when he would leave home. And, much as she dreaded the idea of telling him, even Janice acknowledged that he had the right to know.

But Keith was one of the few moderating influences in Pete's life. Finding out that he was not, after all, his real dad might change the dynamics between father and son, and that, to Janice's mind, could only be a bad thing. She had at one time entertained the idea of persuading Keith to pretend that he was Pete's real dad. But how then could they explain away 'father unknown' on the birth certificate? Not unless Keith also pretended that he had initially abandoned her and the baby . . . she could never ask that of him. And besides, anyone who knew Keith, including Pete, would know that he wasn't capable of doing such a thing.

She picked up a blurred photograph of a Pete aged about six months, strapped in his buggy, wearing a blue corduroy coat and staring crossly at the camera. She recalled with sudden clarity an aspect of Pete's babyhood which, along with many others, she had tried to forget. When he was past the newborn stage, around five months old, Janice refused point-blank to lift him from his cot before seven in the morning, no matter how early he woke.

After a few weeks of prolonged screaming he eventually got the message and lay quiet and wide-eyed until she came to him in the mornings. Back then, as an exhausted single mum on the verge, she realised now, of breakdown, it had been a coping mechanism. With hindsight it looked more like neglect. This insight merely confirmed what she had known from day one: she was, and had been, a bad mother. Guilt consumed her. She'd made him what he was.

Looking at these pictures, it was impossible not to open the floodgates on the past. Her heartbeat quickened as other, more painful memories came crowding in. She set the photos down on the table and took a deep breath to steady her nerves. She wiped the sweat from her palms on the fabric of her jeans and took a deep breath. Best to concentrate on the task in hand, she told herself. She selected a handful of the best baby pictures, and set about arranging them on three album pages she'd laid out on the table. Once she'd decided on a layout, she selected sheets of coloured paper to make the backgrounds and a selection of baby-related stickers, chipboard cut-outs and thin blue ribbon.

Then she pasted a sheet of pale blue paper on the first page of the album and set about cutting out shapes from a contrasting paper. She found plain cream card, cut it into little squares with pinking shears to create crimped edges, and wrote annotations for the pictures. Banal stuff like 'at the park' and 'on the beach', that added nothing to the photos but filled the page nicely. Then she set about gluing everything in position.

She concentrated hard on the task in hand but her thoughts took themselves off in directions she would rather they did not go. Frustratingly, she could not seem to control them. The photos had stirred up the usual disturbing memories, the ones she coped with on a daily basis.

She was nineteen years old, in her second year at Jordanstown. Janice had arrived at university not knowing a soul and hoping that she might somehow be able to shed the skin of her past and emerge like a butterfly, entirely reinvented. In halls she was befriended by two girls, Marie and Katy from Tandragee, County Armagh, a village best known as the home of Tayto, Northern Ireland's favourite brand of crisps.

According to Marie and Katy there really was a Tayto Castle, just like it said on the back of the packets, which housed the crisp factory. Janice had always been sceptical of this claim, even as a small child, but she was glad it was true. She imagined a fairytale Disney-inspired castle, with turrets like needles pricking the sky, and festooned with coloured flags. The reality, Marie assured her, was far more mundane. She maintained you could smell the crisps frying three miles away. The formula for the famous cheese-and-onion flavoured crisps was, Katy said in a conspiratorial tone, a closely guarded secret. Not even her uncle who had worked there for the past seventeen years as a shift manager knew the recipe.

For some unfathomable reason, Marie and Katy made it their business to take her under their wing, not noticing that her lack of confidence and low self-esteem made it hard for her to reciprocate their friendship. She lived with the fear that they would find her out, that one day they would realise that she was not worthy of their acquaintance.

Men on the other hand she understood, or thought she did. She'd spent her first year acquiring a well-justified reputation for sleeping around, constantly trying to bolster a fragile self-worth. So long as she could pull, it kept her chronic insecurity at bay. Other girls began to avoid her, and still Marie and Katy did not abandon her. She gained the impression that they were slightly in awe of her. She imagined they thought her experienced, worldly-wise and sophisticated. She tried not to disappoint.

Janice sat with them in the busy cafeteria at lunchtime, trying very hard not to look self-conscious – she always felt that people were staring at her, subjecting her to scrutiny and uncompromising judgment. She sat between Marie and Katy, not listening to a word either of them said, wondering what she was doing here. She wasn't like most of the other students – bright-eyed, keen, enthusiastic. Or indeed the ones at the opposite end of the spectrum – the ones that feigned no interest in their subjects (while taking care never to actually fail), chain-smoked in public and were at pains to adopt a nonchalant, worldly air. At nineteen Janice was already jaded – she didn't have to pretend.

Three men, dressed in working clothes, came in and Janice, in an effort to calm her wayward thoughts, gave them her full attention. They wore matching fluorescent jackets splattered with mud, hard hats and heavy boots. They were in their early thirties, well-built and bronzed from working outdoors. One of them in particular, the tallest one with thick, dark hair, caught her eye. He got a tray, selected some food, paid for it and went to sit with his colleagues at a table close by.

'Look at him over there,' she said and pointed. 'Now there's a real man,' she added to impress Marie and Katy. 'Not a boy like the rest of this lot.' She glanced deridingly at the skinny, pale-faced physics students sitting at the table next to them.

Marie giggled. Katy said, in that North Armagh accent that made her sound like a softer female version of Ian Paisley, who hailed from the same county, 'They're the builders working on the sports hall extension. I've seen them in their van.'

Marie said, 'You're terrible, so you are, Janice. Don't tell me you're going to chat him up?'

'Watch me.' Janice got up and swaggered over to the table where the men were seated.

'Mind if I join you?' she asked and slid onto the bench beside the handsome man.

He shrugged without taking his eyes off his plate. One of the others said, 'Suit yerself, darlin'.'

She sat down beside the handsome man and crossed her legs, well aware that this hoisted her already short denim skirt up a further two inches. She wore opaque tights and those flat-heeled crumpled ankle boots that were fashionable back then. 'Mind if I have one,' she said and took a chip from his plate.

He scowled and she said, 'You don't mind, do you? I'm starving.'

He carried on eating.

'I'm Janice,' she said and extended a slim hand.

He paused, looked at her hand, and one of the other men sniggered.

'Hmm,' he said gruffly, his innate manners preventing him from ignoring her entirely. He gave her a limp handshake and withdrew his calloused hand quickly.

'So are you working round here or what?'

'Have been these last three weeks,' said one of the other men and gave Janice a grin, revealing a mouthful of rotten teeth like decaying tree stumps. She ignored him.

The third man finished eating, burped, stood up and said, 'I'm off. Need to get some fags. Are you coming, Pat?'

'Reckon I am,' said Pat. 'Two's company, three's a crowd. Know what I mean?' He gave Janice a wink and licked his lips.

When they were alone, the man said nothing until he'd finished eating. Then he pushed his plate away, finished his can of Coke and said, 'What do you want, Janice?'

'Just some company,' said Janice. She placed her elbow on the table, rested her chin on her fist, and tried to look bored. As though all the humanity around her, apart from this man, was beneath her. 'Is that a crime?'

He looked round the vast, high-ceilinged space and then

brought his calm gaze to rest on her. 'Reckon there's plenty of company in here more suited to your age than me,' he said and speared her with a cool glance. His eyes were the same blue-grey colour of the curtains in her bedroom at home.

She squirmed uncomfortably in her seat, glad that Marie and Katy were too far away to hear. 'I prefer the company of older men,' she said brazenly.

He flicked his eyes over her, ran his tongue round the inside of his mouth and said, 'Not ones that are married, you don't.'

'Wanna bet?' she said and gave him a sultry smile.

He regarded her coldly, took a toothpick out of his pocket and picked his teeth. 'Listen, doll,' he said. 'I'm gonna give you some advice. Stop behaving and,' he added, running his eyes quickly over her attire, 'dressing like a prostitute.' He leant close to her and she caught sight then of a silver cross around his neck on a thick belcher chain. He whispered angrily, 'You should be ashamed of yourself. Look at you. You're little more than a slip of a girl and, if you were my daughter, I'd tan your arse, so I would.'

And with that he got up and left her sitting there alone absolutely mortified, her cheeks burning with shame and humiliation. Because she knew that everything he said was true – she did act and behave like a slut. The only difference between her and a prostitute was that she didn't get paid. But glancing over at Katy and Marie, she told herself she didn't care. She put a cocky smile on her face and sauntered back to them and told them lies about the conversation that had just taken place.

A week later she ended up at a post-pub party at a flat on the Shore Road. The flat – she'd no idea who lived there – was cold and desperately unkempt. The blood-red velvet curtains in the lounge were ripped in places, as though someone deranged had slashed them with a knife. In the lounge there was only one battered sofa occupied by a lovey-dovey couple so everyone else stood or sat on the gritty carpet, trying to strum up a party atmosphere. Madonna was playing on a high-tech looking CD player that sat on the floor beside the TV, incongruous amidst the squalor.

In the cramped kitchen, there was a bad smell. The party food consisted of suspicious-looking coarse paté on stale cream crackers, sagging damply in the middle. The paté was drying out, cracked at the edges like mud in a heatwave. There was a story going round about students serving their guests dog food for a laugh. Janice picked up a cracker and sniffed it. It smelt okay. Still, she wasn't going to risk it.

She pinched a warm beer from a Victoria Wine plastic bag on the counter and went back to the lounge where she leant against a wall with her right knee bent, the sole of her foot flat on the faded wallpaper. She would never have got away with that at home. Her mother was obsessively house-proud, fixated on keeping a clean and orderly home. She did housework every day and, apparently, enjoyed it, too busy with appearances to notice the rot within her own family.

The party was full of physiotherapy students from her course and lots of other people she'd never seen before. She'd gone alone because Marie and Katy had gone home for the weekend, as they often did. They'd return on Sunday night laden with home baking wrapped in metal foil and girlish stories of the local young farmers they would, no doubt, one day marry.

Janice had no intention herself of ever going home again. And sometimes, passing yet another tedious weekend all alone, she was envious of her new friends, jealous of their naïvety, their loving families and warm community, their certain faith that life was, and would continue to be, good to them. And most desirable of all, their belief that they deserved it. Maybe that was why she tolerated them, in the hope that some of their magic might wear off on her.

Maybe that too was why she took the crumbs of comfort that came her way in the form of sexual intercourse – the only way she understood back then how to give and receive affection. The workman's scathing words still echoed inside her head and she knocked back bottle after bottle of beer to try and erase them from her mind.

When a thin, bespeckled English lecturer, with a reputation as a letch, approached her in the hall she noted with satisfaction the wedding band on his finger.

He followed her gaze and rubbed the ring with the cracked edge of his right hand as though it might, the opposite of a genie, magically disappear. He sighed heavily and said, 'I . . . er . . . we're going through a bit of a bad patch at the moment. I'm renting a flat down here for a while. Just a temporary arrangement. Until we get things sorted out.'

Men were such lying bastards, Janice thought. The door behind her, to her right, lay slightly ajar. She put the flat of her palm against it and applied gentle pressure with her fingertips – the door yielded. She glanced inside. The room was dark but she could make out the shape of a single bed, the bedclothes in a heaped mess on the mattress. It was a girl's room – she could tell by the smell of perfume and the tangles of female clothing, including white lacy pants, which were strewn across the floor. Whoever lived here was a dirty bitch. But at least that was better than blokes' rooms which were, generally, ten times worse.

'So you're a free man then,' she said and took his hand in hers. It was hot and damp with sweat. He looked eager, pathetically grateful. She turned and entered the room.

She thought how she would boast of this to Marie and Katy on Sunday night – her finest conquest in some ways, given the lecturer's maturity and the fact that he was married. How it would put their mundane little escapades of the weekend in the shade. She was sure they expected no less of her and she would deliver.

So she closed the door tight behind them and became what she thought every man wanted.

Janice shivered, and put her hands to her cheeks. They burned with the same intensity and shame as they had done all those years ago sitting in that cafeteria. She gave her head a shake to clear her mind of the memories which, of course, would not disappear on command. They were stuck with stronger stuff than the glue she had absentmindedly used too much of and which now covered her hands.

As the wife of a prominent lawyer, Janice had reached a position in life where she had a lot to lose. Her sexual exploits, of which she had once been rather proud, were now a cause for embarrassment. By the time she'd met Keith she had a toddler in tow and was living a nun-like existence. He did not realise it, of course, but with his integrity and optimism, he had saved her. He had renewed her faith in men and life – and in so doing had saved her from the cynicism that threatened to destroy her. She took a deep breath, closed her eyes and tried to calm her nerves.

'Come on. Pull yourself together,' she said to the empty room, got up and went to the small bathroom next door and washed her hands.

When she came back into the room she realised that it was already dusk. She flicked the anglepoise light on and the desk flooded with light. She set about gluing the pictures and captions in place on the album pages.

Keith had no idea about her past, and she intended to keep it that way. She feared he might think less of her, or worse, be repulsed by her reckless promiscuity. Of course, she reminded herself, there was no reason why he should ever find out. She just had to be careful, that was all. Watchful.

She glued the last baby picture in place and sat back to admire the three pages laid out in a row on the table. But all she could think about were those awful, excruciating scenes from her past. She must stop torturing herself with these memories of a girl she no longer knew and a life that she wished had belonged to someone else.

'What're you doing?' said Pete's voice in left ear and Janice nearly leapt out of her skin.

'For heaven's sake,' she cried, spinning round in the chair to face him. 'Don't creep up on me like that. You scared the living daylights out of me.'

He backed off a little and held his hands in the air. 'Sor-ry,' he said, in a sing-song voice, elongating the syllables. Poking fun at her.

She knew she was red in the face. Of course Pete couldn't know what she had been thinking about but she felt caught red-handed all the same. And she didn't like him creeping up on her like that. This room was her place. Her sanctuary.

'What do you want?' she said.

'Nothing,' said Pete and he craned his neck to see what lay on the table. 'Are you making another one of those albums?'

'Maybe,' she said without turning round, using her body as a shield. She did not want him to see what she'd done. It would spoil the surprise.

'Hey, isn't that a picture of me? What does it say underneath? "Pete's first shoes",' he read.

'I didn't want you to see that.'

'Why not?'

'It's a . . . well, it's a present. For you.'

He frowned. 'What would I be wanting that for?'

She sighed, wounded. The surprise was ruined now. 'I was

going to give it to you for your birthday. It's going to be an album of your childhood from when you were a baby right up until . . . well, until now I suppose. I thought it would be something you'd like to take to university with you. You know, to remember home by.'

'Oh, Janice,' he said. 'That is totally gross. Thanks but no thanks.'

Janice pursed her lips and simmered with rage. How dare he speak to her like that? Even if he thought the album was naff, why couldn't he just pretend that he liked the idea? That would be the polite thing to do, the sensitive thing to do. But Pete was so incredibly self-centred the thought that he might have hurt her feelings never even crossed his mind. Or, more worrying, perhaps it had.

'You know what, Pete? You can be incredibly rude sometimes.'

'What'd I say?' he said and raised his bony shoulders in a gesture of innocence. 'I'm not going to lie and pretend I want the thing when I don't.'

'Sometimes you ought to think more about how other people feel than yourself. There's nothing wrong with a white lie now and then, you know.'

'Well, I am sorry. But at least I've saved you the trouble of doing the rest of it, haven't I? Better to know now than find out when you're finished.'

She turned away from him then, swivelled round in the seat, and stared at the album pages, tears pricking her eyes. The pictures were artfully arranged, the layout professional – it was one of her best attempts at scrapbooking to date. But there was no point in completing it. Pete did not want it. She threw the pages in the wastepaper bin.

'I'm just going to get something to eat,' he went on, apparently oblivious to her distress. 'And then I'm off out.'

'But I've made a casserole for dinner,' she said, turning to face him once more. 'It'll be ready shortly, if you'll just wait a bit.'

'Naw. I'll just grab a sandwich or something.'

'Okay,' said Janice slowly, trying very hard not to let this annoy her. 'Where are you going?'

'Jason Dobbin's eighteenth.'

'Where's that being held, then?'

'At The Kiln and then back to Jason's for a party.' Technically Pete was too young to be going to The Kiln but she decided to let that go.

'Will his parents be there?'

'I dunno. I suppose,' he said dismissively, like it was a stupid question. 'Can I take your car?'

So that was why he'd come up here – he wanted something after all. She should have known. She would make him sweat it out a bit.

'Lots of kids going from school, then?' she said.

He shrugged, impatient to be gone.

'Are you going straight to The Kiln at this time?' she asked, consulting her watch. 'It's only just gone six.'

'I'm going round to Al's first to watch a DVD. Can I take your car please?'

At least he'd remembered to add 'please' this time.

'Not if you're drinking,' she said.

'I'll leave it at The Kiln and collect it tomorrow.'

'You'd better. How will you get home from Jason's?'

'I'll walk. It's not that far.'

Janice nodded. 'Well, just you be careful. And I don't mean only the driving.'

He threw her one of his well-practised, withering looks. 'I'm not a kid,' he said. 'I know how to look after myself.'

And Janice had no doubt that he did. If there was one

thing Pete was good at, it was looking out for his own interests. She realised that her warning came more from a concern for other people rather than from fear that any harm would come to Pete.

He sauntered out of the room without so much as a goodbye. She could hear him whistling all the way down the narrow stairs to the second floor and into his room. She heard the door slam and the whistling stopped abruptly.

Somewhere along the line, and she couldn't quite put her finger on where exactly, she and Keith had gone terribly wrong in parenting this child. She was his mother, his blood, so she must take the lion's share of the blame. It was her fault and now it was too late.

She sincerely hoped he would find someone to love him – someone who would give him what she had not been able to. Unconditional love. She had done her best and in the end she had been found wanting – her best had not been good enough.

She felt guilty about that, but even guiltier about the fact that she couldn't wait for him to go to university. It was an awful admission to make, but it was true. She blushed with shame.

She retrieved the album pages from the bin. Pete might not want the album but Keith might. She could make it for Father's Day, her way of saying thank you for everything he had done for her. And for being a good and loving father to Pete. Keith would like that – he was a sentimental man.

Janice stared at the earliest photo of her with Pete, a fuzzy, out-of-focus snap taken by Marie at the hospital. How kind Marie and Katy had been, visiting her and bringing gifts for both her and the baby. They were the only true friends she had back then – and her only visitors at the hospital. And she'd repaid them by deliberately losing touch. She often wondered what they were doing now. She wished them well for they deserved it.

In spite of Marie and Katy pleading with her, she'd never told her parents about Pete. To this day they did not know he existed. She had told Keith and, later, Pete that her parents were dead. She hoped they were.

In the photo she was holding the newborn Pete in her arms and staring at the camera unsmiling. Pete's eyes were closed. He may have been asleep – she couldn't remember. His hands were curled up into tight fists ready to take on the world, as though from the moment of his birth he found fault with it. Janice looked like she was in shock, which wasn't far from the truth.

She remembered those hazy weeks after Pete's birth, the numbing exhaustion, the fear and the loneliness. She had been miserable. She remembered how she nearly threw up every time she had to change Pete's nappy, how she could not breastfeed him no matter how much the nurses at the hospital nagged her to do it. She simply couldn't. And she still believed to this day that Pete would have turned out differently had she been able to bond with her newborn son.

Chapter Nine

It was late afternoon at the beginning of April and Patsy was sitting on the desk in the gallery, talking on the phone to Janice. They had just returned from the Art Ireland Spring fair at the Royal Dublin Society Showground, situated in the heart of Dublin. She and the girls – Kirsty, Janice and Clare – had spent a whole day at the fair and a fun night staying in the modern Ballsbridge Inn on Pembroke Road, just minutes from the RDS. The hotel was only three-star but it was perfectly nice, well-located and, most importantly, it was within everyone's budget.

They were discussing a gorgeous painting of red poppies by Barbara Boland that Janice had bought at the fair and arranged to have delivered.

'Has it arrived yet?' said Patsy, with a smile on her face, remembering some of the highlights of the trip. Like the morning Kirsty came down to breakfast with her skirt tucked into her knickers at the back. How they'd laughed. She walked over to the window and stared out at the shoppers, battling against the wind and rain on the High Street. So much for pleasant-sounding April showers. It was a storm out there.

'It came this morning.'

'And what does Keith think of it?' said Patsy.

She did not hear Janice's reply because just then she saw

something that made her freeze. It was Martin, hurrying furtively along the other side of the street, his head turned away from the shop, briefcase in hand, as though he did not want to be seen.

'Janice,' she had the wherewithal to say, 'I've got to go. I . . . something's come up. I'll see you tonight at No.11.'

She walked to the door, opened it and stepped out into the cold rain with the phone still in her hand. She caught a glimpse of the back of Martin's cream raincoat and opened her mouth to shout his name. But before she could call out, he turned sharply into Quay Street, in the direction of the train station, and was gone. She stood there, stunned, for some moments. How peculiar. Why would Martin pass the shop without stopping by to say hello? And where was he going?

A trickle of rain ran down her forehead and into her right eye. She blinked it away and realised that people were staring at her – standing in a short-sleeved blouse in the middle of the pouring rain. She turned and went inside, her heart pounding in her breast. She shut the door, flicked the shop sign to 'closed' and pulled the blind. Then she stood in the middle of the shop, shivering in her wet things, and thought.

Martin had distinctly said he was going to be in Belfast all day today. He rarely went anywhere else and he certainly never worked in Ballyfergus. There were few corporate clients in the small town and none of them was his customer.

Perhaps he had personal business like a dental or doctor's appointment. Or maybe some reason to go and see their lawyer – or maybe the bank about personal finance. But why not mention it to her? It must have been an oversight. She knew he was worried about the performance of the bank and, in the current economic climate, work was no picnic. She reminded herself that he had a lot on his mind.

But still it niggled at her. Why was he going in the

direction of the train station? It was too late in the day to travel to Belfast only to have to turn right round and come home again. She tutted crossly and said out loud, 'Will you stop torturing yourself?' There would be a completely innocent explanation. She told herself she was sure of it.

When she got home, no-one was there. Laura was at hockey practice and Sarah had just left for work. She changed out of her damp clothes, made dinner and ate it with Laura when she came in. Patsy spent the entire meal clock-watching, waiting for Martin to come home, and she was glad when Laura went straight to her room after the meal, leaving her to worry in peace.

It was after seven o'clock when she heard Martin's key in the lock. She got up from the sofa and walked into the hallway.

'You wouldn't believe the traffic coming out of Belfast tonight,' he said, struggling out of his coat. 'There was an accident. Held the traffic up for damn near an hour.'

'You were in Belfast all day then?'

'Of course,' he said, irritably. 'Where else would I be? I left the office at five and it's taken me two hours to get home.'

Patsy felt the colour drain from her face. When she'd seen him on the High Street it was at least four thirty.

'But that's impossible, Martin. I saw you on the High Street this afternoon. In Ballyfergus.'

He stopped battling with the coat momentarily, then resumed his struggle – the arm of the coat, for some reason, was stuck inside out on his wrist. 'Pah! Nonsense!' he said. 'You're imagining things, woman.'

Was she? For sure, she'd only caught a glimpse of the man in the mac but there was absolutely no mistaking him in her mind. It *had* been her husband. She knew his gait, the length of his stride, the slope of his shoulders, the way he held his head.

'But Martin . . .'

'Who makes these bloody coats?'

'Here, let me help you,' she said, seeing at once what the problem was. She went over and quickly released it. The sleeve slid off his arm at last.

'Thanks,' he said and engulfed her in alcohol fumes.

'You've been drinking!'

'So?'

'You never drink after work. Except at Christmas and leaving parties.'

He shrugged his shoulders.

'But you drove the car,' she said.

'I only had a couple.'

'Where?'

'Does it matter?'

'Yes. Who were you with?'

'Ah, for Christ's sake,' he said, raising his voice and chucking the coat onto the chair by the door. 'What is this? The Spanish Inquisition?'

'Martin, I saw you on the High Street this afternoon. Either you're lying or I'm going insane. And you've come home stinking of alcohol. So,' she said, her voice wavering with emotion, 'can you please tell me what in the name of God is going on?'

'Nothing's going on. Can a man not have a few jars after a hard day's work without an interrogation when he gets home?' And with that he stomped into the snug and slammed the door.

Patsy put her hands over her face. Was Martin's problem alcoholism and not, after all, the other possibilities she'd fretted about these last weeks? Or was that just a symptom of something else? Why wouldn't he tell her who he'd been drinking with? Was it because he was drinking alone? Or worse, because he was with someone he did not want her to know about? A woman perhaps?

She dragged her hands down her face and swallowed the phlegm that had gathered at the base of her throat. She could not leave things unresolved like this. She must persuade Martin to tell her the truth, no matter how awful it might be.

She knocked on the door of the snug and, when no answer came, she opened the door. Martin was slumped on the sofa with his long legs splayed apart.

'Martin,' she said. He did not look up. 'Martin,' she repeated. 'We have to talk.'

He rubbed his forehead with the tips of his fingers. 'There's nothing to talk about.'

'You know that isn't true.'

He let out a long, heavy sigh. 'Look, will you just leave me alone, Patsy? Please.' He picked up the remote, turned up the volume and began flicking through the channels. He did not look at her once.

Patsy retreated quietly, went upstairs and sat on her bed and wondered what to do. Something terrible was going on, that much was certain. She ran through all the possibilities in her head yet again – illness, gambling, alcoholism, adultery – and tried to imagine how she would feel if he admitted to any of them. Devastated. Especially if another woman was involved. In all their married life, Martin had never lied to her. Not once. Not until tonight. And what hurt her most was that he would not, or could not, confide in her now. No matter what he had done, she was sure she could've found it in her heart to forgive him. But the bond of trust between them had been broken and, whatever the cause or reason, she wasn't sure that she could ever forgive him for that.

And now what was she to do? She needed to talk to

someone. She wiped the tears from her eyes and thought of her girlfriends. They would know – they had to – because right at this moment she hadn't got the faintest idea. She would go and meet them at No.11 as planned. Quickly, she slapped on some make-up to hide her tear-stained face and threw on a dress and a pair of boots.

Laura was upstairs in her room, alone, when Patsy knocked on the door. She was curled up on her side on her bed, hugging a pillow.

'What're you doing up here?' said Patsy, alarmed. 'Aren't you feeling well?'

'I'm fine,' said Laura and Patsy sat down on her daughter's bed and stroked her head, pushing the blonde hair off her brow with her fingers, the way she used to do when she was a little girl. She had loved the way, with her fine hair tucked behind her ears, she could still see the baby in her daughter's face. Now she had a woman's head of hair, thick and heavy, and although all signs of babyhood were long gone, Laura was immature for her years and sensitive. If her parents' marriage broke up, it would break her heart. Patsy put a smile, like a mask, on her face.

'What is it, darling?' she asked and Laura closed her eyes. Her lashes, thick with black mascara, were like spider's legs.

'Oh, sweetheart, are you worrying about your exams?' cried Patsy. She suddenly realised that she had been so pre-occupied about Martin recently, she had forgotten Laura was facing a challenging time too. The exams were less than six weeks away and as an average student, Laura had to work hard to get good results.

Laura stared at her mother with her hazel eyes, flecks of autumn colour – russet, yellow, moss green and bark – floating in them like leaves in a pond. Tiny red veins, like bloody tributaries of a river, fanned out from her irises.

'Your dad and I know that you're doing your best. And whatever grades you get we will always be proud of you. I was no brainbox at school,' she joked. 'And I've done alright, haven't I?'

Laura gave her a weak smile.

'So no more worrying about it. Promise?'

Laura opened her mouth to speak, closed it again.

'When's your first exam?'

'The thirteenth of May.'

'That's ages away, Laura. You've still plenty of time to study. You've been keeping up all year, haven't you?'

'Yeah, I guess so,' said Laura with the ghost of a smile.

'And you did well in the mocks. You got the grades you need.'

Laura nodded.

'So you really don't need to worry,' she said and patted Laura's thigh, half-hidden under a fleecy pink blanket, a relic from her childhood that Laura could not be parted from. 'But maybe from now until the end of the exams you should only go out at the weekends. Concentrate on the studying, hey?'

Laura plucked the fur on a fluffy zebra one of her friends had given her for her last birthday. Patsy watched her with a vague sense of unease. If Laura was in any way reassured by her words, she wasn't showing it.

'You look nice, Mum. Are you going out?' said Laura, suddenly changing subject.

'I was thinking about it,' said Patsy, glancing down at her dress. 'What are your plans for tonight?'

'Haven't got any.'

'That's not like you, Laura. Staying in on a Friday night,' teased Patsy but all she got in return was a blank face.

Patsy frowned. Laura was uncommonly pale – maybe she

needed iron or maybe she was coming down with something. She wasn't happy leaving her like this. 'How about we watch a DVD together? What about *Pretty Woman*?'

That raised a smile. 'Oh, Mum. We must've watched that old film a thousand times!'

'Something else then?' said Patsy. Since when had *Pretty Woman* joined the ranks of 'old' films, along with *Casablanca* and *Gone With the Wind*?

'No thanks, Mum. You go out and have a good time,' said Laura and she yawned. 'I think I'll do a wee bit of studying and then have an early night. I'm tired.'

She did look exhausted. She had been overdoing it, burning the candle at both ends. Like that eighteenth birthday party for some fella at school she'd been to last Friday night. She hadn't got home until two in the morning and then she'd to get up for a hockey match the next morning. 'I don't like leaving you like this,' Patsy said.

Laura's mood changed like a switch had been flicked. 'Honestly, Mum,' she snapped, 'I'm not a child. I'm perfectly capable of looking after myself. And it's not as if I'm alone. Dad's here, isn't he?'

Patsy stood up, wounded. 'Well, if that's the way you feel, I'll leave you to it.'

She got as far as the door when Laura said, 'I'm sorry, Mum.'

She turned to look at Laura, her hand on the doorframe. 'Yeah, well, you get a good night's sleep and I'll see you in the morning.'

As soon as she walked out she knew, with a heavy heart, that she had failed her daughter. Something was bothering Laura and she wasn't entirely convinced it was the looming A-level examinations. They were still weeks away and, in spite of her consistently average results, Laura had never been particularly fazed by exams before.

No, Patsy had the vague, unsettling feeling that Laura was holding out on her. There was something else wrong but right now Patsy just couldn't face dealing with it. She had too much on her plate already. Whatever was wrong with Laura – probably some fall-out with a friend, boyfriend trouble or other minor drama – it would just have to wait.

She had more important things to worry about. Like a husband who was lying to her.

She put on her coat, grabbed her bag and left the house without speaking to Martin who was still in the snug. She drove to No.11 where, as soon as she sat down at their usual table with her friends, she spilled it all out – what she'd seen that afternoon and what had happened tonight when Martin got home. She told them about the shares too and how they would struggle now to put Laura through college.

There was a stunned silence.

'Martin?' gasped Clare, incredulously. 'Your Martin? Are you sure?'

'I think he's having an affair,' said Patsy and she put a hand over her mouth and blinked at her friends' shocked faces. She fought, and succeeded, in holding back the tears. Kirsty, who was sitting beside her, laid a hand on her shoulder.

'Well, if he is,' said Janice angrily, 'I'll . . . I'll have his balls for Christmas lights!'

Patsy started to laugh at the absurdity of this notion and the fact that sophisticated Janice had uttered these words. The others joined in, including Janice.

'I can't believe I just said that,' she exclaimed and slapped a delicate hand over her mouth.

Soon tears of mirth rather than sorrow were streaming down Patsy's cheeks. She wiped them away and said, genuinely moved by Janice's loyalty, 'Oh, Janice. You're a great pal. So you are.'

Janice blushed and Clare said, 'You need wine, Patsy. Here, take this.'

She thrust a glass into Patsy's hand and watched while she put the glass to her lips.

'There,' said Clare, sounding satisfied, and she sat down in the tub chair beside Patsy. 'That feels better now, doesn't it?'

Patsy gave her a weak smile. Wine seemed to be Clare's solution for most ills. But it wasn't the wine that calmed Patsy's soul. It was the love and concern she saw in her friends' faces as she looked at each of them in turn.

'Thanks, girls,' she said. 'I need all the laughs I can get.'

'Patsy, you mustn't jump to conclusions,' said Clare earnestly, leaning forwards with her hands clasped anxiously between her knees. 'There could be all sorts of innocent reasons for Martin's behaviour.'

'Maybe he's planning a surprise for you both and wants to keep it a secret,' offered Kirsty.

'Like what?' asked Patsy.

Clare glanced sideways, searching for an answer. 'A holiday?' she said at last.

'That's my department,' said Patsy flatly. She wondered if they would ever go on the safari now. If it had all been a pipe dream. 'So much for renewing wedding vows and starting afresh and rekindling romance. At this rate I'll be lucky if we're still together come September.'

'Now come on, Patsy,' chided Janice gently while Kirsty patted her back. 'We all know Martin and none of us thinks him capable of cheating on you. He adores you.'

'Maybe it's some sort of personal crisis,' said Kirsty, removing her arm from Patsy's shoulder. 'That might be why he wasn't in work this afternoon and why he was drinking.'

'A personal crisis?'

'You know. A midlife crisis. Maybe he's under a lot pressure at work. It can't be easy being a banker in this climate.'

'He has been working very hard,' acknowledged Patsy, clutching to the shred of hope offered by this theory.

'And he's bound to be concerned about financing Laura's education,' added Janice. 'It must prey on his mind. Maybe the burden of responsibility is getting him down.'

'So it could be that, couldn't it?' said Clare.

Patsy nodded. 'I guess so.' Perhaps she was imagining the worst. But until Martin confided in her, she couldn't help but let her imagination run away with itself. 'But why doesn't he just talk to me?'

'Maybe,' said Janice carefully, 'he feels he's failed you and the girls.'

Patsy looked into her glass, which was now empty, and bit her lip. She did blame him for the shares disaster. But she hadn't given him a hard time over it, had she?

'I'll just have to try and talk to him again,' she said. 'I need him to open up and tell me what this is all about.'

'That's the spirit!' said Janice.

Patsy smiled, her spirits, if not completely restored, then more buoyant. She was so glad she had come out. As she'd hoped, the girls had helped her get some perspective. Martin had been a loving and faithful husband for a quarter of a century. He wasn't going to suddenly have an affair, was he? The reason for his subterfuge was, as the girls suggested, probably something much more mundane. It could even be a cry for help. And even if Martin didn't want her help, he needed it. Her job was to make him see that. She took her purse out of her bag and asked, 'Can I get anyone a drink?'

'Don't you dare!' Janice grabbed the purse out of Patsy's hand. She held it close to her chest, her fingers gripping the red leather like a vice, and laughed. 'You're not paying for anything tonight, Patsy. The drinks are on us and no arguing.'

Patsy, who was driving, insisted on water and while Janice went up to the bar, Clare raised the subject of the exhibition. 'Listen, Patsy,' she said, 'I'd understand if you don't want to go ahead with it. Or would rather postpone. You've got a lot on your plate just now.'

'Oh, Clare, it's sweet of you to say that,' said Patsy and a look of loss, no, resignation, passed fleetingly across Clare's features. It was as though a shutter came down, closing in her dreams. Well, thought Patsy grimly, her dream of a safari might have to be shelved, but she'd be damned if Clare's dream was going the same way. 'But there's no question of cancelling the exhibition. I contacted Bronson and it's all organised, Clare. I can't pull the plug on it now.'

'Are you sure?' said Clare and the light came back on in her eyes. She bit her lip to suppress a smile. 'I don't want to put you under any pressure.'

'Don't be daft,' said Patsy airily. 'I'm looking forward to it,' she lied. The last thing she wanted to do right now was organise an exhibition. It required energy and enthusiasm, both of which she was low on. But she would do it for Clare.

Janice came back with the drinks and sat down.

'We're talking about Clare's exhibition,' explained Kirsty.

'In fact,' said Patsy, 'that reminds me. It's time I got the invitations out.' She would also have to drum up some media coverage, organise drinks and canapés – on a very tight budget – and hang the pictures. It would keep her busy if nothing else.

'Who'll you invite?' said Kirsty.

'The usual. All the great and the good plus my regular customers. And you lot of course!'

'Would you mind if I gave you a list of names?' said Janice, and she gave Patsy a meaningful stare. 'I think they would be very interested.' By this Patsy understood that they would be willing to put their hands in their pockets – not just stand around knocking back free drinks. Exactly the sort of people she wanted to come.

'That'd be fantastic. You know the more I think about it,' she added brightly, surprising herself with sudden inspiration, 'the more I think that this exhibition is exactly what the gallery needs right now. I need to get people talking about it and get more people through the door.'

If she could earn more money from the gallery it would take some of the pressure off Martin. 'I think,' she said, voicing her thoughts out loud, 'I need to diversify.'

'Into what?' said Janice.

'Oh, jewellery and bags, maybe. I'd make sure everything was of high quality and tasteful, but reasonably priced. I'll still sell original artwork but maybe supplement it with less expensive prints.'

The conversation rumbled on along these lines, everyone pitching in with ideas, empowering Patsy and filling her with some optimism. She might not make a fortune, but she would contribute more to the family finances than she was currently – and shoulder some of the responsibility she had, perhaps unfairly, been too quick to pass on to Martin.

Concious that she had monopolised the conversation too long, Patsy turned to Kirsty. 'How's the job going?'

'Great,' said Kirsty brightly. 'Better than I expected. I love dressing up in my suit for work and my boss Denise and I get on really well. She's pretty much given me free rein to do things my way. I'm organising all sorts of new things for the schools' programme. David's class are visiting next week which I'm really excited about! Though I don't know if he'll be pleased or embarrassed to see me.'

After a short pause, Clare said, 'Has Kirsty told you the latest? She's met someone.' She paused dramatically. 'A man.'

'Oh do tell!' cried Janice.

Kirsty sighed and accepted the inevitable – she wasn't going to get away with not telling them. 'It's someone I've known for quite a while. And nothing's happened between us. Nothing at all. I don't even know if he likes me.'

'But you like him?' said Patsy.

Kirsty squirmed in her seat. 'Quite a lot,' she admitted. 'I hadn't seen him in a while and when I met him recently, I realised that . . . well, my feelings towards him had changed.'

Patsy and Janice leant forwards in their chairs, waiting breathlessly for her to go on.

'That's it,' she said, uncomfortable talking about her feelings and embarrassed to be the centre of attention. 'There's nothing else to tell.'

'Has he kissed you?' Patsy winked at Janice.

Kirsty blushed again and gave Patsy a gentle thump on the arm. 'Of course not! We're just friends.'

'But not for long,' said Clare meaningfully and she ran her finger round the top of her wine glass. 'He sounds very promising,' she added, as though she were talking about an applicant for a job.

'Well, aren't you going to tell us who he is?' said Janice, impatiently.

'Okay, but you mustn't go round telling people.' Kirsty looked over her shoulder, leant forwards and watched the faces of her friends carefully so that she could gauge their first, and honest, reactions. 'It's Chris Carmichael, the gardener.'

Janice exchanged a favourable, if slightly surprised, look with Patsy and said, in an encouraging tone, 'Mmm. He's very handsome.'

'I think so too,' said Clare thoughtfully. 'In a Gordon Ramsay kind of way.'

'Yes, he's all sexy and rugged,' went on Patsy, giving her shoulders a little shake and pouting her lips.

Kirsty blushed in embarrassment. 'Stop that, Patsy!' she said and gave her another playful thump.

'So have you told him how you feel?' said Janice, getting down to brass tacks.

'No, of course not.' Kirsty looked at the table.

'Why ever not?'

Kirsty was horrified at the very idea. 'I just can't march up to him and ask him if he fancies me! What if he said "no"? Plus there's something else.'

'What?'

'I think he mentioned children once. He might be married.'

'Can't you just ask him?' said Janice, sounding a little exasperated. 'You know, slip it into the conversation.'

Kirsty shook her head and put a hand to her chest. 'Oh, no. I couldn't do it without it being obvious I was fishing. Honestly.'

'You don't need to, pet,' said Patsy with authority. 'I can put your mind to rest on that one.'

Kirsty held her breath and waited for Patsy to go on.

'Chris Carmichael's been divorced for over ten years. His ex-wife, Paula, works in the book shop on the High Street. I've known her for years. And as far as I know Chris is not involved with anyone else.'

Kirsty bit her lip and suppressed a smile, her heartbeat quickened by this news. Chris was single! He was a free man. There were then no obstacles to them forming a relationship. There was no reason why it mightn't work out between them. And every possibility it could . . .

Chapter Ten

Wednesday nights in Clare's house had taken on an unwelcome predictability. Invariably, like tonight, there was Izzy, sat at the kitchen table doing her homework, Rachel and Josh running riot and Liam nowhere to be seen.

It had its advantages. One of them was that a fragile camaraderie had developed between Clare and Izzy, based on mutual hostility towards Liam – blatant on Izzy's part, thinly veiled on Clare's. Children, of Izzy's age and intelligence especially, were very perceptive. Izzy was angry at her father's neglect and she had divined, without being told, that Clare was fed up being left holding the fort.

The phone rang.

'That'll be your dad,' said Clare, taking a sip of the teatime gin and tonic she allowed herself every day – one of the compensations for being a stay-at-home mum.

Izzy rolled her eyes. 'I wonder what time he'll be home tonight,' she said in a world-weary tone, far beyond her tender years.

Clare said, 'Let's see, shall we?'

'I'm so sorry, Clare,' Liam gushed into the phone. 'I'd planned to leave early but it just didn't work out. Things have been crazy here since the lay-offs. Tell Izzy I'll be there by seven thirty at the latest. I promise. Love you.'

Clare put the phone down and sighed. 'Seven thirty,' she said.

'Figures,' said Izzy, tugging at the hem of her way-too-short skirt. 'Still, could've been worse.'

Clare tried to be understanding about the pressure Liam was under. As the size of the economy contracted, more and more businesses went bust, and accountancy firms felt the knock-on effects. At Liam's office they'd already let six people go. The reason Liam was often late home, he told her, was because he was literally fighting to keep his job. Part of that battle was being 'seen to be keen'. And if that meant staying late at the office, then that was what he had to do, like it or not.

Clare understood all this very well and she hated seeing Liam under such pressure. That was why it was so important that she get her own career off the ground. Their future as a family would be much more secure if they had two sources of income. And the only way she could secure that future was by being, in the short term at least, a little bit self-centered. Something that, as a mother, she found hard to do. She would just have to try and be more like a man.

Clare looked at the vegetables in the sink, ready to be peeled, and the polystyrene packet of sleek, pink chicken breasts sitting on the counter – the rudiments of a meal for her and Liam. The kids, including Izzy, had already eaten: fish fingers, chips and peas. Then she looked at the clock and did a quick mental calculation. She *had* to work tonight. She didn't have time to cook a meal. With the exhibition just six weeks away she had no choice. She still had to finish off three paintings and do another four from scratch. She was really feeling the pressure but she would not let Patsy down. Or herself.

Liam would just have to fend for himself. She put the

chicken back in the fridge and tossed the vegetables into the basket under the sink.

'Aren't you making Dad something to eat?' asked Izzy.

Clare glanced over at her stepdaughter. 'No. I haven't time. He can grab a sandwich or something when he gets in. I'm going to put Rachel and Josh to bed now,' she said, expecting no response.

'I'll take them up and do their bath if you like,' said Izzy quite cheerfully without raising her head, and Clare was astonished. She put her hands on her hips and stared at her stepdaughter, trying very hard to figure her out. And then it hit her – Izzy was really only comfortable when she was in opposition. She needed an adult enemy on which to project her anger and frustrations.

Until recently Clare had been the relentless target of her foul temper and moodiness. Now – partly through his own fault – it was Liam. She and Izzy would never be friends, she'd come to accept that, but this uneasy truce was a damn sight better than the former status quo. And it wouldn't do Liam any harm to be at the receiving end of his charming daughter's temper. It might open his eyes to what she was really like.

It was sad that it had taken a common cause to unite them, albeit warily and probably only temporarily. It gave Clare an insight into what life could be like if only Izzy would stop blaming the adults around her for messing up her life. Okay, she never got the happy ever after every little girl craves – but she needed to get over it. She saw, underneath the bravado, a vulnerable child crying out for attention. It seemed to Clare that she didn't get enough from either her mother – or her father. Recently, as well as working late, Liam had started catching up on paperwork at weekends, which meant he'd even less time for Izzy.

'Josh! Rachel! Time for bed. Race you to the top of the stairs,' called Izzy as she headed up the hall.

Soon squeals of laughter and the sound of splashing came from upstairs. Clare sighed. It was nice to see Izzy enjoying her younger siblings. But she wouldn't take advantage of her – or give her any opportunity to say that she had. She knew that Izzy would happily paint her in a bad light if it served her purposes.

Clare tidied the kitchen, made a quick sandwich and wolfed it down standing at the sink, followed by a bag of crisps. Then she filled Rachel's bottle with milk, warmed it in the microwave, and took it upstairs.

Amazingly, Izzy had both kids out of the bath, dried and in their pyjamas. Rachel was sitting on the floor looking at *The* Very *Hungry Caterpillar*. She poked a finger through one of the holes in the book which the hungry caterpillar of the story had supposedly chewed. Izzy was on her knees brushing Rachel's fine, wet hair.

Clare went over and put her hand on Rachel's bottom, checking that Izzy had remembered to put a nappy on her.

'I didn't forget,' said Izzy, prickly, as soon as she realised what Clare was doing. Rachel grabbed the bottle and began guzzling down the milk.

'Just checking,' said Clare. 'I'll get a hairdryer.'

She came back a few moments later and said to Rachel, 'Shall I dry your hair, sweetheart?'

'No,' said Rachel with a grin. 'Izzy.'

Clare managed to hide her disappointment. 'You okay with that?' she said to Izzy.

'Yeah.'

Clare plugged in the dryer, uncoiled the flex and gave it to Izzy. She went through to Josh's room, where he was on the floor playing armies. This consisted of lining green plastic soldiers up in rows on the carpet and throwing missiles, in the shape of marbles, at them. They were dead when they fell over. She touched his short, spiky hair. It was almost dry.

'Time for bed,' she said.

'I have to kill these baddies,' he announced.

'Okay,' she said. 'I'll be back in a minute.'

She went into the bathroom. It was a mess. Towels and dirty clothes were strewn across the floor and a big puddle of water lay beside the bath. Nice to know that there were some things a twelve year old couldn't do as well as her, thought Clare. Quickly she dried the floor, hung the towels back on the rail, and put the dirty clothes in the laundry basket.

Back in his bedroom, Josh had finished the game. By the time she'd read to him, settled him down to sleep and went through to Rachel's room, her daughter was in her cot, hovering on the brink of sleep. Clare leant over the crib beside Izzy and kissed Rachel on the forehead. Her eyes fluttered, opened, closed again.

'She's gorgeous like that, when she's all clean and sleepy, isn't she?' said Clare.

'Yeah,' said Izzy, her words a soft breath. She leant over and stroked the top of her little sister's head. 'Night-night, Rachel.'

'Thanks, Izzy,' said Clare. She quietly raised the side of the cot, and together they tiptoed from the room.

Five minutes later, at the precise moment that Clare heard the key in the front door, the atmosphere in the house changed. Izzy looked up from her books, resentment radiating from her like heat.

'Izzy,' warned Clare, reaching for her jacket, which was hung on the back of a chair. 'Don't give your father a hard time. He's not late on purpose.' She started to shrug into the coat.

'Hello,' called Liam. He came into the kitchen wearily, with his tie askew. He gave Clare a hug, kissed her on the cheek and said, surprised, 'You off out?'

'Mmm,' said Clare, giving him a quick peck on the cheek. 'I'm going to the studio.' She took an apple from the fruit basket and put it in her pocket. 'How was your day?'

'You know. The usual madness,' he said and rolled his eyes.

Liam went over to Izzy, who had ignored him when he'd come in and was now pretending to be engrossed in a book that, up until now, she'd barely glanced at.

'How are you, love?' he said and kissed her on the scalp.

'Don't,' she said and ducked her head.

'What's up with you?'

'You're late,' said Izzy and gave him one of her mutinous glares.

Liam let out a long sigh, his shoulders slumped and he said, 'I'm sorry, alright? Something came up and I just couldn't get away.'

Clare put a hand over her mouth to hide a smile. It wasn't right, in fact it was horrible of her, but she couldn't help but take some satisfaction in seeing Liam's discomfiture. Now he knew what she had been dealing with all these years.

'Listen,' said Clare, 'I've got to run. Don't wait up. I don't know when I'll be home.'

'Okay. Something smells good,' said Liam, looking about the kitchen expectantly.

'Oh,' said Clare, airily. 'That'll be the kids' tea you can smell.'

'So what's for dinner?' said Liam and he rubbed his hands together. 'I'm starving.'

Clare busied herself with the zip on her jacket and sidled to the back door. 'I'm afraid I didn't have time to cook tonight.'

He opened his mouth in astonishment.

'Don't look at me like that,' she said, feeling guilty. 'I spent all morning at the surgery trying to see the duty doctor about that rash under Rachel's chin. He got called out on an emergency and we ended up waiting for nearly two hours.'

'What's wrong with her?'

'Just a touch of eczema. He gave me some cream for her chin. And then Josh had a party this afternoon.'

'But couldn't you rustle something up now?' he said forlornly. 'I've had nothing to eat all day.'

She hardened her heart. She wasn't responsible for the fact that he hadn't eaten – couldn't he buy a sandwich at lunchtime like everyone else? 'No, I'm sorry, Liam, but I can't. I need to go now if I'm to get any painting done tonight. Not that I like painting under artificial light, but it seems that's the only time I can get to do it.'

'And what am I supposed to do about that?' he said and glowered at her. 'I'm at work all day.'

'A bit more help at the weekends would be nice. If you looked after the kids a bit more I could work then. You've no idea how long it takes to complete a picture.'

He let out a sigh that sounded like steam escaping from a gasket. 'You're something else.' He shook his head. 'So what am I supposed to do for food?'

'Make something. There's chicken in the fridge.' It won't kill you, thought Clare, wondering when Liam had become so averse to pulling his weight. When they'd first met he was a competent cook – now she couldn't honestly remember when he'd last made a meal. 'Or do what I did. Have a sandwich.'

And with that she left before he could say another word.

Clare drove to the studio, her head full of the unpleasant altercation with her husband. She did feel guilty about him coming home with no dinner ready but what was she to do?

She had come to the conclusion that she simply couldn't do everything. She couldn't be everything to everyone. Something had to give.

She opened the door to the studio, stepped inside and left all thoughts of Liam outside. She couldn't afford to dwell on them. When she entered this world, she had to give her art one hundred per cent attention. Anything less led to mistakes and mistakes equalled lost time – and time was her most precious resource right now.

An hour later, Clare had finished her first glass of wine and was just putting the finishing touches to a complex view of Carnlough Harbour taken from the end of the limestone pier. She loaded the brush with black paint and set to work on a chain mooring a red dinghy to a buoy.

Suddenly there was a sharp tap on the door. Startled, Clare looked up to see Janice smiling in at her through the window. Her heart sank. She looked at the fine, thin brush in her hand and wondered when she would ever get the space and peace to paint. The kids, Izzy, Liam and now Janice. Why did everyone want a piece of her? How was she supposed to be creative under this kind of pressure?

The door opened. Janice poked her head in. 'I saw the light on. Can I come in?'

'Of course,' said Clare. She wished she could say no but Janice had been so very generous to her.

Janice stepped inside, a cigarette dangling from her right hand, and the smell of smoke filled the room almost instantly. Janice only ever smoked if she was drunk or stressed. Tonight she seemed perfectly sober, which suggested to Clare that something was up.

'You don't mind if I smoke in here, do you?' said Janice, flicking a lock of dark brown hair over her shoulder with her left hand. 'It's cold out there.'

'No, it's fine,' said Clare, dropping the brush into clean water. A cloud of black pigment swirled up like octopus ink.

'So. How are you getting on?' asked Janice, glancing at the two empty wine bottles in the bin. Clare gave herself a mental kick – she should've put them in the recycling bin days ago. Janice came closer, wafting the cigarette close to Clare's left cheek. 'Oh, that one's Carnlough, isn't it?'

'It's not finished,' said Clare, suppressing a cough.

'It's very good. Once you've added in the details it'll be a fine picture. In fact, I might bag that one for myself.'

Clare smiled, knowing only too well that Janice and Keith would buy at least one of her paintings and exhort their well-off friends to do the same.

'Thanks for all your support, Janice.'

Janice looked at the polished nails on her left hand, then at Clare. 'Well, I try to do my bit. I know you'll be successful with or without my help, of course, but it's nice to be involved. It's actually very exciting helping someone launch their career. Who knows where it'll lead? And it'll give me something to talk about at dinner parties when you're rich and famous.'

A tingle of excitement ran down Clare's spine. She gave a little shiver and squeezed her hands between her knees. Janice was right. This was the start of a new chapter with, she hoped, many exciting possibilities ahead.

'So where are the finished pictures?' said Janice.

'There aren't any,' said Clare, deadpan. She hid her face behind her hair.

'What do you mean?' said Janice. A look of panic crossed her face. 'The exhibition's only weeks away.'

'"Art is never finished, only abandoned",' quoted Clare.

'Leonardo da Vinci,' said Janice, and she put her hand on her heart and let out an exaggerated sigh of relief. 'Don't do that to me, Clare. You nearly gave me a heart attack.'

'Sorry,' said Clare, struggling to hide a smile.

'Okay, Leonardo, where's your *abandoned* work, then?'

'In that case on the floor,' said Clare, pointing at a black nylon portfolio propped against the wall. It had been a gift from Liam their first Christmas together. He understood then how passionate she was about art – she wondered how he had forgotten.

Janice put the cigarette between her perfectly lined and painted lips, crouched down, pulled out the paintings and spread them on the floor. She took the cigarette out of her mouth and said, 'They're all good, Clare.'

'Some of them aren't good enough. I don't like that one of Ballycastle. The perspective's all wonky. Or that one of Portstewart Strand. The sky's wrong – too much yellow. And the people on the beach at Whiterocks look like ants.'

Janice gave a little laugh. 'Artists are never satisfied with their work. They always see flaws that aren't there.'

She gathered all the pictures together again. 'Well, I think you're being far too critical. Any one of them would stand up to the toughest scrutiny. However, it's your decision. You must have complete confidence in everything you put into the exhibition.' She looked over her shoulder at Clare. 'What about getting them framed?'

'Patsy said she'd take care of that. That reminds me – I need to drop some of those ones off at the gallery so the framer can get started on them.'

'Do you want me to do that tomorrow?' said Janice, leaving the pictures momentarily to throw the cigarette stub out the door. She slammed the door shut. 'I can if you like. I've nothing else to do. It'll save you the bother of dragging the kids all the way down there.'

'That'd be absolutely great, Janice. Thanks.'

Janice came and stared at the picture on top of the pile.

It was one of Clare's favourites – the Black Arch outside Ballyfergus. 'Such talent,' she said.

Clare blushed with embarrassment and, changing topic to deflect the unwarranted flattery, said, 'Let me just take some of those out. Some of them aren't good enough.' She removed several pictures from the folder, set them on the floor by the desk and sat down.

Janice folded her arms and paced the studio, completing two restless circuits of the small room. She came to a standstill at the end of the desk and stared at a box of paints. Unnerved, Clare busied herself: she took the rigger out of the jar of water, wiped it with a piece of kitchen roll and set it to dry on the shallow tray with the other brushes. She screwed the lid on a tube of paint she'd left out and tossed it in the box with the others. Then she put her right thumb in her mouth, chewed what remained of the nail and waited. The long, awkward pause seemed to go on for ever, tension building like heat inside a car on a summer's day.

Just as Clare opened her mouth to fill the air with meaningless chatter, Janice blurted out, 'Do you think adopted people have the right to know who their biological parents are?'

Clare paused, stunned by the question. She considered how to answer it while wondering why on earth Janice was asking her. She picked up a brush and chewed the end of it. 'It depends,' she said at last.

Janice fumbled in her pocket, lit another cigarette, and offered one to Clare, forgetting momentarily that her friend didn't smoke. Clare shook her head and noticed with surprise that Janice's hands were shaking. Janice, who was always so self-assured, so confident. It occurred to Clare that this might not be a theoretical question. Was it possible Janice was asking about herself? She'd always been guarded about her background – she never, for example, talked about her parents. Had she been adopted? Clare could never ask her – personal questions had always been off limits with Janice.

'On what?' asked Janice, pulling hard on the cigarette. She blew out a spiralling, almost beautiful, plume of smoke from between pursed red lips.

'Well, what I mean is, it's everybody's right to know their genealogy – to know where they came from – isn't it? But it might not always be the best thing, in their interests or other people's, for them to find out.'

Janice was staring hard at her. 'Under what sort of circumstances?'

'Well, say a young girl put her baby up for adoption and then went on to get married and have a family later in life. If she never told her husband about the baby she wouldn't want to be contacted, would she?'

'No, I suppose not,' said Janice. 'It might cause all sorts of problems for her and her family.'

'Exactly. Or if a child grew up not knowing they were adopted, more harm than good might come out of telling them. And you might not want to tell a child about a real parent if you thought that parent would be a disappointment or a bad influence – like a drug addict or a violent criminal. That sort of thing.' Clare paused, feeling out of her depth. 'Why are you asking me this, Janice?'

Janice shrugged and said lightly, 'It's just that someone I know isn't sure if they should tell their daughter that she's adopted.'

'Oh, I see,' said Clare and wondered who the friend might be. 'Well, it depends how old she is, doesn't it? If they tell her when she's very young she'll grow up always knowing and it'll be no big deal.'

'She's a teenager. And her parents think that telling her would lead to . . . heartache for all concerned.'

Clare paused, took the brush from between her teeth and said, 'Then maybe they shouldn't tell her.' She shrugged. 'But without knowing the whole story, it's hard to know what to do, isn't it? It's a difficult one.'

Janice nodded gravely, the cigarette burnt to a stub in her hand. She looked at it, went to the door and threw it out into the garden.

Clare shifted uncomfortably in her seat, feeling somehow that her answer had been inadequate, that she had let Janice down. But without the full facts she didn't know what the right answer was and anyway, who was she to advise? What did she know? But perhaps that wasn't what Janice wanted from her. Perhaps, she concluded, all Janice wanted was someone to listen.

'Well,' said Janice, snapping herself out of the sombre mood, 'I suppose I'd better let you get on, hadn't I?'

'I'm sorry,' said Clare, 'that I couldn't be of more help to you.'

'Oh, that's alright,' said Janice, with a forced smile. She picked up the portfolio and swung the long webbing strap over her left shoulder. She walked over to the door and then delivered her parting shot.

'I'll make sure Patsy gets these pictures,' she said, tapping the portfolio with the flat of her left hand.

'Thanks, Janice.'

'And don't worry about my friend, Clare. I know exactly what I'm going to tell her to do.'

It was after twelve when Clare finally called it a night. She washed out the brushes, cleaned the porcelain palette, and rinsed out the jam jars, making sure the studio was shipshape and ready for next time. If Liam was home reasonably early tomorrow night she hoped to finish the Carnlough Harbour picture. After that, she'd need to give some thought to what she was going to paint next.

As she locked up the studio, a wave of exhaustion overcame Clare. She'd been on the go for more than eighteen hours, and she'd be lucky to get five hours' sleep tonight. She was getting used to tiredness though. When she was painting it barely registered. It was only when she was doing other, more mundane activities, that exhaustion hit her like a sledge-hammer.

It was after one when Clare let herself into the kitchen, feeling like a naughty teenager sneaking in after curfew. She locked the back door, hung the key on the hook behind the curtain and slipped off her shoes. She was glad it was so late – Liam had work in the morning and would almost certainly be asleep by now. After their earlier exchange, she had no wish to talk to him. She raised her eyes to the ceiling, anxiety gnawing at her like hunger. She and Liam were never going to see eye-to-eye on the subject of her work and the domestic compromises that were needed to enable her to paint. But she was prepared to fight for them.

She drank a glass of water standing at the sink, left her jacket over the back of a chair and crept upstairs. She was surprised to see light spilling out onto the landing from the opened door of the room she shared with Liam. Perhaps he had fallen asleep with the light on? She would check in a moment – but first she had something much more important to do.

In Rachel's room, she lowered the side of the cot, and rolled Rachel onto her back. She responded by curling into the foetal position and putting her thumb in her rosebud mouth. Clare nuzzled her face into Rachel's neck, inhaled her peachy smell and brushed her lips on Rachel's hot, soft cheek. In Josh's room she performed the same ritual. She ruffled his spiky hair and thought how much younger he looked when he was asleep.

She paused outside the door to Izzy's room. It was firmly shut. She put her palm on the wood and sighed. Poor little Izzy, shunted between her alienated parents like a tennis ball. Her hand slid down the door and fell to her side. She had tried to help her, she really had. But Izzy, she decided, was no longer her problem.

How she loved her children. And how much more she loved them because she felt fulfilled – in spite of the lack of sleep, the difficulties with Izzy and Liam, and the pressure of responsibilities at home. Not to mention the pressure to produce saleable paintings. But she was happier than she had been since before Josh was born. This joy was different from the everyday delight that comes from the wondrous, but commonplace – a clear blue sky or the weight of a sleepy child on your shoulder at the end of a busy day. This happiness came from the fact that Clare was doing something special. She was living a dream.

Yes, it was bloody hard work but she was managing things remarkably well. The balls were all in the air and none had, yet, fallen to the ground. So though she was tired, she was feeling rather pleased with herself when she tiptoed into the master bedroom to be met by Liam sitting up in bed, his face hidden behind a book. Clare's smile evaporated as the memory of their earlier quarrel returned. She still felt guilty about the meal, or rather the absence of it. These feelings of culpability annoyed her. She tried to shake them off but they were stubborn, like ketchup stains.

Liam closed the book and set it on the bedside table without looking at her. 'You're home late.' He had a blank expression on his face but his voice was full of disapproval.

'I had a lot to do,' she said, brightly. 'I thought you'd be asleep by now. You've got to get up in the morning.'

'So have you,' said Liam.

Clare shrugged, slipped her pyjamas out from under the pillow and went into the en-suite bathroom to change. Lately she hadn't felt comfortable changing in front of Liam. She'd always been conscious of her weight and she'd put on a few extra pounds after the birth of the children. But this recent onset of modesty had more to do with the alienation she felt from Liam than from her own body.

She washed her face, brushed her teeth, flicked off the light and slipped into bed. She rolled onto her side facing him, plumped the pillow a few times, and said, 'We'd better get to sleep.'

She laid her head down and closed her eyes. The reading light by Liam's bed remained stubbornly on.

'I don't think we can go on like this,' said Liam, and there was a long pause.

'Liam, it's late,' she said with a soft sigh, a sound that belied her inner turmoil. Her fear of confrontation. 'We both need to go to sleep. Can't we talk tomorrow?' She held her breath.

'When tomorrow, Clare? You're never available to talk. You're either busy doing things around the house or out with your friends or taking off to the studio.'

Clare opened her eyes. 'I've hardly seen the girls these last few months,' she said, letting the air out of her lungs. 'And you make it sound as though I go to the studio to gad about. I go there to work, Liam.'

'You see more of the girls than you do of me.'

'Don't be silly. You see me every day.'

'It's not the same. You're always . . . engaged in some activity. Or rushing off to the studio, like tonight. I was only in the door and you shot out of it like a bullet, leaving me to fend for myself and Izzy.'

'What d'you mean, Izzy? She'd already had her tea.'

'She said she was starving.'

'The wee madam,' said Clare, propping herself up on her elbow. 'She's only taking advantage of you, you know. What did you make to eat?'

'Does it matter?' said Liam, shooting her a searing glance. 'She's only a child, Clare. How can she take advantage of me?'

'Easily,' said Clare. 'She manipulates people all the time. Sure, the other day . . .'

'I wish you would stop talking about my daughter like that,' interrupted Liam.

Clare felt like she'd been slapped in the face. After everything she had done to try to assimilate Izzy into her family. 'Well, I wish you would take care of *your* daughter and stop leaving her in my care.'

He flinched, jerked his head in the opposite direction. 'That hardly ever happens. Only if I get held up at work.' His tone was indignant.

'Or you have to work the weekends she comes to stay,' she said, satisfied she had hit a raw nerve.

'Come on, that doesn't happen often.'

'Often enough.'

Liam's eyes narrowed, the corner of his mouth twitched. 'Are you saying that you object to looking after Izzy? Not that she needs much looking after.'

Clare's pulse raced. 'She needs more attention than Josh and Rachel.'

'Oh, don't be ridiculous.'

'It's a different kind of attention. She's more emotionally demanding. I never, ever relax with Izzy around in case I do or say something that she can report back to her mother. I'm walking on eggshells with her.'

'Don't talk rubbish,' said Liam.

Clare sighed and rolled onto her back. 'You can dismiss that all you like, but it's true. I don't mind looking after Izzy, Liam, difficult as she is. But it's not me she needs to be around. It's you.'

'Do you think I deliberately avoid being with her? You think I choose to be stuck at the office listening to people talking shite, rather than spend time with my own daughter?'

'Of course not.'

They were both silent then. Tears pricked Clare's eyes. All they ever seemed to do in bed these days was argue.

'If you did more to help around the house,' she went on, 'maybe we would be able to spend time together.' These days she seemed to spend her evenings, if not painting, then doing chores. 'How come you have time to sit down and watch TV at night? Do you ever see me doing that?'

Now that the floodgates were opened, she had so many things to say they tumbled out on top of each other. 'Since when did it become my job to remember and shop for every single birthday, anniversary and the like on your side of the family as well as mine? I organise the kids' birthday parties, Christmas, every family holiday. I do all the cleaning, shopping, laundry, childcare and cooking. I even put out the recycling and empty the goddamned bins! Apart from earn a wage, Liam, what exactly do you do for this family?'

'All the cooking. Oh, that's a joke. You can't even be bothered to make an evening meal, Clare.'

'I had to work tonight.'

'And I had to leave for work at seven this morning. When exactly was I supposed to make dinner?'

'You managed tonight, didn't you?'

'We had beans on toast, Clare.'

'That was your choice,' she said, batting away the guilt that threatened to settle on her like a fog.

'I don't think,' he went on with a catch in his throat that, she assumed, was meant to elicit sympathy, 'that it's too much to ask for a hot dinner when I come home from a day's work. I'm not asking for haute cuisine, just a square meal. I think you forget that we depend on my salary for survival. And it's simply illogical to suggest that I do the household chores when I'm at work and you're home all day.'

Her head was spinning with retorts. She hated the way they sounded just like her parents used to. Her head filled with rage and angry thoughts. She counted to ten and managed to form them into something coherent. 'I could make a significant contribution to the household income if you'd just give me the support I need, Liam. I supported you for a year while you did that Diploma in Corporate Finance before the kids were born. I remember us both coming in from a long day's work and me making dinner while you studied. Why can't you do the same for me? The way I see it, you just want an easy life and you're not prepared to put yourself out in any shape or form to help me get my career off the ground.'

Liam shook his head and looked at her sadly. 'You're wrong. I want you to be successful with your painting, Clare. In fact I think it's wonderful that you're motivated to do what you're doing and I'm pleased that Patsy's offered to host an exhibition for you. I don't even mind the money you've spent on art materials.'

'I'll earn that back as soon as I've sold a couple of paintings,' snapped Clare.

He paused momentarily. 'What I object to is your timing. We have two under-fives at home, Clare, and I just think you're taking on too much. I'm worried for you.'

Trust Liam to twist the argument around so that it was about her, not him. 'The timing might not suit your idea of happy families, but it's perfect for me. *I'm* ready for it.'

'I'm not sure this family is. If you'd just give it a few more years . . . wait 'til Rachel starts school at least. It would just be so much easier on everyone.'

'Easier on you, you mean,' mumbled Clare darkly.

'No, I mean everyone. Can't you see that the children are affected by what you're doing?'

'What d'you mean?' she demanded, shocked by the suggestion that she was having a negative effect on either child.

'This mood you're in all the time. It affects the whole atmosphere in the house.'

'What mood?'

'You go about like a martyr, with a face like you've sucked a lemon. If this is what being an artist does to you then you should seriously think about giving it up.'

'It's not the bloody painting, Liam, that makes me miserable. It's everything else I have to do.'

He smiled, utterly humourlessly. 'There you go again. Saint Clare.'

His sarcasm was so cutting, so mean-spirited. He had never spoken to her like that before. She rolled away from him so that he could not see the cold tear slide down the bridge of her nose and seep into the pillowcase.

'If looking after your family makes you so unhappy, Clare, then you should've thought twice about having them in the first place.'

Her heart hardened. 'The children don't make me unhappy, Liam. If I'm disappointed in anyone, it's you. I thought you would make a better father. And a better husband.'

He gave a hollow laugh. 'Now that's the pot calling the

kettle black. You're not exactly the original Stepford wife, are you?'

The light went out then, followed by much sighing, rustling of bed linen and creaking of the mattress as Liam made a show of settling down to sleep. She lay as close to the edge of the bed as possible – she could not bear for him to touch her, even unintentionally.

'I'm going through with this, Liam, whether you like it or not,' she said into the darkness but there was no reply.

She wasn't just talking about the exhibition. She realised that what she wanted was a sea change, a fundamental reappraisal of the roles within their marriage. She was fed up being a doormat.

Neither of them spoke again. Clare lay for a long time listening to the sound of Liam's breathing, believing that he would relent, that he would admit that he had taken too much for granted, that he would say he was wrong. But his shallow breathing deepened and slowed and soon she knew he was asleep.

Clare's heart was seized by anxiety. They had just done something terrible. Something that her parents did all the time. Something they had sworn to each other on their wedding day that they would never do. To someone looking in on the marriage from outside, it might not seem so awful. But for Clare it was a measure of just how bad things were between them. They had let the sun go down on their anger.

Chapter Eleven

The first two weeks in April which, happily, coincided with the school holidays, turned out to be exceptionally warm – summer had come early, everyone said. The back door to Kirsty's kitchen was wide open, and Candy lay stretched out contentedly in the shaft of midday sun that beat down on the tiled floor.

Outside, in the back garden, Chris had set the sprinkler up to give the grass a soaking and the boys, bare-footed, were taking turns to jump over it. The objective, supposedly, was to time the leap to avoid a complete drenching. But once Adam discovered there was much more fun to be had when the jets of water were pointing directly up his shorts, that went out of the window. Boys, thought Kirsty, and shook her head and smiled.

She lifted down a glass pitcher from the shelf above the cooker. The shrieks of laughter coming from the garden filled her heart with joy – the sound of heady, carefree days, echoes of her own, happy childhood. She took a bottle of elderflower cordial, Chris's favourite, from the cupboard, poured an inch of the thick syrup into the pitcher and then filled it with cold water. It frothed up like bubble bath, then died down as quickly – as though she'd thrown a bar of soap in the jug. She set it on the draining board, leant her hands on the edge of the Belfast sink and looked out of the window.

The cherry tree was almost in full blossom and at its foot, white and pale yellow narcissi waved delicately in a gentle breeze. Deep purply-blue irises, highlighted with bright yellow streaks, red tulips, and all manner of primulas peppered the borders – cerise pink, red, yellow, salmon, blue and orange. Some of the early flowering clematis on the garden fence to the right were already in bloom, cascades of star-shaped white flowers tumbling down to the ground. Scott had laboured to ensure that the garden had 'interest all year round'. The garden, and the boys, were his lasting legacy to her.

Chris toiled in the flowerbed beside the garden shed. He was down on one knee in the shadow of the tall hedge that separated the garden from the public path along the back of the house, tugging something out of the ground. He wore a sort of uniform of khaki shorts, revealing strong, tanned legs and an air-force blue shirt with the sleeves rolled up. Grey patches of sweat spread out in circles beneath each arm. Now and again he glanced over at the boys, still running in and out of the sprinkler, and smiled.

Kirsty took four clear picnic tumblers from the cupboard beside the fridge. She set them, one by one, on a green melamine tray. Four was such a pleasing, even number. So many products were aimed at the ideal family size of four. Every time she bought a pack of croissants, a box of breaded haddock, a pack of doughnuts or muffins she was always left with one over – an almost daily reminder, even now, of Scott's absence.

The boys came in shivering with the cold and Kirsty sent them upstairs to change out of their wet things. She arranged chocolate biscuits on a melamine plate and placed it and the jug of cordial on the tray along with the glasses. After a few minutes of giggling and shouting the boys appeared back downstairs, racing to see who could get their wet clothes in the washing machine first. Then they ran out into the garden.

Kirsty touched her hips lightly with her hands, looked down at her figure. She had taken care with her appearance. She wore red linen trousers and a tailored white linen shirt. On her feet were red flip-flops from Accessorize embellished with sequins and beads. She tucked a stray lock of hair behind her right ear, lifted the tray and walked into the garden.

'Chris,' she called and he looked up, his eyes shaded by the baseball cap on his head. She set the tray on the table. 'I've got some cordial here if you fancy a drink,' she shouted.

He nodded, stabbed the point of the trowel into the bare earth, stood up and walked slowly over to the patio where Kirsty and the boys were seated on slatted wooden chairs arranged around the table. Chris removed his leather gardening gloves that had once been a pale tan and were now muddied and worn. He threw them on the bench under the kitchen window, sat down heavily and sighed. His forehead was beaded with sweat.

'There's some heat in that sun.'

'You'll be ready for this then,' said Kirsty, filling the tumblers with the eerie pale greenish-yellow liquid. She picked up a glass and handed it to Chris. 'It's elderflower cordial.'

'My favourite,' he said and Kirsty smiled shyly, pleased he'd noticed.

'Do I like that?' interjected Adam, eyeing the glass in front of him suspiciously. 'It looks like pee.'

'Adam!' cried Kirsty and she blushed. 'Don't use language like that. It's rude.'

Chris put a hand over his mouth to hide a smile. But

Adam saw it and took it as encouragement. 'But it does, Mum,' he persisted, with a sly glance at Chris.

'That's enough now. Just try it, will you?' said Kirsty, trying to sound cross and suppress her laughter at the same time.

Adam closed his eyes, screwed his face up and put the glass to his lips. The tip of his tongue barely touched the drink. 'Yuck!' he cried, slammed the glass down, grabbed the base of his throat and made spitting noises. 'It's disgusting.'

Kirsty sighed. 'Go and get a carton of Ribena out of the fridge then. They're in the door, on the bottom shelf.'

'Thanks, Mum,' said Adam, making a remarkable recovery. He shot his brother a triumphant grin, grabbed a biscuit and disappeared.

On the other side of the table, David pulled a face. 'I don't like it much either, Mum. It tastes a bit sour,' he said and then added bravely, 'But I'll drink it if you want me to. It's not that bad.'

'That's okay, son,' said Kirsty. 'Go and get some Ribena if you want it.' And he too scurried off, before Kirsty could change her mind.

Chris chuckled. 'Looks like I'm the only person round here that likes this stuff.'

'I like it too.'

Chris drained the glass in one draught and Kirsty refilled it. She pushed the plate of biscuits towards him. 'Have one.'

'Don't mind if I do,' he said. He broke it in half, then into quarters and set the pieces on the teak table, bleached to a pale grey by the sun and rain. He put a piece in his mouth and squinted at the garden. Kirsty followed his gaze across the lawn, then closed her eyes and raised her face to the sun's rays.

She could feel his presence like she could feel the sun on her face. Everything inside her was orientated towards him, like the way the narcissus bulbs in the pot on the kitchen windowsill tilted towards the light. When the pot was turned a hundred and eighty degrees the plants simply began the process of leaning, once more, to the thing they needed to survive. She was attuned to Chris all the time, when she was with him and when she wasn't. She realised that she thought about him constantly.

'That *Prunus lusitanica* needs cutting back,' he said.

She opened her eyes. 'Pardon?' His knowledge of gardening was encyclopedic.

'The hedge at the back,' he said and pointed to where he'd been working earlier. 'You know, the Portugal laurel. It's due a trim.'

'Oh yes.'

He crunched another piece of biscuit. 'And the hydrangeas need dead-heading.'

'Keep some for me – I might put them in a vase indoors.' Kirsty had always thought the faded flower heads far nicer than the bright blue ones of summer.

'Sure thing. And do you want those asters split? They could be divided and some used to fill in that bare patch over by the bird table. Now's the time to do it.'

'Sounds like a good idea,' she said.

She and the boys were booked to go to Scotland next week to visit her parents. She stared at Chris. He was looking down, the top part of his face hidden by the peak on the cap. He reached out a bronzed arm, took the third triangle of biscuit and ate it. Even a week seemed too long to be away from Ballyfergus.

'And I'll need to prune that fuchsia and buddleia back hard too. Loads to be done at this time of year. Though if you can get on top of it now, it's easier to manage for the rest of the season.'

'Can I help?' said Adam, who had crept up and was standing beside Chris's left elbow. David loitered a few feet away.

'Of course you can, wee man,' said Chris, using his pet name for Adam. 'Now let me see,' he said and rubbed his chin. 'I'll tell you what needs doing. I could do with a bit of help to hoe those beds over there.' He pointed to the borders behind the pond. 'Do you remember how to hoe?'

'I do,' said David, taking an eager step forwards. 'I know how. I can show him.'

'That's great, big man.'

David led the way across the lawn. 'We need to get the hoes out of the shed first, Adam.'

'What's hoes?'

'A hoe is what you dig the weeds up with,' said David, his voice growing fainter as they crossed the lawn, heads bent together. 'Don't you know . . .'

'Great kids.' Chris popped the last piece of biscuit in his mouth and rubbed his fingertips on his shirt. 'So how's the job going?'

'Really well,' smiled Kirsty. 'My boss is really nice and she's been very flexible. She said I can fit the job in around school hours and I get Fridays off as well.' She glanced away from him then and focused instead on a cluster of crimson tulips growing in the narrow border by the wall. She did not tell him, of course, that the main reason she had negotiated Fridays off was because that was the day Chris came to do her garden.

'Sounds perfect,' he said.

'Yes, I think so. Harry and Dorothy said they'd help out during the holidays. And though it's early days I'm sure I'm going to love it. It's an exciting time, coming up to the summer. That's when the museum gets most of its visitors.

Lots of Americans and Canadians come here, you know, trying to trace their family histories.'

Chris was staring at her. 'I'm sorry,' she said, and felt her cheeks redden. 'I'm rabbiting on a bit, aren't I?' She took a long sip of cordial and avoided looking at him.

'No, not at all.' Chris brushed the crumbs off the table onto the patio with a cupped hand. 'For what it's worth,' he went on, bringing his gaze to rest on her, 'I think you're doing the right thing. It's what, over three years since Scott died?'

He had never mentioned Scott before, either by name or in passing. Kirsty nodded.

'I think you're very brave taking these first steps towards rebuilding your life, Kirsty. The danger with a loss like yours is that you never move on. I've seen it happen.' He leant forwards in the chair then and fixed those clear blue eyes of his on her like lasers. 'You have a whole new future ahead of you. You must grab it and make the most of it.' He held his hands up, formed into two tight fists. 'And one day I hope that you find happiness, because you deserve it, Kirsty, you really do.'

Kirsty was taken aback by the passion in his voice and in his demeanour. Was he going to say what she hoped? She blinked and put her hand to her breast. Her heart was pounding against her ribcage, the roof of her mouth so dry her tongue felt thick and too big.

'Not only,' he went on, 'are you one of the nicest people I have ever met but you're too young and beautiful to be on your own. You deserve to be loved. Just be careful who you let into your life. Not all men are worthy of a woman like you. But there is someone out there for you, Kirsty, I'm sure of it. You just have to open your heart and you'll find him. Or he'll find you.'

Kirsty felt the colour drain from her face. Her heartbeat steadied, her pulse stopped racing. He saw himself as an advisor, a protector, a benign confidant to a younger woman in need of a friend. Not a potential partner to her.

'Well,' he said after a pause and looked a little sheepish. 'Now look who's talking too much!'

It was certainly true that she had never heard him say so much all at once. Kirsty gave a hollow little laugh. She could not bring herself to speak. He relaxed back into the chair, folded his right leg across his left. He took the baseball cap off and hooked it over his knee. His hair was flat against his head, dark with sweat. There was a short silence and then he cleared his throat.

'Talking of your new job,' he said, his eyes fixed on the boys working in the border by the pond, 'I'm thinking of a change myself.'

Kirsty swallowed with difficulty, licked her dry lips. 'What sort of change?'

'A complete one. New job. New place.'

'A new place,' repeated Kirsty. 'But . . . but I don't understand. I thought you liked your job. And you've spent years building up the business. You can't just throw that away.'

He gave her one of his gentle smiles. 'Being my own boss has a lot going for it. But it's got its drawbacks too. I'm not getting any younger and I'm not sure how long I can carry on with hard physical labour. If I'm ill, there's no-one to do my work. If I can't work, there's no pay. And then there's the difficulty of finding enough work to survive the winter months.' He shook his head. 'No, it's time for a change.'

'What sort of change?' said Kirsty, filled with dread. What if he moved away from Ballyfergus? She might never see him again. All of a sudden, the sun seemed too bright, the wind too cold. She shivered.

'I'm not sure yet. I haven't really been looking, not with any focus, so I'm not sure what's available.'

Kirsty wet her lips. 'And you'd consider moving away from Ballyfergus?'

'For the right job.'

Kirsty smiled and tried to look like she did not care. Her hands were shaking so much she hid them under the table.

Chris looked over at the boys again who, hoes now abandoned, were kneeling on the grass at the edge of the pond. David had a stick in his hand that was half-submerged in the water, prodding the frogspawn. 'Because of the divorce, I've never had a particularly close relationship with my daughters. It's the one thing I regret.'

What if he relocated and she never saw him again? There was only one thing for it, she had to tell him how she felt. She swallowed and tried to drum up the courage to speak.

But before she could open her mouth, Chris sighed, took the cap off his knee and looked inside it before placing it on his head. 'But that's the way it is. So you see there's nothing to keep me here.'

She closed her mouth, stunned. His words cut her to the quick. She felt like something had been placed over her, dulling her senses, like a fire blanket over a blaze. Cutting off air and light. All she felt was hurt. If he had any feelings for her, any at all, he would never have said such a cutting, hurtful thing.

'Well, I'd better get on,' he said, stood up and rolled his shoulders backwards, and cricked his neck to the right, then the left. 'That's the problem with tea, or in this case cordial, breaks. Once you stop you don't want to start again!' He laughed, went over to the bench by the window, and picked up his gardening gloves.

'Chris?'

'Yes?' He paused in the process of donning the second glove, and looked at her.

She wanted to say something but she did not know what.

He watched her expectantly, waiting for her to speak. 'About the new job,' she said at last. 'I hope you find something you want.'

'Thanks.' He smiled and walked past her. She almost reached out for him. Instead she gripped the arms of the seat with her fingers and sat there staring at his retreating back as he walked slowly across the lawn. She wanted to call out to him but what would she say? She wasn't brave enough to share her emotions and, anyway, there were no guarantees that he would reciprocate the feelings.

If fact, if this conversation was anything to go by, his reaction would be quite the opposite. He had shown absolutely no interest in her, apart from a brotherly sort of concern. And actions spoke louder than words, didn't they? It was time for Kirsty to face up to the facts. If Chris cared for her at all he would not be making plans to move away from Ballyfergus. She was quite sure that if she told him how she felt, not only would she have to suffer the humiliation of rejection, but she would risk losing him as a friend.

Tears pricked her eyes and she brushed them angrily from her cheeks. It was time for her to let go of the romantic notions she had harboured concerning Chris Carmichael. Clearly he had a lot more sense than Kirsty in recognising what she had been so determined to ignore – a relationship between them was never going to work.

'Mum! Mum!' called Adam. 'Come over here. You've got to see this.'

Kirsty closed her eyes, opened them and took a deep breath. 'Just a minute,' she called.

Her children were the only thing that really mattered. Now and again she needed to be reminded of that. She had got the job she wanted, the independence she craved. She should be content. But all she'd thought about for the past four months was herself – her own needs and desires. And that was indulgent and self-centred. Her boys were still young. They needed her. She was ashamed of herself.

'Mum!' cried Adam. 'Quick! Come and see this. We think it's a tadpole.'

'I'm coming,' she called and hauled herself to her feet. She felt a sudden chill and rubbed the goosebumps on her bare arms. The breeze had picked up, whistling between the heads of the tulips and daffodils and sending a dry leaf from last autumn skittering across the patio, like a mouse on a kitchen floor. The day wasn't what it had, at first, seemed. She had been fooled by an April day masquerading as summer, just as she had been fooled into thinking that her relationship with Chris was something more than a friendship.

'Quick, Mum! Hurry up.'

She set off across the lawn, her legs as heavy as her heart. Every step was an effort. She fixed her gaze on the boys to stop herself from glancing in Chris's direction. Adam looked up as she came close, his wide blue eyes full of wonderment. She pasted a smile on her face.

'What is it, darlings?' she asked.

'Look, Mum. Look,' said David, his voice little more than a whisper and he held up a white plastic bucket for her inspection. The same one she had used to soak their stained BabyGros and vests in. 'I think it's a tadpole.'

It was too early for tadpoles. She bent at the waist to stare into the bucket and yes, the creature in the bottom, circling round the perimeter of its watery prison, was a tiny fish. But she would not tell the boys that, not today. One shattered dream was enough.

'Do you know what? You may be right,' she said, 'You may be right.'

Chapter Twelve

Patsy stood in the gallery at lunchtime on Thursday, staring at the delivery that had just arrived – two big cardboard boxes full of Radley leather handbags. Two weeks had passed since Martin had lied to her and in spite of Patsy's best efforts she had been unable to get him to open up. If anything, he had withdrawn into himself even more. He left early for work, came home late and was short with her and the girls. It was almost as though he was spending as little time as possible at home. She tried to get him to talk about the pressures of work, but he spurned every one of her efforts. His character had changed so much she hardly recognised him these days.

And she still had no idea what he was hiding from her.

She gave one of the boxes a desultory kick with the toe of her boot and sighed sadly. When she'd told Martin about her plans to diversify, with the objective of shoring up the family's finances, he'd given her an odd, twisted smile and said enigmatically, 'Well, I wish you the best of luck.' There'd been no warmth in it, no enthusiasm. She wondered now if he was indeed suffering from depression. She had tried to help but he would not let her.

The invoice for the handbags needed checking, and each handbag had to be individually priced. Outside the day was grey and miserable, matching her mood, and keeping customers at home. Rain pounded the deserted pavement relentlessly.

She didn't care about the handbags or the gallery. All she cared about was saving Martin and her marriage. And she was so tired – worn out with worry and grief, and the strain of keeping up appearances in front of the girls and the rest of the world while her life at home was falling apart.

She had run out of energy, of resources. She couldn't do it any more. Patsy closed up shop, put on her raincoat, and went home.

Ten minutes later, she parked the car in the drive and dragged herself to the front door. She put her key in the lock but, when she turned it, the door was already open. How odd. She pushed it open, went inside, closed the door behind her. She shook the rain from her hair and called, 'Hello? Anybody home?'

And only then did she remember that Martin and Sarah were at work and Laura was at school – she'd dropped her off there herself this morning. Either one of them had forgotten to lock the door, or there was someone in the house. Her heart thumped against her ribs.

She heard a noise from the kitchen at the end of the hall. She started to back towards the door, her hand groping behind her for the door handle. Her hands found it, she held her breath, depressed the handle and . . . a figure appeared in view at the end of the hall.

'Ahh!' she screamed, and put her hand on her heart when she saw that it was Martin. 'Jesus Christ,' she cried. 'You scared the living daylights out of me!'

Then she laughed with relief but Martin did not. If she was scared, Martin looked truly petrified. He stood there in his work trousers and white shirt, with slippers on his feet, holding a broadsheet in his hand. His face was frozen in horror.

The smile instantly fell from her face. She took a few steps up the hallway and her eyes locked with Martin's. She knew instantly from the expression on his face that something was terribly wrong.

'Martin,' she said quietly. 'Why are you not at work?'

He held her gaze for some moments and shook his head and in that instant she saw pure terror in his eyes. Then he blinked and it was as if a veil came down between them, filtering the truth once more.

'I . . . I . . .' he stumbled. 'I thought I'd work from home today.'

He turned sharply and walked back into the kitchen. Patsy followed. The remains of breakfast were on the table – tea and toast and the marmalade jar with the lid off. Bits of the newspaper were strewn across the surface. There was no sign of his briefcase or bank papers.

'You never said anything about working from home today.'

Quickly Martin snatched a section of the paper off the table and folded it under his arm. But not quickly enough. Patsy glimpsed the word 'Appointments' at the top of the page – it was scribbled on all over and circled with blue biro.

'Are you looking for another job?' she asked. 'Why didn't you tell me? I didn't know you were that unhappy at the bank. You should've told me.'

He did not answer. He stood with his head bent, looking at the floor.

'Is this what your moods have all been about?' She found that she was angry with him for not confiding in her. For causing her so much heartache. Her throat constricted with emotion, her voice rose to a pitch. 'You've no idea what you've put me through these past weeks. I thought you were ill or having an affair . . .'

'An affair! How could you think that? I'd never do that to you.'

'What was I to think? You lied to me about being in Ballyfergus that day. And all along it's been about work and some sort . . . sort of effing midlife crisis. We've been married nearly twenty-five years, Martin, and you've never kept . . .'

Suddenly she became aware of a small noise and she realised it was coming from her husband. She stopped shouting and looked at him. He was weeping.

'Martin?' she said hesitantly. Her anger was justified but it oughtn't to have reduced her big, strong husband to tears.

Brusquely he wiped the tears from his face with the back of his hand. Then he raised his red-rimmed eyes to meet hers.

'Oh, Patsy,' he said. 'I've lost my job.'

Patsy sat down abruptly in the nearest chair, stared at the things on the table and tried to make sense of it all. When she'd collected her thoughts, she said quietly, 'But why?'

'Cutbacks. There's almost no lending going on. I knew it was coming. I could see the writing on the wall. But there was nothing I could do.'

'Oh, my God,' said Patsy as the full realisation of what he'd said hit her. She squeezed her eyes shut. Panic took hold and spread through her like a fever. How would they manage the mortgage and all the other bills? How could they put Laura through university? Would they even be able to put food on the table? Her blood ran cold when she thought of the healthy deposit she'd paid up front for the safari. But that was the least of her worries.

They'd ploughed almost all their savings into shares and buying the gallery. They had only a few thousand in savings on top of that, and the modest income generated by the gallery.

Patsy opened her eyes. 'What about a redundancy package?' she asked, hopefully.

Martin shook his head. 'I've been with the company for less than a year, Patsy. It's peanuts. Enough to tide us over for a month or two, that's all.'

Patsy bit her lip. They were the victims of bad timing and bad luck. Martin had been with the Bank of Ireland for fifteen years before jacking it in to take a higher paid and, as it had turned out, much less secure position with his current employer. If he didn't get a job soon they'd have to raise capital. They'd have to sell something. But the shares were virtually worthless . . .

Patsy put her hand over her mouth. 'We might have to sell the gallery.'

Martin nodded miserably and Patsy tried not to cry.

'So long as we have each other that's all that matters,' she said bravely, trying to convince herself as much as Martin. 'And our health and the girls. That's all that really matters, isn't it?'

He nodded mutely.

'But I wished you'd told me, Martin. I would've faced this with you, shoulder to shoulder, like we've always done. Like we're doing now. Why didn't you tell me?'

Martin pulled out a chair and sat down on it as though his long legs could no longer support the weight of his body. He hunched forwards with his clasped hands between his legs, his shirt pulled taut across his back and stared at the floor.

'I didn't want to worry you. At first I thought I could ride the storm out and hold onto my job but things just kept getting worse and worse. And the worse they got the more

I wanted to protect you – and the girls.' He glanced up at her, his brow furrowed with pain.

She felt an overwhelming rush of affection for him. 'You still should've told me,' she said, and smiled sadly. But she couldn't be angry with him – though misguided, his motives had been honourable. He had acted out of love.

'I know.'

'Oh, Martin,' said Patsy. She got up and went over to him, pressed his face into her bosom, and kissed the top of his head where his dark hair, once so thick, was starting to thin.

At least he wasn't having an affair. And he wasn't ill or an alcoholic, or a gambler. Redundancy, unwelcome though it was, was definitely the lesser of these evils. And Martin was a clever, capable man – he'd get another job soon. Wouldn't he?

Something was still puzzling her, though. 'But what were you doing in Ballyfergus that day? And why did you lie to me?'

She felt him stiffen in her embrace and then he pulled away. 'Patsy,' he said, and she knew from the tone of his voice and the way he stared up at her with wide, remorseful eyes that she would not like what was coming. She tensed.

'What?'

'I lost my job four weeks ago.'

'Four weeks ago,' repeated Patsy, reeling from the news like a physical blow. He had been unemployed for a month. Getting up every morning, putting on a shirt and tie and pretending to go to work. Deceiving her. She thought she knew this man and yet he was capable of this? Tears pricked her eyes.

'How could you, Martin?' she said, a well of hurt expanding inside her as she spoke.

He hung his head and said, 'I knew how you'd worry – I didn't want to upset you. I was going to tell you as soon as

I'd got another job, I swear. I thought I'd get one straight away but . . . that didn't happen.'

'But we tell each other everything, Martin. At least we used to,' she added bitterly. She put a hand on her heart, bruised with pain.

'I'm sorry, Patsy.' He sounded broken.

'I knew something was wrong. I just never thought it was this . . .' said Patsy, thinking back over the past month. 'And all the things I thought it could be are much, much worse than this. You've no idea the heartache you caused me. If you'd just told me . . .'

'I know. I should have. I'm sorry. What else can I say?'

'You've broken the trust between us, Martin, that's what you've done.'

He nodded, his face ashen. 'Can you forgive me?'

Patsy said sorrowfully, 'I'm not ready to yet.'

There was a long silence during which she raked over every incident in the last four weeks, looking for clues she should've picked up on.

She brought her gaze back to Martin. 'What did you do every day? Where did you go when you left the house in the morning?'

'I drove about. Enniskillen. Armagh. Omagh. Londonderry. Coleraine. I've been all over. I even drove to Dublin and back in the same day.'

'Doing what? What did you go there for?'

He shrugged. 'Looking for work.'

'And that day I saw you in Ballyfergus?'

He blushed and looked at the floor. 'I was going to the Station Bar.'

Patsy tried not to be angry, thinking of the money wasted on fuel for these pointless journeys and squandered in the pub. She thought too, that if she'd known the truth she would've reined in her spending, not carried on like there was no tomorrow. As a result of Martin's foolishness they were even worse off financially.

'So any leads?'

He shook his head despondently, and played with the pen lying on the table. 'The country's awash with unemployed bankers, Patsy. My CV's with several recruitment agencies but I haven't even had so much as a phone call. They're all saying the same thing. There aren't any jobs, not for someone like me.'

Patsy felt her bottom lip quiver. Martin wasn't going to get a job quickly. They could lose the gallery. And the safari . . . it wasn't going to happen now. She had struggled to keep that dream alive, even after the shares fell so dramatically in price, but she could do so no longer.

'I'll have to cancel,' she said out loud.

'Cancel what?'

Patsy blushed, remembering then that Martin, of course, had no idea what she was talking about. All her secretive planning and dreaming had come to nothing in the end. 'I booked a safari in Botswana for our twenty-fifth wedding anniversary in September. It was,' she said, her voice breaking down, 'going to be a surprise.'

Tears of self-pity ran down her cheeks and this time it was Martin who got up and came to her. He knelt beside her, put an arm around her waist and she leant her head on his shoulder.

'I paid a deposit of a thousand pounds,' she sobbed. 'We won't get a penny of it back.'

'Don't worry about the money,' said Martin.

'But it was going to be our second honeymoon, Martin. The exotic, exciting one we never had. I thought we could even renew our wedding vows.'

Martin moved and she lifted her head. He took her head in his hands and he said fiercely, 'Don't say that. We had the most romantic honeymoon anyone could've wished for. Just you and me, alone, in the middle of a lake in Fermanagh. Don't you remember? All we wanted was each other, Patsy. Do you remember what we used to say? So long as we have each other and somewhere safe and warm to live, we don't need anything else. And it's true, Patsy.'

She smiled, and the tears dried up. Martin was right. Back then, when they had so little, they'd wanted for nothing. Life had seemed so simple. But somewhere along the way, it had become complicated and the life they led now required endless streams of cash to support it. Things would have to change – and dramatically.

'It'll be okay, Patsy. It really will. You'll see. We'll go back to the way we used to be. And we'll be happy. I promise.'

Patsy closed her eyes and tried very hard to believe him.

Janice waited uncomfortably in No.11 for the others to arrive. All she could think about was Pete and the fact that the time when she must tell him he was adopted loomed closer with each passing day.

She ran the palm of her hand along the cool leather arm of the chair, remembering what the place had looked like before the makeover seven years ago. Back then it had been all big floral fabrics and patterned carpet. This is where she and the girls had come for their very first drink together on the evening of that last art class fifteen years ago, and it had borne witness to almost all the landmark events in their lives since.

It was here Kirsty told them she was pregnant with David, where Clare had announced she was to marry Liam, where Patsy broke down and told them her mother had terminal lung cancer. It was here too that Kirsty had broken her heart, time and again, in the weeks and months following Scott's death.

But in all those years, Janice had always held back, sharing little with her friends, bar everyday problems like what she should do about Pete's behaviour at school. She wondered if they'd noticed. Janice swallowed, her heart brimming with emotion, and stared at an arty monochrome print on the wall. She'd always kept her past carefully segregated from her new life, as if in fear of contamination. But now past and present were merging, like watercolours on a sheet of paper, and it was impossible to keep them apart.

Keith was agitating to tell Pete the truth about his adoption. Pete would need his birth certificate to register at university – they absolutely couldn't hide it from him any longer. She'd always known he would, one day, have to be told. But she had always resisted. And now that day was hurtling towards her and she wasn't ready for it. She had spent years grimly holding back the tide of truth, and now it was about to come down crashing over her.

'Hey you,' said Clare, arriving with Kirsty, startling Janice from her thoughts.

They sat down and, before they'd even taken their jackets off, Kirsty looked at Janice and said, 'What's wrong?'

Janice sniffed and shook her head. She blinked hard and bit her lip and glanced at her friends. The concern on their faces was almost unbearable. Silent tears slid down her powdered cheek.

Clare gave Kirsty a sideways glance and said, shrugging off her coat, 'This calls for a drink. And quickly.'

Kirsty nodded and got up and started fussing with coats and handbags and finding a tissue for Janice. Clare came back quickly with a bottle of wine and four glasses, and when they were settled round the table, Kirsty rubbed Janice's arm and said, 'Janice, please tell us what's wrong.'

'It's Pete,' she blubbered into the scrunched-up hankie in her hand.

'Pete? What's wrong with him?' said Clare, holding her glass suspended in mid-air.

The two of them sat and waited for her to go on, their faces strained.

'Nothing.'

Janice dabbed at her eyes, composed herself and found that she felt a sudden urge to unburden herself. Telling it the first time would be the hardest, it was bound to be. And if she could do that, if she could form the words and hear them issue from her own mouth, it would be easier the next time, when she told Pete. Her friends would not judge, or jump to conclusions. She feared a much less benign reception from Pete.

'When we moved here to Ballyfergus, I lied about Pete,' she blurted out.

'You what?' said Clare.

Patsy arrived just then and approached the table with her mouth open, ready to speak. But Clare raised a hand in the air, like a policeman directing traffic, and said firmly, 'Here, sit down, Patsy. Janice is in the middle of telling us something very important.' She stared meaningfully at Patsy – and she, picking up on the cue, slid silently into a chair, with her coat still on.

'I told you Keith was Pete's dad. And he is,' Janice added hastily. 'What I mean is, he's the only dad Pete's ever known. But Keith isn't his biological father. He adopted him when we got married.'

Relief flooded the faces of her three friends and she knew then that they didn't understand. How could they?

Patsy shook her head, and said what the others were thinking. 'But what's the . . . I mean, I don't understand. Lots of people are adopted. Why are you so upset, Janice?'

Janice sighed and felt some of the terror subside. The tight feeling across her chest eased off and she picked up the wine and took a long, welcome drink. She set the glass down carefully and began the tricky process of stepping through the truth, like a field full of landmines.

'We never told Pete that Keith wasn't his father. That was my fault,' she admitted. 'Keith always said we should've told him from day one.'

'But why didn't you?' said Kirsty gently.

Of course they should have, but Janice had been unable to then, as she was now. How could she ever expect Kirsty to understand? So she shook her head and went on.

'Now that he's eighteen and about to go off to university after the summer, Keith says we have to tell him. He'll need his birth certificate to register at uni.'

Patsy wriggled out of her coat, threw it over the back of her chair, and said, 'He does have a right to know, love.'

A tight little sound escaped Janice. Kirsty touched her forearm lightly. Janice composed herself and said, 'I know. But once we tell him, he's going to want to know who his real father is, isn't he?'

There was a long, silent pause as the others considered this statement.

Kirsty spoke first, in her soft Scottish burr. 'What does it say on the certificate, Janice?'

Janice looked straight at Kirsty and steeled herself. 'Father unknown.'

Another silence, this time more uncomfortable. Clare looked at the floor. Kirsty bit her lip, and Patsy said, carefully, slowly, 'You're not so worried about him finding out he's adopted, as him wanting to know who his real father is, aren't you, love?'

Janice nodded, the tears dried now but her heart still heavy with worry. She cleared her throat. The skin on her face felt taut, like a canvas stretched over a frame. 'I do know who Pete's father is.'

Another pause, the air between them heavy with anticipation.

'But I can't tell him. I won't ever tell him,' said Janice, her resolve hardening. 'He'll just have to accept what it says on the birth certificate. I'm not telling him anything more.'

The women glanced at each other and Janice held her chin up, resolute.

'But he's bound to ask questions, sweetheart,' said Patsy tentatively, her voice little more than a whisper. 'What explanation will you give him then?'

Janice shrugged. 'I'll just refuse to say anything.'

'But he might think that . . .' began Patsy, and her voice trailed off, unable in the end to articulate her thoughts.

'I don't care *what* he thinks!' cried Janice, sudden anger rising inside her. She clasped her hands together so tightly they hurt.

The others glanced anxiously at each other and Clare said, after an awkward pause, 'When are you planning on telling him?'

'At the end of May, when his exams are over.'

There was a long silence which Kirsty broke with, 'You poor thing, Janice. You must be worried sick.'

Janice forced a nervous laugh. 'Let's just say I've not been sleeping the best lately.'

Kirsty put a hand out and touched Janice lightly on the knee. 'It'll be alright. Worrying about something is usually a whole lot worse than actually doing it.'

Janice thought of her son's nature and wished she could believe this as surely as Kirsty, with her wide, green eyes and earnest expression, clearly did. She folded her hands in her lap and looked down at them, and said, 'Well, we'll have to see,' a signal to the others that she was finished talking about this topic. She was glad she had told them at last, but it didn't make the prospect of telling Pete any more palatable.

A long silence followed, broken by Clare. 'How are you and Martin coping?' she said to Patsy, bringing the welcome change of subject Janice had hoped for.

Patsy looked tired. Janice could see the black circles under her eyes, through her heavy make-up. She was dressed drably, all in black, even though it was the end of April. It was only two weeks since Martin had told her that he'd lost his job. And Patsy was still reeling. She let out a weary sigh.

'Well, you've just got to get on with it, haven't you? Nothing else for it,' she said stoically, though there was no warmth in her voice. She looked like a much older, severe version of the Patsy that Janice knew and loved.

'It must've been such a shock to find out that he'd been unemployed for four weeks before he told you,' said Clare.

'Shock doesn't come near to describing it,' said Patsy grimly, and she pressed the thumbnail on her right hand into her left palm. 'In fact the more I think about it, the more angry I get. It's not Martin's fault he lost his job but not to tell me . . . to go about pretending like that for a whole month.' She paused, ground her teeth as if chewing, and went on, 'I find it hard to forgive him that.'

'Oh, Patsy,' said Janice. 'I'm sure he had good reasons for not telling you.'

Patsy sighed again, relenting a little. 'He says he was trying to protect me and the girls. He thought he could land another job before having to tell us.'

'I'm sure that's the case,' said Clare.

'I'm sure it is too. But he still should've told me. He made me feel like a fool.' said Patsy, shaking her head. 'If I'd known, I wouldn't have gone on that shopping spree with the girls . . . or ordered that new fridge freezer. The old one was fine . . .'

'Well, maybe something will come up soon,' said Kirsty, hopefully.

'I don't know,' said Patsy, shaking her head. 'His CV's been with a recruitment agency for six weeks and they haven't come up with a single prospect for him. They say they're inundated with applications like his.'

This was met with a despondent silence.

'And it's affecting the girls. Well, Laura anyway.'

'Maybe she's worried about the exams,' offered Janice. 'If it's any comfort, Pete's definitely out of sorts.' If possible, he was being even more difficult and rude than normal.

'I don't know,' said Patsy, doubtfully. 'You know Laura's always had to work for her grades, but she's never been bothered by exams before. And they're still two weeks away.'

'Maybe it's something else? Boyfriend trouble?' suggested Janice.

Patsy shrugged. 'She's not seeing anyone, as far as I know, though she does like this one boy, Kyle . . . but I honestly don't think it's that either.' She paused, rubbed her chin and added, 'Mind you, she said she wasn't feeling well when she came in at lunchtime.'

'That'll be it then,' insisted Kirsty. 'She's just a bit under the weather.'

'Has she been doing a lot of studying?' asked Janice.

'She's been spending a lot of time in her room.'

Janice nodded. 'It could be stress.'

'I know how she feels,' replied Patsy darkly and a ghost

of a smile crossed her face. 'I feel like I'm revising for those bloody exams with her. I'll be glad when they're over!'

'I heard Martin got some bad news,' said a male voice behind them and they all looked up, startled, to find Danny, the barman, standing over Patsy.

Patsy gave Danny a very bright smile. 'Ach, he's not the only one,' she said off-handedly, blinking rapidly. 'I'm afraid banking isn't the secure career it once was.'

'Well, listen here,' said Danny, reaching over Patsy and pressing his hand on her shoulder. 'Here's a wee something on the house to cheer youse all up.' He placed a steel cooler, filled with ice and an unopened bottle of wine, on the table in front of Patsy.

'I can't accept that . . .' began Patsy but Danny stilled her with a squeeze of his hand.

'Sure you can. I'd be hurt if you didn't. Now tell Martin I was asking after him.' He gave Patsy a parting squeeze on the shoulder, and moved to the next table to clear away glasses.

'What a sweetie,' said Patsy, with the first real smile Janice had seen all day.

Patsy shared out the wine and Janice, making the most of the lighter mood, said, 'Look, I think we all need something to look forward to. Why don't we finalise that trip to London now? Let's look at dates in September.'

'Mmm,' said Patsy and she touched her lips with the tips of her fingers. Her eyes were glassy with tears. 'It's just that . . . well, we were supposed to go to Botswana in September.'

Janice was annoyed with herself for her thoughtlessness. 'Is there no way you can go now?'

'No,' said Patsy firmly. 'The safari's out of the question. Not until Martin gets another job – and God knows when that'll be.'

'I'm so sorry, love,' said Janice. The safari had meant so much to Patsy. It broke Janice's heart to see her friend disappointed. 'I'll give you the money,' she blurted out suddenly, without hesitation.

Patsy, startled, took a few moments to reply and when she did her response was a considered one. 'That's sweet of you, Janice. It really is. And I'm touched. But you know I can't accept.'

'Look upon it as a loan,' said Janice, trying to make her offer more acceptable. 'You can repay me when Martin gets a job.'

Patsy smiled and reached over and gave Janice's hand a firm squeeze. 'It's a lovely gesture. But no. Thanks. We really don't want to be taking on debt, especially not for something like a holiday.'

'But I know how much this one meant to you,' said Janice quietly.

Patsy nodded, withdrew her hand and said bravely, 'There'll be other holidays.'

'Listen, if you don't feel up to going to London in September we can always postpone,' suggested Clare.

'No, don't do that,' said Patsy, 'I'd like to go. With cheap flights and free accommodation, it's not going to cost much. And if I put the money aside now, we'll not notice it when September comes.'

'That's the spirit,' said Janice, determined that she would make sure Patsy had a wonderful time in London. Of all of them, she needed it the most.

When they'd finished making their plans nearly an hour later, Clare said, 'Janice, did I see Pete driving up Main Street in a new car yesterday? A black Volkswagen GTI?'

'That was him alright,' said Janice. 'I told Keith it was far too much for his eighteenth.'

'Lucky boy.' Clare whistled through her teeth and Kirsty said, 'Did he have a party?'

'No. Funny enough, he said he didn't want one. To be honest, we were relieved. I heard that the Dobbins' house was trashed after Jason's eighteenth party.'

'Trashed?' exclaimed Patsy.

'Things were broken, including a Waterford crystal bowl, and there were beer stains on the carpets they couldn't get out. I met Alison Dobbin in the hairdresser's the other day and she told me all about it.'

'Do they know who was responsible?' said Patsy, sounding concerned. 'I mean, she wasn't implying Pete had anything to do with it, was she?'

'Oh no, not at all,' said Janice truthfully, glad that for once her son wasn't the cause of trouble. 'But then they did go out and leave the kids to it. What did they expect? Apparently there were quite a few gatecrashers. It's not the kids you know that you have to worry about. It's the ones that turn up uninvited.'

'That's funny,' said Patsy, frowning. 'Laura never said anything to me.'

Janice shrugged. 'Maybe she didn't want to get into trouble?'

'It's not like her,' said Patsy, quietly, pushing the untouched glass of wine away.

'What's Laura doing for her eighteenth in June?' said Clare.

'What?' said Patsy, giving her head a little shake. 'Laura's birthday? You know, it's odd but she hasn't asked for a party either. In fact she's hardly mentioned her birthday at all.'

'She'll be too preoccupied with revising for her exams,' said Janice. 'Can't get a word out of Pete these days.'

Patsy stood up suddenly. 'You know what, I think I'll call it a night,' she said. 'I have to work in the morning.'

And she was gone in seconds, leaving Janice and the others pondering if she was really coping with Martin's redundancy, or falling apart.

When she got home at ten thirty, Patsy drove into the driveway, parked bumper to bumper behind Sarah's car and cut the engine. Then she sat in the quiet stillness for a few moments, staring straight ahead. She tried to put aside the nagging unease she felt concerning Laura. Her daughter was facing a difficult time what with exams looming and now her father's redundancy. Of course she was worried and out of sorts – they all were.

Janice's news about Pete had shocked her and she felt for her friend in her distress. Whoever Pete's father was, Janice was quite determined that Pete should never find out. Janice must, Patsy concluded, have sound reasons for not wanting him to know. And none she could think of was a pleasant scenario . . .

Patsy counted her blessings, an exercise learned on her mother's knee and one guaranteed to make even the most dire situation seem better. She had what millions of people all over the world would never know – a warm and comfortable home, food on the table, access to healthcare and a healthy, happy family. On top of that she and Martin had enjoyed many luxuries: two cars, foreign holidays, nice clothes and all the trappings of a middle-class lifestyle. The girls had never wanted for anything.

Yes, Patsy knew she ought to be grateful every day, and was ashamed that she had not been. Not until her lifestyle was threatened had she truly appreciated it.

Martin would get a job eventually, she told herself, and meantime, if they had to tighten their belts, it would be good for them all. It would make them appreciate what they had all the more. They would find a way to get Laura through uni. Everything, she told herself, was going to be alright.

She got out of the car and glanced up at the house, where lights were blazing in almost every window. The girls hardly ever switched the lights off when they left a room. As part of their new economy drive, that was a habit that would have to change. Not only did it waste money, but it was environmentally unfriendly as well. Patsy smiled, seeing for the first time how saving money had the potential to provide a feel-good factor. She tripped lightly up the steps to the front door, put her key in the lock, turned it and pushed the door open.

As soon as she stepped across the threshold, she knew that something was wrong. All the recessed spotlights in the hall were on, flooding the place with light like a stage. And when she caught sight of Sarah at the end of the corridor, carrying a box of tissues in her right hand, her daughter froze. She stared at Patsy and then, as though she could not bear to look at her, she disappeared into the kitchen without a word.

Patsy pushed the door closed, dropped her bag on the floor and walked slowly up the hall. She thought she heard the sound of crying. Cold fear gripped her. She put her hand to her breast, her chest so tight it was difficult to breathe.

'Sarah?' she called but there was no answer. She could hear the sobbing more clearly now and the muffled sound of a man's voice. Then the tap-tap-tap of knuckles on wood.

The crying was coming from the downstairs loo. She was drawn towards the sound, mesmerised with fear. When she reached the end of the corridor and the door came into view, she saw Martin leaning against it, his left cheek pressed against the wood and his right fist held aloft, bunched into a ball. His eyes were red-rimmed and watery, and his nose was red like an alcoholic's.

When he saw her, Martin closed his eyes, opened them again and his Adam's apple moved up and down. His fist dropped to his side and he stepped away from the door. He could not look her in the eye.

'Martin?' she said. She reached out a hand and touched him on the bicep. He responded by turning his face to the wall. Fleetingly, she wondered if he'd cracked. If the pressure had led him to have some kind of breakdown.

But that would not explain the sobs coming from the loo. She stared at the pale oak door. Sarah had gone into the kitchen. It had to be Laura in there. Something was wrong with Laura. And, whatever it was, it had reduced her father to tears. Her heart began to pound but she took a deep breath and willed it to slow again. Panic would only make things worse.

'Martin,' she said, surprising herself with the calm, low voice that came from within her. 'Tell me what's wrong.'

'It's Laura. She's . . .' he began and faltered. He held his left hand out towards the door, the way an usher shows you to your seat in the theatre, as if that gesture by itself explained all. Then his hand dropped to his side. He pressed the thumb and forefinger of his right hand on the bridge of his nose, unable to speak.

Patsy turned her attention to the door once more. Her heart was racing now, out of her control, and she no longer tried to contain it. She tried the handle – locked, and put her hand on the brass fingerplate, adrenaline coursing through her veins. She considered if she had the strength to kick it down. 'Laura?' she called but there was no answer, only quiet weeping from within.

'Is she hurt?' said Patsy, her hand still on the door handle.

Martin shook his head.

'What's wrong with her, Martin?' she shouted, all semblance of calm gone. 'For God's sake will you tell me what's wrong?'

'Mum,' came a voice from behind. It was Sarah. 'Come away from the door. Come into the kitchen. Laura's . . . she's fine.'

Immediately Patsy's heartbeat slowed. She wiped the perspiration from her palms on her skirt. But if Laura was fine, then who was crying behind that door?

Patsy swivelled round to see her eldest daughter standing in the doorway to the kitchen. Her arms were folded across her chest, her hair was scraped back severely from her pale and sallow face, the colour of uncooked pastry. Sarah turned and walked into the kitchen. Patsy followed. Sarah came to a halt in the middle of the room and Patsy noticed that her mascara was smudged under her eyes and she was shaking, like a puppy removed for the first time from its mother.

'Please, Sarah. Will you just tell me what's going on?' urged Patsy.

Sarah glanced at her father who had followed Patsy into the room – and in the end it was he who spoke. He stood between the women, equidistant from them both, the third point of a triangle. He ran a hand through his dishevelled hair.

'Laura's pregnant, Patsy.'

Chapter Thirteen

'Dear God, no,' said Patsy.

She looked at Martin's face, then Sarah's, then looked away because their expressions confirmed what she did not want to know. She cupped her hands over her mouth and nose and, at the same time, her legs buckled beneath her. But Martin was there. He caught her under the arms, held her upright and she heard him say, 'Let's get you sitting down. Sarah, get your mother a glass of water.'

Next thing she knew, she was sitting on one of the kitchen chairs with a glass in front of her. She did not touch it. Laura pregnant? It was simply impossible. She was little more than a child herself. She didn't have a boyfriend. And yet . . . she thought of the changes she had noticed in Laura over the past few weeks and how she had attributed them to the stress of exams. Had she been too busy worrying about Martin that she had closed her eyes to Laura's plight?

She remembered that night when she'd sat on Laura's bed and stroked her hair. Had Laura tried to tell her she was worried then? Had she been too preoccupied to notice? Had she failed her? Not just then but before. Were she and Martin, by some deficiency in their parenting, responsible for this catastrophe? She looked up at Martin.

'Please tell me it's not true,' she whispered.

He put both hands on her shoulders and kissed the top of her head. 'I wish I could.' Then he sat down and folded his arms. He stared straight ahead, his lips set in a tight, grim line.

Sarah sat down opposite her mother at the table and let out a long, weary sigh. 'I can't believe she's been so stupid.'

No-one refuted the comment – it lay there on the table between them, small and mean, until it occurred to Patsy that they were all making a huge assumption.

'Sarah,' she said, her face tight with pain, 'did she say how it happened?'

Sarah shook her head. 'No.' She looked at her father.

'She came into the kitchen and I'd just made a cup of tea and she sat down here beside me.' Martin pointed to a chair, his face pale. 'She just started to cry and then she told me.'

'Did she say how many weeks? Who the father is? When did it happen?' Patsy catapulted the questions at the blank faces of Martin and Sarah. 'Has she been seeing someone, Sarah?'

Sarah shook her head. 'Not that I know of.'

Had she been raped? Patsy put her hand on the cross around her neck, closed her eyes and said a silent prayer.

'Patsy,' said Martin's voice. She opened her eyes. 'We don't know anything. As soon as she said it, she ran out of the room and locked herself in the loo.'

'Oh, Martin,' said Patsy and a lump formed in her throat. All her dreams and hopes for Laura flashed before her: university, graduation, a career, husband, children. A pregnancy – a *teenage* pregnancy – would jeopardise it all.

Patsy heard the click of a door opening and the three of them looked up. Laura came into the room, shuffling like an old woman. Her lovely blonde hair was all messed up, her face was bright red and she had black rings of kohl around her eyes. As soon as she made eye contact with Patsy she burst into tears.

Immediately Patsy went over to her, put her arms around her daughter and pulled her to her breast. Laura rested her head on her mother's shoulder and wept, her entire body vibrating with each sob. Silent tears ran down Patsy's cheek and she stroked the back of Laura's head and whispered, 'Sweetheart, sweetheart,' over and over. And all she could think about was that some man had defiled her precious child.

'Laura, love,' she said at last, when Laura's cries had eased a little. 'Shush, there now. Listen, sweetheart, there's something I need to know.' She lowered her voice and whispered into Laura's hair, 'Did someone force you to have sex with them?'

Laura pulled away, dabbed at her face with the saturated tissue and said, with a vehement shake of her head, 'No.' Then she peeled away from her mother, threw the soiled tissue on the table and ripped another one from the box her sister had left there.

Some of the tension that was built up inside Patsy like a tightened elastic band subsided. Laura had not been raped, thank God.

Patsy followed her daughter over to the table and sat down. The anxiety she had experienced on first hearing the news had been replaced by an indescribable sadness.

'Laura,' she said. 'Talk to us.'

Laura eyed her warily and Patsy blinked and said, 'No-one's going to be cross with you.' She looked at Martin. 'We just need to . . . to find out a few facts.'

Laura sat down and put a strand of hair in her mouth and chewed on it – something she had done from childhood when stressed or worried.

'Are you absolutely sure you're pregnant, Laura?' said Patsy.

'Yes,' she said and sniffed. 'I bought a kit from Boots. I did the test twice.'

Patsy swallowed and, fighting back the tears, thought of all the things she wanted to know – and the things she didn't. But the hurt was so deep. The disappointment was like a physical pain in every bone in her body. So instead of asking questions about the where, when and who, she found herself saying, 'How could you, Laura? How could you throw everything away?'

Fresh tears cascaded down Laura's face, and Sarah said, 'This isn't helping, Mum.'

Martin cleared his throat. 'Your mum's just upset, Laura. We both are. We just can't understand how . . . how this could've happened to our . . .' He broke off then and held a closed fist to his lips.

Laura lifted her head and blew her nose and when she was composed again, Patsy said, 'Will you tell us what happened, Laura?'

She nodded. 'It was at Jason's party. I was there with Louise and Catherine.'

Patsy thought back to what Janice had told her about the party – the house trashed, the gatecrashers. It sounded like a seedy affair. Laura should never have been there. Patsy should've made sure she wasn't.

'We were all just hanging out,' said Laura. 'And Kyle Burke came in and me and him got talking.'

'Kyle Burke!' exclaimed Patsy and she looked at Martin.

'It's not Kyle,' said Laura quietly and she stared red-faced at her hands folded in her lap.

Patsy covered her mouth with her hand, resolving not to interrupt again.

'Kyle and you were talking . . .' prompted Martin gently.

'Yes and we . . . well . . . we were all just hanging out. You know. Having a laugh.'

'Were you drinking?' said Martin.

Laura nodded, still staring at her lap.

'What? What were you drinking?'

'Bacardi Breezers mostly.'

Martin looked at Patsy, nodding slowly, as if confirming something to himself. 'Were you drunk?'

'I don't think so. I mean, I had a few drinks. But I wasn't off my face.' This brought forth a fresh wave of tears. But Laura quickly wiped them away and composed herself.

Patsy thought back to the night of the party. She and Martin were in bed asleep when Laura came in very late. They had not seen her until the next morning. They should have checked on her. They should not have given her so much freedom. They should not have trusted her so blindly.

No-one spoke. Dripping water from the tap drummed out a rhythmic beat on the stainless steel sink. Patsy waited for Laura to go on, to tell them what they were all waiting for. She bit down on her knuckles until it hurt.

'It was about twelve and we were thinking of leaving,' said Laura at last. Patsy held her breath. 'And then they came in.'

'Who? Gatecrashers?' said Patsy, releasing her breath in a rush, unable to hold back any longer.

'No, Pete Kirkpatrick and his friends.'

The blood drained from Patsy's face at the mention of Pete's name. What had he got to do with this?

'Pete came straight up to me and starting chatting like we were old buddies. And you know the way he's kind of good-looking and some of the girls fancy him – well Amy Ritchie does anyway.' She sighed heavily. 'I don't really know what happened after that . . . well, I do know. But I don't know why I went along with it.'

'But I thought you didn't like Pete?' said Patsy, her voice choked.

'I don't. Not really. But he was there and he was telling me how gorgeous I was. When he asked me to go upstairs with him, I went.'

Patsy covered her ears with her hands but she could still hear what Laura said next. 'Don't do that, Mum. I'm not a child. It's not as though it was my first time.'

Patsy closed her eyes and stifled the strangled cry that almost escaped her lips. Not her first time! Laura had had casual, mindless sex with someone she didn't even like – and it wasn't the first time!

'I thought he would've had condoms,' went on Laura, talking so matter-of-factly it made Patsy blush. 'But he didn't and by then it was too late.'

No-one said anything. Patsy was truly shocked. She looked at Sarah, who was staring at Laura in astonishment.

Patsy felt the anger build up at Laura. She made it sound like a recreational activity, like tennis or shopping. She and Martin had somehow failed to instill in Laura the notion that sex was something valued and sacred, something to be cherished and shared with someone you loved. Not some guy who picked you up at a party. Not a creep like Pete Kirkpatrick.

'Oh, Laura,' said Sarah. 'Since when did Pete Kirkpatrick ever give you, or me, the time of day?'

Laura looked at her sister with those big blue eyes and frowned. 'What're you saying?'

'Didn't it occur to you that he was after something?'

Laura, wide-eyed, shook her head. 'Not at the time. But afterwards, he went off with his friends and ignored me for the rest of the night. I knew I'd done a stupid thing. I came home and just tried to forget about it.'

The naïvety of this woman-child broke Patsy's heart. Laura had been foolish, certainly, but she had also been used. Pete Kirkpatrick had taken advantage of her.

Martin, who had been quiet for some moments, suddenly brought his fist down on the table so hard it made everyone jump. 'The little shit! That little bastard,' he said, staring at the kitchen wall. Then he turned his gaze on Laura, specks of spittle on his lips. 'I'm ashamed of you.'

Laura hung her head and let out a little sob. Sarah put her hand on her sister's back and rubbed it in a circular motion.

Martin's face was tight with rage, every muscle tensed. His eyes bulged in his head.

Patsy put a restraining hand on his forearm. His muscles were taut like Patsy's nerves. She applied gentle pressure with her fingertips and his fist unfurled slowly like a flower.

'Why did you go with him, Laura? Why?' said Patsy. 'You don't even like him.'

Laura shrugged in a defeated, worn-out way. 'I don't know.'

There was a long silence. The facts, in all their lurid detail, lay on the table. Patsy's imagination stepped up to fill in the missing gaps in the story, too lucidly for her liking. She couldn't bear to think about Laura and Pete together. It made her feel sick. If she had never warmed to Pete Kirkpatrick, now she hated him with every fibre in her body. 'Does he know?' she asked.

'No,' said Laura and tears seeped from her eyes again. 'I tried to tell him a couple of days ago. But he wouldn't listen. He told me to stop bugging him. He said that I was an embarrassment.'

Martin swore, using such colourful expletives, it made Patsy wince. Fury swelled up inside her. Pete was even worse than she had thought. He was a monster. Then her fretting mind latched onto the fact that Laura was about to sit the most important exams of her life so far.

'Oh, God, what about your exams?' said Patsy.

Laura sniffed. 'What about them?'

'You can't sit them in this state. There must be some sort of process by which you can defer them.'

'On what basis, Mum? That I'm pregnant?'

The words stung Patsy like little darts. 'The doctor would give you a letter, I'm sure. To say you were suffering from . . . from stress.'

'And then what? I'd lose my place to study psychology at uni. I'd lose a whole year.'

'Laura,' said Patsy and she looked involuntarily at her daughter's stomach. 'What makes you think you'll be going to uni in September?'

The colour drained from Laura's face. 'I hadn't thought,' she said. She touched her flat belly and Patsy had to look away. The idea of Pete Kirkpatrick's baby growing there was grotesque. 'I know that sounds stupid but I hadn't thought that far ahead . . . I can't picture myself with a baby.'

And neither could Patsy. Laura was little more than a child herself, not so much physically but emotionally. She wasn't ready to be a mother, in any sense of the word. But a baby was on its way and, unless something was done about it, Laura would be forced to become a mother whether she liked it or not.

Patsy looked at Laura's tear-stained face and she was fuelled by two emotions, compassion and fury, the latter of which threatened to spill out at any moment. She thought it better that Laura went before she said something she regretted. 'Laura,' she suggested suddenly, 'why don't you go to bed now? It's very late. You must be exhausted.' Patsy stared hard at Sarah, who nodded, got up and took Laura by the arm and led her out of the kitchen. Martin and Patsy sat in shocked silence.

Patsy sighed and pressed her forehead with the tips of her fingers. 'You know, I always worried about Sarah more than Laura. I was always on at Sarah to go out more, to spend more time with her friends. I told her that she sat at home too much and that she should socialise more like her sister.'

She thought back to how, only a few months ago, she'd congratulated herself, and Martin, on their parenting skills. There was no doubt about it, Janice and Keith had raised a heartless, self-centred, arrogant child. But had she and Martin done much better with Laura? They'd produced a promiscuous daughter who appeared to have difficulty distinguishing right from wrong and who was either too naïve or too stupid to know when she was being used.

'I just can't believe I was so blind. There's nothing wrong with Sarah, Martin. She might be a bit sensible but she's grounded. It was Laura I should've been watching all along.' She paused, trying to pinpoint what it was, in this whole debacle, that troubled her so deeply – apart from the fact of the pregnancy itself. It was Laura's attitude. 'Laura doesn't seem to have a moral sense, Martin. She doesn't seem to think that what she did was wrong. Stupid, yes. But wrong, no.'

'Pete Kirkpatrick's taken advantage of her,' said Martin through thin lips. 'I know she's no angel but to use a girl like that . . . my girl . . .' He raised his closed fist to his mouth, unable to go on.

'Are we responsible?' asked Patsy, staring at the back of her hands which suddenly looked old. The skin was loose and wrinkled at her finger joints like the knees of an elephant.

'How do you mean?' he said, turning to look at her for the first time. 'Pete Kirkpatrick's responsible.'

'We let, no, we encouraged, Laura to go running here, there and everywhere. Were we too liberal with her?'

'She had the same upbringing as Sarah, Patsy,' he said and paused, allowing this thought to sink in. 'And they've turned out completely different. It's as much to do with her personality as anything we did.'

'But she's been sleeping around, Martin. She admitted it. Where did she learn that that sort of behaviour was okay?'

'I don't know.' He shook his head. 'From her friends?'

'Well, it certainly wasn't from us.'

Tears flooded Patsy's eyes but she blinked them back. She could cry for ever about what had happened but what was needed right now was clarity of thought. Laura had had unprotected sex. She would have to be tested for STDs and, she closed her eyes at the thought, HIV. Patsy looked at Martin's murderous face and could not bring herself to share this with him. She sensed that he was trying to hold onto what was left of the image he had of Laura – that of a sweet, innocent little girl. Well, that girl was long gone.

'What are we going to do?' said Martin.

Patsy put her head in her hands. 'I don't know,' she said. 'I can't imagine Laura with a baby. She's not ready to raise one and neither am I – I can't do it for her, Martin.'

'The baby could be put up for adoption.'

'God, no! Can you imagine what that would do to her? Can you imagine what it would be like to carry a baby to full term and then hand it over to some stranger? And never see it again. I think that would break her, Martin – it would break any woman.'

'What's the alternative, then? She keeps the baby?'

Patsy said nothing but she looked at Martin, held his gaze for a few moments and then they both looked away. Both thinking the same thing that they would not utter: abortion. Even the sound of the word was repugnant.

'I believe in the sanctity of life, Martin. But I put Laura's interests before those of a baby that doesn't even exist yet.'

'It does exist.'

'It's not a baby yet. It's a foetus.'

'I hate that word,' said Martin. 'And I don't feel comfortable having this conversation. I know neither of us goes to church, but there are certain things I believe in, Patsy.'

'And I believed in them too, Martin. It's easy to believe in things when they don't affect you. It's easy to be all morally superior and tell other people what's right and wrong. But when it's your own flesh and blood . . .'

'Are you seriously saying that you would let her have a termination?'

'It's not up to me. It's up to Laura. But if you're asking me, then yes, I would.'

Martin put his elbows on the table and buried his face in his hands. 'I can't believe we're having this conversation.'

'Well, what would you have her do, Martin? Go through with a pregnancy when she's little more than a child herself? Have her raise a child alone? Because, believe me, Pete Kirkpatrick isn't going to want to know. It'd ruin her life, Martin.'

'I know that. But children are a gift from God.'

'This one isn't.'

Martin removed his hands from his face and looked at her as though he was seeing her for the first time. 'When did you get so hard?' he said.

Patsy was defiant, unapologetic. 'About fifteen minutes ago when I walked through that door and you told me my youngest daughter was pregnant.'

Martin did not respond, he just looked away. Patsy put

her hand on the table and held his. His fingers were long and elegant, with the sinewy strength of a pianist's. Bluish veins stood out on the back of his hand like ghostly tributaries of a river, winding their way through a forest of dark hairs. It was a manly hand, capable and strong. The hand of her protector and Laura's. Yet Martin had not been able to protect Laura from this catastrophe. She wondered if he felt a sense of failure as a parent. She certainly did.

'But it doesn't matter what I think,' said Patsy, quietly. 'It's Laura's decision.'

'You'll try and influence her.'

'I swear to God I won't. I don't want her to go through with this pregnancy but I don't want her to have an abortion either. Yet I do know that whatever she does, she's going to be affected by it for the rest of her life. And I don't want to be responsible for forcing her hand either way.'

'It's up to her then,' said Martin.

'It is,' said Patsy. 'And, whatever she decides to do, we have to support her.'

And they both sat in silence then and stared at the wall, Patsy wondering how they could've permitted such disaster to befall their family. How had Pete Kirkpatrick slipped under their radar and done this?

Chapter Fourteen

Saturday morning just after nine found Janice in front of the computer in the study in her pyjamas. Keith was golfing. Pete was still in bed and wouldn't surface until nearly lunchtime. As with pretty much everything else about him, even his circadian rhythms were out of sync with his mother's.

It was exactly thirty-one days until Pete finished his exams. Unlike most parents who were praying for them to be over, Janice counted down every day wishing they could last for ever. Because when Pete had done his last exam, Keith would tell him something that she was sure would alter his relationship with them, at least with *her*, for good. She had tried to persuade Keith not to tell Pete he was his adoptive father. And she had failed. Keith was adamant.

Thinking about it induced a horrible feeling in the pit of her stomach like seasickness. She tried to quell this nausea with logical thinking. Pete would be shocked to find out he was adopted. But Keith was the only father he had ever known and he was a good one. She hoped their father-son relationship would survive the revelation unscathed. There was no reason why it should not.

But Pete would be curious about his real father. It was only natural that he would want to know. Of course she would never tell Pete the truth. And that was going to be the hard part.

Janice gave her head a little shake and tried to put these thoughts out of her mind for they were in danger of consuming her. She hated the way it was all she thought about, every bloody waking minute. It had taken her years to come to terms with what had happened and crowbar those memories into the recesses of her mind. And now they were being hauled out and aired like winter woollens, forcing her to confront a past that should never have happened.

In an effort to distract herself, she busied herself with booking flights to London for herself and her girlfriends in September. She was watching a copy of the flight confirmation churn out of the printer when the phone rang, startling her.

Who would be calling so early on a Saturday morning? Had something happened to Pete? Maybe he wasn't along the landing comatose in his bed as she had assumed. She glanced at the door, got up, sat down again. Maybe something had happened to Keith on his way to the golf club? She snatched the receiver up and pressed it to her ear. She was relieved to hear Patsy's voice on the end of the line.

'Hey, Patsy,' she said, 'guess what I've just done?'

Silence. Janice felt vaguely uneasy.

'Patsy, are you still there? I've just booked our flights to London. What do you think of that?'

Patsy cleared her throat.

'I didn't ring to talk about the trip to London, Janice.'

'Oh,' said Janice, taken aback by Patsy's frosty tone. She put both hands on the receiver and strained to listen. Patsy's voice sounded muffled, far away.

'Martin and I want to come round and see you. And Keith.' It was a demand, not a request.

'Well, sure. Any time,' said Janice, hesitatingly. 'That would be nice. When were you thinking of?'

'Tonight,' said Patsy in a tone Janice had never heard her use before. It was . . . direct, businesslike. And yet, behind the clipped tone, Janice sensed a well of emotion.

'Will you be in tonight?' asked Patsy.

'Well, no, actually,' said Janice, bristling a little. 'We're going out to a party.'

'What time?'

'I really don't think tonight would suit . . .' began Janice but Patsy cut her off.

'This isn't something that can wait,' she snapped.

'Patsy, what's wrong?'

'I . . . I . . .' There was the sound of rustling and Martin's voice in the background and Patsy came on the line again. 'It's not something I wish to discuss over the phone.'

'Okay,' said Janice slowly, 'but can't we talk about it another time?'

'We'll be there at seven.'

The line went dead and Janice looked at the receiver. 'What the hell was that all about?' she said out loud to the empty room. Her mind was racing. She couldn't ignore the tone of the conversation. Patsy had been anything but friendly – in fact she'd been downright rude. But why?

Janice thought back to the evening before in No.11. Nothing had happened to account for Patsy's attitude. Perhaps she was having second thoughts about the London trip? Was she annoyed that Janice had gone ahead and booked the flights without further consultation? Or had she inadvertently caused offence in some other way? If so, why would Patsy not talk about it over the phone? And why involve Martin? Janice's stomach churned with anxiety.

She wished Keith was here. He would be able to rationalise

the situation in a way that Janice could not. She always suspected the worst; he always assumed the best. There would be some perfectly logical explanation for that very weird phone call and Keith would know what it was.

Janice showered and dressed and spent the next two hours doing chores, while the worry settled in her stomach like a rock. She put on a load of washing, folded laundry, watered the plants, tidied every room downstairs and changed the towels in all the bathrooms. She emptied the bins and chopped vegetables for carrot and lentil soup.

When Pete finally emerged from his bed at noon, crumpled and crusty-eyed, he was as uncommunicative as usual. He got himself some Shreddies and sat at the kitchen table in a t-shirt and pair of boxer shorts and read the *Saturday Times*.

'Are you going out tonight?' she asked, tossing carrot peelings and onion skins in the bin.

'No plans. Why?' He turned the page of the paper, rubbed his nose with the back of his hand and scanned the headlines.

'Oh, just asking,' said Janice. It occurred to her that if there was going to be any unpleasantness tonight she didn't want Pete around. But she kept coming back to the same old question – what on earth could have upset Patsy?

While Pete showered, Janice served herself a bowl of soup and ate it with some oat crackers. Then she tidied up and waited for Keith to come home.

When she heard his car pull up at the front of the house, she ran to greet him. As soon as he got out of the car, she forced a cheery smile and said, 'There you are!'

He looked relaxed and a little amused. 'I'm not late, am I?' He consulted his watch. 'I'm not usually home before now.'

Then, giving her a concerned look, he said, 'What's eating you?'

She let out a sigh. 'Am I that transparent?'

'Yes. Come into the kitchen and tell me all about it.'

'It's Patsy,' she said, following him. In the kitchen he filled the kettle and made tea in a mug while she proceeded to tell him all about the disturbing phone call and her worries that she had unwittingly offended her friend.

'I don't think you've offended her.'

'You don't?'

'No.'

'So what do you think's going on?'

'Think about it a minute, Janice. What's happened to Martin?'

'He's lost his job,' said Janice a little impatiently. 'So what's that got to do with anything?'

'Money's a concern, isn't it? You told me that they'd all their savings in bank shares that are worth almost zilch, right?'

'So?'

'I think, if the Devlins are coming here together, Janice, it's probably to ask for financial help.'

'Oh,' said Janice. Then she shook her head, recalling the tone of the phone call. 'I don't think that's it. She sounded really . . . frosty on the phone. Not like Patsy at all.'

'She was probably upset. Maybe she was embarrassed to have to ask. Maybe Martin put her up to it.'

Janice recalled that she had heard a man's voice in the background. Perhaps Keith was right . . . It was such a welcome insight that she threw her arms around him and hugged him.

'Hey, what's brought this on?' he said, pulling back a little so that he could look at her face.

'I was really worried that Patsy was angry with me,' said Janice, feeling more than a little foolish. 'But what you've said makes perfect sense. Why didn't I think of that?' She grinned with sheer relief.

'That's what you've got me for,' he said. 'Among other things. Here, have a cup of tea.'

She took the proffered mug and nursed it in her hands. 'So, what'll we do, Keith? If they come here asking to borrow money, should we lend it to them?'

'I'd like to help them,' said Keith. 'I'm sure the difficulties they're experiencing are only temporary. Martin's a really clever guy – I'm sure he'll get another job soon. So yes, if we can help, then we should.'

'Okay,' she said and smiled, thinking that Keith had a good heart. This evening wasn't going to be comfortable but at least it wouldn't be unpleasant. She was so glad that she had Keith to talk sense into her.

By seven o'clock that evening, Janice was dressed in an off-the-shoulder royal blue cocktail dress that came to just above the knee, sheer skin-tone tights and black heels. She wore her hair in an up-do and a pretty blue enamelled necklace that Keith had bought her on a trip to Rome. Keith was smart in a light grey suit and pink-and-blue tie.

Janice surveyed the drawing room with satisfaction. A bottle of gin, tonic water and lemon slices were arranged on a silver tray along with some olives and pretzels. The evening sun streamed in across the oak floor, filling the whole room with a warm orange glow. Money was never a good subject to discuss between friends and there was bound to be a little awkwardness. So it was important to get the atmosphere just right. She wanted the Devlins to feel comfortable – but not so comfortable they didn't want to leave. She hoped they'd take a hint from her, and

Keith's attire and remember that, business done, they were meant to be somewhere.

The bell rang precisely at seven. Janice took a moment to compose herself, then opened the door wide with a welcoming smile on her face. She wanted to make this as easy for her friends as possible. What greeted her on the doorstep wiped that smile away at once.

Patsy wore a cream raincoat over dark trousers and flat shoes. She had no handbag and her hair was wild and unkempt. Martin loomed behind Patsy, dressed in jeans and an old sweatshirt. He jiggled the car keys in his hand and would not look at Janice.

Janice, puzzled, stepped back without a word, and let them in. Patsy walked straight into the hall, without making eye contact with Janice, placed her left hand on the newel post and craned her neck to look up the stairs. 'Is Pete here?' she said.

'Yes,' said Janice, shocked by Patsy's appearance. 'He's studying in his room.'

Keith, who had just joined them, shot Janice a concerned glance and said, 'Why don't you come through here?' He gestured towards the drawing room.

Martin gave Patsy, who was still staring up the stairs, a little push and said, 'Go on.'

They walked in and stood awkwardly by the coffee table which was flanked by sofas on three sides. Keith said, 'Can I take your coat, Patsy?'

'We won't be staying long,' said Martin.

'Care for a drink?' said Keith.

Martin shook his head slowly and stared at Keith with a look of hatred on his face. Janice, standing beside Keith, put her hand on her breast. Keith was mistaken. They weren't here to ask for money. Something was wrong. Very wrong. She took Keith's hand in hers and squeezed it tight.

'What is it?' she whispered.

Patsy's bottom lip began to quiver and she touched her temple with the tips of her fingers as though suffering from a blinding headache. Martin, standing over a foot taller than his wife, put a protective arm across her shoulder. Janice glanced fearfully at Keith and steeled herself for some terrible news. Dear God, had someone died?

'Our daughter Laura,' began Martin and his voice wavered. He paused for a moment to compose himself and went on. 'Laura . . . she told us last night that she's pregnant.'

'Oh, God, I'm so sorry,' said Janice and she reached out a hand to touch Patsy's arm. Her friend flinched.

'Patsy?' she said, looking at her fingertips then at Patsy's wretched face. Patsy turned away.

Martin pressed on grimly. 'She says that your son is the father.'

Janice's legs trembled and she reeled backwards until her calves hit the edge of the sofa. She sat down involuntarily because her legs would no longer support her.

'What?' said Keith, squaring up to Martin, defensive, challenging, refusing to believe what Janice knew instinctively and immediately to be true. Her knees began to tremble, and she pressed them between the palms of her hands.

'You heard me,' said Martin. 'Your son took advantage of our daughter at a party.'

Had he really done that to Laura? How could Pete 'take advantage of' Laura? It struck Janice as such an old-fashioned saying. From what she had seen and heard, teenage girls nowadays were perfectly capable of looking after themselves. Unless Laura had been forced. Or been drunk or high on drugs and not known what she was doing. Janice's eyes filled with tears because she suspected that what Martin said might very well be true. But not pretty, bubbly Laura, her dearest friend's little girl. She put her face in her hands.

'Now, steady on,' said Keith. He let out a loud puff of air and pulled at the shirt collar around his neck as though it was suddenly too tight. 'You're making a lot of assumptions here.'

'Are you calling Laura a liar?' said Patsy, spitting out the words like bullets.

'No, of course not,' said Keith, his lawyer's voice conciliatory and smooth. 'This is a terrible shock for all of us. But Janice and I just need to hear all the facts. Please. Come and sit down.'

Patsy looked at Martin and he nodded. They inched forwards and sat down gingerly on the edge of the sofa. Such a change from when they were last here for dinner – was it only a matter of weeks ago? – before Martin lost his job and before this . . .

'Now, tell us what Laura said, exactly,' said Keith. He leant forwards, his head cocked to one side.

Patsy spoke, looking directly at Keith. 'She said that she and Pete had . . . slept together at Jason Dobbin's eighteenth birthday party.'

Janice let out a little gasp. Pete had definitely been at the party, that much was certain.

'Where exactly?' said Keith.

'For God's sake, does it matter?' said Patsy. 'Do you want every gruesome detail?'

'I'm sorry, Patsy. I know this is difficult but I'm just trying to piece together what happened.' In his smart suit, Keith looked, and sounded, every inch the lawyer.

'One of the bedrooms upstairs,' said Martin, the words slipping out, against his will it seemed, from tight, thin lips.

'I see,' said Keith and he nodded slowly. 'And Laura . . . she's definitely sure it's Pete?'

'Keith!' gasped Janice, appalled that he was questioning Laura's story and, worse, suggesting that she had slept with someone else as well as Pete.

'Of course she's bloody sure,' said Martin through gritted teeth, the tendons on the side of his neck standing out. 'What the hell are you suggesting?' His hands, resting on his long thighs, clenched into fists.

'How dare you, Keith,' whispered Patsy, and she stood up, her face twisted in rage. Her voice rose. '*How* dare you.'

'Okay. I'm sorry,' said Keith and he raised a palm, like an admission of guilt. 'I just . . . have to be sure. Please, Patsy, sit down.'

She glanced at Martin, he nodded and she obeyed. 'That's very odd,' said Keith, looking at Janice. 'Pete hasn't said anything to us about Laura, has he?'

Janice shook her head. 'No.'

'And the party was the first time?' said Keith.

'Yes,' said Patsy.

'And did it happen again?' said Keith.

'No, certainly not. Apparently, once he got what he wanted, Pete refused to have anything to do with Laura,' said Patsy. 'He's been telling her to stop pestering him.'

Janice put a hand over her mouth, removed it and said, 'So he doesn't know about this . . . this accusation?'

'It's not an accusation, as you call it, Janice,' said Patsy coolly, and she stared hard at Janice. 'It's a statement of fact.'

Keith said, 'Martin, you said that Pete took advantage of Laura. What did you mean by that?'

Martin paused, looked at Patsy and ploughed on. 'From what we can gather, it seems that Laura might have . . . well she might have had a drink.'

'Jesus, Martin,' said Keith and he glanced at Janice with a horrified expression on his face. 'Let's just get this straight.

Are you saying that she was drunk and Pete . . . Pete raped her?'

'No,' said Martin and he shook his head violently. 'No, not rape.'

'Then they had consensual sex?'

Patsy, red in the face, said, 'Laura's not used to alcohol. Her judgment was . . . clouded. She didn't know what she was doing, Keith. And Pete did.'

'Is that what she said?' said Keith. Patsy and Martin looked at each other. 'Is that what she told you?' persisted Keith.

'Will you stop splitting hairs over semantics, Keith?' said Patsy.

'I'm trying to establish the facts, Patsy. You can't come in here casting allegations about without being absolutely sure that what you're accusing my son of is true.' Keith counted on the fingers of his left hand with his right thumb as he spoke. 'One – Laura and Pete are both over the age of consent. Two – Laura's judgment may have been impaired by alcohol. Three – that said, Laura willingly consented. None of this adds up to a crime on my son's part. He and Laura have both made a terrible and foolish mistake.'

'That's easy for you to say,' said Martin angrily. 'It's not your daughter that's pregnant.'

Keith stood up. 'I think it's time we heard Pete's side of the story.'

'Yes, let's,' said Martin and he inched closer to the edge of the sofa, as though he was about to stand up.

Janice put a hand to her throat. 'I'll go and get him.'

She escaped the room and climbed the stairs to the landing. Her legs felt like they were made of lead, her fine clothes suddenly seemed ostentatious and inappropriate. The door to Pete's room was slightly ajar. She could see his head bent over his desk, the anglepoise lamp shining down on the opened book in front of him. Had he really done what the Devlins claimed? Had he coerced Laura into having unprotected sex with him? She rapped the door with her knuckles and, when she spoke, found that she was shaking.

'You're needed down in the drawing room,' she said, without crossing the threshold of the room. With its dark blue walls, Black Watch tartan curtains and insufficient lighting – all Pete's choices – it was like a dungeon. It was her least favourite room in the house, and she found it slightly menacing.

'Huh?' he said, looking over his shoulder with a frown to demonstrate his irritation at being interrupted.

'Now, Pete,' she said and something in her tone arrested him for he got up without further comment, and followed her out of the room and down the stairs. She entered the drawing room first, head down, and went over to the sofa to sit beside Keith, opposite the Devlins. Behind her, Pete came to a halt in front of the coffee table and put his hands in the front pockets of his jeans.

He raised his shoulders, sharp beneath a thin white t-shirt, and said, 'What?' to the four sombre faces staring at him.

Keith spoke first and to the point. 'Laura Devlin's pregnant, Pete. And she says you're the father.'

A ghost of a smile crossed his face, as if he found this statement mildly amusing. 'You've got to be kidding.'

'I wish I was,' said Keith and he sighed heavily. 'Did you or did you not sleep with Laura at Jason Dobbin's eighteenth birthday party?'

The corner of Pete's mouth turned up in what looked like a smirk and then it was gone. 'I . . . er . . . I may have done.'

'You either did or you didn't,' said Janice sharply, incensed by his smart-ass comment. She could feel the tension between

Martin and Patsy from across the room, like a taut elastic band, ready to snap at any moment.

'Okay, then. I did.'

Keith's face crumpled and Janice put her hand on his knee. He had really believed in Pete up until this point. He had so much more faith in him than Janice had.

Martin bent his head like a great weight was pressing down on it. Patsy's eyes filled with tears but, chin up, she kept her composure.

'Did you use any protection?' said Janice.

Pete shrugged, and shook his head. 'That's her problem, not mine,' he said, raising a sardonic eyebrow. 'If she's gonna lay it out, she should know how to look after herself. Anyway, how come you're so sure it's me that got her preggers?'

Janice never even saw Martin leap out of the seat, he moved so fast. Before she realised what was happening he was standing in front of Pete. He pushed him roughly with the flat of his right hand and sent Pete sprawling backwards onto the floor. A cry escaped Janice's lips. Then Martin stood over Pete, hands formed into fists, choking with anger. A string of expletives, words that Janice had never heard mild-mannered Martin use before, poured forth. He was so pumped up with adrenaline, she was afraid he might set those fists to work on her son. She reckoned he was capable of beating Pete to a pulp. She found she was loath to intervene.

Quickly, Keith got between Martin and Pete, locked his hands on Martin's biceps and looked into his face. 'You've got to calm down, Martin. This isn't helping.'

'Did you hear him? Did you hear what he said?' shouted Martin, his face puce with rage, straining to look past Keith at Pete. 'Talking about Laura like that. Like she's some sort of slut.'

'I know, Martin. I know,' said Keith and he looked over his shoulder. He glared angrily at Pete who still lay on his back on the floor, his legs splayed out, his feet bare. Pete looked down at his chest, at the place where Martin had struck him.

Janice went over to him and helped him to his feet.

'I'm alright,' he mumbled, and brushed her hand from his arm. 'Did you see that? That was assault.'

'Oh, for God's sake, Pete,' cried Janice and only just managed to restrain herself from slapping him across the face. 'Don't you know when to shut up? You're lucky he didn't do a lot worse.' She paused and examined his face. His chin was tilted up slightly, his eyes narrowed a little. He looked proud, unrepentant. Janice lowered her voice, and looked directly into his eyes. 'Have you no idea what harm you've done, Pete? What this means for Laura? For all of us?'

He stared back at her, challenging her with his arrogant, steady gaze. He did not answer but he didn't need to. His expression said it all – he refuted any culpability. He accepted no responsibility, displayed no shame or remorse. Janice stepped away from him and took a sharp intake of breath.

Keith managed to manoeuvre Martin back to the sofa and pushed him gently into a sitting position. The fight had gone out of him all of a sudden. Janice returned to her place on the sofa, leaving Pete to stand alone, his weight on one leg, hands shoved into the back pockets of his jeans.

'Let's all just calm down a minute,' said Keith, sitting down. 'Pete, I want you to apologise to the Devlins for slandering Laura's character.'

'Sorry,' said Pete quickly, without looking up. It was said so ungraciously, Janice closed her eyes in embarrassment and was surprised that it didn't bring Martin to his feet once more.

Patsy, who had been quiet for some time, spoke suddenly. Her voice was dripping with disgust. 'Look at what you two have raised,' she said and shook her head. 'A heartless monster, who doesn't give a damn about anybody but himself. Look at him! He doesn't care about Laura – or the baby.'

Pete made no attempt to defend himself. He redistributed his weight to the other foot and let out a bored-sounding sigh. His blue eyes sparkled with defiance. Janice realised he was actually enjoying this.

'I've always believed that children are a reflection of their upbringing,' said Patsy. 'Which says a lot about you two, doesn't it?'

Keith ran his hands through his thick, greying hair and said quietly, without looking at his son, 'Go back to your room, Pete.'

When he'd gone, there was a long silence. Keith, for once in his life, was speechless – a measure of his despair. Janice felt his disappointment and shared it. Pete had exceeded even her worst expectations. Janice looked at Patsy's wretched face and knew that this would drive a wedge between them. Their friendship would never be the same. Pete had destroyed Laura's life and refused to accept responsibility for his actions. But she would do everything in her power to make amends. To demonstrate that she accepted Pete's culpability, even if he didn't.

'Has Laura decided to keep the baby?' she asked.

Patsy ignored the question. 'Well, it's clear that Pete has absolutely no interest in Laura or the baby. Therefore she can't count on any sort of support from him whatsoever. Personally, I'm glad, because I wouldn't want that excuse for a human being involved with my daughter in any way.' She glared at Janice.

Janice hung her head, letting the blow glance off her. Keith stared at the empty fireplace. His face was white. He appeared not to be listening.

'As for the baby,' Patsy went on. She paused and looked at her hands clasped in her lap so tight the knuckles were white. When she spoke again her voice was a whisper. 'I think she should get rid of it.'

'Patsy!' said Martin.

Patsy looked at him, her eyes full of tears and said, 'What else can she do? If she has the baby, it'll ruin her life, Martin. All our hopes and dreams for her . . . her future, everything . . . shattered.'

Janice had never before felt so much compassion for another human being. She pressed her hands to her mouth and fought back the tears. Her son had brought this misery right into the heart of Patsy's family. And he thought he could simply walk away from the wreckage. Pete had disgraced her before, but nothing came close to the shame she felt now.

'I'm sorry,' said Janice. 'We both are.' She looked at Keith for support and he nodded grimly, quiet now, the stuffing knocked out of him.

'Well, sorry isn't a great deal of help to us right now,' said Martin. 'Though it might have made us feel better to hear it from Pete. But that's not going to happen, is it?'

Janice swallowed. Keith spoke up, in a voice that was flat and broken. 'As Pete's parents we accept full responsibility for what he's done. And we want you to know that whatever Laura decides to do we will help in any . . .'

Patsy snorted, cutting him off. 'You think we want your money? Is that what you think we came here for?'

Keith shook his head. 'No, of course not.'

Janice said, 'Keith's only saying that we will be there for Laura whatever she decides to do. If she has the baby, we'll . . . we'll help with whatever it needs. Practically as well as financially.'

'And you think that we'd accept help from you?' said Patsy, and she pretended to laugh. 'Let me tell you something. If – and it's a big if – Laura decides to have this baby the last people in the world we'd want to come anywhere near her or the child is anyone remotely connected to Pete Kirkpatrick.' She paused, allowing the words to sink in, and shook her head. 'I always had my reservations about Pete, Janice.'

Janice's head snapped up – this was the first she'd heard of it. 'What do you mean?'

'I always thought he was a strange child – cold and aloof. I put a lot of it down to shyness but I see now that my instincts were right. He's arrogant and selfish and entirely lacking in any sense of right or wrong.'

Janice swallowed bravely, trying not to let Patsy's words hurt so much but they stung like knife cuts. But weirdly, Janice also found solace in the pain – someone else had seen in Pete what she thought only she could see.

'If you didn't come here for money, Patsy,' said Keith, 'what did you come here for?'

The question seemed to take her by surprise. 'I honestly don't know,' she said sadly and looked at her husband.

'You needed to know,' said Martin, addressing Keith. 'Pete needed to know. And we thought . . . well, I guess we hoped that Pete would . . .' He stopped abruptly, thought for a moment and then said simply, 'We wanted to hear Pete say he was sorry.'

It wasn't much to ask, Janice reflected, but based on Pete's performance tonight it was a wish that was unlikely to be granted. She felt her cheeks redden yet again, mortified by her son's behaviour.

'Martin,' snapped Patsy. 'We're finished here.' She stood

up and started to walk towards the door, then stopped abruptly and turned to face Keith and Janice once more. 'There is one more thing. I don't want a word spoken about this. If Laura decides to have the baby, everyone will learn about it soon enough. And if she doesn't, there's no need for half of Ballyfergus to know our business. So help me God, if I hear that Pete's going around blabbing . . .'

'You won't,' said Janice firmly. She dug her nails into her palms. 'We'll make sure that Pete doesn't talk about it to anyone. And neither will we.'

Patsy gave a tight little nod and made for the door without so much as a glance at Janice or Keith. Neither of them made any move to follow her.

Martin put his hand on the door handle and paused. He turned around, took a step back into the room and stood with his hands hanging by his side, the car keys still clutched in his left fist.

'Just in case my wife hasn't made it absolutely clear,' he said, pulling himself up to his full height, 'I want you to know that we wouldn't take a penny from you. Not if we were living on the street and starving.'

As soon as the door closed behind him, Janice started to weep. She had never been so humbled. She and Keith had had the arrogance to assume that Patsy and Martin wanted to borrow money from them. They thought Patsy and Martin were coming to them, cap in hand, begging. But it was they – Keith and Janice – who ought to be the ones begging. Pleading with their friends for forgiveness for the sins of their son.

Keith put an arm across her shoulder but there was little comfort in it – shattered, he had little to give. His face was ashen, the light in his eyes gone out. 'I can't believe it,' he said softly and shook his head. 'I can't believe that Pete was so stupid. I thought I'd told him enough times about unprotected sex. And I'm horrified that he would treat a girl so badly.'

'It doesn't surprise me.'

'Don't say that, Janice. It's not true. You're as shocked as I am.' He removed his arm.

She did not argue. What good would it do? What use was 'I told you so' now, when it was too late? A young girl's life was damaged and whatever route Laura decided to take there was no way out of the situation that would leave her unscathed. Janice remembered the night of the New Year's Eve party after everyone had left when she had tried to warn Keith about Pete. He would not listen. He had not wanted to hear. But, in ignoring Pete's faults he had given them room to take root and tighten their grip on his fledging character – like the rust-red fungus in the shower that, left too long, refused to budge no matter what you tried to clean it with. Keith had heaped all his affection on Pete and made the erroneous assumption that Pete was, like him, fundamentally good.

She remembered her premonition back then that something bad was going to happen. She put her hands on her hot cheeks. She never imagined it coming true in this horrible way. Not only had Pete managed to destroy a young girl's life but he had driven a wedge between his mother and her dearest friend – a rift that, right now, seemed too great to ever heal. Had he set out specifically to injure Janice, it was hard to think of a more effective way to do so.

Chapter Fifteen

'At least pretend that you're pleased for me,' said Clare. She hauled an old red jersey dress out of the wardrobe and stared at Liam's reflection in the mirror mounted on the inside of the wardrobe door. He was standing behind her, in a pair of navy trousers, struggling to remove a pair of cufflinks from a pale blue shirt. His face was pinched. She tried not to let his grumpy mood infect her – another tough week at work, he'd said – but it was hard and she resented it. This was her night, her exhibition. And he was spoiling it.

'Oh, Clare, of course I'm pleased. I just . . . damn, I can't get these out.'

'Here, let me help,' said Clare and she quickly threaded the cufflinks through the holes. 'There. What were you saying?'

'Nothing,' he said and untied the blue-and-red striped tie around his neck. 'You'd better hurry up or you're going to be late.'

Clare decided not to pursue the conversation. She would not be drawn into an argument. 'I don't know what people will expect me to look like,' she said, holding the dress against her body and looking in the mirror. She pulled the stretchy fabric taut against the curve of her waist and could hardly bear to look at the heavy woman who stared back at her.

Someone slightly eccentric or arty-looking, she thought, not a fat, frumpy housewife. It was no wonder she and Liam hardly had sex any more. Who would find her attractive? She threw the dress on the bed and sighed. 'I think they'll be disappointed when they see me.'

'I don't know what you're worrying about, Clare,' he said, without even looking at her. 'People are coming to look at your paintings, not you. You should just be yourself.' He threw the tie on the bed, turned his back on her and disappeared into the en-suite, the back of his untucked cotton shirt full like a sail.

It was sound advice but delivered with such a lack of interest, it crushed her spirit. She put the dress back in the wardrobe, pulled on black trousers and a black shirt and tied her hair back with a clasp the way she always did. As a concession to the occasion, she applied some bright red lipstick. It didn't look right, and so she rubbed it off with a tissue. The reflection that looked back at her was severe – all in black, she looked, not like an artist, but the way she imagined someone in fashion or an architect might appear. Except they would be slimmer.

Liam came back into the room and unbuttoned his shirt unselfconsciously, revealing a smooth golden chest. He was still in good shape; his trim figure matched his boyish looks but the glimpse of his torso did nothing to excite desire in Clare. She remembered how it used to be, looked away and bit her lip.

'That's a terrible business about Laura and Pete,' he said and shook his head.

Clare sighed, her heart heavy with worry for her friends, but grateful also for the distraction from her musings over the state of her marriage. 'I know. It's just awful. Patsy's so upset. I tried to talk her out of the exhibition but she was adamant that she wanted to go ahead. She said that being busy helped to take her mind off things.'

She paused, glanced at Liam and considered this statement. She understood exactly what Patsy meant. Her busyness over the past few months meant that she had been able to avoid addressing the problems in her marriage. Once the exhibition was behind her, though, she vowed she would spend more time with Liam. She was sure he felt neglected and, if she was honest with herself, he had been. As for herself, she felt increasingly distant from him.

'I'm surprised Patsy's invited Janice and Keith tonight,' said Liam, pulling on a freshly laundered white shirt.

'It's going to be very difficult for her,' said Clare. 'But she's doing it for me. She knows that if she vetoed Janice and Keith coming, their friends might not come as well. And they're the people who are most likely to buy my pictures. Patsy knows that.'

'Well, whatever happens,' he said, doing up the shirt buttons, 'I can't see things between the Devlins and the Kirkpatricks ever being the same again.'

The knot of anxiety, which had been lodged in Clare's stomach since Patsy had confided the whole terrible story to her and Kirsty only two days ago, tightened. 'Don't say that,' she said.

'It's true, Clare. There's nothing people feel more emotional about than their kids.'

Liam was right. She didn't know if fathers felt the same but the maternal instinct to protect and defend was ferocious. Patsy's anger towards Pete and, by extension, his mother was so intense Clare seriously doubted if she would ever be reconciled with Janice. Selfishly, she thought about the female friendship that meant so much to her. The dynamic of that relationship would be altered for ever.

She thought about the things they'd done together over the last fifteen years – nights out, parties, spa days, weekends away, shopping, but most of all the simple, innocent pleasure of shared fun and laughter. It wouldn't be the same if they were all no longer friends. Something unique and special would be lost. She'd been looking forward so much to the trip to London to celebrate their amazing friendship. Now, unless Patsy and Janice were reconciled, it looked as if that too was under threat.

'Maybe they'll make up,' said Clare optimistically, slipping her feet into a pair of sensible black ballet pumps. 'It seems a bit unfair to blame Janice for what Pete's done. After all Pete and Laura are both adults – well, almost in Laura's case. She had to know what she was doing.'

Liam tucked the shirt into his trousers. 'Maybe. But imagine if Rachel came home one day and told us she was pregnant. You'd want to blame somebody, wouldn't you? It'd be hard to accept that your daughter wasn't the little angel you thought she was.'

Clare shuddered, tried and failed to turn her mind to the impossible task of imagining such a scenario. She couldn't picture her babies grown up, never mind engaging in sexual relationships. 'I suppose so,' she said thoughtfully and then added, 'Now, you're not to tell anyone. Patsy told me in the strictest confidence.'

'What do you take me for?' demanded Liam, sounding peeved.

'Patsy's anxious that as few people as possible know. I think she has in mind that if Laura has an abortion it's not something she'd want bandied about.'

'Poor kid.'

'I know,' she said and then, glancing at the digital display on the radio alarm, added, 'Look, I'd better go, Liam. The kids are watching TV and the babysitter'll be here shortly.' She went over and gave him a kiss on the cheek.

He gave her a distracted peck in return and said, 'Okay. I'll see you down there.'

She walked onto the landing. When she heard Liam call her name, she stopped and smiled. She knew he wouldn't forget to wish her luck – he knew, after all, how much tonight meant to her. She turned around and went back and stood expectantly in the doorway to the bedroom.

'Yes?'

'Remind me, again, would you, Clare? What's the babysitter's name?'

And Clare smiled and told him and began to wonder if, like a puzzle with too many missing pieces, she was ever going to be able to piece her marriage back together. First she must get tonight over and done with – and tomorrow she would address the other areas of her life that seemed so out of kilter.

Patsy was in the gallery alone when Clare arrived, arranging small wine glasses on a tray by the cash register. She was wearing a knitted dress, her breasts like twin granite peaks underneath the marled grey fabric. Below the hemline, which stopped just above her knees, she wore opaque black tights and incredibly high red patent Mary Janes. Round her neck was a thin, sparkly silver-grey scarf and a chunky red necklace. Immediately Clare felt dowdy and underdressed. But if Patsy noticed, she passed no comment. She greeted her friend warmly.

Patsy put the last glass on the tray. 'What do you think of the pictures?'

Clare's pictures were arrayed along one wall of the little gallery, Bronson's on another. This was wise, for Bronson's work was so much bolder in medium (oil as opposed to watercolour), brushstroke and colour that her detailed, muted watercolours would've been overwhelmed. Bronson's pictures, ranging in subject from still life – fruit and vases of flowers – to landscapes, were very good. Clare worried that hers weren't.

But viewed as a group, each one in a fine gold frame with handsome cream mounts, Clare's paintings held their own. Looking at them like this, framed behind glass, was almost like seeing them for the first time, and Clare was surprised at how striking they were. Some, like the one of Carnlough Harbour, were beautiful.

'Oh, they look fantastic, Patsy,' she said and put her hands up to her face as though they could draw the heat of her embarrassment.

'That's because they are fantastic,' said Patsy and her smile was like armour donned not to protect her from outside threats, but to contain the pain that lay within. Clare would never have used the word lacklustre to describe Patsy but tonight it seemed to fit.

'Clare,' her friend went on, looking at the bottle in her hand, 'would you give me a hand to pour the wine? I'm expecting forty or so.'

They worked in companionable silence. While Patsy wrote prices on small white textured cards with a black fountain pen, Clare filled the glasses as instructed, her hand trembling. This was the most exciting thing that had happened to her, professionally speaking, in years – and she wanted so much to enjoy it. She needed to calm down.

'Do you mind?' she said to Patsy and held the bottle up.

'No, help yourself.'

Clare did. Turning her back to Patsy, she downed three glasses of white wine in quick succession, like whiskey shots. The glasses were very small after all. Within minutes a calmness started to radiate through her bones and she tried to think of something other than the state of her nerves.

She stole a glance at Patsy. Her friend finished writing the last of the cards, blew on it and went over to a largish moody-looking landscape and Blu-Tacked the little notice underneath.

'How are things at home?' said Clare, breaking the silence.

'Awful.'

'I'm sorry, I shouldn't have asked.'

Patsy stared at the display of oils for a few long seconds and then turned and looked at Clare. 'Why shouldn't you ask?' she said airily, her voice raw with hurt. 'It's all I think about these days. And now and again it's nice to talk to someone other than Martin about it. Laura's been lucky. She hasn't had any morning sickness. Though I think the reality of her situation's just beginning to hit her.'

'And she's going ahead and doing her exams?'

'She's been absolutely insistent that she carry on as normal. She won't even let me speak to the school.'

'Is that wise? Surely she's not going to do as well under these circumstances?'

Patsy sighed. 'She's nearly eighteen, Clare. At that age you can't force your will on your children. You can advise them, that's all.'

There was a pause. Patsy walked over to the window, folded her arms and stared out onto the main street, nearly deserted now that the shops were closed for the day. On the opposite side, a man hoisted a metal shutter onto the shopfront of the hardware store and padlocked it in place.

Clare asked, 'Has she decided what she's going to do about the baby?'

Patsy shook her head. 'Not yet. And we haven't pressed her for a decision. We want her to get her exams out of the way first. Her last one's on the second of June. There's time yet if she wants a termination.'

This last phrase hung in the air between them like the sea mist, thick and menacing, that settled on the town in hot summers, sometimes for days at a time.

'If she did go down that route, Patsy, it's not going to be easy. Do you remember all that hoo-hah last autumn about extending the provisions of the Abortion Bill to Northern Ireland? It never even got a reading at Westminster.'

'Yes, I do remember though I'm ashamed to say I didn't pay it a whole lot of attention at the time. It didn't affect me, you see. Not then.'

'She'll not get an abortion here in Northern Ireland, Patsy.'

Patsy frowned. 'But surely under the circumstances . . .'

'Abortion's effectively illegal here.'

Patsy shook her head. 'It can't be.'

'Doctors will only perform an abortion under the most restrictive of circumstances, like if carrying the baby to full term endangers a woman's life,' Clare pointed out, wondering why her friend wouldn't listen to what she was saying.

Patsy gave a little snort. 'But we live in a civilised country, Clare. I'm sure it'll be okay.'

Clearly, Patsy didn't want to hear any more. Clare decided that now wasn't the time to discuss it further. She ducked her head, swallowed and said, 'Perhaps you're right. Laura's GP would be the best person to advise you.' Then she cleared her throat and added, 'Anyway, before everyone arrives, I just wanted to say thanks for agreeing to let Janice and Keith come tonight. I know it's not going to be easy for you.'

Patsy managed a wry smile. 'It's business, Clare. And I won't let any argument I have with the Kirkpatricks come between you and them. Janice is still your friend, after all.'

Clare's heart sank. This meant, she supposed, that Janice

was no longer Patsy's friend. Patsy went on, 'And more importantly – as far as tonight is concerned anyway – she's also a great admirer of your work. When the Kirkpatricks buy, as I'm sure they will, I'd be grateful if you handled the transaction. Here.' She picked up the card machine. 'It's very easy. Let me show you how to use this.'

Bronson arrived some ten minutes later. He was in his early sixties, a broad-shouldered man of average height with thick white hair and the tanned, rugged face of someone who spent much of his life outdoors. He had a white goatee beard and his face was creased with a permanent, contented smile. He wore a brown leather jacket over brown corduroy trousers and a white shirt. A hairy belly peeked through the strained buttons above his belt buckle. Patsy lit up when he kissed her warmly on both cheeks.

'So this must be the lovely Clare,' he said, and embraced her in a bear hug, his belly pushing against her like a big, soft cushion. He smelt of expensive aftershave and peppermint. Clare pulled a face at Patsy over his shoulder and she held her stomach and laughed, the first genuine chuckle Clare had heard from her in a while.

He released Clare. 'Now, let me see your work, dah-ling,' he said, putting emphasis on the last word and rolling his eyes at Patsy in self-mockery.

He put an arm across Clare's shoulder and leant heavily on her but there was nothing threatening about his overfamiliarity. He was warm and cuddly and Clare thought him the closest thing to a living teddy bear she had ever met.

He examined a few of her paintings with such great gushes of enthusiasm that Clare blushed. 'You are a talented little thing, aren't you?' he said and winked at her. 'Patsy, you old tart, I do believe I have real competition at last.'

With his praise ringing in her ears, the door opened and

the public began to arrive. People who had come here to see – and to buy – her work. Bronson peeled off to greet an elderly couple who'd just come in and Clare turned to Patsy, her palms wet with sweat. She wiped them on her shirt. 'He's sweet, isn't he?' she said. 'I know he's only saying that to make me feel good but it works. It's awful nice of him.'

'Bronson is a sweetie,' said Patsy, 'but believe me, he's not saying those things to make you feel good. If Bronson admires something it's because he believes it has genuine artistic merit. And he's a harsh critic.'

Patsy walked over to a huddle of well-dressed women who'd just stepped into the shop and Clare, stunned, looked at her pictures with a fresh eye. They were good. As good as any original watercolours she'd seen for sale in the gallery or hanging in other people's homes. Maybe her plan to make a living from painting wasn't such a far-fetched fantasy after all. She crossed her fingers and prayed that some of her pictures sold. If so, she'd have a cheque in her hand. That would show Liam. He'd have to take her painting seriously then.

The place filled up quickly and Clare took the opportunity to knock back another glass of wine – just to bolster her confidence. Thankfully, by the time Kirsty arrived with Janice and Keith the small gallery was packed and Patsy could pretend not to notice them. She busied herself meeting and greeting other people while Clare went over and got her friends drinks.

They all toasted her success and it didn't take long for Janice and Keith to buy not one, but two pictures. As soon as Clare had applied the red 'sold' sticker to the second painting, a woman with long blonde hair, thick make-up and a curvaceous figure encased in a tight black dress teetered over to them.

'Janice Kirkpatrick,' she teased. 'I was after that one of Carnlough!'

'Well you'll have to be quicker off the mark, Lorna,' said Janice. 'Pictures of this calibre aren't going to hang about. Excuse the pun,' she said and everyone laughed. 'Lorna, have you met the artist herself?' Introductions were made and Janice said, 'Clare is a very good friend of mine. And my tip, if you want to own one of her pieces, is to buy tonight because you won't be able to find them at these prices in the future.'

'In that case I'd better hurry up,' said Lorna. She bought one of Fair Head. Soon another sticker appeared and then another. Clare's head was dizzy with excitement and wine.

'So this is what you do with yourself when you're not being Mummy,' said Zoe's icy voice, stopping Clare dead in her tracks. She spun round. As slim as a girl, and dressed completely in sleek black, Zoe looked like the fountain pen Patsy had used earlier. Her eyebrows were raised in a challenge, her dune-coloured lips closed over her teeth. Zoe was hanging onto the arm of a man about Bronson's age who was tall and slim and pleasant-looking. Clare's heart sank. What was she doing here?

'Yes, as you can see I manage both very well, Zoe,' said Clare bravely, surprising herself with the quick-fire retort. Zoe stared at her, stony-faced, and said, 'Well, I think that's a matter of opinion – on both counts.'

Clare's heart pounded against her ribs – but she was too angry to reply. Suddenly, Zoe's companion put out his hand and shook Clare's limp one, forcing her to drag her eyes away from Zoe and look at him instead. 'Didn't know you two knew each other,' he said genially.

'Clare's my replacement,' sniped Zoe, cold as a north wind.

Her companion frowned, not understanding and Zoe added, 'She married my ex – after I had finished with him.'

Clare smiled and the man said, 'Old Bronson seems quite taken with you, my dear, and that is high praise indeed. I understand this is your first exhibition. Congratulations.'

Zoe scowled and Clare felt herself grow two inches. She beamed at the friendly stranger. 'Thank you.'

'Alex,' roared Bronson's voice, which grew louder the more wine he drank, and the stranger responded by looking over at Bronson and smiling. Zoe had not even bothered to introduce him by name. 'Will you get yourself over here? Debbie wants to hear that story about the nun, the fish and the skateboard.'

'Ah, the master summons me,' said Alex, returning his attention to Clare. 'A pleasure meeting you, my dear.'

Zoe looked away, as if she was bored already, and the pair of them moved off.

Clare watched them move across the room, and decided that she was, after all, glad Zoe came. Clare could tell she hated every minute of her success. It felt a little like revenge for all the mean things Zoe had said and done to her in the past. She resolved never to let Zoe make her feel small again.

It was nearly eight thirty when Liam finally arrived. Clare waved over but she was immediately diverted by Patsy asking her to pour some more wine.

'Now where is Patsy's latest protégé?' said Bronson in a voice loud enough to be heard by everyone in the room. 'Ah, there you are!' He came over to Clare, put his arm around her waist and whispered in her ear, 'I want you to meet a very good friend of mine.' Then in a loud voice he cried, 'Coming through! Coming through!' while propelling her across the room. Clare blushed and laughed, embarrassed to be the centre of attention. He deposited her among a group of well-dressed people. Soon Clare found herself in conversation with the Director of Arts Development for the Arts Council, Northern Ireland, a fine-looking woman with bright blue eyes and shoulder-length blonde hair.

When there was a natural pause in the conversation about funding Clare looked over at Liam again. He was in conversation with Kirsty, a glass of red wine in his left hand. Janice came up behind Clare, placed her hands on Clare's hips and said quietly, 'We're going now.'

'Oh, so soon?' asked Clare. She excused herself and moved away from the people she had been talking to with Janice.

'Yes, I'm afraid so.' Janice threw a brief glance in Patsy's direction. 'We have another engagement.'

'Oh, okay. Thanks so much for coming and for buying those pictures. I really appreciate it. If it hadn't been for you and Keith I'm not sure anyone would've bought anything.'

'Oh, they would, Clare.'

'Well, I think it made all the difference. You got the ball rolling.'

'I can see it's been a great success,' said Janice, sidestepping the praise. 'All but one of your pictures have sold.' She squeezed Clare's arms lightly. 'Well done.'

'Thanks, Janice. Thanks for the studio and for believing in me. Thanks for everything.'

'What are friends for?' said Janice warmly and then she added, with a swift glance at Patsy, 'Would it be possible, do you think, to take the pictures now? Rather than come back and collect them another day?'

'Yes, of course,' said Clare, moving towards the till. 'I can deal with that.' She took the pictures off the wall, covered them in bubble wrap from a big roll underneath the counter, took the credit card payment and bade her friends goodbye. She was just making her way over to Liam and Kirsty, when Patsy came up.

'So they've gone, have they?' said Patsy, glowering at the shadows of Janice and Keith as they passed the window, the pictures under Keith's arm a black rectangle in the fading light.

Clare nodded.

'And good riddance. Oh, by the way, Clare, I won't be taking commission on those two sales. Martin told them we would never take a penny of their money.' Patsy's upper lip turned up in a sneer, an expression of hate Clare had never seen before. 'And we won't. Ever.'

Clare opened her mouth to plead the case of Janice and Keith, whom she felt could not be held accountable for their son's actions. But before she could say anything, someone dragged Patsy off. Clare looked again for Liam but, just then, one of Keith's golfing pals came over. He talked at length about a commission for a painting of Slemish, a local landmark, while Clare watched Liam and Kirsty over his shoulder.

Kirsty glanced repeatedly at her watch. When Clare was finally free, she went over to them and Liam said, 'I'm going to give Kirsty a lift home now, Clare. I'll see you back at the house.'

'Oh, right. Okay,' said Clare, slightly taken by surprise. She had hoped Liam would stay to the end, and maybe join her, Patsy and Bronson in a celebratory drink. She hadn't even had the chance to introduce him to the other artist.

'I'm afraid I've got to dash,' said Kirsty. 'Dorothy's babysitting and I told her I wouldn't be late. Congratulations on a wonderful exhibition,' she added, leaning close to her friend. 'I'm sorry that I couldn't afford to buy a picture.'

'Oh Kirsty, just having you here has been wonderful. I need all the moral support I can get.'

The room emptied quickly after that and soon it was just Clare, Patsy and Bronson and a rash of red stickers across both walls. There were some gaps where pictures had been removed but most remained, to be paid for and collected another day. Now that everyone had left, Clare felt suddenly deflated, sorry that it was all over. And at the back of her mind was a vague sense that something wasn't right between her and Liam – even more so than usual.

Patsy, smiling, filled three glasses and said, 'Here's to a very successful night. Bronson, to a complete sell-out as usual. And Clare, your first exhibition has been an unqualified success. All but one picture sold.'

Clare knocked back most of the wine, wondering what was wrong with Liam. Or was she imagining things?

'I think you might find you're mistaken there,' said Bronson, and he lifted the sheet of stickers from where they lay on the counter amidst a cluster of used wine glasses. He went over and stuck a red sticker on the last remaining picture of Clare's – the Black Arch outside Ballygalley.

'Bronson,' protested Clare, greatly embarrassed. He was only buying it out of charity. So that she would be able to say – for the rest of her life – that her first exhibition was a sell-out. It was sweet of him but she couldn't let him do it. 'You don't have to do that. You don't really want it, do you?'

He shook his head and sighed. 'You're an accomplished painter, Clare,' he said kindly. 'But what you lack, my dear, is self-belief. Overcome that and you have a very rosy future.'

Clare blushed and, not knowing how to respond, drained the rest of the wine in her glass. Tonight had been a huge confidence booster – but Bronson was right, she had to believe in herself.

Bronson left soon afterwards and Patsy said, 'You go on home, Clare. You must be exhausted after all the excitement.'

'I wouldn't leave you to clear up all this on your own, now would I?'

'Oh, Clare, you are an angel,' said Patsy, manually totting up figures on a sheet of paper.

Clare loaded the tray with dirty glasses. 'Why don't I get started on this lot?'

'That'd be great. The kitchen's through the back,' said Patsy, pointing to a door on the back wall of the gallery. 'Thanks a million.'

Clare gingerly carried the tray through the door into a brightly lit large storeroom, with not much in it apart from some old furniture and bubble-wrapped pictures leaning against one wall. She held the door open with her behind, the tray balanced precariously in her hands, and said, 'Gosh, there's loads of room through here.'

'Yeah, there is,' said Patsy absentmindedly, the end of a pen in her mouth.

Clare let the door close and went through to the small but perfectly adequate kitchen. She worked quickly at the stainless steel sink, looking up now and again at her reflection in the curtainless window, the sky outside inky blue. She hummed to herself, reliving every moment of the evening. It had passed off very well and she was especially glad that any unpleasantness between Patsy and the Kirkpatricks had been avoided. The only thing that disturbed her was the fact that she'd hardly spoken to Liam.

She stopped humming, a hard knot forming in her stomach. It couldn't be helped. She'd been too busy networking and meeting people, which was just as important in building a career as actually painting pictures. Liam would understand, wouldn't he?

When Patsy had finished her paperwork she came through, stood shoulder to shoulder with Clare, and dried the glasses. 'What're you going to do with the proceeds of tonight's sale, Clare?'

Clare plunged her bare hands into the warm soapy water and fished out the last glass. 'First off, I need to pay back what I used of our savings to buy materials. After that, the first thing on my list is a chandelier for our bedroom. I've seen one in the new Laura Ashley catalogue. It's gorgeous – dripping in crystals, with five dinky black pleated silk shades.'

'Sounds fabulous.'

Clare rinsed the glass and set it upside-down on the draining board. 'The only thing is, it'll make the rest of the bedroom look shabby!'

'Well, you can do it up with your future income stream,' said Patsy, turning to smile at her friend. 'Because this is only the start for you, Clare.'

Clare beamed happily. She dried her hands, filled a bucket and quickly mopped up some red wine that had been spilt on the gallery floor. When she was done, she poured the dirty water down the loo and put the mop and bucket back in the cupboard.

'Patsy?' she said, standing with her back to the cupboard, staring into the middle of the dusty storeroom.

'What?'

'Does this room get any natural light?'

'Yes,' said Patsy, coming to stand beside her with a glass and drying cloth in her hands. She pointed above. 'Look, up there. There's a cupola in the roof. It runs along the length of the building. You can't appreciate it now – it's too dark – but it's quite pleasant during the day. Floods the place with light.'

'Have you ever considered opening this up? You know, extending the gallery through here?'

Patsy shrugged her shoulders. 'I've never needed the space.'

'It wouldn't take much to do it up, Patsy. Everything's in good shape. All it needs is a lick of paint.'

Patsy shrugged.

'You know the way you were talking about diversifying?' said Clare.

'I was and then this thing happened with Laura and, well, I haven't really given it any more thought.'

'Do you know what I think would be wonderful?'

'What's that?'

'A café. This would make the most fabulous café.' Clare stepped into the middle of the room, between a broken chair and a pile of boxes. She threw her arms wide and turned around slowly. 'You could have pictures for sale all round the walls, and serve homemade scones and cakes. And tea and coffee in old-fashioned china cups. People would love it.'

Patsy laughed and took a step forwards. 'The thought hadn't crossed my mind. Me, running a café?'

'You'd be great at it. You know you would. You've such a lovely warm way with people.'

'Now you're embarrassing *me*,' said Patsy, smiling broadly.

'It would get a lot more people across the door, and then you could sell them all the other things you talked about before – bags and jewellery and handicrafts. And it wouldn't cost much to do it up. Look, this wooden floor's relatively new.' Clare pressed the floor with her toe.

'The previous owners had that laid just before I bought the place. And it's not had much wear and tear since.' Patsy folded her arms, looked at the floor, at the cupola, at the smooth, bare walls. 'I wonder why I didn't think of that before. This town could do with a decent coffee shop.'

'Bet you could get your catering stuff second hand from some business that's gone bust.'

'That's a cheery thought, Clare,' said Patsy and raised one eyebrow.

'I'm only saying that you could do it without investing very much. You could buy second-hand bone china – nobody wants it nowadays. You could pick boxes of it up for next to nothing at auction. Even the loo's in good nick.'

Patsy tilted her head to one side, considering. 'I suppose I could get Martin to do most of the work. It's not like he's got anything else to do at the moment.' She paused and sighed. 'Though emotionally I don't think either of us are up for a project like this at the moment.'

'I understand,' said Clare. Her enthusiasm evaporated like a popped balloon. 'Well, it's maybe something to think about once things with Laura are . . . are resolved.'

Patsy gave her a tight-lipped smile. 'At the moment it's hard to think of anything else. It's the first thing I think about when I wake up and the last thing I think of when I'm drifting off to sleep.'

Clare went over to Patsy and put her arms around her. Then she pulled away and said, 'I'm grateful to you for tonight, Patsy.'

Patsy shook her head. 'I've enjoyed it. It's true I wasn't really looking forward to it but it's given me something else to focus on. And I'm so pleased it was such a success. Come on, let's lock up and go home. It's late.'

Outside the gallery on the all but deserted street, Clare turned to Patsy and said, 'Can I ask you something?'

'Sure, honey. What?'

'Is Bronson gay?'

Patsy chuckled. 'You need to ask? He's as bent as they come, love.' And she sauntered off towards her car, her hips swinging like a metronome.

When Clare came through the back door the kitchen was in darkness and the phone was ringing. She stood on one of Josh's toy cars, it scooted out from under her foot, and she only managed to save herself from crashing to the floor by grabbing onto the towel rail by the door. By the time she'd righted herself and got her breath back, the phone had stopped. Either Liam had taken the call in another room or whoever it was on the line had given up rather prematurely. She glanced at the clock; it was after eleven thirty. Very late for a phone call. She felt suddenly sober.

There was no-one downstairs – all the lights were out and the front door locked for the night. Clare crept upstairs and, anxious to see Liam, went straight to her bedroom door without looking in on the children. She put her hand on the doorknob and paused. She could hear Liam's voice from inside, low and soft. He was talking on the phone. But to whom? Someone from work? Not at this time. His mother? His sister? Not unless . . . unless there was something wrong. Her heart fluttered and Liam spoke again, his voice a murmur. She relaxed. If there was something wrong, he wouldn't sound like that.

She turned the door handle, opened the door and went in. Liam was sitting up in bed, bare-chested as usual, propped up by two pillows behind his back. The phone in his hand was pressed against his right ear. As soon as he saw her he froze, his mouth slightly open. But this lasted only for a few seconds, no more. He quickly removed the phone from his ear, and hit a button on the handset, presumably ending the call. He cleared his throat and set the handset on the bedside cabinet as though it was suddenly too hot to hold.

'Who was that?' she said, walking over to her side of the bed. She sat down with her back to him and kicked off her shoes.

'Someone from work.'

Clare frowned. 'Awfully late to be phoning you at home.' She got up and put the shoes in the wardrobe.

'Did all your paintings sell in the end?' he said, not understanding that her comment was actually a question. But she let it go. She was glad to talk about the exhibition.

She closed the wardrobe door then sat on the bottom of the bed so that she was facing him. 'Bronson bought the very last one,' she said and smiled when she thought of what she'd achieved. She brought her hands together and squeezed them against her chest, thrilled with her success. 'Isn't it fantastic? It means my first exhibition was a complete sell-out.'

'That's good.' He sounded uninterested.

'To tell you the truth, I think that's why Bronson did it. Just so I could always say that my first exhibition was a sell-out.' She wondered all of a sudden why Liam hadn't bought the last picture. It would've been a bit of an academic exercise of course, with the money coming out of the household finances and going straight back in again. But it would've been an act of support, of solidarity.

'Good for him.'

She could tell that Liam was annoyed. She stroked the silken bedspread with the flat of her hand. 'I'm sorry I didn't get to introduce you to Bronson.'

'You didn't introduce me to anyone,' said Liam, picked up a book, and pretended to read.

'I know and I'm sorry. It was just so manic. All these people wanted to talk to me. Do you know that the Director of Arts Development for the Arts Council was there? She seemed very interested in my work. She gave me one of her business cards.'

'You hardly spoke to Kirsty,' he said from behind the book.

'That's not true. She arrived with Janice and Keith right at the beginning and I spoke to all of them, for a little while anyway. Janice and Keith bought two pictures, you know.'

Liam closed the book abruptly and dropped it on the bedside table. 'So you made time to speak to everyone but me?'

'Oh, Liam, it wasn't like that. And you know it. Tonight was a social occasion for the guests but very much a working one for me and Patsy. We were rushed off our feet getting people drinks, selling paintings and networking.' She looked down at a loose thread and plucked at it. 'I was disappointed that you didn't stay behind and have a drink with us at the end. It would've been nice. And you could've met Bronson then.' She looked up at him, with a small, conciliatory smile on her lips.

'I wasn't asked,' he said bluntly.

The smile fell from her face. 'You don't need an invitation. You're my husband, for heaven's sake.' Why was he being so infantile about this?

'Well, it'd be nice if you acted like it now and again.'

He was hell bent on finding fault with her tonight. It was almost as though he was determined to maintain distance, his prickliness like an unassailable electrified fence.

'And it'd be nice if you acted like my husband now and again. You left just as soon as you could.' She paused, took in his pained expression. 'You'd no interest in being there tonight, had you, Liam?'

Liam expelled a puff of air through his nose. 'I'll tell you what interests me,' he said. 'How you couldn't make time to talk to me and yet you were all over Bronson Gaffney like a rash.'

'Oh, don't be ridiculous,' she snapped. She would not allow Liam to make her feel as though she had done something wrong. 'I was just being sociable. He's very well connected. He introduced me to some important people – people who might be able to help further my career.'

'And that's all that matters to you, isn't it?'

The partial truth of this statement made her blush. 'I have been a bit preoccupied lately,' she admitted, and stared at the closed curtains. Bringing her gaze back to Liam she added, slightly hopeful, 'Are you jealous?'

He frowned, as though giving this great consideration. Then, his features relaxing again, he said at last, 'Maybe I am.'

Her heart lifted. 'Bronson's gay, Liam, didn't you know?'

He let out a soft sigh. 'I wasn't talking about Bronson.'

She cocked her head to one side, wary. The conversation was slipping away from her into unfathomable territory.

'If I'm jealous of anything,' he went on quietly, 'I'm jealous of you. Your life. Your freedom.'

Clare fought the immediate instinct to defend the injustice of this statement. Her life, ruled by the demands and routines of two young children, was anything but free.

'You're doing what you want to do, Clare, raising your children and painting. And good for you,' he said without rancour. 'I struggle to remember what that's like. I feel as though I've spent most of my adult life doing things to please other people. First Zoe and now . . .'

'Don't include me in the same sentence as that woman.'

He folded his arms, bowed his head. 'I do admire what you've done, Clare. I admire your focus and your determination and your passion. But . . .' His voice trailed off.

'But what?' said Clare, her pulse pounding in her head, every sense suddenly alert to the danger she sensed now lay ahead.

'I think what I'm trying to say . . . what I want to say is this. We don't seem to have much in common any more.' The words came quickly, rushing out like water through a breached dam.

'I see,' she said. She felt light-headed and suddenly afraid. She sat in silence, his words ringing in her ears, while her heart pounded against her chest. She must get him back from the brink. 'I think that's a bit of an exaggeration, Liam,' she said carefully, feeling like she was trying to pedal backwards, trying to undo something that was tightly knotted – she wasn't exactly sure what. 'I know the last few months have been difficult for both of us and I do appreciate the support you've given me.'

Liam's chin dropped dejectedly on his chest.

'But it's over. I earned over a thousand pounds tonight, Liam. Isn't that great? I know it's not a lot really, not for the amount of hours I put in, but think what we can do with the money. First off,' she said and looked up at the ceiling, 'I'm going to buy a new light fitting for this room. Do you know that I hate that paper shade with a vengeance?' She forced a smile. If she could just get the conversation back on familiar, practical territory all would be well.

'You have mentioned it once or twice.'

He was coming round. She could tell. Encouraged, she went on. 'And how about we put the rest towards a summer holiday? We could take the kids . . .'

'Clare,' he said, and there was something about the way he jerked his head up that made her stop in her tracks. His gaze was unflinching, his blue eyes like the sky on a sunny winter's day. 'You know the way I said that I was speaking to someone from work?'

Immediately her gaze fell upon the phone on the bedside table. 'You weren't?' she said and held her breath.

'No, I was.' She let her breath out. For a minute there she imagined that he was going to confess he was seeing someone. What a silly notion. She realised how thoughtless and self-centred she'd been. If someone was calling from work at this time of night, it must be something serious. And there she was giving Liam a hard time about the exhibition, when he was dealing with some crisis at work. 'Who was it?' she said and settled her hands on her lap, ready to listen to some long, convoluted tale about office politics.

'Gillian Spencer.'

'Oh yes, I remember her. I met her at the office Christmas party, didn't I?' She was a glamorous woman, younger than Clare, with a slim figure and blonde hair. Clare remembered her white silk shirt open at the neck and a sharp black business suit. They'd talked briefly. 'She was friendly enough, as I recall.'

Liam said nothing, just continued to stare at her, his mouth a thin pale line.

'What did she want?' said Clare and when this did not elicit an immediate reply she added, 'Is something wrong at work?'

Liam shook his head.

'What, then?'

It took him a long time to speak. 'She needed someone to talk to.'

'About work?' said Clare.

'No. The call was personal.'

'Personal! What's she doing calling you? And at this time of night?'

'I told her to.'

It seemed as though everything in the room froze for a few moments, like in a photograph: Liam motionless in the bed, his arms still folded defiantly across his chest. Clare, holding her breath, felt momentarily removed from her body as if watching the scene from above. Then she began to tremble and her voice, when she spoke, was reedy.

'Isn't she married?'

'Yes.'

'And her husband doesn't mind her phoning other men at half eleven at night?'

'They're separated.'

Clare shivered, suddenly chilled. 'Liam, are you trying to tell me something?'

'I honestly don't know.'

She stared at him, speechless, for what seemed like a very long time. 'Are you having an affair with her?' she said and braced herself for his answer.

'No.'

She closed her eyes and said, 'Then what, if anything, is going on?'

'We're friends. Good friends.'

'Better friends than you and I?' she heard herself say and opened her eyes.

'At the moment that wouldn't be hard, would it?' he said with a derisive snort and then, seeing her wince, he added solemnly, 'I'm sorry. But let's be honest with each other, Clare. We haven't been getting along very well this past while, have we?' He paused and looked at the duvet. 'I have to be honest with you. Gillian and I . . . well, we're very close. Not in a physical way. Nothing has happened between us. We just . . . well . . . we just talk. I don't know how to explain it . . . we seem to be on the same wavelength. I feel a real connection with her. We seem to have so much in common.'

Clare stared at him, her heart aching with hurt. She still loved Liam. And there were two innocent children sleeping next door whose lives would be devastated if he left her.

'Liam,' she said and waited until he looked at her. She fought hard to keep her voice calm and controlled. 'Are you in love with this woman?'

He looked away and swallowed, the Adam's apple at his throat bobbing like a float. 'I don't know. I think I might be.'

She sat in silence, the anger rising in her like sap. Yes, she had neglected him – she was the first to admit it – but instead of talking to her, instead of trying to repair things between them, he had found solace in the company of another woman. When at last she spoke, her voice was tinny with emotion. 'So this is what you do at the first sign of trouble, Liam? Run into the arms of another woman.'

'That isn't fair, Clare. I told you – nothing's happened between us.'

'And you think the absence of a physical relationship makes it alright, Liam?'

He sighed deeply, his chest rising and falling like a bellow. 'I didn't say that. I didn't set out to form a relationship with Gillian, Clare. It just happened. I've tried to do the right thing. I've tried to keep it just friends.'

'If you want to give our marriage a chance you have to stop this relationship now. Before it goes any further.'

'I'm not sure I can do that, Clare,' he said and stared hard at her. 'She's my best friend.'

His comment ripped through her like a knife. She remembered a time when they had been soulmates, unable to bear being out of each other's company even for a few hours. 'I used to be your best friend,' she said and hated the way she sounded – needy and resentful.

'Likewise,' said Liam, and he looked at her then with tears in his eyes. 'But it's been a long time, hasn't it, Clare, since you and I felt any real connection?'

'I'm sorry that you feel like that,' she said, looking away and not answering his question because it was a painful truth she did not want to admit. 'It's hard with a young family and you working late all the time. We've had so little time together, just the two of us.'

'Other people make time. But you haven't wanted to, have you? And the truth is, neither have I.'

She sat in silence for a few minutes, biting her bottom lip. With a soft sigh, Liam turned out his light and rolled over on his side, facing away from her.

'Is that it?' she said.

'There's nothing else to say, Clare,' he said flatly. 'It's late. You'd better get some sleep. The kids will be up early.'

'Liam?'

'What?'

'Are you going to leave?' said Clare.

There was a long silence and then he said quietly, 'No. Not unless you want me to.' Another pause. 'Do you?'

'No.'

Too shocked to say any more, Clare took her pyjamas, got changed in the en-suite with the door firmly locked and, when she came out, crept into Izzy's bedroom. She crawled under the pink 'princess' duvet and pulled it over her head. The pillow smelled of coconut and cheap perfume. She buried her face in it, and wept silent tears. Her marriage was as good as over.

It was little comfort to know that the relationship between Liam and Gillian wasn't a physical one – it was much worse than that. Gillian was the one he confided in, to whom he bared his soul and shared jokes with in a way he no longer did with her. Gillian was the one he whispered to late at night on the phone. She imagined Liam unburdening himself to her, moaning about his awful home life. She was quite sure that he talked about his wife to this woman with her smart suits and her painted nails and her salon-styled hair.

She would pay rapt attention to what he said, laugh at

his jokes, make him feel important and valued in a way Clare clearly did not. Gillian was a fantasy, fulfilling Liam's emotional needs that were not sated at home. Clare, on the other hand, represented real family life – punctuated by moments of great joy, yes, but generally messy and untidy, distracted and relentlessly exhausting. How could she hope to compete?

She had reached for the stars, thinking that she could count on Liam's support no matter what. Believing that their love would survive anything. And she had succeeded – she had proved that people valued her work and were prepared to pay good money for it. But her achievement had come at great cost. Her marriage was on the rocks. Liam said he wasn't going to leave, but how long would that resolve last?

She wanted him to stay but she was, suddenly, very angry. She pulled her knees up to her chest, tight with rage, her stomach cramped with fury. How could he betray her in this way? And how could she have been so stupid as not to see what was going on? The working late, the lack of interest in her, the lack of support prior to the exhibition. If they did manage to weather this storm, and it was a big if, Clare wasn't sure she could ever forgive Liam.

The tears dried up, leaving crusty trails on her temples and wet patches on the pillow. She lay on her back and stared at the glitter ball suspended from the ceiling above Izzy's bed until her eyes adjusted to the dark. In the absence of light bouncing off the tiny mirrored squares, the ball was a dark grey orb, like a dead planet. She wondered how Izzy felt lying in this bed at night in the home of a woman who was not her mother. Alienated? Lonely? Angry? And she wondered too if the same uncertain future awaited her own children. Clare waited for a long time, believing that Liam must've heard her cry, that he would come and sit on the edge of the bed and tell her that he was sorry. That it wasn't too late, that he wanted to save their marriage. It was a long time before Clare finally drifted off to sleep. But Liam never came.

Chapter Sixteen

In Clare's kitchen, Kirsty watched her friend take an already opened bottle of white wine from the fridge and pour it quickly into one of the thin-stemmed wine glasses on the counter. Some of the yellow liquid sloshed onto the granite surface but Clare, talking all the while, appeared not to notice. The sound of children's TV drifted in from the room next door where Josh and Rachel were watching cartoons.

Clare, who looked like her hair hadn't been washed in days, picked up the glass and thrust it at Kirsty. 'Here, take this.'

Kirsty, having spent the best part of the last hour listening to Clare's revelations about her marriage, was sorely tempted. But she shook her head. She followed strict rules about daytime drinking which, except on the rarest of social occasions, was simply not on. Clare shrugged and, pausing only to gulp down some wine as if it were water on a hot summer's day, continued babbling nineteen to the dozen.

Kirsty glanced discreetly at the clock and bit her lip. It was four thirty on a Monday afternoon – far too early to be drinking, especially when in charge of young children. And she should know. Hadn't she been there once herself? And if she'd learned anything after Scott's death it was that alcohol was not the answer.

'So when did all this happen?' said Kirsty, when Clare finally paused for breath.

'Friday night,' said Clare, her face twisted with bitterness. 'After my hugely successful exhibition.'

'I'm so sorry, Clare. I'd no idea you and Liam were going through a rough patch.'

Clare let out a little peal of nervous laughter and took a gulp of wine.

'It's not unusual, you know,' Kirsty went on. 'What he's doing.'

Clare snorted. 'What? Having an affair with a work colleague?'

'Well, technically he's not having an affair. The relationship isn't in any way physical, is it?'

'Not yet,' said Clare darkly.

'So it's more of a . . . a meeting of minds. It's like having a best friend at work. A confidante. Someone who understands the pressures you work under because they work under them too. The term for someone like her is an "office spouse".'

Clare necked some wine and glared at Kirsty. 'A what?'

'An "office spouse". I read an article about it in a Sunday supplement.' Kirsty folded her arms across her chest and went on. 'What you've got to understand, Clare, is that, in his mind, because he hasn't actually been unfaithful to you, he probably doesn't think he's done anything wrong. All he's done is talk to this woman, albeit on an emotional level. Now to you and me that sounds very much like a betrayal but men don't operate on the same emotional level as women.'

Clare bit her lip and stared out of the window.

'This isn't helping, is it?' said Kirsty and she touched Clare's arm, dipping her head. 'I'm sorry.' There was a long pause and Kirsty said, quietly, 'So where do you go from here?'

Clare shook her head. 'I have no idea. We hardly spoke to each other all weekend. Liam worked most of Saturday and I took the kids over to his parents on Sunday while he played golf. Thank God Izzy wasn't here. I don't think I could've handled her on top of everything else.'

'I'm sure you can work things out,' said Kirsty, feeling like a fraud for dispensing marriage advice. What did she know about making a marriage work? She often wondered if she and Scott would still be together if he had lived. 'Look, I really have to go. I'm sorry. Dorothy and Harry were expecting me to pick the boys up forty-five minutes ago. They'll be wondering where I am.'

'Of course. I'm so sorry for keeping you back,' said Clare in a slightly startled manner, as though waking from a daydream. 'Thanks for coming round.'

'I knew something was wrong as soon as I heard your voice on the phone. I just wished you'd called me earlier.'

Clare shrugged. 'I needed a bit of time, you know, to myself.'

Kirsty forced a smile and glanced at the glass in Clare's hand. 'Look, are you going to be alright?' she said, reluctant to leave her friend in this state.

'Oh, I'll be fine,' said a suddenly animated Clare, waving the wine glass in the air. 'I have my Chardonnay to keep me company!'

Kirsty cleared her throat. 'That's what I'm worried about,' she said quietly and stared hard at Clare. There were black rings under her eyes.

'What?' asked Clare, and she held the wine glass out in front of her and looked at it, as though focusing on it properly for the first time. 'Are you suggesting I'm drinking too much?'

'Look, I hope you don't mind me saying this, Clare. But alcohol doesn't solve anything. In fact it just makes things worse. And I'm speaking from experience.'

'Oh, you don't need to worry about me. I know when I've had enough.'

'You really shouldn't be drinking when you're in sole charge of the children,' persisted Kirsty.

'Oh, don't fuss so. Liam'll be home soon. He can take care of them. For a change.'

Kirsty let out a long loud sigh.

'Honestly, Kirsty. I know what I'm doing.'

'Well, just promise me one thing.'

'What's that?'

'Promise me you won't drive after having a drink.'

'You know I'd never be *that* stupid.'

'Well, that's good to know.' Kirsty picked up her car keys and handbag and gave Clare a kiss on both cheeks. 'Chin up, sweetheart. I'm sure everything's going to be alright between you and Liam.' She added lamely, 'It sounds like you two need to sit down and have a good long talk.'

'I think it's going to take more than a long talk to fix this mess,' said Clare.

'Well, it's a start, Clare. And you have to start somewhere.'

'I suppose so.' Clare forced a smile and looked at Kirsty. 'Life just seems to be full of disappointment, doesn't it?' she said bitterly. 'Look at you. You finally meet someone you like and what does he do?'

'He hasn't gone yet,' said Kirsty bravely, trying hard not to adopt Clare's morose mood. But inside her heart ached at the idea that Chris might one day soon walk out of her life for ever.

'I still think you should tell him how you feel, Kirsty.'

Even the idea of it made Kirsty's heart pound and a fine

beading of sweat came out on her brow. 'There's no point, Clare. I've told you what he said before. He's not interested in me.'

'I'm not so sure.'

'If he cared for me at all,' said Kirsty quietly, wiping her brow with the back of her hand, 'he wouldn't be leaving, would he?'

Clare shrugged. 'You won't know unless you ask.'

'Look, I really have to run,' said Kirsty. 'Bye.'

Outside in the car, Kirsty checked her mobile. There was a message from Dorothy to say that she'd set off for Kirsty's house with the boys, she on foot, the boys on their bikes. They would be home by now. Kirsty paused, cast one last anxious glance at Clare's house, and drove off.

Troubles never came alone. First Martin had lost his job, then Laura fell pregnant and now Clare's marriage was in crisis. And Chris was going to find another job and she would never see him again. The prospect brought tears to her eyes. She stopped at lights, braking too late and screeched to an abrupt halt just inches from the bumper of a Ford Focus. The driver waved his fist at her and she blinked hard to hold back the tears.

She had spent the last three years building a secure future for herself and the boys, supported by loving friends who had never said a cross word to each other in all the time she'd known them. And now, suddenly, everything – or so it seemed – was thrown into chaos. Rifts had arisen between her dearest friends that she seriously doubted would ever heal.

And Chris was going to leave her. The lights changed to green. Brutally she shoved the car in gear and drove home, wondering why everything was falling apart.

'Is everything okay?' said Dorothy, rushing to greet Kirsty

as soon as she came through the door. She wore a pale pink jersey tracksuit (which she euphemistically referred to as a leisure suit) and bright white trainers that had never graced a running track in their life. Her face was rigid with worry, her hands clasped so tightly together the tips of her fingers were pink.

'Didn't you get my text?' said Kirsty, slightly irritated by Dorothy's over-reaction. She was only a little bit late home from work. You'd think, from Dorothy's reaction, that she'd just returned from an expedition up Mount Everest.

'Yes. But you didn't say where you were or what had caused the delay.'

'Well, I'm sorry I'm late. I got a call from a friend who needed a shoulder to cry on.'

'Nothing serious, I hope,' said Dorothy, her brows knotted with anxiety.

'Yes. And no. Man trouble,' said Kirsty vaguely, not wishing to discuss Clare's personal life. She hung her handbag over the newel post at the bottom of the stairs and kicked off her work shoes.

'Usually is,' said Dorothy wryly and visibly relaxed.

Kirsty followed her into the kitchen where the tiled floor was pleasantly cool under her hot feet. The boys were kicking a ball around in the garden. The ironing board was set up in front of the kitchen sink. On the table was a pile of Kirsty's knickers including three black thongs, well past their best, which she wore under tight trousers. They had all been ironed and carefully folded.

'I thought I might as well make myself useful while I was here,' said Dorothy brightly, not noticing Kirsty's discomfiture. The older woman picked up the iron, positioned the point of it over the crotch of a pair of black lace knickers and pressed with precision.

'There's no need to do that,' said Kirsty and she grabbed the knickers and scrunched them into a ball in her right fist. 'You know I never iron underwear. It's a complete waste of time.'

'Don't you, love?' said Dorothy, as though hearing this for the first time. 'I iron everything. I think it just makes everything so much more . . .' She glanced at the pile of Kirsty's knickers on the table, folded neatly like a stack of pancakes. 'So much more comfortable, don't you think?'

'No, I don't. No-one ever sees your pants, for heaven's sake.'

'Oh,' said Dorothy and she tucked her chin in and said again, resolutely, 'Oh.'

Kirsty sighed. 'It's good of you to think of doing the ironing. But you really shouldn't. There's no need,' she said, walking the tightrope between causing offence and making a stand in her own home. 'Will you look at the time!' she added, changing subject – and tone. 'I'd better get these two something to eat. They'll be starving.'

'I gave them their tea at our house. I hope you don't mind? When you texted to say you'd be delayed, Harry and I were just about to sit down at the table. I'd made a chicken pie. You know how the boys love it,' said Dorothy, justifying herself in a slightly subservient manner. It made Kirsty ashamed. Dorothy was only doing what she had always done – helping out in any way she could. There was a time when Kirsty would've been thrilled to come home and find the ironing done. She had changed the goalposts, not Dorothy.

'Sounds lovely. That's very kind of you,' she said, meeting Dorothy's wounded eyes and looking quickly away. 'Thank you very much.' She opened the back door. 'I'll just let the boys know I'm home.'

'I'll be off then.'

'Are you going to walk?'

'Yes,' said Dorothy firmly. 'The exercise'll do me good.' And before Kirsty could say another word, Dorothy slipped past her into the garden. She kissed both boys goodbye, ruffled their hair and disappeared out the side gate without so much as a backward glance at Kirsty.

Kirsty closed the door and sat down at the table. She unfurled her fist, looked at the pants in her hand and shook her head. Her privacy had been invaded tonight. No, worse than that, it had been violated. The over-familiarity with her in-laws now felt stifling.

She could bear it no longer. She didn't want to end up living alone, with Dorothy and Harry wandering freely in and out of her life, and home. Insidiously undermining her with their unwanted kindnesses and well-meant concern. Her job at the museum had given her a taste of a new, independent life, outside the tiny orbit of her home, and she loved it. She yearned for more.

And suddenly it was very clear to her what she did want – Chris. She should have listened to Clare. What had she to lose by telling him how she felt? Only face and the chance of happiness. If she let him walk out of her life without telling him how she felt, she would regret it for the rest of her life. And never knowing would be a whole lot worse, she told herself, than rejection. He was a decent man – if he did turn her down she was sure he would do it kindly.

Her mind was made up, she told herself. This Friday, come whatever, she would tell him how she felt. Before he found another job. Before it was too late.

The rest of the week dragged by, and all Kirsty could think about was Chris. She rehearsed what she would say over and over, until it was as familiar as a prayer, her emotions fluctuating between hope and despair, certainty and doubt. And when Friday dawned at last, a bright, breezy May morning, Kirsty was ready, as ready as she was ever going to be. She got up early, showered, dressed and applied her make-up with care. She ferried the boys to school, came back home and waited. Chris had no fixed schedule. He could appear at any time.

When she finally heard the growl of Chris's beaten-up Land Rover pulling into her drive mid-morning, her heart stood still. She listened as the engine died, the car door creaked open, slammed shut again, the scrape of metal tools being hauled out of the back of the trailer, the click and thud of the side gate as Chris made his way into the back garden. She got up, wiped her sweaty palms down the thighs of her jeans, touched her hair. There was, she told herself firmly, no time like the present.

Downstairs, she stepped out into the garden where Chris was bent over with a rake in his hand, removing leaves and other debris from the surface of the pond. The breeze was chilly and small white clouds skittering across the sky.

Chris looked up when she came alongside him, then returned his gaze to the surface of the pond. 'I'm hoping those new plants I put in last month will help control the algae this year. You don't want it taking over.'

Kirsty folded her arms and peered into the murky waters of the pond, her banal response stuck in her throat.

There was a pause. He looked at the pond, back at her, and then at the pond again as though he wanted to get on with his work but didn't want to be rude and say so. Time to cut to the chase. Time to say what she had rehearsed all week. She took a deep breath.

'Chris . . .'

'Kirsty . . .' he said at the same time.

'What?'

'No, you go first,' he said.

She took a deep breath. 'There's something I want to ask you.' She paused – and could not go on. 'But . . . it'll . . . it'll keep. What was it you were going to say?' She smiled brightly and blushed. She was such a coward.

'I went over to Dubai for five days last week.'

'Dubai?' she said. 'On holiday?'

He shook his head and said, looking confused, 'I thought I'd mentioned it to you before?'

'Mentioned what?'

He shrugged and said, 'Oh, well, it must've been someone else. I've been offered a job there.'

Kirsty's legs felt weak and her head light. Dubai. It was worse than she'd thought. She took a deep breath.

'One of my friends has a very successful business out there,' went on Chris, oblivious to her distress. 'He's been badgering me for years, on and off, to come out and work for him.'

'I see,' said Kirsty faintly and started to shiver. She wrapped her arms around herself.

'I'd be project manager of the team out there, which would mean no more physically demanding work. And the pay's good.'

She tried and failed to think of a valid objection. Only that she loved him and she could not bring herself to say that now – not now that it was so obvious he didn't care for her.

'I start at the end of August, in three months' time.' He paused and looked at his feet.

She pressed her fingers into the flesh of her upper arms so hard they hurt. 'Oh. That's . . . that's great.'

He looked over his left shoulder and cleared his throat.

'It'll give me time to wind down the business, sell the van and tools and clear out the house. I'll not sell the house just yet – I think I'll rent it out. Best to keep my options open in case things don't work out.'

'Yes. Quite.' Her voice was a whisper.

She was too late. His mind was made up. He was going to Dubai. What on earth had made her think he cared for her? Thank God she hadn't delivered her planned speech. She would just have embarrassed him – and felt like a complete fool.

'Oh, cheer up, Kirsty. Don't look so glum.' He showed his teeth in a smile and the corners of his eyes creased like fans. 'I'll make sure I find someone reliable to take over from me. I wouldn't leave you in the lurch, now would I?'

She forced a smile.

He shifted his weight to the other foot and pinned his gaze on her, his eyes the colour of the blue stripe on her kitchen china. 'Now, what was it you wanted to ask me?'

She stared at him, her heart pounding against her chest.

He waited. 'Just there now. You said you wanted to ask me something.'

'I . . . I . . .' she said and glanced desperately around the garden. Her eye fell upon a buddleia bush, the purple cone-shaped flowers half-obscuring the lounge window. 'I was wondering if you could cut back that buddleia,' she said and pointed. 'It's cutting out quite a bit of light into the lounge.' He followed her gaze and she closed her eyes momentarily.

'Are you sure? I cut that back in the spring. And it's in flower now. You'd need to leave it 'til next year,' he said.

She opened her eyes. 'I forgot. Yes, of course.'

He looked at her oddly and his brow furrowed. 'Are you alright?' he said, and he rubbed his chin, the rough skin on his palms rasping against the stubble on his face.

'Yes, perfectly,' she said with a smile that felt like it might crack her face.

He nodded and returned to his work, dismissing her or so it seemed. She took three slow steps backwards, away from him, and then turned and ran inside, closing the back door behind her. She turned the key in the lock and leant her back against it, barricading herself inside. Then she put her face in her hands and cried silently.

How she would miss Chris. How much she wanted him to love her, but he did not. That much was clear. Just as she could not make herself love Scott again, she could not make Chris love her. It simply was not to be and she must accept that. But, oh, it was hard.

After some time had passed and she had no tears left, she took a deep breath. She was being indulgent, self-centred. It was a disappointment, yes, but one that she could, she must, overcome. She dug her nails into her palms in an attempt to ground herself – to abandon this fantasy and face up to reality. She had her health, her boys, her friends, and a job she loved. And she had the support of Dorothy and Harry. She had a good life and, if it wasn't entirely fulfilled, then she must learn to live with that, to appreciate what she did have, and not to mourn what was missing.

Later, after she'd composed herself, she took a glass of cordial out to Chris and, just to prove to herself that she could do it, she chatted like old times about everything but Dubai. And then she left him and went to collect the boys from school. But she had swallowed a bitter pill that left her with a burning ache in her chest that would not go away. And though she tried to put a brave face on it, she knew that something inside her had died that afternoon in the garden.

'Mum, can I ride my bicycle?' asked Adam later that afternoon.

Kirsty opened her mouth to tell him that he, along with his brother who was playing on the Wii next door, had to tidy his room instead. But he stood there in his long shorts, freckles dusted across his nose like wet sand, his little face alive with excitement. The battered and scraped cycling helmet, a hand-me-down from his older brother, was already on his head, the strap secured under his chin.

'Look, Mum! Conor and Aidan are out on their bikes,' he said, pointing out of the window at the twin brothers who lived two doors down.

'Sure,' said Kirsty, watching the twins race each other up the road on their matching red bikes. 'Why not?' Why spoil everyone's happiness just because her own was destroyed? 'Just make sure you stay on our street and watch out for cars,' she said but, when she turned around, he was already gone.

She shrugged and resumed her position at the window. Even though he was only six, she tried not to worry about his safety out on the road. Olderfleet Road, though not a cul-de-sac, was quiet and residential and mostly everyone who used it lived around here. There were no parked cars on the road to shield a vulnerable child from a driver's view; no-one speeded, everyone knew kids played in the street.

The memory of the time immediately after Scott's accident skidded across her brain, a jumbled mass of images and sounds and a tightness across her chest. She took a deep breath. She mustn't let what had happened to Scott make her paranoid about the boys and their bikes. All the other kids rode their bikes in the street, even little Jenny Clark who was a year younger than Adam. The other parents wouldn't let their kids do it unless it was safe, or as safe as riding a bike on a street could ever be, would they? No. The risk was minimal. She would have to learn to switch her brain off, to relax. Nothing was going to happen to Adam.

There he was, sitting on the kerb with the twins, the bikes abandoned on the pavement. In a few minutes they would no doubt run into someone's house to play, the novelty of riding their bikes already worn off. She turned and walked out of the room.

She went into the kitchen, weary with exhaustion, took an apron from the peg on the back door, pulled it over her head and tied the strings around her waist. It was time to make the kids' tea. As for herself, she couldn't care less if she never ate again.

It was then that she heard a dull thud, muffled and quiet like the sound of a car boot slamming shut on a snowy day. She listened but heard nothing more. She shrugged, got a box of chicken out of the freezer, flicked the oven on and tipped the sandy-coloured nuggets onto a tray. Then she poured frozen peas, hard like pellets, into a Pyrex bowl, covered them with water and put them in the microwave.

Dring-dring went the doorbell and then again and again, too loud, too fast. She tutted to herself. It would be Adam. He quite often rang the doorbell when he wanted something, instead of simply opening the door and walking in. It was laziness – he didn't want the hassle of having to take off his shoes and come looking for her. It was easier to summon her to the front door.

Bang! Bang! Bang! Kirsty frowned. If he banged any harder he would break the glass. Then she remembered the odd sound she'd heard only minutes before. A chill ran down her entire body like an electric shock. She moved into the hall. Through the frosted glass she saw an outline, not of a child, but an adult. Kirsty flung the door open.

It was Mary Clark, Jenny's mum, wearing fluffy pink

slippers on her feet. 'Come quick, Kirsty. There's been an accident.'

'Is it Adam?' she said.

Mary opened her mouth, closed it. Didn't answer. Kirsty pressed her teeth together so hard it hurt and pushed past Mary down the garden path, onto the pavement, looked right then left.

It was then that she saw them. Less than a hundred yards away, where Olderfleet Road and Fleet Street met at the T-junction. A group gathered around the base of the lamp post. And a big blue four-wheeled car abandoned, the front wheels up on the pavement, the driver's door hanging wide open.

Kirsty did not cry out. She did not scream. She ran straight up the middle of the road. The ballet pumps on her feet flew off and she did not stop. All she could think about was the fragment of Scott's skull embedded in his brain – the thing that had killed him – and Adam on his bike, his skinny limbs as fragile as twigs.

Please God. Please God. Please God.

Her feet pounded the tarmac, blood crashed in her head like waves in a storm. Distracted by Chris she'd taken her eye off the ball – the only thing that mattered. Her child. Her Adam. The sound of rushing air filled her ears.

Please God. Please God. Please God.

She should never have let him out on the road on his bike.

If He spared him, she never would again.

Chapter Seventeen

The small crowd parted as Kirsty approached. People stepped back out of her way, heads bowed. And there in the middle of the crowd, lying on his side, was the slim unmistakable form of Adam. He was on the pavement, eyes closed, on top of the mangled front wheel of his bike. Someone was leaning over him, their hand under the small of his back.

She found her voice at last. 'Adam!' she screamed. She fell to her knees. 'Oh, my God! Adam!' She put her hands to her face, closed her eyes, opened them. 'Please God,' she said to the picture-book white clouds whipping across the azure sky. 'Please God, save him!'

Adam opened his eyes and made a sound.

'It's me, Adam. It's Mum,' she gasped and touched his arm. He moaned and closed his eyes. 'Adam! Adam! Adam!' She could hear the rising hysteria in her voice but was powerless to stop it. Tears filled her eyes, she could no longer see clearly. She cried out – a long, low howl, a sound with no form, a primeval cry of pain.

A hand pressed down on her shoulder, hard, forcing her to look up. It was Phil O'Brien, the twins' father.

'Kirsty! Look at me. Kirsty!'

She tried but could not see him through the tears and the fog of her grief. She felt two meaty hands on her shoulders now, holding her upright. She blinked and Phil's green eyes came into focus as he said, 'Listen to me, Kirsty. He's okay. He's going to be alright. Look.'

Suddenly silenced, she stared at Adam again. Incredibly, he was sitting on the pavement with his legs stretched out in front of him, staring at his bloodied knees. 'You're scaring me, Mum,' he said, plugged his thumb into his mouth and promptly burst into tears.

'See,' said Phil's deep voice though she could no longer see him. She was focused only on Adam – everything else was a blur. 'He's absolutely fine. Just a few cuts and bruises, that's all.'

'Was he unconscious?' asked someone.

'No, I don't think so. He just got a nasty shock. Here, let's get that helmet off you, wee man. Where does it hurt?' Kirsty remembered with eternal gratitude that Phil, the leader of the local scout troop, was a qualified first aider.

'Here. And here,' sobbed Adam, pointing to his knees and right elbow.

'Can you bend your elbow for me?' asked Phil, removing the boy's helmet. 'That's a good boy. No, nothing broken. It's just going to be a bit sore for a day or two.'

Kirsty pulled Adam onto her knee. He was howling now, the wonderful, joyous, shocked, indignant cry of an injured child. The sort of cry that tells you no real damage has been done. It's when they don't make noise that you know you have something to worry about.

She held Adam close and kissed the top of his head, sweaty from the helmet, and cooed, 'It's okay, now. Mummy's here. Everything's going to be alright.' She looked up at Phil who was still leaning over her, and wiped away her tears. 'I'm sorry,' she said quietly. 'I over-reacted. I thought . . . I thought . . .'

'You've no need to apologise, Kirsty. It's that bloody

idiot who knocked him off his bike who should be apologising. Where is she?' He stood up, glowering, his big belly protruding over the waistband of his jeans, his hands on the place where, had he been slimmer, his hips would have been.

'Over there. Sitting over on the grass,' said Mary's voice. 'Bawling her eyes out. The stupid cow. She could've killed him.'

'Did she hit him?' said someone.

'No, but he had to swerve to avoid the car and that's how he ran into the fence. Poor wee mite. Must've got the shock of his life.'

'Looks like she's been drinking,' said someone else.

'She has not!' said a horrified voice. 'There's a wee girl in the back of the car.'

'Right. That's it. I'm phoning the police,' said Phil and he pulled a mobile phone out of his shirt pocket and dialled.

'We'd better get the child out of the car,' said Mrs Renton, a widow, from number twelve. She and two other adults moved off towards the car. Someone laid Kirsty's shoes gently on the grass beside her.

Adam's weeping subsided and he picked at a nugget of dusty grey gravel lodged in his knee. Kirsty stood up, brushed the gravel from the knees of her jeans and pulled Adam gently to his feet. She slipped her feet into the pumps. 'Come on, love. We'd better get you home.'

He winced and hobbled a few steps, and Kirsty felt a lump in her throat. He was such a brave little boy. If the person who did this had been drunk . . . she thought she might be capable of causing them actual bodily harm. She tried to put the thought out of her mind. Let the police deal with it. Her priority was to get Adam home and into a hot bath to soak the gravel out of his bony little knees. She raised her face to the sun. Thank you, God.

She glanced over at the car to see a slim, dazed-looking girl emerge onto the road. A girl about the same age and size, and with the same hair colour, as Izzy. Wait a minute. It *was* Izzy. And the car. She recognised it. Clare had one just like it. She sometimes used this road on her way to, and from, the nursery.

'Adam,' she said and she pushed him gently towards Mary. 'You go with Mary. Just for a wee bit. I'll be back in a minute.'

Kirsty stared hard at her neighbour. 'Mary, can you take Adam home with you please? I just want to have a . . . a word with the driver of the car. I'll collect him in a few minutes.'

Mary nodded, laid her hand on Adam's shoulder and looked over at the blue car, her lips pursed together as tight as a mussel. Then she led Adam away with the promise of an ice-lolly from the freezer.

Kirsty walked to the back of the car and round the other side. And there, as she expected, was Clare, sitting on the grass with her face in her hands, her shoulders shaking. Her feet were bare, sequinned turquoise flip-flops lying on the grass. Jean Ross from number seven, wearing orange leather gardening gloves, was standing beside her like a grim sentinel, her arms folded across her chest, deliberately looking away from her charge in disgust.

'The police'll be here any minute,' she said when Kirsty approached. 'We'll see what they have to say when they breathalyse her.'

'Clare?' said Kirsty, too focused on ascertaining for herself exactly what had happened to pay any attention to Jean.

Clare's tear-stained face looked up and she gushed, the words tumbling out one on top of the other, 'Oh, Kirsty. Thank God you're here. I don't know what happened. One minute I was driving along, the next . . . I . . . I lost control of the car and nearly hit this little boy on his bike. I didn't hit him, thank God. I went into the lamp post. But he fell off his bike. Is he alright?'

'As far as I know,' said Kirsty evenly, taking deep breaths. 'What happened, Clare?' She dropped to her knees and leant close into her friend's face.

Clare stared at her blankly for a few seconds and then said, 'I really don't know. One minute I was taking the corner. The next I was heading towards the lamp post.'

The unmistakable smell of wine on her breath made Kirsty nauseous. She sat back on her heels and took a deep breath. Then she got up, walked over to the car, kicked the back tyre with the toe of her right foot and counted to ten before coming back again. She stood over Clare, still sitting on the grass, feeling sorry for herself.

'You promised me you'd not drink and drive, Clare,' she hissed. 'You promised me.'

'I know and I wouldn't have, only I thought Liam was going to pick the kids up from nursery and then he phoned at the last minute to say he was late and he couldn't do it. Just typical, isn't it? Though you think I'd be used to him letting me down by now, wouldn't you? It's only a short drive. I thought it'd be alright.'

'Jesus, Clare. How could you be so bloody stupid? Izzy was in the car, for God's sake. She could've been hurt. And what about Josh and Rachel? What if you'd had an accident with them in the car on the way back?'

Clare hung her head.

'How could you do it?' Kirsty's voice rose to a scream. 'You promised me! You stood in your kitchen four days ago and you promised me you wouldn't drink and drive.'

A few onlookers, drawn by the shouting, stood at a distance watching.

Clare blinked and said, 'I know. I shouldn't have done it. I'm sorry.'

'Have you any idea the trouble you're in? The police are on their way. You're going to get done for drunk driving, Clare.'

'No,' said Clare, shaking her head. 'I only had a couple of very small glasses. Not nearly enough to be over the limit.'

'You don't need to be over the limit to be a danger to yourself and to others!' shouted Kirsty.

Clare rose to her feet. 'For God's sake, will you stop screaming, Kirsty. Get a grip on yourself. Alright, I made a mistake. But there's no harm done. No-one got seriously hurt. I've learned my lesson. I'm sorry.'

Kirsty's ears burned with rage. She saw Adam's bloodied knees and his freckled face smeared with tears and snot. Her head filled with a rushing sound like standing beside a waterfall. She put her hands on the top of her head in a vain attempt to stop the throbbing inside.

'It was Adam, Clare,' she screamed and she felt the veins stand out on her neck. Her voice started to break. 'It was Adam,' she said, choking on tears. 'You knocked Adam off his bike. I thought he was dead.'

Clare's face drained of colour and she pulled herself awkwardly to her feet. She took a few uncertain steps towards Kirsty and held out an arm towards her. 'Oh, my God, Kirsty. I'm so sorry.'

'Don't,' warned Kirsty and her voice came out hoarse and vicious. She put a hand up. 'Don't come anywhere near me. I swear to God if you . . .'

'Come on, Kirsty,' said Phil's voice and he put a hand on her arm and forced it slowly, gently, down to her side. 'She's not worth it. Let's get you home. Adam needs you.'

She stared at him and blinked, suddenly deflated, all anger spent. 'Yes. Adam. I need to go home.' She looked down at herself and realised she was still wearing her apron, smeared with her son's rust-coloured blood.

Everything was going to be alright, she told herself, fighting against the panic that threatened to overwhelm her. Nothing was broken. No real harm had been done. Not physically anyway.

No, the worst thing was that the awful memories from three years before had been catapulted right into the present. It felt as though everything was happening all over again, all the pain and grief and shock, as raw as the day Scott died. And all this anguish had been caused by Clare.

She could not forgive her for drinking and driving. She could not forgive her for breaking her promise.

So she let Phil put his arm around her shoulder and lead her away from the woman she had once regarded as her best friend. And she didn't look back.

Clare sat in the back of the police car flanked by an officer on her left and one in the driver's seat in front. The policeman held a small machine in his hand. It beeped, he peered at the display screen, then held it up to her face and said, 'Please breathe sharply and steadily into the mouthpiece.'

She inserted the clear plastic tube in between her lips and blew hard. And when she was done she sat there and waited, silent tears seeping out of the corners of her eyes.

A man Clare recognised as Kirsty's neighbour walked over to the police car and almost stuck his head in the driver's window. 'Are you going to take her in?' he demanded.

Clare ducked her head, hiding behind her long hair. She was too ashamed to be seen. Even now she still couldn't fully understand what had happened. The afternoon was a blur. She'd spent most of it in her room, sobbing into her pillow, and had only emerged when Izzy turned up, on foot, at about four o'clock. Yes, she'd had two very small glasses of wine, one at lunchtime and one just before she'd left the house, but she was far from drunk. She'd hardly slept for a week – not since Liam had told her about Gillian. If her judgment was impaired it was through lack of sleep, not excess alcohol.

The officer in the driving seat puffed up his chest. 'Sir, we're trying to do a job here and you're obstructing police business. Now will you stand back from the car please? Thank you.'

His colleague, sitting in the back of the car with Clare, said, 'The reading's thirty.' The officers exchanged glances in the rear-view mirror.

'What does that mean?' said Clare.

'It means you're within the legal drink-drive limit of thirty-five.'

The officer beside Clare let out a sigh that spoke of wasted time, and started to pack away the breathalyser equipment in a hard protective case, the inside padded with grey moulded foam. Clare, numb, gave no reaction to this news.

'Have you taken statements from all the witnesses, Colin?' said the officer in front.

'Yes.'

'That's us done, then.'

There was silence.

'Mrs McCormack?'

'Yes?'

'You're free to go.'

Clare looked out at the small crowd, still hanging about on the pavement.

'Though that lot aren't going to be happy,' said Colin. 'They look like they're ready to lynch you.'

Clare bit her lip and forced back the tears.

'I don't think you're in any fit state to drive,' said Colin, his voice full of disapproval. 'I'd suggest you park your car safely on the road and leave it here for now. Can someone come and collect it? The damage's only cosmetic.'

'My husband. I'd better ring him.' She fumbled in her bag for her mobile and called Liam's number. Miraculously, he answered.

'Liam, I've been in a car accident.'

'What?'

'Everything's okay. I just need you to . . .'

'Are you okay? Where are you?'

'I'm fine. I'm on Olderfleet Road, Just down a bit from Kirsty's house. The police are here.'

'And the kids?'

'Izzy's with me. Liam, I need you to collect Josh and Rachel from nursery. They should've been collected half an hour ago.'

'Is Izzy alright?'

'She's fine.'

'I'm almost there.' He hung up.

Clare slipped the mobile back in her bag. The officer beside her got out of the car and started dispersing the crowd of onlookers.

'Mrs McCormack?' said the policeman in the front of the car.

'Yes?'

'Can you get out of the car please and park your vehicle safely by the kerb? Then we'll run you and your stepdaughter home.'

Clare got out of the police car with her head bent and walked quickly over to her car, fumbling in her bag for the keys.

'Bloody disgrace,' said someone.

'She should be locked up,' shouted another voice.

'Move along now. Move along,' said the policeman. 'The show's over.'

Fighting back tears and shaking like a leaf, Clare reversed the car off the pavement. After cutting out the engine twice she managed to park it alongside the kerb. She got out, locked the vehicle and put the keys in her bag. Izzy was sitting on the kerb with her long legs bent up like a newborn colt's, her arms wrapped around herself. A woman in red jeans was talking to her. Clare wanted to go over and comfort the girl but she was immobilised by shame. So she stayed where she was and looked at the ground.

Moments later, Liam's car pulled up. The door opened, and he got out and scanned the people by the roadside. His gaze hovered momentarily on the front of her bashed car. And then he saw Izzy and ran straight over to her, leaving his car door wide open. She jumped up, flung herself into his arms and they exchanged a few words. Clare was suddenly, irrationally jealous.

Then the policemen said, 'Liam?'

Liam nodded and said to his daughter, 'You go and get in the car, Izzy.' She did as she was told and the policeman walked over to Liam and spoke briefly with him in low tones.

Clare felt invisible. They were talking about her, of course. As though she wasn't there. When they were done, Liam made a beeline for her and, without preamble, said, 'I'm going to take Izzy home to Zoe.'

'But she was supposed to be spending the weekend with us. I got tickets for that new Hannah Montana film.'

Liam glared at her. 'What planet are you on, Clare? She's just been in a car crash. She wants to be with her mother. And personally, I think she'd be a lot safer there, don't you?'

Clare blushed. 'It wasn't a car crash. It was an accident. A very minor accident.'

'I've phoned the nursery,' he went on, ignoring her. 'They

know what's happened. The staff are going to stay on and give the kids tea. I'll collect them later.'

'Oh,' said Clare, feeling suddenly redundant. Stripped of her maternal responsibilities she was left exposed, useless.

'The police will take you home,' he said coldly.

'Liam, why are you acting like this?'

'Like what?'

'All . . . all frosty. And self-righteous.'

He lowered his voice. 'Jim Petticrew, the policeman . . .'

'You know him?'

'We went to school together. He just told me that they breathalysed you, Clare. And that you narrowly missed a kid out on his bike.'

'I wasn't over the limit,' protested Clare, annoyed that the officer had shared these details with Liam. She would've done, of course, but in her own time.

Liam's face coloured. He looked down at his feet, then brought his gaze up to meet hers. 'I don't want to talk about this now, Clare. Let's just do what has to be done to sort out this . . . this mess.'

'Okay.' Clare bit her lip and looked away. Everybody hated her. Even her own husband. He turned away without another word, got into his car and drove off. And she was left standing there on the grassy verge, feeling lonelier than she had ever done in her entire life.

It wasn't until the police car had dropped her at home, and she was sitting in her own eerily silent kitchen, that the seriousness of what she had done slowly began to dawn on Clare. She'd driven the car into a lamp post on Olderfleet Road with Izzy in the back seat. She'd nearly knocked down Adam.

And it was Izzy's fault. The little cow had done nothing but whine and moan, like she always did, and Clare had finally snapped. She'd lost control of her temper – and the car. She took a deep breath. But was it really fair to blame a twelve year old? She had been drinking. Only two glasses but, combined with sleep deprivation, had it been enough to slow down her reflexes? Enough to distort her judgment? If she hadn't had the wine, would she have reacted to Izzy like that? Would she have lost control of the car? She began to think perhaps not. She'd been under the limit, but only just. She never should've got behind the wheel. It was the stupidest thing she'd ever done in her entire life.

She remembered the way Kirsty's neighbours had looked at her – like she was some kind of vermin. They hated her. And so did Kirsty.

Kirsty. She thought of all the awful things Kirsty had said to her and put her hands over her face. In the heat of the moment she hadn't made the connection but now it was glaringly obvious. Scott had been knocked off his bike and killed by a motorist. And for a few minutes Kirsty must've thought the same thing had happened to Adam. How could she do that to one of her dearest friends? Would Kirsty ever forgive her?

Added to Liam's revelations about Gillian it was too much too bear. Clare folded her arms on the table, rested her head upon them, and wept. And wondered, in all sincerity, if the world would be better off without her.

When Liam came in the back door almost an hour later, Clare was still sitting at the table, staring into space, wondering how a life could fall apart so quickly. Only a week ago she'd been on cloud nine, a happy wife, mother and successful artist. Now her life was in tatters.

Liam carried Rachel inside on his shoulder, fast asleep. Josh held his hand but, as soon as he saw Clare, he broke free and ran to her.

'Now, Josh,' said Liam. 'It's very late. Kiss Mum goodnight. I'm putting you to bed tonight.'

Clare pulled Josh to her breast and squeezed him tight. She kissed him on the cheeks, the nose, the chin. Were Josh and Rachel the only people who wouldn't vilify her? Who would love her no matter what? The thought of anyone harming so much as a hair on their heads brought tears to her eyes. She understood, in that moment, just how much Kirsty must hate her.

'That's a good boy, Josh,' said Liam, in a synthetically cheerful tone, refusing to make eye contact with Clare. 'Now come on, let's get you ready for bed.'

Josh, with a last glance at his mother, his little brow furrowed with confusion, followed his father out of the room. But there was no protest. He must've sensed from the atmosphere – indeed, it would've been hard to miss – that something was up. Liam rarely put the kids to bed.

Clare remained where she was, listening to the sounds from above, afraid to go upstairs. Liam's non-verbal signals had warned her off – she daren't upset him any more than she'd already done. Once, she heard Rachel cry out, 'Mummy!' and then the shooshing sounds of Liam's voice, soothing her to sleep. And still she stayed rooted where she was. The message from Liam was loud and clear: by her behaviour, she had forfeited the right to be Mum. Tonight at least.

When Liam came downstairs some twenty minutes later, Clare said, 'I'm perfectly capable of putting the children to bed, you know.'

Liam loosened his tie, got a tumbler out of the cupboard and poured himself a glass of water. He drank it standing at the sink, his hand trembling.

He finished the water, let out a little gasp and said, 'You've had a shock, Clare. I don't think you should be taking responsibility for anybody just now.' He rinsed the glass and set it upside-down on the draining board.

Her heart leapt, latching onto the shred of kindness in this statement. In spite of everything, it showed that he still cared for her.

'I wasn't drunk, you know, Liam. I was under the limit.'

'By a hair's breath, Clare,' he said, holding up the forefinger and thumb of his right hand, like a vice. He brought them together until the pads of the finger and thumb were just a centimetre apart and held them up in front of his contorted face. 'You were this close to getting done for careless driving.'

'Don't be silly, Liam. You're exaggerating. All I did was momentarily lose control of the car and run into a lamp post.'

'I'm not exaggerating, Clare. I've just spoken to Keith Kirkpatrick on the phone. He said that because the only car involved was yours, and no-one was seriously hurt, the police probably won't press dangerous driving charges. Kirsty might see it differently though. You're lucky you didn't kill her son.'

At the mention of her friend's name, Clare hung her head in shame. If only she'd taken that corner thirty seconds earlier, or thirty seconds later, the coast would've been clear. She would still have hit the lamp post, but not a child. Not that she had actually hit the boy, of course, but no-one seemed to care about that distinction. Of all the kids in that street, why did it have to be Adam?

'I just can't believe that you drank two glasses of wine and then got in the car with Izzy.'

'Because I had no choice. You were late, Liam. You were supposed to collect them.'

'Of course you had a choice. Why didn't you call someone? Kirsty? Janice? Patsy? One of the mothers in the street? Any one of them would've picked the kids up – you only had to ask.'

It was a perfectly reasonable question that she was too ashamed to answer. How would it have sounded, having to ask someone to collect her kids because she'd been drinking during the day? 'I know. I know,' said Clare, rubbing her temples with the heels of her hands. 'I wasn't thinking straight.'

'Damn right you weren't. You were drunk.'

'Will you stop saying that,' said Clare. 'It's simply not true.'

'Well, what other explanation can you give for driving into a lamp post in broad daylight?'

'Sleep deprivation.'

He shot a brief glance in her direction. 'I'm tired too, Clare. But I don't go around wrapping my car round lamp posts.'

Clare took a deep breath. 'And Izzy was doing her usual. Sulking and –'

Liam put up a hand. 'Stop right there,' he said, his voice tight with rage. 'Don't tell me you're going to try and pin this one on Izzy?'

'I'm not saying it was all her fault. But she was –'

'That's good, because,' he said, interrupting again and glaring at her until tears pricked her eyes, 'for a second there I thought you were going to blame a twelve-year-old child.'

It wasn't fair. Liam should be the one consoling her, holding her in his arms and telling her that, no matter what, he would stand by her and love her. She wanted him to admit his part in this disaster – by causing her so much upset over the past week that she had been unable to sleep. She wanted him to take her in his arms and tell her how much he loved her. That Gillian meant nothing to him.

Instead he said, 'Where's the keys to your car?'

'What?'

'The keys to your car.'

'In my handbag. Why?'

He picked the bag up off the table, tipped out the contents

and picked up the car keys. He made no attempt to restore the scattered items to her bag. 'I have to walk round to Olderfleet Road now and pick up your car.'

'I can get it tomorrow.'

'I want it off that street as soon as possible. It'll have to go into the garage for repairs straight away. You can't drive it like that.'

'The policeman said that the damage was only cosmetic.'

Liam tossed the keys from one hand to the other and snorted. 'Do you have any idea how much it costs to get a car repaired these days? And this isn't just a scratch. You've dented the bumper, the bonnet and buckled the driver's side panel. You can kiss goodbye to that cheque you brought home last Friday night, Clare. After we've paid for a new bike for Adam, and paid for the car repairs, there'll be nothing left.'

'Is Adam's bike ruined?'

'Looked like it to me. The front wheel was badly mangled. After what the wee lad's been through, I think buying a new bike is the least we can do.'

Clare nodded in agreement. Adam loved that bike – Dorothy and Harry had bought him it for his last birthday. She would buy him the best bike she could possibly find. And a big box of Lego – his favourite. But no amount of material gifts could compensate for the harm she had done. She knew that. She just hoped Kirsty could find it in her heart to forgive her.

'But what about my car insurance? Won't it cover the cost of the repairs?'

'The excess is two fifty. Don't you remember? We opted for a higher excess to try and keep the cost down. And you'd lose your no claims bonus. It's probably not worth claiming.'

So much for all her hard work – it had been for nothing. There would be no chandelier for the bedroom, no money towards a special summer holiday. She tried not to be self-indulgent. Wasn't it self-pity that had gotten her into this mess in the first place? Perhaps, if she thought of others more, instead of herself, she could make things better.

'Is Izzy okay?' she said.

'She's fine. Just a little shaken.' Liam shook his head and looked out of the window. It was nearly eight o'clock and still daylight outside. 'But you should've seen Zoe. You'd have thought she was the one in the car, not Izzy. She was almost hysterical. She says Izzy is never to come here again.'

'But she can't do that!'

'Legally no, but you know Zoe. She's making as much capital out of the situation as she can. You should've seen her when Izzy told her you were breathalysed.'

Clare squirmed in her seat, and humiliation reddened her cheeks. This would confirm Zoe's opinion that Clare was an unfit mother. She could just see her telling all her friends about Clare's daytime drinking – one of the few remaining taboos, among mothers in charge of young children anyway. She would exaggerate, make out that Clare had nearly killed her daughter. And no doubt she would convince Izzy that this was true, thereby undoing all the progress they had made in their relationship.

'Things with Zoe were prickly enough,' went on Liam. 'Though I thought lately that we'd reached a workable compromise. This is just the excuse she needed to pull up the drawbridge.'

'Oh,' said Clare, taken aback by a repercussion she hadn't seen coming. 'I'm so sorry, Liam.'

'She says I can see Izzy but she's not to come here.'

'Liam, she really can't do that. You have a legal right to see your daughter and have her here to stay. I haven't been convicted of a crime. I . . .' She was about to say she had done nothing wrong and then thought better of it.

'I know that, Clare. But it's not worth it, fighting her. It just makes things worse for Izzy. In the end, it's her who suffers. I'll just have to placate Zoe for a while and hopefully, once she's calmed down a bit, she'll relent.'

'I'm sorry, Liam.'

He shook his head. His crumpled suit looked shabby, his hair untidy. His face was a picture of misery. 'The damage is done.' He turned and looked upon her for the first time and she squirmed under his scrutiny.

'What can I do to make things right?' she said.

Liam held the car keys in his right hand as if weighing them. 'I have to go and get your car.'

Her eyes filled with tears. How she longed for him to hold her and tell her everything was going to be alright. 'Talk to me, Liam.'

'No,' he said sharply and she winced. 'I think,' he went on, 'that if this conversation continues, I might say something I regret.'

Clare bowed her head and suddenly realised that, amidst all the chaos, neither she nor Liam had had anything to eat. 'You must be starving,' she said and stood up. He loved her cooking – when she could be bothered to make something good. She would rustle up a nice supper and start the process of making up for what she had done. 'I'll have something ready for you when you get home.'

'Don't bother. Why don't you just go to bed and get some sleep?'

He walked to the back door.

'I'll see you soon,' she said lamely.

He opened the door and paused with his hand on the doorknob. He looked at the floor and said quietly, 'Don't bother waiting up, Clare.'

And then he was gone.

Chapter Eighteen

'Last exam today,' said Pete, almost skipping across the slate floor in the kitchen. He was wearing black socks and his school uniform. He looked handsome, clean-cut, smart – everything a mother would want in a son. Only Janice standing by the sink, measuring out teaspoons of ground coffee, knew it was a façade.

Unusually Keith was going into the office late. He was seated at the table in a shirt and tie eating a piece of toast and jam. He looked up and smiled at Pete. 'It's been a long slog, son, but it'll be worth it. You'll see.'

A little shiver went down Janice's spine. Since they'd found out about Laura she could hardly bring herself to speak to Pete civilly. But Keith hid his anger and disappointment better than she did. Or perhaps he didn't feel it as keenly. Either way, he was capable of interacting with Pete the way he had always done. As though nothing had changed.

Pete sat down at the table and helped himself to corn flakes.

'How do you think you'll do in this one?' asked Keith pleasantly. 'Maths, isn't it?'

'Mmm,' said Pete, his mouth full of food. He finished chewing and added, 'Yeah. Should do alright. I think.'

They had only talked with Pete about Laura twice since the night Patsy and Martin visited them, and both times Pete had been uncommunicative and withdrawn. Keith said Pete was traumatised by the whole affair – he needed time and space to sort out his feelings towards Laura and the idea of fatherhood. And, with exams coming up, it was vital they gave him the space he needed. Janice thought Pete couldn't give a fig about Laura or the baby. And yet still she shared Keith's anxiety that he should do well in his exams.

If he didn't, she worried that he might fail to get into university and end up living at home indefinitely, the way so many young people seemed to do these days. So they had let the matter drop, for fear that pressurising him might affect his results.

And now the time had come, almost, to tackle the issue again. And, of course, to tell him that Keith was his adoptive father. Janice stole a glance at Pete and mentally steeled herself for both events.

She set the cafetière in the middle of the table and sat down in the seat opposite Pete. She couldn't help but feel that he was getting off too lightly. Of course she concurred with Keith's argument about not upsetting him at exam time. But she *wanted* to see him upset. She wanted to see him hurting in the way Laura and her family were hurting. She wanted to see him suffer for destroying her friendship with Patsy.

Janice glared at Pete and there was an awkward silence. Pete, his eyes fixed determinedly on the morning paper, continued eating. Janice pushed the empty cereal bowl in front of her away, her appetite gone, and poured herself a cup of coffee.

'Look,' said Keith. 'Why don't we all go out for a meal to celebrate the end of your exams, Pete?'

Janice stared at Keith in amazement. She wasn't sure she could sit across a table from her son and make small talk.

Pete looked up from the paper. 'Sure.'

'We can go to The Mill,' said Keith. The Mill was a popular

restaurant on the Old Glenarm Road. It served good, traditional food and they used to go there quite often when Pete was younger. Before he grew up and decided it was no longer cool to be seen out with his parents. 'How about Sunday night?'

'Okay,' said Pete.

Janice's heartbeat quickened. Sunday was the day they had agreed to tell Pete that Keith wasn't his real father. Surely Keith wasn't planning on telling him in public? She didn't know how Pete would take the news – he was bound to be upset, angry even. He might cause a scene.

Pete pushed back his chair and got up, leaving his dirty dish sitting on the table. 'Gotta run,' he said.

'Good luck,' said Keith.

Janice stirred her coffee disconsolately, set the spoon down and pushed the cup away, the smell of the coffee, for some reason, suddenly repellant. 'I'm not sure I'm up to a celebratory meal, Keith. It doesn't feel like there's much to rejoice in at the minute.'

Keith nodded his head and looked at the table. 'I know how you feel.'

Janice doubted that he had any idea. And she could not tell him. For what would that make her? A vengeful witch? Or, worse, some kind of monster – isn't that how women who despised their own offspring were regarded? Mothers were meant to love in spite of, no matter what, always and for ever. An unconditional love that, try as she might, Janice had never been able to muster for her son. It wasn't that she didn't love him at all. She did – but not fulsomely, unreservedly. Not like a mother ought.

Keith cleared his throat, brightened a little. 'But it would be wrong to let a milestone in Pete's life like this go unmarked. I wouldn't want us to look back and regret it, Janice. I wouldn't want this business with Laura to overshadow his achievements.'

'Well, it kind of does, Keith. And no pretending can make that otherwise.'

Keith pressed his lips together, and looked sad. Immediately she regretted what she had said. Not because it wasn't true but because of the effect her words had on Keith. Optimistic, cheerful Keith, who didn't deserve any of this. All he wanted was a happy family.

'But I suppose you've got a point,' she said and his head lifted just a little. 'A neutral venue might make for a better atmosphere.' She listened for the sound of Pete's car engine revving and when she heard it drive away from the house she said, 'You weren't thinking of telling him about being adopted at The Mill, were you?'

'Lord, no. Let's tackle one thing at a time. We'll have an early dinner and maybe try to talk to him about Laura – in a non-threatening, supportive way?' He cast a meaningful look at Janice but did not wait for her to respond. 'And then I think we should tell him about being adopted when we get home.'

Janice nodded, resigned to the fact that this was going to happen whether she liked it or not. In two days' time Pete would know that Keith wasn't his birth father. 'Okay,' she said bravely. She squeezed her sweaty palms together under the table so hard it hurt. The pain helped to distract her brain and stopped the panic in its tracks.

'What are we going to do about Laura?' she blurted out, anything to stop having to think about Pete's father.

Keith paused, then said in a low voice, 'In some ways it might be better if she had an abortion.'

'Oh, Keith. How can you say that?'

He leant back in his chair and folded his arms across his chest. His Adam's apple moved in his throat, an indication that, though his features were hardened and his voice was even, he was upset. 'I'm thinking of Laura as much as Pete,

Janice. A baby at her age would ruin her life. And Pete's not ready to be a father. He's not going to be any support to her. She'll be on her own and poor Patsy and Martin'll end up pseudo-parents to the baby.'

'It doesn't have to be like that,' said Janice quietly. 'I managed on my own.'

Keith put his hand out and covered hers where it lay on the table. 'I'm sorry, love. That was insensitive. I forgot for a moment that you were a single mum before I met you. It can't have been easy for you.'

'It wasn't.'

He put her hand to his lips and kissed the back of it. In all their years of marriage they had rarely discussed Janice's life before she met Keith. She had told him once that it was something she wasn't comfortable talking about and he had respected that.

Keith stared at her, his nut-brown eyes softening. 'So we're agreed. We tell Pete on Sunday, after the meal.'

'Oh, I don't know,' said Janice, withdrawing her hand from his grasp and seeing a way out. 'I'm having second thoughts. Maybe it's not a good time with all this bother with Laura. Maybe we should wait until it's blown over. It might be very . . . upsetting for him.'

'I do worry about that. I'm afraid that he . . . that he might reject me.'

Janice rushed to reassure him. 'Oh, Keith, that's not going to happen. You're the best father in the world and he loves you.'

'Thanks, love.' He paused and went on, 'But we've been putting it off for years. There's always a reason not to tell him. I don't think we can let it drift any longer. If he's old enough to father a child, he's old enough to hear the truth, don't you think?'

Janice stared out the window. 'I guess so.'

'Anyway, I want to get it off my chest. I don't like lying to him. Well, it's not lying exactly. I don't like misleading him. I never did. I'd rather he knew the truth, even if it hurts both of us.'

Janice got up and went over to him, kissed the top of his head and rested her hands on his broad shoulders. 'It'll be alright, Keith. You'll see,' she said, without much confidence. Keith was such a good man. Pete was lucky to have him as a father. She just hoped her son had the maturity to see it that way.

She sat down again and folded her hands in her lap. She twisted her wedding ring round and round her finger. 'I'm afraid too,' she said, and she started to tremble. It wasn't often she confided the true nature of her feelings to her husband. And yet the extent of her terror was such that she felt compelled.

'I know,' said Keith.

Janice put her face in her hands and whispered, 'I can't tell him, Keith, who his real father is. You have to understand that.'

'Hey, it's okay. No-one's going to make you,' he said, reaching across the table and touching her arm.

She removed her hands from her face. He stared at her for several long moments, his black pupils dilated. 'You know what I think.'

She closed her eyes briefly, opened them again, anticipating what was coming next.

'I think you ought to tell him,' he said gently.

She took a sharp intake of breath. Every muscle in her body tensed involuntarily, resisting this idea.

'Listen, Janice, please. Not just for Pete. I think it might help you exorcise the ghosts of your past. It breaks my heart to see you upset like this. I can't begin to imagine what must've happened to cause you so much distress, even now, all these years later.'

'Please, Keith. Don't,' she said firmly, unable to bear his kindness. She did not want to cry. She had to stay strong.

He raised his hands in surrender, and said, sounding defeated, 'Okay. I won't talk about it. If that's what you want.' He stacked the cereal bowls and stood up.

Janice knew her inability to confide in him hurt him deeply, but there was nothing she could do to change that. How could she make him understand? She hardly understood herself. All she knew was that everything she had built for them, everything she had worked for – a safe, loving and happy marriage – would be destroyed if she started burrowing around in her past. She had learned to cope and she would go on coping, if only she could keep her past where it belonged. It was a deadly virus that would contaminate, and destroy, everything it came in contact with.

Keith carried the dishes over to the sink and glanced out of the window. 'There's Clare.'

'Really?' said Janice, embracing the distraction eagerly. She stood up immediately and looked out of the patio doors just in time to see Clare stride quickly from the car to the studio, her hands in the pockets of her long grey cardigan. The wild part of the garden, down by the studio, was a carpet of flowers and wild garlic, each head a cluster of snow-white five-pointed stars, albeit past their best. Golden narcissi and daffodils, on the wane now, bobbed in the breeze. The summer was coming. But Clare, her chin tucked on her chest, looked at none of it. Janice sighed.

'That's the first she's been here since the exhibition,' said Janice. 'I'd better go and talk to her. I haven't seen her since the accident.'

'I thought you'd spoken to her.'

'Only on the phone.'

'She had a narrow escape if you ask me,' he said. 'She's lucky the police didn't press charges.'

Janice sighed. She loved Clare and she felt sorry for her because of the marital difficulties she was going through, but it was hard to hide her disapproval. Clare had done an awfully stupid thing and one that threatened to tear to shreds what was left of their little group. Though of course Pete had dealt it the initial, far more deadly, blow.

'Well, I guess there's no time like the present,' said Janice, reaching behind the linen curtain for the key to the patio doors that hung there on a hook.

'Maybe she's come here for a bit of peace and quiet,' said Keith. 'After all, if she wanted to talk to you, she would've come up to the house.'

Janice paused for a moment to consider this. But she knew, more than anyone, that it's when people don't ask for help that they need it most. She smiled ironically to herself. Of course, if anyone ever needed help, it was her. But the absolute last thing she would ever do was ask for it – or accept it. That was why she had kept her secret all these years.

'Perhaps,' agreed Janice. 'But I reckon that if Clare ever needed a shoulder to cry on, it's now.' She opened the patio door.

'You're a good friend,' said Keith. 'And a good person.'

Janice looked over her shoulder and gave him a shy smile, trying very hard to feel worthy of his praise. Then she stepped out onto the patio into the sunshine, took a deep breath of the fresh morning air, and headed towards the studio.

'It's been a while since we've been here together as a family,' said Keith.

It was Sunday teatime and Keith, Janice and Pete were sitting at a window table in The Mill looking out on a wet and dismal scene. All day the wind had howled like a banshee and heavy showers, interspersed with fleeting, bright spells of sunshine, soaked everyone hardy enough to venture out. Now, black clouds were gathering for another downpour.

'Yes, it's been years,' said Janice, toying with the stem of her wine glass, and trying very hard to get into the spirit of happy families for Keith's sake. She had dressed carefully for the occasion, in spite of the weather. Her cream linen suit felt like armour.

Keith sat across from her at the rectangular wooden table in his usual smart-casual outfit of short-sleeved shirt, chinos and leather loafers. Pete was beside his father, in a crumpled t-shirt and dark jeans. He was slumped in a leather bucket chair, staring distractedly out of the window. Janice's white leather handbag sat in the chair beside her, the place where the fourth member of their family – a girl, she had always imagined – would have sat. But they hadn't been blessed with a child and Keith didn't believe in interfering with nature. So they never went for investigations. It was something that she now deeply regretted.

Pete yawned, without covering his mouth. She saw his tonsils, pink and healthy.

'Late night last night?' said Janice.

Pete stretched, raising closed fists above his head and revealing a pale slender midriff, rippled with muscles. 'Yep. I didn't get in 'til after three.'

The waitress came and took the order and Janice said, reluctant to let the subject drop, 'So you went to that party after all?'

Pete raised his eyes lazily to meet hers. 'I couldn't see any reason why not.'

Janice pressed her lips together. 'I thought your father and I made it clear that you weren't to go to any more parties.

Not,' she said, glancing at Keith, 'after what happened at the last one.'

'Look, let's not argue,' said Keith. 'Let's try and keep things . . . pleasant.' He lifted his glass and said, 'I propose a toast to Pete. Congratulations on finishing your exams.'

Janice put the glass to her lips and glanced sourly at Pete. The starters came – watercress soup for Janice and Keith, barbecued chicken wings for Pete. They ate in silence for a few minutes and then Janice put her spoon down and laid her napkin on the table. 'Have you seen anything of Laura these last few weeks, Pete?'

Pete pulled meat off a wing with his teeth and said, 'Not much.'

'And have you spoken to her at all?'

He licked the fingers of his right hand. 'No.'

'Don't you think you should?' said Keith, finally stepping up to the mark.

Pete shrugged and shifted in the seat. 'I don't know what to say, do I? I mean, what is there to say?'

'You could say sorry,' said Janice flatly.

'She's expecting your baby, Pete,' said Keith. 'At the very least you should tell her how you feel about that and whether you're willing to support her in any way. Though of course if she decides to have the baby and keep it, you'll be legally bound to pay maintenance until the child is independent.'

Pete slouched even further into the seat, his legs sticking straight out in front, his neck supported by the back of the chair. He folded his arms across his chest. 'But that's ridiculous. How can I support a baby? I don't have any income.'

'You could always get a job,' remarked Janice acidly.

'A summer one, maybe,' said Pete, not noticing, or perhaps choosing to ignore, her sarcasm. He'd never had a job in his life. Another mistake. Money and creature comforts had always come too easily to Pete. It occurred to Janice then that she and Keith had failed him. He was so ill-prepared for independence. But it was an uncomfortable thought – if they had failed as parents, how much of what Pete was could be laid at their door? She knew she was to blame, but it seemed unfair to hold Keith responsible for a child that wasn't even his own.

'But I'm going to be at uni for the next three years,' he protested. 'I won't have any income worth talking about. I'll be surviving at subsistence level.'

Hardly, thought Janice. Not with a father as deep-pocketed and generous as Keith.

'There are other ways of providing support besides money,' said Keith.

'Like what?'

'Taking your responsibilities seriously. Being a proper father to the child in the long term, emotionally as well as financially. And once you graduate and start working you'll have a good job and you'll be able to afford maintenance then.'

Pete stared at Keith, horrified.

'For up to nineteen years.'

'Nineteen years! But I didn't ask to be a father. And I don't want to be one.'

'At least he's honest,' observed Janice drily, and she couldn't help but take some pleasure in his discomfort. She took a swig of wine. 'Though it's a pity you didn't think of that *before* you got Laura pregnant, Pete.'

He glared at her from under his pale eyebrows and she thought back to the sacrifices she had made to raise him. The education she might have had – and still mourned to this day. 'And while you're busy feeling sorry for yourself, have you given any thought to the effect this'll have on Laura's life? If she has the baby, she'll probably never get to uni. Or if she does, she'll have to take a year out and it'll be a real struggle for her. In fact, without the support of her family, it'll be absolutely impossible. And is it fair that Patsy and Martin should . . .'

'Okay,' said Keith, cutting her off.

She swallowed the anger – rage not only at the injustice for Laura but for her own lost dreams, her sacrificed ambition.

Pete raised his eyebrows, gave a small shrug. 'She shouldn't have it then. She should have an abortion.'

Janice counted to ten. Before she'd got that far, Keith said glumly, 'That's what I thought. But it's not your – or my – choice to make. It's entirely up to Laura. But it's only fair to let her know where you stand, Pete. You can't just ignore her and pretend it never happened. You did sleep with the girl.'

'I didn't *sleep* with her. That makes it sounds like it was more than it was. It was just a quick shag.'

'Pete!' cried Janice, so loudly people turned to look.

Keith face went red. 'Don't talk like that in front of your mother. And don't talk about Laura like that. It's disrespectful.'

'Why should I respect her?'

'Because she's carrying your child. And you've known the girl all your life. Doesn't that count for something?'

Pete shrugged.

Keith shook his head. 'You just don't get it, do you? This isn't just about you, Pete. You've potentially ruined Laura's life and you've destroyed the relationship between us and the Devlins. They were among our closest friends. And now they won't even talk to us. Your mother rang Patsy the other night and she put the phone down on her. Can you imagine how hurtful that is?'

Pete scowled. 'I'm sorry about that. But it's not like I did it intentionally. As I told you before, things just got a little . . . out of hand.'

'You're telling me,' said Keith grimly. He took a long drink of water, and stared out of the window.

'Everyone finished here?' said the waiter. Janice nodded at the bowl of congealing green soup and Pete pushed his plate, half of the chicken wings untouched, into the middle of the table. The waiter cleared away the unfinished food without a word, laid fresh cutlery on the table and disappeared quickly. No wonder. You could've cut the atmosphere with a knife.

Pete's mobile bleeped. He pulled it out of the back pocket of his jeans, read a message and started typing a reply. 'Will you put that thing away?' said Keith, uncharacteristically testy.

Pete glanced up at him with a surprised look on his face but did not comply straight away. He pressed a few more buttons, watched the screen for a few seconds, then slipped the phone back in his pocket. He fidgeted for a few moments and then picked up a clean fork and pressed the prongs into the back of his hand. He removed it and examined the row of regimented red marks imprinted on his pale skin. He laid the fork on the table. 'Alright. I'll talk to Laura.'

'Good,' said Keith, bringing his gaze back to Pete and brightening up. 'That's a step in the right direction, isn't it, Janice?'

Janice, not so readily mollified as Keith, replied, 'What are you going to say to her?'

'Dunno yet. I'll have to give it some thought.'

'Good lad,' said Keith, and he actually smiled. 'I knew you'd do the right thing.'

Pete gave him a sideways glance, the tiniest hint of a sneer on his upper lip. Pete might have fooled his father but he hadn't fooled Janice. She would reserve judgment until she saw what he did next. And try, perhaps, to give him the benefit of the doubt.

'Look, can we talk about something else?' said Pete. 'I thought we were here to celebrate the end of my exams.'

Keith let out a long sigh, sounding relieved that, having tackled the subject of Laura, he could now put that particular unpleasantness behind him. 'We are here to celebrate, son.' He looked at Janice. 'What am I thinking of? This is no way to have a celebration. Waiter! Can we have some champagne over here?'

In the car on the way home, with Pete in the back seat of the Range Rover, and Keith driving, Janice's head began to throb. She hadn't wanted the champagne; she'd forced it down to please Keith. Now, combined with a glass of wine, and the strain of being civil when all she wanted to do was slap Pete, she felt a bad headache coming on. She pressed the heel of her hand against her forehead. She shouldn't have had anything to drink. She should have kept a clear head. She'd thought a few drops of alcohol would help her relax and cope better with what was about to come. But it had only made things worse.

Her heart pounded against her chest and a rising panic constricted her throat and made it hard to breathe. The headache made it hard to think. She must keep calm. And she must be careful. She mustn't say more than she had planned, more than was safe. She must stick to her story and hold fast in the face of whatever Pete might throw at her. She would let Keith tell him the bare facts but, in the end, Pete would look to her. His history came down to her – what she knew and what she was willing to tell.

She rummaged in her handbag, found two ancient-looking paracetamol and popped them in her mouth. With nothing else to hand, and desperate for relief from the pounding inside her head, she washed them down with the stale dregs of a water bottle lodged in a recess in the passenger door.

'Are you feeling alright?' said Keith

'Just a sore head. Must've been the champagne. Once these tablets kick in, I'll be okay.'

Of course, she could be wrong. Pete might not be interested in his real father. He might not want to know. He might not press her for answers. There was always that slim chance. She grabbed onto this hope, wrapped it like a bandage round her frazzled nerves.

As soon as they stepped through the front door, Pete said, 'I think I'll pop over to Al's.'

Keith looked at Janice, his usually affable face rigid with fear. She suddenly realised how much it was costing him to do this thing. 'We'd rather you didn't,' he said. 'Your mum and I want to have a talk with you.'

Pete let out a loud sigh and slapped a fist into the palm of his hand. 'Tell me this isn't about Laura. Again!'

Keith glanced at Janice and gave her a brave smile. 'No. It's not about Laura,' he said quite evenly. 'It's about something else entirely.'

Pete softened. 'Oh.' A short pause. 'What?'

Neither of them answered him and he fell silent, sensing at last that something was up.

'Come into the kitchen. Let's talk in there.' Keith led the way and Pete followed, with Janice in the rear. Keith had forgotten to take his jacket off.

'Can't this wait?' said Pete, casting an uneasy glance at his mother. 'I want to go out now.'

'No, I'm afraid it can't wait,' said Keith firmly and he looked at Janice. 'Not any longer.' But his decisive words could not hide his anxiety. He fidgeted with something inside his jacket pocket, then took his hand out and patted the pocket softly. His left cheek twitched involuntarily. He had never seemed old before, but he did tonight.

They all sat down round the table. Keith took up his usual position at the head of the weathered oak table and Janice sat down across from Pete. She wished now that Keith had chosen the drawing room. He probably thought this a less intimidating environment but Janice found it too uncomfortable sitting there staring at each other across the empty table. In view of what he was about to hear, she wished for greater distance between herself and Pete.

'Well?' he demanded, clearly irritated.

Janice took a deep breath, counted to three, let it out again. Her headache had diminished to a dull, intermittent twinge.

Keith cleared his throat, gave Pete a tentative smile and mirrored him, resting his own forearms on the table. He clasped his hands together loosely and looked at Janice, then back at Pete.

'You know that your mother and I love you dearly,' he began.

Pete turned his head slightly away from Keith and looked at him out of the corners of his eyes. He frowned, his expression guarded. He wasn't used to hearing either of his parents talk openly about their feelings for him. Janice imagined that he found it embarrassing.

'And we would never do anything to hurt you.' Keith paused and looked at Janice for support. She tried to turn the corners of her lips into a smile, but her features were frozen.

'Sometimes we do things that aren't right but we do them with the best of intentions. I want you to know that your mother and I have always done what we thought was best for you. With your happiness and welfare uppermost in our minds.'

'What are you talking about, Dad? Are you getting divorced?'

'No, of course not! There's something that your mum and I should have told you a long time ago. But the time never seemed right and the truth is, as time went on maybe we were a little afraid to tell you.' Keith paused, ran his hand over his lips. There were beads of sweat on his upper lip.

'In some ways it's a momentous thing but in others, it doesn't matter at all. It doesn't change anything. Not for us. Not for me.'

Pete's frown had deepened. He tapped the table with his nails. *Rat-a-tat-tat. Rat-a-tat-tat.* The sound bore into Janice's skull like a drill. Pete never took his eyes off Keith.

'But you're eighteen now and soon you'll be leaving home. And it's only right that you should know the truth.'

Janice could not bear the suspense. She wished, suddenly, that Keith would say it – just say the thing she had dreaded all these years from the moment Pete opened his mouth and called Keith 'Dad'.

'Please, Keith,' she whispered. 'Just tell him.'

'Yes, tell me,' said Pete, with a quick, sharp glance at Janice. 'You're freaking me out, Dad.'

Keith faltered and bent his head. And then after some long moments had passed he raised his eyes to Pete, held his gaze firm and true and said, 'I am not your biological father, son.'

'But of course you are,' said Pete quickly, a reflex response and he gave a nervous laugh.

Keith shook his head sadly. 'No. I'm not. I met your mother when you were two-and-a-half years old. We married six months later. I adopted you the following year.'

Pete opened his mouth to speak but nothing came out. 'But . . . I . . . it can't be,' he said at last and his voice trailed off. He leant back in the chair, his arms hanging redundantly by his sides. He shook his head, and it gathered momentum until he was swinging it vehemently from side to side. 'I don't believe you.'

Keith put his hand in his pocket, pulled out a square of folded paper and laid it on the table in front of Pete. His hands were shaking as he unfolded it and carefully smoothed it flat with the palm of his hand.

'Read it,' he said quietly.

Pete scanned the paper briefly and shook his head. 'What is it?'

'It's your birth certificate. Peter Andrew Moody. Look, there,' persisted Keith, his voice gentle as a caress. He placed his finger on the paper. 'See where it says "father"? Read it, Pete.'

'Unknown. It says unknown.' Pete looked up at Keith and there were tears in his eyes.

'That's right, son,' said Keith, his voice choked with emotion.

Pete put a hand to his face and quickly rubbed his eyes. He sniffed and stiffened. 'Why didn't you tell me?' he asked.

'I don't really know,' said Keith vaguely, protecting Janice. Avoiding the truth that it had been her all along that had not wanted Pete to know. She who had insisted they put off telling him, year after year, until they could do so no longer.

'This doesn't change anything between us, does it, Pete? I wish I was your real father but I've tried to be the best dad I can.'

Pete smiled bravely and Janice wanted to reach out and touch him. To take away some of the pain, some of the shock so evident in his ashen face. But physical intimacy between her and Pete had always felt awkward.

'No, Dad. It doesn't change anything between us,' said Pete and Janice smiled with relief for Keith. Maintaining his relationship with Pete, intact and unscathed, was what mattered most.

The tension in Keith's face dissipated, his entire body relaxed. 'I'm so glad, Pete. I'm so glad you feel that way. It's a privilege being your dad.'

Pete touched the birth certificate, ran his fingertip over the words inscribed there. 'I couldn't have asked for a better dad,' he said, his voice tight with emotion. 'But why choose to tell me now? Why tell me at all?'

'We knew we'd have to tell you one day – when you were an adult. Ultimately you have the right to know. And we knew you'd need your birth certificate to register at university in the autumn.'

'And yet you kept it a secret for so long.' Pete paused, still staring at the paper in front of him. 'What were you afraid of?'

Keith looked at Janice, warily, and ducked his head as if avoiding a low-flying missile. 'I was afraid . . . I was afraid you might not love me once you knew.'

'And you?' said Pete, and he turned his steady gaze on Janice. 'What were you afraid of?'

Janice blinked, her eyelids snapping open and closed like a camera lens. Her chest tightened and her breath came in shallow, silent gasps. 'I . . . I wasn't afraid of anything. Keith is the only father you've ever known. As far as I am concerned he is your father.'

'But that's not what it says on my birth certificate.' His gaze was unflinching. She felt her cheeks grow hot with shame. She looked away.

Slowly, Pete pushed the piece of paper under her nose. She could not look at it.

'It says "father unknown".'

'I know.'

'But I have the right to know, isn't that right, Dad?' Pete turned his head towards Keith but never took his gaze off

Janice. Keith did not respond. 'I have the right to know who my real father is.'

'I can't tell you,' she managed to squeeze out, so quietly that she had to repeat it a second time. She put her hand to her throat. 'I can't tell you.'

Pete regarded her with a sort of detached curiosity. 'Is that because you don't know? Or because you don't want me to know?'

Keith interrupted. 'Look, Pete. This is between you and your mother. I'm not sure I should hear this. Do you want me to leave the room, Janice?'

'No,' snapped Janice and she grabbed his arm. 'I won't be saying anything you can't hear, Keith.'

'Do you not know who my father is?' persisted Pete.

She shook her head.

'Or do you just not want to tell me?'

She shook her head again and he gave a short burst of mirthless laughter. 'It's one or the other, *mother*. It can't be both. You either know who he is, or you don't.'

'It's for your own good, Pete,' she blurted out. 'I'm just trying to . . . to . . . protect you.' She would never tell him. She would die first.

Keith put his hand over her trembling one and squeezed it. But the trembling did not stop.

Pete started to snigger, a heartless, hysterical chuckle that soon became a full-blown laugh.

'Pete,' said Keith at last. 'Will you stop that? What the hell is so funny?'

Pete wiped tears from the corner of his mouth and the laughter ceased immediately. His expression was suddenly poker straight. 'You don't know, do you, Janice? You don't know who my father is.'

Janice slid her hand out from under Keith's. She could

allow Pete to believe this, unsatisfactory as it was, or she could tell him something a little closer to the truth.

'I do know,' she said quietly, lifting her chin up, meeting his gaze. 'It happened at university.'

Pete laid his forearm on the table and leant across. 'Who was it?'

'I . . . I . . .' She was aware of Keith staring at her in surprise. 'It was . . .' She could not say it, not now, not ever. 'I never saw him again. It was . . . just a . . . a one-night stand.'

'Just a one-night stand,' repeated Pete flatly. He sat back and looked at her as though she was something on the sole of his shoe. Pete shook his head, mocking her. 'You can't remember. You old slag!'

'Pete,' bellowed Keith and he rose to his feet, knocking the chair backwards onto the floor. He rolled his shoulders, still strong, and lifted his fists as though ready to strike out at the slightest provocation. Though Janice knew he would never hit Pete. 'How dare you talk to your mother like that! Apologise at once.'

Pete stood up, face to face with Keith, nothing in it between them height-wise. Pete shook his head defiantly, the way he used to do when he was a kid. 'Do you know what? I don't feel inclined to.' He let out a hollow laugh and looked at Janice. 'You two crack me up, do you know that? You've done nothing but bang on and on about poor old Laura and how badly I've behaved. You tried to make me feel like a piece of shit for knocking her up when she was just as much at fault as I was. Ramming your middle-class morals down my throat. But who are you to talk to me of what's right and wrong?'

He snatched the birth certificate up and held it in a tight fist in front of his chest, crumpling the edges of the document. 'You had a bastard,' he said, addressing Janice. 'And you don't even know the name of the father.'

The words bounced off Janice like arrows, each one piercing a little hole in the invisible armour she had constructed over the years, her shield against the world. Each one taking with it a tiny bit of her sense of self. But she held firm, she did not break down. It didn't matter what he said. It didn't matter what he thought. She could live with his hatred. For this was better, so much better than the truth.

He screwed the certificate into a tight ball and fired it at Janice. She flinched when it hit her chest, though she hardly felt it. It bounced off her and fell to the floor. Pete rested his closed fists on the table and he leant in close to Janice's face. 'Don't you ever try to tell me what to do again,' he breathed. He looked so much like his father – he even sounded like him. And he was rotten too, like him, bad to the core.

'Get out!' screamed Keith. 'Get out!' He pointed to the door. But it was too late. Pete had said everything he wanted. Everything he would ever say to her on the subject.

He left the room and it was only then that Janice put her hands over her face and started to sob. She felt Keith's arms around her and heard his whispered words of comfort. But she remained stiff-backed, resisting the urge to collapse against him. She must be strong. She mustn't weaken, not now, not after all these years. The worst was over and she had weathered it. She had done her duty as a mother.

'You do know I don't care, don't you?' said Keith, stroking her hair, his lips close to her ear. 'It doesn't matter to me how Pete came into this world. Or how you lived before I met you. You do understand that, don't you, Janice? It doesn't change anything as far as I am concerned. It doesn't change the way I feel about you at all.'

What a good man he was. He was ready to forgive her anything. But even he might find the truth hard to stomach.

Chapter Nineteen

Two days after her last exam, Laura came into Patsy's bedroom late one night and sat on the edge of the bed. Patsy, who had been lying awake for over an hour, stared at the outline of her daughter in the darkness, fearing what was coming next, and waited.

'I've decided what to do,' she said and Patsy's stomach lurched. 'I've decided to have an abortion.'

Patsy, who realised that she had been waiting for this all along, put her face in the pillow and wept. She cried over the gruesome practicalities of the procedure itself and the emotional damage it would wreak on Laura. She cried because she had allowed herself, fleetingly, to imagine what this grandchild might look, and feel like, in her arms.

'Please don't cry, Mum,' said Laura, stroking her head, her voice crackling with emotion, and immediately Patsy felt ashamed.

She should be the one supporting Laura, not the other way round. Quickly she sniffed back the tears and sat up in bed. They were alone in the room – Martin was in the study trawling the web for jobs. The room was in darkness save for the shaft of yellow light seeping through the half-closed door from the landing. It cast a golden halo round Laura's head.

'I'm sorry, Laura. It's not helping, is it? Me, bawling my eyes out.'

'I cry too, Mum, every night.'

Patsy felt like someone had stabbed her chest. 'Oh, darling.'

'I'm afraid.'

'You don't have to do this, Laura.'

There was a long silence. Patsy could not tell if Laura was crying, or not. Perhaps that was how Laura wanted it to be. When she spoke her voice was surprisingly steady. 'I always thought I'd have children one day, Mum. But not like this. I'm not ready to be a mother. And I want my children to have a dad who loves them.'

'Are you sure, Laura?'

'Yes.'

Patsy took her daughter's hands, soft and smooth, in her own. 'Are you absolutely sure?'

'Yes.'

'The other option is to . . . to put . . .' She paused, steeled herself. 'To put the baby up for adoption.' She had never said the word baby out loud. Doing so now, hearing the word come out of her own mouth, brought fresh tears to her eyes. She swallowed and fought them back with all her might.

Laura made a sound, a low whimper like an animal in pain. 'I couldn't do that, not in a million years. I couldn't have a baby and then give it away.'

'No,' said Patsy and she squeezed Laura's hand. She hated the idea of abortion and had at one time – in her youth and before she knew any better – been opposed to it. And there were too many abortions; it was used too freely by ignorant women as a form of contraception.

But experience had taught her that life was never as black and white as the moralists would like it to be. There were situations, and Laura's was one of them, when bringing a child into the world was just not the right thing to do – for the mother or the child.

'Mum?'

'What, love?'

'Will you help me?'

Patsy patted the back of Laura's hand, trying to instill confidence in her daughter though she had never felt so out of her depth, or so terrified, before. 'Of course I will, darling. I'll be there for you every step of the way.' She paused, and added, 'But if this is what you want and you are absolutely certain of that . . .'

'I am.'

'Then really, pet, the sooner it's done the better.'

Five days later, Patsy sat at the computer in the study searching for flights to London. So often had she booked flights online, to Edinburgh, London, cities across Europe and further afield – each occasion a happy one, a cause for celebration. Never before had she undertaken the task with such sorrow in her heart.

And in addition to grief, her heart was full of anger and bitterness. Incredibly, Clare had been right about abortion in Northern Ireland. Dr Sullivan had confirmed it when Patsy went to see him the morning after Laura announced her decision.

According to Dr Sullivan attempts were made only last year to bring abortion law in Northern Ireland into line with the rest of the UK, but all the political parties in Ulster resisted it. And the British government backed down because, it was widely believed, pushing it through would threaten the stability of the peace process.

The more Patsy pondered this legal anachronism, the more enraged she became – at the politicians and churchmen and pro-life campaigners, sanctimonious in their certain belief that they knew what was best for women.

The staff at the Marie Stopes Clinic, in Brixton, South London, couldn't have been more helpful. They said they had thousands of women across their door from Northern Ireland every year seeking abortions, fugitives from an archaic province. It made a farce of the whole system. Denying women abortions didn't stop them wanting them, or getting them, they just, like Laura, had to endure an arduous, expensive and shame-faced journey simply to obtain what was, for women in the rest of Britain, a basic human right.

Martin came in and stood behind her. Patsy tried to let go of the rage, tried to concentrate on what she had to do to help Laura.

'She says she doesn't want me to come,' said Martin.

'Did you want to?'

'No. But I would've if she'd wanted me to.' He sounded relieved.

An abortion clinic was the last place for a man, thought Patsy, but she did not voice this for fear of hurting Martin. 'She might feel uncomfortable talking about . . . you know . . . medical, personal things in front of you, Martin.'

He nodded glumly.

Patsy turned her attention back to the computer screen. 'We'll go over for two nights.'

'Is that going to be long enough?' he said.

Patsy swivelled round in the chair and looked up at him, her facial muscles strangely immobile. She imagined her face wiped clean of all expression, mirroring what she felt inside – worn out, exhausted, numb. 'Apparently. So long as she's under twelve weeks they can do a vaginal aspiration and technically she could travel home the same day . . .'

Martin put his hands over his ears. 'Stop! Please! I don't

want to hear it, Patsy. I don't want to think about what's involved. I'm sorry. But I just don't think I can bear it.' He stumbled backwards and sat down on the green sofa-bed. His face was grey, his eyes bloodshot. He'd hardly slept since Laura had shared her decision.

Neither had Patsy. But she would *have* to bear it, and familiarise herself with every gruesome detail so that she could ensure Laura knew exactly what was involved. So that she could support Laura during it and when it was all over. Her shoulders just weren't broad enough to carry all the burdens placed upon them. But somehow she must.

'Martin, can you cover for me in the gallery those two days? I'd rather not shut. I don't want people asking questions. You could just say I'm on a buying trip if anyone asks.'

'I'll do whatever you need me to do. Look, don't worry about the cost of the flights, Patsy. Just book the most convenient. And don't skimp on the accommodation either. I don't want you two staying in some grotty dump somewhere. Or eating rubbish. Eat in decent restaurants.'

Patsy forced her lips into the semblance of a smile. It was a nice sentiment but where did Martin think the money was going to come from? They were living on her earnings from the gallery, Martin's unemployment benefit and, slowly, eating their way through their little pot of savings. She tried not to think of money at such a time, but it was hard when the life they had lived so happily seemed to be crumbling all round them.

It was Laura's eighteenth in less than a fortnight. What kind of a birthday could they give her? What could they do, or say, to take away the misery? And even if they had an endless supply of money, it wasn't in their gift to give Laura what she really wanted – to somehow turn back the clock and undo what had been done. Nothing would change the fact that what should've been one of the highlights of her young life would for ever be utterly overshadowed by this event.

'Patsy, I know how hard this is for you.'

She lowered her eyes. He could still read her mind after all these years. When she looked at him again, he was crying silently, rivulets of tears running down his face and onto his white t-shirt, spotting the fabric with the palest shade of grey.

She knelt on the floor and took both his hands in hers. She pressed her forehead against his and she said, 'Please, Martin. Please don't cry.'

'But I feel like such a failure. I'm Laura's father. I'm supposed to protect her, keep her safe. That's my job, isn't it? And I let this happen.'

'You couldn't have stopped this from happening, Martin. No father could. You can't be there every minute of every day.'

'It doesn't feel like that. I feel like I should've been.' He pressed a fist to his breast.

'You are not to blame. No-one could've protected her from Pete Kirkpatrick, Martin. If you're looking for someone to blame, look to him.' She hadn't thought it possible, but her hate hardened around his name even more.

She released his hands. He ran them over his face, wiping away the tears. 'I'm sorry, Patsy. Sometimes it just gets to me.'

'Me too,' she said bitterly.

A week later and she and Laura were back from London, both traumatised and, in Patsy's case, numbed by the experience.

It had all gone to plan. They'd stayed in a perfectly adequate two-star hotel in Streatham recommended by the staff at Marie Stopes. It was big enough to afford Laura the anonymity she craved, and less than two miles from the clinic. The morning after their arrival, they walked to her appointment in the warm June sunshine, navigating with a map Patsy had printed off the internet – she was too embarrassed to ask the hotel staff for directions, or a taxi to the Marie Stopes clinic. Laura wasn't committing a crime, she ought not to be ashamed, and yet the very fact that they had been forced to leave their home in secrecy to seek out this treatment reinforced those feelings.

Looking back, she needn't have bothered taking such precautions. The hotel staff were efficient and polite but, in spite of her and Laura's conspicuous Northern Irish accents – which seemed so much more exaggerated away from home soil – not one enquired as to the nature of their visit to London. Perhaps they had seen too many dazed, gaunt-eyed mother-and-daughter duos passing through the hotel's door to ask too many questions.

The doctors and nurses at the clinic were utterly professional while managing to convey a sense of compassion that Patsy found particularly hard to bear. But the worst thing was not being allowed to stay with Laura while she underwent the procedure. Patsy walked the streets, aware of nothing around her, only the pounding of her feet on the hard, unforgiving pavement and the hot sun on the back of her neck. Seeing nothing, feeling nothing, her feet burned with pain and still she would not stop, while a doctor in a white coat did what Patsy could not bear to think about.

On the morning of their departure, Patsy and Laura came downstairs with their small black suitcases. Laura went and stood by the window staring out, arms folded, shoulders hunched, putting on a brave face, literally – her full make-up, applied like armour, made a good job of hiding the ghostly pallor beneath. Patsy paid the bill. The receptionist, an ample-bosomed woman about her own age, smiled sadly at Patsy, her big brown eyes so full of kindness that Patsy had to look away. And when the woman pressed the receipt into Patsy's open palm, she caught her wrist with the other brown hand, her bare nails a natural shade of luminous pink like the inside of a shell.

'Your daughter's gonna be alright now, honey,' she said in a lilting, sing-song accent. 'I bin there. You jus' wait and see.'

And now, standing in her kitchen ironing on the Saturday after their return, the memory of that simple act of solidarity brought tears to Patsy's eyes.

Martin had gone to play a round of golf with some pals. In an effort to cheer her sister up – to replace the lacklustre Laura that had come back from London with something resembling her old self – Sarah had organised a day out as an eighteenth-birthday treat. She'd taken Laura up to Belfast to have her hair done at some trendy salon on Bradbury Place. They were going to have lunch somewhere nice and then go shopping. Patsy had been asked along, of course – to their credit, her daughters always willingly included her in their shopping trips – but she had not wanted to go, using the gallery as an excuse. In the end she'd closed at lunchtime and came straight home. She needed some time alone to be miserable, worn out with trying to keep everyone else's spirits up.

It was Laura's birthday on Thursday and Patsy was dreading it, for she knew none of them, least of all Laura, would feel like celebrating. She and Martin had splashed out five hundred quid on a Raymond Weil watch for Laura they could ill afford. If ever Laura deserved a little spoiling, it was now. They wanted her to have something wonderful to remember her eighteenth birthday by, not just misery.

She lifted a damp top out of the laundry basket and her stomach heaved. It was the pretty summer blouse that Laura had worn to the clinic – a blouse made of fine printed cotton with short puffed sleeves and tiny pearl buttons. A garment of extraordinary detail, considering Laura wouldn't have paid more than a few quid for it in H&M or New Look. It was, she knew, one of Laura's favourites.

But it would for ever remind Patsy of the abortion, the pink roses and tiny curling leaves a reproachful reminder of her failure as a mother. She gave the blouse a vigorous shake, then laid it on the ironing board and smoothed out the worst of the creases. Then she placed the iron very carefully on the front of the garment, right across the chest where it would be most visible and impossible to disguise. She pressed down hard.

The doorbell went. Patsy paused, lifted her head and gently, as if letting go of a tiny child's hand, released the iron from her grasp. She walked to the door that led into the hall and glanced back. Then, slowly and deliberately, she made her way to the front door.

It was Janice, her face partially covered by a pair of over-sized sunglasses, making it impossible to read her expression.

Patsy put her hand on her chest, so surprised to see her there that she was, for a moment, quite speechless.

'Hello, Patsy.'

Miriam Thompson was in her garden next door, weeding. She lifted her head, and waved at Patsy. 'I was just saying to Janice that this is the best June I can remember in years.'

Patsy managed a weak smile, mindful of the need to keep up appearances, to protect Laura at all costs. She hissed at Janice through gritted teeth. 'What do you want?'

'I'd like to talk to you.'

But before Patsy could answer Janice cried, 'What's that smell? Why, there's smoke coming out of the kitchen!'

Patsy did not move nor turn around. Janice pushed past her into the hall. Patsy closed the door, blocking out Miriam's inquisitive, prying gaze. She followed Janice slowly into the smoke-filled kitchen just in time to see her lift the smouldering iron from the blouse and set it safely in the metal cradle. Patsy noted with satisfaction the brown scorch mark on the blouse, the exact size and shape of the iron.

Janice ripped the smoking garment off the ironing board, opened the back door and tossed it out into the garden. Then, quickly, she darted about the room, closing the doors into the hall and utility room. She opened all the windows and then came to an abrupt standstill in the middle of the room.

She waved her hand in front of her face and gave a little affected cough. 'You're lucky that didn't catch fire! You could've burnt the house down. That blouse is completely ruined.'

Patsy shrugged, stared at the scorch mark on the ironing board. 'Just like Laura.'

Janice's shoulders sagged. She put a hand on the back of one of the kitchen chairs.

'I saw him the other day, you know,' said Patsy. 'He was in his car with two other boys. Men, I suppose I ought to call them now that they're all eighteen. Jamie Hamill was with him and those other two he hangs around with all the time. What are their names? Al Knox and Ben Curran, isn't it?' she went on without waiting for a reply. 'The windows were rolled down and loud music was blaring out into the street. Pete had his elbow on the sill, holding the wheel with just his fingertips. People stopped to look when they passed.

And they were all singing along to the music, so happy and cocky. Not a care in the world.'

'Patsy, please.'

'I absolutely hate him. I have never hated anyone the way I hate him.'

Janice removed her glasses. The whites of her eyes were crazed with red, and she squinted in the light. 'I didn't come here to talk about Pete. I came here to talk about us.'

'There is no *us*, Janice. Not after what's happened. Pete is as much a part of you as Laura is of me.'

Janice shook her head. 'No. Our friendship exists separately from our children. In spite of them, even.'

Patsy looked out of the window, folded her arms. 'What friendship?' she said bitterly.

'I heard about the abortion,' said Janice softly. 'I'm sorry. It must have been awful.'

Patsy winced. Her head dropped just a little but she raised it again, jutting out her chin ready to take another blow. She gave Janice a withering look. 'I don't want your pity, Janice. In fact I don't want anything from you. And I certainly don't want your friendship.'

'I gathered as much,' said Janice, and she seemed to shrink and become smaller with every word. 'Nights out in No.11 aren't the same without you, Patsy. I miss you.'

Tears sprung to Patsy's eyes but she hardened her resolve. She would not let Janice manipulate her. 'Well, in case you hadn't noticed, I've had a lot more to worry about lately.'

Janice nodded. 'I left three messages on your answer machine.'

'I know. I got them all.'

'You never called back.'

'That's right.'

Janice let out a long, sad sigh. 'We've been friends for

nearly fifteen years, Patsy. We've come through so much together. You're my best friend. You can't throw all that away.'

Patsy glared at her. 'I can't forgive this, Janice.'

'I'm not asking you to. I'm not proud of Pete, you know. But he is an adult. Keith and I aren't his keepers.'

Something inside Patsy snapped. 'You're continuing to support him though, aren't you?'

Janice put a hand to her throat. 'He's our son, Patsy. What do you expect us to do? Throw him out onto the street? Would you do that if it was your child? And what would it achieve anyway?'

Patsy dropped her hands to her sides and balled her fists. 'It might teach him that what he's done is wrong. That there are repercussions, sanctions. That he can't just do what he did and . . . and get away with it. While our Laura has . . . has . . . suffered so much.'

The tears came freely but she did not break down. Rather they coursed unbidden down her face, as solid and implacable as stone.

'Patsy, please,' said Janice, her voice breaking. She crossed the room towards Patsy, extended her arm and touched her on the shoulder.

Patsy shrugged her off, made no attempt to wipe the tears away. She wasn't ashamed of them – they weren't a sign of weakness. Not as far as her resolve concerning the Kirkpatricks was concerned. 'Don't touch me,' she said.

There was a long, tense silence broken at last by Janice. 'Neither of us can be held responsible for the actions of our children, Patsy. And, from what I can gather, both of them are culpable. Yet you seem determined to foist one hundred per cent of the blame on Pete.'

Patsy stiffened. 'It's not so much what happened as how he behaved once he found out.' This was not completely true;

his behaviour had enraged her and Martin but they also held him entirely to blame for the pregnancy in the first place. 'He's treated my daughter like some sort of . . . sort of leper. He hasn't even had the grace to come here and talk to her, approach her in school or phone her. What effort does it take to pick up the phone? He left her to deal with this entirely on her own.'

'But he said he would!' cried Janice. 'Keith and I talked to him about it and he promised he would talk to Laura. That he would face up to his responsibilities.'

Patsy snorted. 'Well, there you go. How come I'm not surprised by that?' She paused for effect and added, 'Well, you needn't trouble yourself with it any more. He doesn't have any responsibilities towards Laura. And thank God for that. I can't imagine a worse fate for any daughter of mine than being associated with your son.'

Janice's face, to Patsy's satisfaction, went red from the neck up.

'And I'm sorry, Janice, but I don't agree with you about parents not being held responsible for the actions of their children. After all, we raised them, didn't we? I still blame you – and Keith – for the way you raised that . . . that monster.'

Janice bit her bottom lip and looked at the floor. She looked thin and insubstantial all of a sudden, like the stuffing had been knocked out of her. Just the way Laura looked in fact when she walked into the clinic waiting room after the abortion.

Patsy swallowed and reminded herself where her loyalties lay – with her family. 'I don't believe our friendship can ever recover.'

Janice looked up and a single tear slid down her powdered face. 'I wish I could say something to change your mind. I wish I could, but . . . but I can't.'

'No, you can't,' said Patsy firmly. 'My daughters are the most precious thing to me. More precious than anything. I would die for them before I'd let anyone harm a single hair on their head. And so would Martin.'

'They are lucky girls, to be loved so much.'

'Yes, they are. But it wasn't enough, was it? Love. It wasn't enough to prevent this. And Martin and I have to face up to the fact that we have failed her.'

'I failed Pete too. That's what I'm trying to tell you, Patsy.' Janice put both hands on the back of the chair and held on so tight her knuckles went white, like her dress.

'Yes, you did.'

'I did the best I could,' said Janice and she bent her head, addressing herself, or so it seemed, as much as Patsy. 'Under the circumstances I did the best I could . . .' Her voice trailed off.

Patsy looked at her unpityingly. 'Well, clearly it wasn't good enough.'

Janice let out a quiet sob, touched her face with her hand and Patsy's tone softened. Not because she relented in any way. She stood firm by what she had said. But she still grieved for the friendship that had been lost.

'Look, Janice. I imagine we will continue to see each other occasionally in company, at parties held by mutual friends, and the like. It's impossible to avoid people altogether in a place like Ballyfergus. I can't speak for Martin, but I won't go out of my way to shun you because I don't want to make other people, particularly Clare and Kirsty, feel uncomfortable.'

Janice raised her head, her teary eyes full of hope. Patsy thought it best to deal any misplaced optimism a quick and decisive blow. 'But as far as any friendship between us goes, we're finished.'

Janice took a few unsteady steps towards the door, clutching her bag to her chest. She leant momentarily against the doorframe and then, collecting herself, walked quickly out of the room.

'Excuse me,' she said and Patsy spun round, shocked, to find Sarah standing in the hall with her car keys in her right hand and two House of Fraser shopping bags in the other. She moved aside to let Janice pass and watched the front door slam shut in amazement. She walked into the kitchen, her face ashen. 'Oh, Mum,' she said and sat down heavily on one of the kitchen chairs, dropping the bags on the floor.

'What are you doing back so soon?' demanded Patsy. How long had Sarah been standing there?

'Laura had a headache. We decided to come home early.'

'I didn't hear you come in.'

'I gathered that.'

'Where's Laura?' said Patsy, suddenly anxious. Was a headache one of the signs to look out for in case of post-operation infection? She didn't think so. But she'd better check, just to be sure.

'In her room, crying. She bolted upstairs as soon as she heard you and Janice arguing.'

Patsy put her hand over her mouth as if she could cram her words back in. She looked up at the ceiling. 'How much did she hear?'

'From the bit where you said Pete Kirkpatrick had treated her like some sort of leper.'

'Oh, my God.'

Sarah gave her mother a blunt look, her brow furrowed crossly. 'Why couldn't you be more discreet, Mum?'

'I never heard you come in, Sarah.'

Sarah shook her head. 'We had a great day. She was laughing and smiling and trying things on in H&M. She was almost like her old self, until the headache came on, that is. And now she's up there bawling her eyes out.' Sarah paused, and they both raised their eyes upwards to gaze at the ceiling and listened. Patsy could hear the muffled sound of weeping from the room above the kitchen. It ripped through her heart.

She slumped in a chair. 'I don't take back anything I said to Janice,' she said sullenly. 'I meant it all.'

Sarah frowned and sniffed. She cocked her head to one side. 'What's that smell?'

'I accidentally burnt something with the iron.'

'You've never burnt anything before.'

'There's a first time for everything, Sarah.'

She regarded her eldest daughter closely. Her hair was tied back severely in a ponytail, and she wore little make-up. She had pulled the sleeve of her cream hoodie right down over her hand and sat like an amputee with the handless arm resting on her thigh.

'You've been so supportive of Laura since this happened,' said Patsy, trying to find some words of encouragement for Sarah, who had been somewhat overlooked recently. 'I'm proud of you.'

Sarah shrugged and ducked, letting the praise slide off her like butter off a hot knife. 'She's my sister.' There was a pause. She put her left thumb in her mouth and chewed at a rag-nail, then took the thumb out and examined it. 'Mum, some of the things you said to Janice, things about Pete Kirkpatrick. They were a bit harsh.'

Patsy shifted in her seat. 'I don't think so. I thought I was . . . entirely fair.'

Sarah nodded, bit her bottom lip and eyeballed her mother. 'Did Laura ever tell you why it happened?'

Patsy's head snapped round so fast the vertebrae in her

neck clicked. '*Why* it happened? I don't know what you mean.'

Sarah took a deep breath. 'She told me that she did it – slept with Pete Kirkpatrick – because Kyle Burke told her at the party that he didn't want to go out with her.'

Patsy looked stunned. If true, it meant that Laura had taken a much more proactive role than she had led her parents to think. 'What the hell are you talking about, Sarah?'

'After Kyle told her that, Laura saw him snogging Amy Ritchie – you know, that girl in her year she hates?'

'Yes,' said Patsy vaguely.

'Well, she decided there and then to get back at him, show him, you know, that she could get another guy. She wanted to make Kyle jealous. And Amy Ritchie fancies Pete, so Laura thought it was the perfect way of getting back at them both.'

'But that's . . . that's so infantile,' gasped Patsy in dismay.

'That's Laura,' said Sarah flatly, without rancour. 'The really sad thing is that she thought it would work. Of course it never made Kyle jealous. He couldn't care less.'

Patsy felt a sickening feeling rise in her stomach. 'Are you sure? How do you know this?'

'Laura told me. She made me promise to keep it a secret. You mustn't say I told you.'

Patsy was incredulous that Laura had kept this information to herself. Information that cast, if not an entirely new light on the evening, then at least a very different one. 'But why didn't she tell us?'

'Isn't it obvious? She saw how furious you were with the Kirkpatricks and she was afraid you'd be angry with her, I guess. And you would've been. You were so quick to point the finger at Pete that I think she thought it easier just to say nothing and let you get on with vilifying him.' She paused, put her fist to her mouth as though stemming the tide of words.

'What?'

'There's something else.'

Patsy had always thought Laura was open and honest with her. She thought she confided in her. She thought she *knew* her daughter. 'What, Sarah?' she said coldly, because she couldn't help but feel that Sarah was almost enjoying this.

'She said she was drunk. Out of her head, in fact.'

'But she said she'd only had a few!'

Sarah sighed. 'I never saw her that night – I was already in bed when she got in. But she told me she threw up in the toilet when she got home. She said she was pissed. She told me all this in confidence, Mum. Promise me you won't say anything to her?'

Patsy said nothing. Her heart ached with disappointment and a sense of betrayal. Laura had lied about that night. Patsy let out a heartfelt sigh.

But she would not say anything, either to Laura or Martin. Because Laura had suffered enough for her foolishness – she had learned her lesson. What was the point of raking over the coals of a past they were all trying very hard to forget? And the knowledge would break Martin's heart. He couldn't bear it.

'I promise. But there's one thing I don't understand, Sarah. Why are you telling me now?' Patsy was annoyed at being burdened suddenly with something she did not want to know. Something that challenged her perception of events. Something that interfered with her righteous anger and blurred the lines between right and wrong.

'Because it isn't right to put all the blame on Pete. And I don't want to see you and Janice fall out over this.'

'We've already fallen out.'

'Well, I don't see why you should. Why should you lose your best friend over something stupid that Laura – and Pete – did?'

Patsy put her head in her hands. 'I think it might be too late for me and Janice.' She thought of the things she had said in her rage. 'Sometimes you can't take things back.'

She looked up and Sarah was regarding her curiously. 'You know,' she said, 'it's kind of ironic that this has happened to Laura.'

'I don't see anything remotely ironic in it,' said Patsy wearily.

'I was the one you worried about. You were always nagging me to go out more, see more of my friends. You more or less told me that I was weird, wanting to spend my spare time at home.'

Patsy sighed. 'I never said that.'

'Not in as many words. But I got the message loud and clear. And all along it was Laura you should've been worrying about, not me.'

Patsy rubbed her temples with the tips of her forefingers. 'Sarah, where are you going with this conversation?'

Sarah smiled crookedly. 'I know that Laura's always been your favourite.'

Patsy's heart missed a beat, then raced the way it did on the very rare occasions when she exercised. 'I never favoured Laura over you,' she said, choosing her words carefully, feeling like she was walking into a mine field. 'I always treated the two of you exactly the same.'

'Materially, yes. But she's the one that makes you light up when she walks into a room, not me. It was never me. And I think that blinded you. You let her get away with far more than me at her age, you were always on at her to go out and enjoy herself. Like she could do no wrong, do whatever she liked. Well, she certainly did that.'

Patsy stared at her eldest daughter, appalled by the resentment in her voice. The cold hand of fear gripped her heart. All these years she had striven to convince herself, as much as the girls, that she loved them equally. And she had completely failed. Had she been so transparent? Was she responsible for creating the sibling rivalry between her daughters that she had so feared?

'You sound as though you hate Laura.'

'I don't. I love Laura. I just think that maybe if you hadn't been so indulgent with her, then maybe this might never have happened.'

It was her fault then. Just as she'd suspected. 'I'm sorry, Sarah. I'm sorry if I made you feel that way.'

Sarah shrugged. 'I don't mean to make you feel bad, Mum. It's just better, I think, if we're all completely honest about these things,' she said sanguinely, impressing Patsy with a maturity well beyond her years. 'At the end of the day, I'm alright. It's Laura that's come out of this the worst.'

And it was true. It was Laura who would carry the scars of this with her for the rest of her life. And so would Patsy.

Chapter Twenty

The summer holidays came and Clare welcomed them with relief. Because it meant that Zoe took Izzy on holiday to Cyprus for the first two weeks of July.

Lucky them, she thought enviously, as she pushed Rachel around the local park in the buggy on a fine warm day. Either Zoe's shops were doing really well or Liam was paying her too much maintenance. But it had been nice these past two weeks not to have to deal with either of them.

After three weeks of refusing to allow Izzy anywhere near Clare or the house, Zoe had relented and things had returned, more or less, to the status quo, apart from the stipulation that Clare wasn't to take Izzy 'anywhere in the car, *ever* again'. She said she was only agreeing for Izzy's sake so she could see her father. But the fact that Zoe's stance had lasted less than a month had more to do, Clare suspected, with the restrictions Izzy being around all the time imposed on Zoe's lifestyle.

Clare had seen Izzy only a few times after that, before she went off on holiday, and she hadn't had much to say to her stepmother. She had reverted to her old self – secretive, reserved and cautious. Aside from injuring Adam, that was Clare's greatest regret. She wondered how much of Izzy's attitude was a survival response in the face of Zoe's renewed hostility towards Clare.

Josh ran erratically along the path beside the buggy in a pair of combat shorts and matching t-shirt, and a floppy sun hat on his head, looking like a cute mini-soldier. The trees in the park were in full, vibrant leaf, the ferns, wild flowers and tall grasses in the wild part of the park were at their zenith. Every now and then Josh would be captivated by something and stop dead in his tracks, mesmerised by a fallen leaf, a stick, a clod of earth. He found two battered pine cones that had been lying in the long grass all winter. He gave one to Rachel, who squealed with delight.

Clare wished she could live in the moment, like the children. But her problems weighed too heavily on her mind.

Liam, Zoe, Izzy, Kirsty. There was so much to be put right, Clare didn't know where to start. And that wasn't even counting the quarrel between Janice and Patsy, not that there was much she could do to solve that dispute. She looked at her babies and thought of what Laura had been through and shivered involuntarily even though the sun was blazing and it was in the twenties.

Clare had met both women recently for coffee, separately of course, and Janice was anything but defensive of Pete. In fact, she was furious with him. It wasn't as if she and Keith were defending what he'd done – but Patsy wasn't swayed. She remained strident in her views. It saddened Clare to think that the four of them might never meet again as friends. She missed their get-togethers terribly. She missed Kirsty most of all. She could still see Janice and Patsy on their own, of course – but it wasn't the same. The spark had gone from all of them, it seemed to Clare.

Just as the spark had gone from her marriage to Liam. She tried to remember exactly when it had happened – round about the time she decided to start painting. Had she been selfish in single-mindedly pursuing her dream? Had she asked too much of Liam to support her ambition, when the children were so young and demanding? Had she put her needs above those of everyone else in the family? The answer was probably yes, at least some of the time. But isn't that what men did all the time? The weekend game of golf, for example, was taken as a God-given right. When had Liam ever expressed guilt about spending upwards of three to four hours on the golf course, while she kept the children occupied almost every weekend?

She sighed and tried to put him and everyone else out of her mind, just for now. Just so that she could have one afternoon of peace and tranquillity without being eaten up inside by anxiety.

Eventually, they came over the brow of the gentle hill and the play-park came into view. It had been refurbished the previous year with new equipment, the chief attraction being a 'flying fox' – a wire attached between two poles down which shrieking children, clenching a small button-shaped seat between their legs, launched themselves. There was a crowd of kids around it now, all much older than Josh.

Josh cried, 'Swings!' and immediately set off at a canter across the grass. Rachel screamed to be released from the buggy and Clare bent down and undid the safety restraint. The toddler spilled out and followed her brother, stumbling across the grass in a remarkably effective manner. Soon she was many yards ahead of Clare, who found herself obliged to run across the grass to keep up.

It was then, jogging breathlessly, the wheels of the buggy clogging up with the damp, recently cut grass, that Clare saw Kirsty. She was sitting on one of the benches facing the play-park, wearing a pink t-shirt, white jeans and a black baseball cap on her head. An opened book lay in the palms of both hands. Clare stopped, and put her hand to her heart. She hadn't seen or spoken to Kirsty since the accident. She'd sent a letter of heartfelt apology but received no reply. Should she approach her? Should she risk being shunned?

Kirsty lifted her head, looked in Clare's direction, then quickly dipped her head. She had seen her, Clare was sure of it. Kirsty closed the book and stood up. Swiftly she collected garments off the bench and put them, along with the book, in a rucksack by her feet. She walked away from Clare, towards the Coast Road exit, hoisting the bag over her shoulder and calling to the boys as she went.

After a few moments' delay, David and Adam emerged from the gaggle of children swarming over the play equipment. They ran over to the bench, picked up bikes that were lying on the grass and mounted them. Adam's was bright red – the one Clare had had delivered to Kirsty's house three days after the accident. She was pleased to see that the gift had been accepted, that Kirsty had allowed her to make some reparation at least. The boys sped after their mother, standing on the pedals and zigzagging haphazardly across the grass. Kirsty did not once look back.

Abandoning the buggy by the edge of the barked area, Clare reached the play-park in time to scoop Rachel out of the path of a well-built twelve year old whizzing down the flying fox. She deposited her and Josh on the roundabout and gave it a brutal shove. The roundabout spun round and round and the children waved at her, their little faces illuminated with pleasure.

She stood with a smile on her face, the muscles on her neck taut with anger. She was fed up being ostracised. How long must she be treated like a pariah? It was ridiculous. The punishment far outweighed the crime. She knew she had done wrong, she had tried to make amends.

But it would not be enough in a small town like Ballyfergus.

Every detail was pored over, repeated a hundred times, exaggerated a hundred more and each telling glazed with a liberal dose of indignant outrage. Clare wished some other, more juicy piece of news would hurry up and eclipse her embarrassing tale. Until then she was the hottest topic for local gossips.

No-one had the nerve to say anything to her face, of course. But she knew people were talking about her. At the last playgroup before the holidays, groups of women clammed up and scattered like chickens when she approached, as if they'd suddenly found a fox in their midst. And she knew for a fact that her reading group, an informal affair of like-minded women, had held a meeting without telling her. And now Kirsty had walked off.

Only Janice and Patsy had shown her any compassion. Liam had shown her little. She ought to be able to count on his support no matter what. If the roles were reversed and he had done something stupid she would be there for him, standing up for him, fighting his corner. Liam's apparent unwillingness to do this for her hurt most of all. And to Clare this said more about the sorry state of their marriage than anything else.

She watched Kirsty's retreating figure, now just a speck-sized dolly mixture on the other side of the park, and something inside her snapped. Enough was enough.

How many of them could put their hand on their heart and swear that they had never, in their entire lives, taken a drink before driving a car? Probably only a handful would pass that test. She had to keep reminding herself that she had been within the limit because, the way everyone was getting on, you'd think she spent her entire life behind the wheel of a car tanked up on bottles of gin and running down hapless cyclists.

The irony was that it wasn't the drink, primarily, that had made her lose control of the car. It was Izzy. Demanding to know why her dad was late again and why she had to go out in the car to collect Rachel and Josh. Why couldn't she stay in the house? Why was Clare treating her like a baby? Who did she think she was? On and on she went, until Clare's knuckles, clutching the wheel, were white with tension and her head, a pressure cooker of exhaustion and misery, felt like it would burst.

Of course, at twelve years old, Izzy was perfectly capable of being left alone in the house for a while, but there was no way Clare was allowing that. Zoe would find some way to turn it against her – she would no doubt accuse her of neglect and irresponsibility. In the final analysis (and Clare had scrutinised the events of that day ad nauseam) a combination of factors had led to the accident. Drink was just one of them.

She remembered looking over her shoulder at Izzy, screaming 'Shut up! You self-centred little cow,' and the next thing she knew she was sitting in the car face to face with a lamp post. It was the first and only time she had ever used such language to Izzy. She was deeply ashamed. And that was why she hadn't told Liam the entire truth about what had happened that day. And Izzy hadn't either. In the end both of them were to blame.

Liam had never offered an explanation as to why he was late home the night of the accident and Clare couldn't help but imagine him cosying up to Gillian over an after-work drink. The thought that this might have been the cause of his lateness enraged Clare. If he had been on time, none of it would even have happened.

'Do it again!' shrieked Rachel, as the roundabout wound down slowly to a gentle halt.

'No! I want off,' cried Josh, holding up his arms. 'I want to go on the swings.'

‘Me too! Me too!’ hollered Rachel, her voice like a foghorn.

The children scrambled off the roundabout and ran over to the swings. Clare trailed in their wake, hoisted them into the baby seats and set them off swinging. It was hard work, keeping both of them in motion at the same time.

‘Faster!’ cried Rachel.

‘Higher!’ shouted Josh.

She pushed harder, higher, sweat forming on her upper lip.

Liam had not mentioned Gillian since the accident and Clare was too scared to ask him about her – too afraid to find out that he was still seeing her, or worse, that their ‘friendship’ had developed into something more intimate. Since the night of the accident Liam had been even more remote, disconnected from her. He was never rude or unkind and he helped around the house as much, or as little (depending on how you looked at it), as he had always done.

He treated her with a formal kind of respect, which felt like disdain. He was quite often home from work late – he said he was very busy at the office. Nights, he either played golf, worked at the dining table in the lounge ’til late or watched TV. He blamed her for the accident, that much was clear, and for the renewed difficulties between him and Zoe. Clare, for her part, could not forgive him over Gillian. She was deeply upset that Liam had chosen to make a confidante of another woman. But her overriding feeling when she thought of Liam was one of disappointment, on many fronts.

And so they reached a frosty truce, which involved living pretty much separate lives. After the children had gone to bed at night, and the many household chores were done in preparation for the next day, Clare would retire to her room with a book. She was always asleep before he came to bed.

Well, it couldn’t go on. She’d had enough of living in an

emotional vacuum. It was worse than arguing all the time. At least she felt alive then. If this was the best the marriage could offer both of them, perhaps it was time to get out. And it was certainly time to ask Liam the question she had avoided for the last six weeks: what did he really want? If the answer was the end of their marriage she had better get ready to face that too.

'More! More!' cried the kids and she realised she had stopped pushing and was standing with her hands on her hips, tears streaming down her face. She brushed the tears away and put her shoulder to the wheel, lunging and pushing and heaving until the two little bodies were flying through the air screaming with delight, and she was soaked with sweat.

Clare was in no hurry to leave. Izzy was coming to stay tonight, her first visit since her return from holiday, and Clare was dreading it. But here, in the park, if she tried very hard, she could pretend there was no Izzy and no Zoe and her life with Liam was perfect.

Eventually, though, the children started to complain about being hungry. She gave them a mottled banana each and set off for home with a heavy heart. It was time to face up to reality.

When she arrived at the house, Liam and Zoe's cars were parked in the drive and the front door was open. Rachel had fallen asleep in the buggy and so Clare left it parked outside at the bottom of the steps leading up to the front door. Josh climbed the steps on tired legs and stumbled through the door. He ran to Liam and wrapped his arms around his right leg. Zoe, dressed in white linen, with a tan the colour of an old leather bag, completely ignored Josh as usual. Liam looked up and nodded at Clare as she stepped into the hall. She gave him a weak smile. When she heard Zoe's voice her stomach tightened with anxiety.

'. . . and don't forget she starts hockey summer school tomorrow at ten,' Zoe was saying. 'Her kit's in that bag. She'll need a lift over there in the morning.'

Izzy was standing between her parents, with her thin arms folded, two bags at her feet, a bored expression on her face. She wore a tartan mini-skirt and a t-shirt and she was brown all over like a sun-kissed Californian teenager from an American TV show.

'Hello, Josh,' said Izzy, kneeling down so she was at the boy's level. 'Where have you been?'

'At the park. And I'm tired.' He let out a sad little sigh that made Izzy giggle.

Liam ruffled Josh's hair. 'Good to see you, pal.' Then he said to Zoe, 'You know I won't be able to take her, Zoe. I have to go to work.'

'Hello, Izzy,' said Clare quietly, feeling sorry for her, caught yet again in the middle of one of her parents' squabbles. Izzy raised her face to Clare, gave her a tentative smile and rolled her eyes.

Zoe let air out through her nose noisily. 'Well, you can't expect me to do it, Liam. I have to be over at the shop in Ballymena for nine thirty. I can't be in two places at once.'

'Neither can I, Zoe.'

Izzy stood up and they both looked at her as though she could somehow offer a solution to the dilemma. And, surprising them all, she did.

'Why can't Clare take me?' she asked, with a little shrug of her slender shoulders.

There was a long silence. Clare wished the ground would open up and swallow her whole. Liam looked at the floor.

'You know you're not allowed in the car with Clare,' said Zoe, glaring at her daughter.

'Remind me why that is again, Mum?'

Zoe simmered. 'You *know* why. You could've been killed.'

'Anyone can make a mistake. Clare's a good driver.'

Clare gasped in astonishment. Was Izzy actually standing up for her? She looked at Liam and he too was staring open-mouthed at Izzy. Even Josh, somehow, grasped the enormity of the moment. He slumped to the floor and sat there on his bottom, staring up at Izzy with something approaching awe on his face. Either that or he was just plain exhausted.

Zoe tucked her chin in and took a hard look at her daughter. She seemed, for once, lost for words.

'Don't you think it's time you and Dad,' said Izzy, with a sharp glance at Liam, 'gave Clare a break? She said she was sorry. What more do you want?'

Liam, taken by surprise, took a step back suddenly and pushed out his chest.

Zoe, flush-faced, brandished her mobile. Ignoring Izzy and glaring at Liam, she said, 'I suppose I'll just have to get on the phone and ring round some of the other mothers – see if one of them can take her. Though why you can't do that beats me. Why does it always have to be me who sorts these things out?'

Clare thought she had a point. Zoe stabbed buttons on the phone, her bracelets clanging like chimes, and held it to her ear.

'You two are such hypocrites,' said Izzy, diving back into the conversation, clearly determined to have her say.

'Izzy!' exclaimed Liam.

'What did you say?' Zoe removed the phone from her ear.

'I said you two are such hypocrites. I've seen you get in the car after a drink, Mum. On lots of occasions. And you spent the entire time in Cyprus with a drink in your hand. All you wanted to do was lie in the sun and sleep and talk to Alex. You wouldn't play tennis or go swimming or do *anything* with me. I've never been so bored in my life.'

Zoe might have blushed but her face was too deeply tanned to tell. At any rate her face fell and, for a millisecond, Clare almost felt sorry for her. Then she bit her lip to stop herself from smiling.

'Izzy, that simply isn't true,' protested Zoe.

Izzy ignored her mother. 'And you're no better, Dad. Clare makes one little mistake and you won't let her forget it. What about all the mistakes you've made? All the times you've let me down? And Clare.'

Liam looked at Izzy in astonishment and said, 'I really don't think you should be talking to me like this.'

Sensing she had the upper hand, Izzy ploughed on. 'You made Clare cry because you've been seeing some woman from work. And you've been so mean to her lately. If anything made her crash the car, I think it was that.'

Clare felt her face go red. Zoe, glancing over at her, brightened at this news and gave Clare a self-satisfied look that managed to convey, simultaneously, both pity and triumph.

Liam bristled. 'That is not true, Izzy. I am not seeing anyone.'

'Well, what about this Gillian? I heard you on the phone to her.'

'She's . . . she's just a friend, a colleague from work. Nothing more.'

'Strange way to talk to your friends, if you ask me.'

Liam opened his mouth to speak, then thought better of it. Rachel started to grizzle and Zoe shoved her phone in the pocket of her white linen jacket. 'You're in charge tomorrow, Liam, not me,' she snapped. 'You can sort out a lift for her.'

'You needn't bother, Dad. Clare'll take me. Won't you, Clare?'

Clare nodded dumbly and held her breath. Having found

the most unlikely ally, she had no idea what would happen next. She realised, in that instant, that everything was at stake. It was a defining moment of her life. Without exaggeration, her future depended on it. If Liam sided with Zoe then their marriage was, in her opinion, over. If, however, he sided with his daughter, there was hope. It was his last chance to prove where his loyalties lay.

The moment seemed to last for ever. Rachel's whining grew louder but no-one moved. Clare was pinned to the spot. Dust motes danced in the sun streaming through the front door. The tropical smell of after-sun lotion filled the air, and sweat oiled her palms as she clenched her fists, waiting. Everything rode on what Liam said next.

'That's perfectly okay with me,' he said, staring coldly at Zoe, and Clare breathed again. Tears pricked her eyes and she blinked to hold them back.

'Looks like it's three against one, Mum,' said Izzy matter-of-factly, folding her arms again. 'So you're outvoted.'

Zoe took a deep breath and said, 'What you can and cannot do, Izzy, is not decided by popular vote, and especially not one that includes people who are no relation to you.' She glanced briefly at Clare when she said this.

'Everyone here is related to me,' said Izzy stubbornly and Clare wondered how one so young could keep her nerve and her composure. Her self-possession was unnerving. Clare had always thought her a clever girl but she was far more mature than she had ever realised.

Liam cleared his throat. 'Perhaps Izzy has a point, Zoe. I think you forget that Clare wasn't convicted of any crime. It was just an accident. Caused by more than one factor, perhaps, but an accident nonetheless.'

He looked at Clare and gave her a small, awkward smile. It wasn't much but it was a start. Clare's heart soared.

Zoe looked at Liam, then Izzy and finally back at Clare. Her lips turned up in a sneer and she said to Clare, 'If you so much as hurt a hair on her head, you'll . . . you'll have me to answer to. You're nothing but a drunk and a . . .'

'That's enough!' said Liam. 'I won't have you talking to my wife like that, not in my home.'

He stepped forwards and put an arm round Clare's shoulder. It felt heavy and a little awkward but it felt good too. She put her hand up, found his and held it.

Zoe stood there trembling with rage as the realisation dawned on her that she was defeated. Her domination had come to an end. She glared at Liam. 'If you let Izzy ride with her, you'll have to take full responsibility for anything that might happen. I wash my hands of it.'

Rachel let out a loud wail.

'I'll get her,' said Izzy and she bolted past her mother and out the front door. A few seconds later, Rachel's cries ceased.

'I think that's something we can live with, isn't it, Clare?' said Liam, and she looked at him in astonishment.

Zoe turned and stomped out of the door, her wooden wedges thwacking each step on the way down. They listened to the sound of her car engine rev, a door slammed, tyres screeched on the tarmac and then she was gone. Josh, hearing Rachel's giggles from outside, got up and wandered outside.

'Are you alright?' asked Liam, removing his arm from Clare's shoulder.

Clare turned to look at him. Their faces were inches apart. She was shaking but filled with a wondrous sense of release. Zoe no longer had a hold over her any more. She no longer had the power to make her life a misery. 'I think so. And you?'

Liam filled his cheeks and let out a puff of air. He looked tired. 'A bit shocked, that's all. The way Izzy stood up to Zoe was amazing.'

'Yes, it was. And so were you.'

He put out a tentative hand and touched her cheek. 'I'm sorry if I made you cry, Clare. I didn't realise I'd hurt you so much.'

She lowered her eyes, looked at the buttons on his shirt. She took a deep breath. 'Liam?'

'Yes?'

'Are you still, you know, seeing Gillian?'

'I never was.'

'You know what I mean.' She raised her eyes and looked into his. They were intense, fiery.

'I haven't spoken to her, on a personal level I mean, since the accident.' He paused, swallowed and added, 'The accident gave me quite a shock. It made me realise how precious life is and how easily I could've lost you. I realised that the only woman I love is you, Clare.'

'You didn't act like it, Liam. You were horrible to me that day,' said Clare, the memory bringing forth a wave of self-pity.

Liam hung his head. 'I was angry. I was angry with you for putting Izzy and yourself in danger like that and for hurting Adam.'

Clare let out a little sob. 'I thought you were going to leave me. I thought you loved Gillian.'

Liam put his hands on her shoulders and looked into her eyes. 'I don't want Gillian. All I wanted from her was what I couldn't get from you, Clare. Your time and attention. You were so wrapped up with the exhibition you hardly noticed if I was there or not. No, that's not fair. You did notice but I felt you saw me only in terms of a carer for the children. Every time I came in, you cleared off to go and paint. I was just lonely. I'm sorry. Do I sound pathetic?'

She nodded. 'A little bit. But I understand too.'

It would be easy to harbour resentment towards Liam. The recriminations – which she had catalogued and archived relentlessly over the past weeks – sprung to her lips like incantations. His support for her painting had been less than lukewarm. If only he'd worked with her, instead of fighting against her, how much easier that period would have been on everyone. He'd been prepared to parachute out of his marriage at the first sign of trouble and he had not accepted any blame for driving her to distraction and drink that had, ultimately, led to the accident. And until tonight, he had never stood up in her defence against Zoe. She could go on and on.

Now was not the time – she would not jeopardise this fragile peace. She must let these things go, for now at least. She would have to face up to the fact that they might never see eye-to-eye on these issues. What mattered now, most of all, was whether Liam had the desire to work through their problems and save the relationship.

She took a deep breath. 'Liam, do you think we can make our marriage work again?'

'I'd like to try.'

'Me too.'

He gave her a winsome smile and shook his head. 'You're a very complicated woman, Clare. Do you know that?'

She smiled uncertainly, not sure if this was a compliment or a criticism.

'It makes you very hard to live with,' he went on. She opened her mouth to retort but he silenced her with, 'But it also makes you absolutely irresistible.'

She smiled, flattered, but only briefly. Her heart was full of anxiety. 'You do realise that we're going to have to work at it? Both of us.'

'Sure,' said Liam, his voice smooth like melted chocolate.

He put his arms out to pull her to him. It would be so easy to fall into them and make up, and never address what had got them to this impasse. And that would be a mistake, for unless the fundamental issues were addressed, nothing would change in the long term.

She placed the flat of her hand on his chest. 'I'm serious, Liam. There's no point in picking up where we left off without addressing the things that caused our problems in the first place.'

He nodded. 'I'm sure we can talk things through. Things will soon be back to the way they were.'

'I don't want to go back to the way they were,' she blurted out. 'I want it to be . . . better. I'd like for us to go to marriage counselling. Together.'

'Counselling?' he echoed. 'Do you really think that's necessary?'

'I do. There's lots of stuff we need to sort out.'

Liam frowned. 'I thought that's what we're doing?'

'We are. But this is just the start. We need to decide how we're going to change things going forward.'

'Like what?'

'Like how we run two careers without family life, and our relationship, suffering. We need to manage Zoe better in the future so that she doesn't come between us. And stop Izzy manipulating both of us.' Liam raised his eyebrows.

'She does, you know,' persisted Clare, afraid that this might happen. Afraid that he would not take her concerns seriously. 'We both have to acknowledge where we've gone . . .'

'Wow!' said Liam and he put up a hand. 'Okay, I get the picture.'

Clare put a hand on her heart – it pounded against her chest. 'So will you go to counselling?'

He stared at her for some moments. 'Alright. If you want me to.'

'I don't want you to do it just to please me. I want *you* to want to.'

Liam suppressed a smile. 'Okay,' he said slowly and deliberately. 'I want to go to counselling, Clare. Happy?' He ducked his head and looked at her from under raised eyebrows.

She nodded and smiled. Her heartbeat slowed. There was real hope for them after all.

'Now,' he said, holding out his arms. 'Can I please have that hug?'

'There's nothing I would like more,' she said. And though her eyes filled with tears, she was smiling and her heart was full of gladness.

Later, when Liam was putting the children to bed and Izzy was downstairs watching a rerun of *Hollyoaks*, Clare sat down beside her on the sofa. 'Mind if I talk to you a moment?' she said after they had sat in silence for a few moments.

'Sure,' said Izzy, without taking her eyes off the TV.

'Do you mind turning the volume down just for a minute?'

Izzy found the control and muted the sound. She waited for Clare to speak, twisting a lock of sun-bleached hair round the forefinger of her right hand. She glanced at Clare then looked back at the screen. 'What?' she said.

'Izzy, can I ask you what happened earlier?'

'What d'ya mean?'

'Why did you stand up for me and say all those things to your mum and dad?'

Izzy shrugged and looked embarrassed. 'I just told it like it was.'

Clare nodded and said nothing. Izzy shifted in the seat and pulled her legs up underneath her bottom. They both stared at the screen in silence. It was hard to believe that this reticent creature had spoken so eloquently in Clare's defence only hours before. Clare cleared her throat. 'I just wanted to say that I'm sorry for the way I spoke to you in the car on the day of the accident.'

Izzy shrugged her shoulders. 'That's okay.' She slipped a sly glance at Clare, and an embarrassed smile briefly crossed her lips. 'I kind of asked for it, didn't I?'

'Well, I still shouldn't have said it.'

'That's okay.' There was a long silence. Clare inched forwards on the sofa and was just about to stand up when Izzy spoke again. 'Did you and Dad make up, then?'

Clare sat back down again. 'Well, we've started. We're going to go for marriage counselling to help us . . . get things back on track. Sometimes adults need help to sort out their problems.'

Izzy returned her gaze to the screen. 'Good.'

Had that been her objective all along? To get her and Liam back together? Was she trying to make amends because she felt guilty about her role in the accident? Did it matter? Not to Clare. Izzy had done an extraordinarily brave thing, standing up to her domineering mother. And the slate between Izzy and Clare had been wiped clean. It was time for a fresh start. And perhaps, in time, they really could be friends.

Izzy sighed, reminding Clare that she was just a kid with a boredom level to match. 'Can I watch this now? Please?'

'Sure,' said Clare, with an indulgent smile. 'But there's just one thing I want you to know. I'm grateful to you, Izzy, for what you did.'

'That's okay,' said Izzy with a wide, girlish smile that Clare so rarely saw and which imbued her features with real beauty. She would be a stunner when she grew up.

Clare smiled back and then adopted a slightly formal tone. 'I don't think your mum was very happy, Zoe. You will make up with her, won't you?'

Izzy gave Clare an impish smile. 'When I'm ready,' she said, reminding Clare just how manipulative she could be. She and Liam were going to have their work cut out keeping her in line. But even so, Clare couldn't help but smile. There was something so charming about Izzy when she was just herself – when she wasn't trying to be super-cool and aloof and grown-up.

'Well, make sure you do it soon. It's important that you and your mum get along. She . . . she only wants the best for you.'

Clare said this, not because she believed it necessarily to be true, but because she wanted Izzy to believe it. She could cite plenty of occasions from the past when Zoe's actions did not seem to be in her daughter's best interests. What she did believe, however, was that Zoe loved her daughter very much. Her behaviour, Clare suspected, was primarily governed by fear of losing her daughter's affections. Perhaps that's why she hated Clare so much – not because she had married her ex-husband but because she feared Izzy might come to like Clare more than her own mother.

'You only get one mum,' said Clare, gently. 'You have to take care of her.'

Izzy shrugged. 'I know. But then I have you as well. You're not my "real" mum of course. But you're the next best thing.'

With that she picked up the remote and the room was filled with noise. And that, Clare reckoned with a happy smile (which she did her best to hide from Izzy), was as close as she was probably going to get to an admission of affection from her stepdaughter. But it was enough for now.

Clare finished doing up the red buttons on her new

short-sleeved red striped blouse and checked her appearance in the mirror. She'd bought the top last week, after her and Liam's first appointment with the marriage-guidance counsellor, a middle-aged woman called Valerie, in Ballymena. Valerie had talked about making an effort, not taking each other for granted, and Clare was trying very much to take her words to heart.

Hence the blouse – an attempt to take more of an interest in her appearance, to show Liam that she cared what he thought of her, to demonstrate that she wanted to please him and be desired. In addition, she'd started a diet and this time she meant to stick to it. She was determined to get back to the size she had been before the children were born. Meanwhile she tried to see the positive; although her hips were large, she still had a waist and the blouse, which clinched in nicely just beneath her chest, showed off her shape. And cutting out the daytime drinking would help her lose weight too. She'd only been doing it to dull the pain but she didn't need it any more – not now that everything was okay between her and Liam again. Looking at her reflection now, she felt more attractive and desirable than she had for many months.

It was very early days but the atmosphere in the house had changed overnight after the confrontation with Zoe. It was as though a malevolent spirit had been exorcised from the building. Of course it wasn't fair to blame their problems on Zoe – she'd only come between them because Liam, by not confronting her over the issues he should have, had allowed her to exert such an influence over their marriage. Like all bullies, once they stood against her, united, she had melted away. Now, when Zoe came to the house, she was reserved and polite and, if not exactly likeable, then almost pleasant. As Clare's mum used to say, you can go a long way on good manners.

It was such a relief to be reconciled with Liam and liberated from Zoe's tyranny. Clare had not realised how much stress she had been living under since Liam told her about Gillian. And before that, there had been the stress of getting ready in time for the exhibition, albeit that the pressure was self-imposed.

But there was still one troubling issue to resolve and it had preoccupied Clare for the last week – Kirsty. A few weeks ago Clare had woken up in a sweat after a bad dream in which she was chasing Kirsty down a dark alleyway, lined with bins and piles of rubbish. No matter how hard she screamed and how fast she ran, Kirsty would not look round and she could not catch her. Clare reckoned she'd been watching too many American crime shows. But she also acknowledged that unless she tackled Kirsty face to face they would remain estranged for ever.

It broke her heart every time Josh asked why he couldn't play with Adam, whom he adored. So, the morning after the dream she started a painting of Ballgalley where she and Kirsty had taken their children on numerous days out over the years. On the beach she painted herself and Kirsty sitting on a rug talking and around them, four children – her own and Kirsty's – playing in the sand and at the water's edge. It took her three weeks to complete the picture and when it was finally done to her satisfaction, she had sent it to Kirsty with a note asking to meet tonight in No.11.

Clare sighed. Of course there was always the possibility that Kirsty would not turn up, never mind grant her the forgiveness she sought. And without that forgiveness they could never be friends. The prospect filled her with panic. Clare inhaled deeply, held her stomach with her right hand, closed her eyes and let the breath out slowly. She had missed Kirsty terribly these last six weeks. She dreaded being rejected but she dreaded a life without her friend even more. In order to break this deadlock, one of them had to proffer the olive branch. She was ready to do it. But, oh, she was so scared.

She was the first to arrive at No.11. It was a Tuesday night and the place was dead. A couple of men stood at the bar drinking pints and watching football on the screen suspended from the ceiling. Danny was on duty and he looked up when she came in and gave her a big smile.

'Hey, Clare. Good to see you,' he said and automatically reached for a bottle of white wine from the fridge.

'Actually, Danny, can you make that a sparkling mineral water?'

She hadn't gone teetotal overnight but she had got her drinking under control. It was important that she demonstrate to Kirsty that she didn't need alcohol to function. That she wasn't a lush.

Danny raised one eyebrow just a millimetre to signify his surprise. 'Sure,' he said, returned the bottle to the fridge and poured a glass of water instead. He placed a beer mat on the bar and set the drink on it carefully. 'Tell me, what's up with you and your pals? You haven't been in here together in weeks. You used to come in all the time.'

'Yes, it's been a while,' she said vaguely, aware that Danny would not know about the fall-out between Janice and Patsy – and the cause of it must for ever remain a secret. 'It's just . . . we've all been . . . busy.'

Danny threw the empty water bottle into a crate under the bar with a clink. 'Ach, it's a sad day when life's too busy to sit down and have a chin-wag over a drink with your best pals.'

Clare held out the money for the drink and nodded gravely. 'You're right there, Danny.'

She took a seat by the window and waited, her stomach

tied in knots with anxiety. She stared out onto the quiet street, and rehearsed what she would say to Kirsty.

'Hello, Clare.' Kirsty, standing, held a small glass of orange juice in her hand. She was simply dressed in a pair of jeans, a royal blue t-shirt and flat pumps. She wore little make-up but, then again, Kirsty had never needed to.

'Hello, Kirsty. Please, sit down.'

Kirsty sat down on the chair opposite Clare, set her glass on the table and dropped her bag on the floor. Her gaze rested momentarily on the glass of water in front of Clare – then she looked away. 'I can't stay for long.' Her voice was cold.

Clare took a deep breath. 'Thanks for agreeing to meet me, Kirsty.' She paused but the other woman said nothing. 'Did Adam like his bike?'

She looked away. 'Yes,' she said frostily. 'Didn't you get his thank-you note?'

'Yes, yes I did,' said Clare, the nerves inside her like a swarm of bees. 'I know you were very angry with me, and you probably still are, but I'm glad you let him keep it. I thought you might've returned it.'

'I would have, only he saw it by the back door with his name on it and I didn't have the heart to say he couldn't have it. Not after what happened to his other one.'

Clare swallowed and because she could not bring herself to look at Kirsty, stared at the beads of condensation on the outside of her glass. 'And the Lego? Did he like that?'

'I think he said so in his note, didn't he?'

Clare nodded. 'Josh and Rachel have missed playing with David and Adam. Josh especially.'

Kirsty gave her a cold stare. 'You know buying things doesn't make it better, Clare. It doesn't put right what you did.'

Clare risked a glance at her. She was frowning crossly. 'I

know that,' said Clare quietly. 'But I hope you understand, as I said in my letter . . .'

Kirsty sat up straight, with her hands on her lap, taking on an imperious air.

Clare pressed on. 'I hope you believe me when I say how very sorry I am for harming Adam and for causing you so much pain. I know that the accident must've brought back terrible memories for you, Kirsty. And I am so sorry about that.'

Tears filled Kirsty's eyes. She opened her mouth to speak, then closed it and stared out of the window.

Clare felt a single tear, wet on her cheek. She made no attempt to wipe it away, because she knew it would soon be followed by others. 'I wish I could go back and change that day. It's the most irresponsible thing I've ever done. I'm ashamed of myself.'

Kirsty looked at her watch, then stared coldly at Clare. 'Is that what you wanted to say? That you're sorry?'

'Yes.'

Kirsty picked up her bag and stood up. The orange juice remained untouched. 'Well, you've said it now.'

Clare's heart was swollen with sadness like a storm cloud black with rain. She held her grief in check and, finally, found the words to ask for what she wanted. 'Please, Kirsty. I want you to forgive me.'

Kirsty's chest rose and fell. She sat down, nursing the bag on her lap. She leant forwards and hissed, 'You let me down.'

'I let myself down.'

'You promised me that you wouldn't drink and drive.'

'I know.'

'You broke your word.'

Clare felt like Kirsty was raining blows on her head with something both soft and heavy. Her head bowed under the weight of the recriminations.

'You could've killed someone, Clare,' said Kirsty, losing her cool. 'You could've killed Adam!'

'I know,' said Clare and she put her head in her hands and let out a single wrenching sob. 'There's not a day goes by when I don't think about it.'

'Why, Clare? Why did you do it?'

Clare raised her face, crusty with tears. 'You know why. I was upset about Liam, I'd hardly slept for a week. I wasn't thinking straight. None of these is an excuse, I know.'

'They sound like excuses to me,' said Kirsty sullenly.

'I'm not trying to justify what happened. What I did was wrong, plain and simple. And I deeply regret my actions.'

There was a long pause. They stared into each other's eyes. Clare could almost hear the beat of her own heart, it pounded so wildly against her chest. She had laid her soul open for Kirsty's scrutiny and judgment. She could do no more. She would ask one last time. 'Do you think, Kirsty, that you can find it in your heart . . . to forgive me?'

Kirsty broke eye contact and shook her head sadly. She looked down at the bag on her knee and fiddled with the silver clasp. 'I don't know.'

'I've missed you, Kirsty. I want us to be friends again.' Saying this truth, articulating it, brought a relative sense of calm to Clare even though she did not know, yet, how Kirsty would respond. But she had given it her all. There was nothing more she could do. Everything lay in Kirsty's hands now.

'I've missed you too, Clare,' said Kirsty quietly, her face wretched with misery, and Clare's spirits rose. 'But I don't know if I can ever trust you again.'

There was a long tense silence.

'Everyone makes mistakes,' said Clare at last.

'This is very difficult for me,' said Kirsty and she bit her bottom lip. She had not said no, not yet. Clare saw the chink in Kirsty's armour, the glimmer of hope, and went for it.

'What can I do to win back your trust?'

Kirsty gave her a ghost of a smile. 'Well, for a start, don't lie to me ever again.'

'Oh, Kirsty,' said Clare and she clapped her hands together and held them, palms together, under her chin. 'I won't. I promise I won't. Not as long as I live. Does this mean we're friends again?'

'It means we're going to give it another go,' said Kirsty shyly.

Clare extended her arm across the table and Kirsty did the same. Clare clasped Kirsty's hand and realised it was shaking. She squeezed hard and smiled. 'I promise you, Kirsty, you'll not regret this.' She let out a long happy sigh and released her friend's hand.

There was an awkward pause then and Kirsty said, 'So, how are things between you and Liam?'

Clare brightened. 'Much better, thanks.'

Kirsty set her bag on the floor, crossed her legs and took a sip of juice. 'Last time I spoke to you it sounded pretty bad. You'd just found out about that woman Gillian.'

'It was bad,' said Clare, her smile fading at the memory. 'But we're sorting things out now.' Clare went on to tell her about the confrontation with Zoe, and Izzy's role in it, about her reconciliation with Liam and the counselling.

Kirsty listened intently and when Clare was finished said, 'That's wonderful news, Clare. I'm really pleased for you. Are you managing to paint in the midst of all this drama?'

'I've just started doing two sessions a week. I go up to the studio on a Thursday night when Liam gets home early, and do either first thing on a Saturday or a Sunday morning. I can put in three hours and be home by ten. It hardly impacts on family life at all.'

'I'm glad you're managing to work. It would be a great shame to see all the momentum and interest generated by the exhibition go to waste.'

'That's what Liam said. He's been very encouraging. I have a couple of commissions to do and Patsy's going to hang a few pieces in the gallery for me on a permanent basis and we'll see how it goes from there.'

'It sounds like it's all come together.'

Clare nodded, considering this. 'Yes, I suppose it has. And now that you and me are friends again, well, everything's perfect.' She smiled broadly.

Kirsty raised an eyebrow. 'Well, not quite. Don't forget about Patsy and Janice.'

Clare's face fell. 'Oh, yeah,' she said dully. 'Are things just as bad between them?'

'I'm afraid so.'

'Oh, I'm sorry to hear that,' said Clare, suddenly feeling very self-centred. She'd been so focused on getting her own life back on track that she'd given only a passing thought to Janice and Patsy. 'With all that's been going on at home I haven't been much of a friend to either of them. I was hoping it might have all blown over by now.'

Kirsty pursed her lips and said grimly, 'This one isn't going to, I don't think. Patsy is so bitter about what happened. She's changed, Clare. She's not the bubbly, happy Patsy we used to know. She says she can never forgive Janice and Keith.'

'Don't you think that's a little unfair? To blame them for what Pete did?'

'I do. But the way Patsy sees it, Pete's got off scot-free. Though Keith did stop Pete's allowance and told him that if he wanted money this summer he'd have to go out and earn it himself.'

Clare nodded. Liam had mentioned that Pete was now working behind the bar at the golf club.

'The final straw came when Janice and Keith found out that Pete had made no effort to contact Laura – after promising them he would face up to his responsibilities. According to Patsy he'd not even picked up the phone, never mind gone to see her. He left her to sort out the mess by herself.'

Clare took a sharp intake of breath. 'That is bad.'

Kirsty nodded, took a sip of juice and said sanguinely, 'For right or wrong, Patsy's looking for someone to hang the blame on. And on top of Laura she's worried sick about Martin not getting another job. She's got a lot on her plate.'

'But if you and I can patch things up, surely there's hope for them?'

Kirsty sighed. 'You'd think so,' she said but shook her head.

'I miss our nights out,' said Clare.

'Me too.'

'It's just awful, the four of us not being able to go out. Do you think we will ever all be friends again, Kirsty? Do you think it possible that things can ever be the way they were before?'

'I don't know the answer to that, Clare,' said Kirsty, folding her arms across her chest. 'But I do know that I'm fed up being piggy in the middle between Janice and Patsy. I don't want to side with one over the other because I can see both points of view.'

Clare nodded in agreement. 'I hear Laura's got a summer job as a lifeguard in the sports centre.' Laura had always been a great swimmer.

'Do you think she's going to be alright?' asked Kirsty.

'I don't know,' said Clare and she bowed her head. 'I'm

sure it was for the best. In the end,' she said quietly, not sure if she believed this, 'she's only a girl herself. Far too young to be thinking of raising a baby.'

Kirsty shook her head sadly and stared out of the window. She squinted as if focusing on something far away. 'Chris has taken a job in Dubai,' she suddenly blurted out. 'He starts at the end of August.'

'Oh, dear,' said Clare slowly. 'And he's still no idea how you feel about him?'

Kirsty shook her head. 'I left it too late and now all the arrangements are made. And if I'm honest with myself I know that had he cared for me one jot he never would've taken the job in the first place.'

'That's not necessarily true,' said Clare carefully. 'Chris could well be taking the job precisely *because* he cares for you. Maybe he thinks he doesn't stand a chance with you and that's why he's going away.'

'You are a hopeless romantic, Clare,' said Kirsty with a crooked smile. 'And it's sweet of you to say that to try and make me feel better. But you and I both know that just isn't the case. I do love you for it though.'

'Oh, Kirsty,' said Clare with a heavy sigh.

'It's okay. I've a lot to be grateful for, I really have. And I'm getting used to the idea that I might never meet someone.'

'You mustn't give up hope, Kirsty.'

'I'll try not to. But as far as Chris Carmichael is concerned, it's over.'

Much later Kirsty, unable to sleep, wandered the house in her pyjamas. She stopped by the front window, the curtains never closed now against the long, light evenings, and stared out onto the street where, hours before, a horde of squealing children had played. The sky had faded to a pale yellow-grey, dark clouds drawn across it like skeins of navy-blue wool.

The street-lamps cast pools of orange light all along the road, illuminating the signs of family life – old scooters and bikes abandoned in front of garages or on well-worn lawns, bunting tied between trees at number seventeen (left over from a child's birthday party) and hop-scotch chalked onto the pavement.

After Adam's accident, the residents had clubbed together and put up warning signs that read, 'Slow! Children at Play'. Under the word 'Slow' on each of the bright yellow signs was a picture of a child on a scooter. Mary Clark had ordered them from Amazon and got her husband to hammer them halfway up old wooden telegraph poles at either end of the street, and one directly opposite the junction where Adam had been injured. They were quite illegal of course, as Keith had pointed out, but Mary had said that they were coming down over her dead body. The council, displaying rare wisdom, had decided to leave well alone.

A residents' committee had been formed with Phil O'Brien as chair and they were campaigning to have speed bumps installed along the road. People were so very good and Kirsty was grateful, but it did not stop the hard knot of terror forming in her stomach every time one of the children ventured beyond the front garden.

She realised her reaction stemmed from her over-protectiveness towards her sons. Scott's early death had brought home to her the fragility of life. She knew how easily it could be snuffed out – literally in an instant, with no time for goodbyes or regrets or reflection. And she had clung to the life left behind in the form of David and Adam, fretting over every conceivable danger they might encounter daily. She was in danger of suffocating them. Soon David would seek independence beyond the confines of home, school and their immediate neighbourhood.

And when that time came, Kirsty prayed she would have the wisdom to give it to him.

As for the fear, she would have to learn to live with it, plain and simple – a private, daily challenge she fought to overcome. She resented this insidious legacy of the accident, still lingering long after Adam's scars had healed and the brand-new sheen had worn off his red bike, the envy of the street. Sometimes it made her angry with Clare but she tried not to hold it against her. She had, after all, just given her forgiveness. She only wished Patsy could find it in her heart to do the same for Janice. Patsy had just announced that she wouldn't be going to London and none of them had the heart to make the trip without her. Kirsty tried not to take the blow too hard, but right now there seemed precious little to look forward to.

She went through her nightly ritual of checking on the boys, who still shared a room. She pulled down pyjama legs that had ridden up above the knee, tucked duvets under chins, smoothed hair off brows, kissed foreheads and placed each child's favourite toy in the crook of their arm.

Then she went into her own room, crawled under the cool cotton sheet and closed her eyes. And thought of Chris as she did every night, except tonight her analysis was cold and critical. She had mistaken his kindness for affection when, all along, it was mere pity for a lonely young widow. She had been foolish to think they had a future.

Kirsty rolled over and put her hand on her heart, so full of heaviness it ached. And as she lay there in the dark, unable to get to sleep, she realised what had changed – all hope had, finally, been put to rest.

Chapter Twenty-One

It was several weeks before Kirsty saw Chris again. Instead of making sure she was at home every Friday, she now took care to be out of the house whenever possible. She took to leaving an envelope with his money in it under a flowerpot by the back door so that she would not have to talk to him. And when that was unavoidable, she faced up to him with as bright and breezy an air as she could muster, determined to betray no sign that her heart was slowly crumbling as the day of his departure approached.

But this warm and cloudless Friday she was stuck at home waiting for the DHL delivery man. She readied herself for the inevitable meeting with Chris, boxing up her feelings like the parcel of books she awaited and sealing it with determination.

The children, on holiday from school for the summer, were still in their pyjamas watching TV and she was upstairs when she heard Chris's car pull up. She listened for the click of the side gate, then went and stood half-hidden behind the curtain in the boys' room, unable to resist watching. She loved the measured, smooth way Chris moved across the lawn, bending now to pick up a bucket and walking unhurriedly over to the patch of roses by the pond.

It was the beginning of August and the garden was at the

peak of perfection, bursting with flowers and fruit. In a few weeks the inevitable decay and slide into autumn would begin – the time of year Kirsty hated most. Not just because autumn, the season of death, was so depressing in itself, but because it would be the fourth anniversary of Scott's death in November. She already dreaded it, fearing most of all the way the boys would struggle manfully to recall a father whose memory faded with every day, no matter how hard she and her in-laws tried to keep it alive.

Chris took a pair of red-handled secateurs from his back pocket and started to dead-head the roses.

After some minutes Adam appeared, running across the grass barefoot in his pyjamas, his Spider-Man dressing gown billowing out behind him like a cape. Chris looked up and smiled when he saw the boy. Immediately he stopped what he was doing, and called him over to the pond where they both hunkered down on the grass and Chris pointed at the water. Adam sat, listening intently, his face raised to Chris like the sun, hugging his knees with his arms.

Kirsty turned away then, wondering why the image of man and boy, heads tilted towards one another, touched her so. Perhaps because she had once upon a time pictured that scene with Scott in it – it made her so sad to think of all the simple fatherly pleasures he would never know. And how cruelly her sons had been robbed of a good father.

She went downstairs to find Adam back in front of the TV with his brother, both of them staring at the screen like zombies. She switched it off to a howl of protest and said, 'It's ten thirty. Time to get dressed, you two.'

'Let's go outside,' said David, jumping up and looking out of the window. 'Let's see if anybody wants to play tig.'

'Okay,' Adam followed his brother out of the room on

tiptoes, swinging the ends of the dressing-gown belt in his hands.

Minutes later they were both back downstairs fully clothed in the crumpled garments they'd worn yesterday. Their hair stuck up on end and neither of them, judging by the speed with which they had dressed, had done their teeth. Kirsty sighed and smiled and decided to let it go just this once. They opened the door and ran outside.

'Be careful on the road now and don't go any further than Milly Campbell's. Or Darren Weir's at the other end! And don't,' she called after them, her voice rising to a shriek, 'whatever you do, play on the road.' She put her hand to her neck, felt the throb and heat of her anxiety.

David suddenly stopped, turned around and ran back to her. He took her hands in his, folded them one on top of the other, like she did when she was having a serious chat with him – a caring gesture that signified that, for the first time and just for this moment, the tables had been turned. He looked up at her, squinting in the sun, his nose sprinkled with freckles like spilt pepper on a creamy white tablecloth.

'We're going to be perfectly alright, Mum. Now will you stop worrying?' he said, mimicking her words and tone of voice and she had to laugh – and hold back the tears at the same time.

In the kitchen the sun was beating through the windows making the room hot and stuffy. The breakfast things were still on the table and the smell of stale cat food filled the air. Kirsty opened the back door and Candy slid past her legs into the garden. A strong breeze gusted in. Kirsty wedged the door open with the back of a chair and resisted the urge to glance outside. She scraped out Candy's food bowl, filled it with water to steep and flung open the window above the sink. But the breeze was stronger than she'd realised and, in opening the window and the door together, she'd created a wind tunnel.

The breeze filled the green gingham curtains all at once and blew them inwards like miniature sails. One of them caught the edge of a dusty silver-framed photograph sitting on the highest of the decorative shelves that finished the run of kitchen units along the wall. The photograph inched forwards a few centimetres. Kirsty saw what was about to happen and stretched out a hand to push it back onto the shelf, but she was not tall enough. Even on tiptoes, she could not reach. Another gust of wind and the curtain flicked the picture off the shelf. She tried to catch it, but she was too slow, too clumsy. It slid past her like a shadow, hit the kitchen counter with a crack and bounced to the floor. There was a loud crash as the frame hit the tiles. Kirsty cried out. The glass splintered into tiny pieces and showered across the floor like diamonds.

Kirsty took a step backwards and steadied herself against the solidness of the kitchen units. Scott's face stared up at her, the photograph now released from its glassy prison. The picture had been taken by one of Scott's biking pals on a ride in the Sperrins the summer before he died. He was wearing a black tight-fitting biking top and had taken his cycling helmet off for the photo. He stood astride his bike, squinting at the camera, while behind him was the beautiful rolling scenery of the Glenelly Valley. He was smiling broadly, happy and carefree.

Kirsty knelt down and picked the photograph up gingerly, little shards of glass tinkling to the floor. Then she started to cry. The man staring out from the picture seemed like a stranger to her, but still she grieved for the love they had once shared. She wept for Scott, for the life he had lost and her little boys too.

But most of all she cried for what might have been with Chris. She cried because she truly believed that she would never know love again, that she would live the rest of her days in lonely widowhood. And she cried for other things too – the friendship lost between her friends, what had happened to Laura, Adam's accident. It all came out in one great flood of misery. And she made no attempt to hold it back.

'Kirsty!' came Chris's voice from behind her. 'Are you alright?' She struggled to her feet, the picture still in her hand, and turned around. He was standing with a bunch of small, shiny courgettes, weeping at the ends where they had been severed from the mother plant, in his hands. She nodded.

Hastily, he set the vegetables on the table among the cereal packets and came over to her. 'I was just bringing these in when I heard a crash and then your scream. Are you hurt?' He held out an arm as though he was about to touch her and then thought better of it. The arm fell to his side.

Kirsty sniffed, looked at the photo and started to cry again.

'Here, let me,' said Chris and he took the picture gently from her grasp and held it up to the light in his big calloused hands. He let out a long sigh when he saw what it was. 'It's okay, Kirsty. Honestly. It's not damaged at all. All you need is a new frame and it'll be right as rain. Here, let me shut that window.' He stepped around her and the broken glass, secured the window and came and stood in front of her again. He gave her a reassuring smile which for some reason made the tears come all the more freely.

The smile fell from his face. 'I know photographs have great sentimental value, Kirsty, but you have no need to cry. The photograph is perfect. Look, let me help you clear up this mess.'

He held the photograph between his thumb and forefinger and extended his arm, expecting her to take the picture, but she shook her head. He looked at it and frowned, not knowing what to do.

'I'm not crying over the photo,' she managed to say between tears, and was consumed once again by a bout of weeping. She bent towards him like a reed, her heart aching for his touch, for the safety and security of his arms. She wept like she had not done since Scott died. When she glanced at him finally, he was standing awkwardly, looking away, his face flushed with embarrassment.

Kirsty wiped the tears from her face and tried to compose herself. But she was tired of being brave, of coping, of pretending. 'I'm crying about a lot of things,' she said flatly.

His face relaxed and he smiled sympathetically, evidently relieved that she had stopped weeping.

'I'm crying because I don't know how I'm going to manage when you go away, Chris.'

'Sure, I've got a new gardener lined up for you. A good guy who knows what he's doing. Someone you'll feel comfortable having around you and the boys. I was going to bring him over next week to meet you. If you want me to.'

Her answer was knee-jerk. 'I don't want to meet him.' She realised how petulant she sounded – like a spoilt child.

Chris opened his mouth a little and cocked his head to one side. 'Kirsty?'

She had no control over the words that came from her mouth. Even as she primed herself for rejection, she could no longer suppress what she felt. 'I don't want someone else around the place. I want you, Chris.'

She stared at him, shocked by her boldness, amazed that she had simply blurted out the thing she had agonised over for so long. And now that she had done it, she immediately regretted it. Embarrassment engulfed her like a crippling paralysis. Her cheeks flamed with mortification. What had she done? Was she mad? She could not take her eyes off Chris. She waited for him to do something, say something. Anything.

'But . . .' he said and then, slowly, realisation dawned. His eyebrows came together, a deep line forming between them like a scar. He sucked in his upper lip until it disappeared. He looked perplexed. Confused. Embarrassed. She closed her eyes.

She realised in that instant that even though she knew there was no hope – she had resigned herself to that – she needed him to know that she loved him. And with the words came a sense of release, of freedom. She was no longer a prisoner to her fears. The worst was done. She opened her eyes.

Chris cleared his throat in a theatrical manner and set Scott's photograph down carefully on the nearby kitchen counter. 'Do you mean what I think you mean?' he said.

The air was thick with tension. Kirsty could hardly breathe. Their eyes were locked together, unblinking. He held her gaze, his blue eyes intense, unflinching, for what seemed like a very long time. She could not speak. She nodded almost imperceptibly.

All of a sudden he sucked air in loudly and turned away so that his back was towards her. He bent his head, the skin on the back of his neck brown and leathery with the sun, and put a hand to his face. His broad, work-honed shoulders strained against the yoke of the shirt, worn with age and use to a pale sky-blue.

He stood like that for a few moments, while Kirsty's cheeks burned with shame. What had she done? In unburdening her feelings had she simply encumbered Chris with them?

Placed him in the uncomfortable position of having to let her down gently? Had she spoiled the lovely friendship they had shared these last few years? Tears of regret welled up inside. A lump lodged in her chest.

At last Chris straightened up and turned to face her once more, manoeuvring his big feet carefully between the shards of broken glass. He had a resigned look on his face, the face of someone about to deliver bad news. Kirsty bit her lip and steeled herself, ready to take it on the chin.

He glanced at the photo of Scott before speaking. 'I . . . you've taken me by surprise, Kirsty. That was the last thing I expected to hear.'

She lifted her head and stared at him. She could hardly bear the tears of pity in his eyes. She looked away and chastised herself. Why couldn't she have left well alone? Chris would be gone in a few weeks' time and she could've saved herself, and him, from this excruciating encounter.

'I know it can't be easy raising two boys on your own, though you do a fantastic job.'

Under normal circumstances she would have basked in this praise. Today, though, it sounded like a kindly prelude to letting her down.

He paused and his glance was drawn to the photograph of Scott again. He averted his gaze quickly. 'I understand how much you miss your husband, Kirsty, and the pain must still be very raw.'

She blushed then. But she didn't miss him, not in the way Chris meant anyway.

He went on, 'Sheer loneliness can drive you to do and say all sorts of things, Kirsty – things that, in the cold light of day, you realise that you don't really mean. I know. I've lived alone since my marriage broke up. Sometimes . . . well, sometimes you'd do anything just for a bit of human companionship.'

She stared at him and shook her head. He thought that she loved Scott still.

'I would never presume to have a chance with you, Kirsty, and I want you to know that.'

Kirsty's brain felt stuffy and slow. Did he think she was some sort of deranged widow pouncing on any available man who came her way? She thought of the ill-advised date with Vincent Agnew and cringed. 'I don't understand. Why do you say that, Chris?'

He smiled at her kindly. 'I'm just saying that I think you're very vulnerable right now. And I think it would be wrong of me . . . of any man . . . to take advantage of that.'

A tiny spark of hope flickered inside Kirsty's heart. He might believe it wrong to take advantage of a vulnerable woman, but the question was – did he *want* to?

'You think I'm still in love with Scott, don't you?'

He jolted in surprise. A little frown nested on his forehead and he said, 'Why . . . yes. It's obvious. His pictures are everywhere.'

He held out a hand, stained with dirt, in a sweeping gesture. It came to rest, pointing, at the picture of Scott and the boys hanging on the wall on the other side of the room. Kirsty looked at it and at the photograph on the counter. He was right. They were everywhere: on the walls, clustered on the dresser in the lounge, on each boy's bedside cabinet. Their wedding picture had pride of place in the porch as you came in the front door. There was even one of Scott's football team from his student days hanging in the loo. They were part of a desperate attempt to keep Scott's memory alive – but they were not there for her.

'They're there for the boys, Chris, and Dorothy and Harry too, if I'm honest. I want the boys to remember their dad and to know how much he loved them.' She paused, and added sadly, 'But it doesn't work, you know. Every day his memory fades a little more and I wonder sometimes if Adam remembers him at all.'

She shook off the melancholy and tried to smile. 'But the photos aren't there for me, Chris. In spite of what you, and everyone else, might think.'

His eyebrows came even closer together. 'What do you mean?'

Kirsty took a deep breath. 'If I tell you something, Chris, will you promise you'll not tell another soul?'

He considered this for some moments, staring at her. The sound of children playing in the street drifted in through the back door. Somewhere, a dog barked. And when Chris finally said, 'I promise,' she knew he meant it.

She glanced at the doorway that led into the hall, checking that one of the boys hadn't sneaked in unnoticed. 'I want the boys to be secure in the belief that Scott and I had a happy marriage.'

'I see,' he said slowly, tilting his head to one side as though to hear her better. 'And did you?'

'To start with, yes. But we drifted apart. It wasn't anybody's fault.' She rubbed her hands, damp with nervous sweat, on her hips. 'When the children came along, and we weren't doing things as a family, we seemed to spend less and less time together. Scott loved his cycling.'

She picked up the photograph and ran her fingertip over the glossy surface. 'He was obsessed with it, you know. He would go off for hours on these long rides with the cycling club, all year round, and I used to be left with the kids. At first I resented it and then I realised that, actually, I quite liked being on my own with the boys. Don't get me wrong,' she added and glanced anxiously at Chris. 'He did spend time with the boys and he was a good father. I think he would've grown into even a better one. But that was when I realised our marriage was in trouble. In the end, the only thing we had in common was the children.'

She paused. 'I've never told anyone that before, Chris. I've never been able to. When he died everyone just made . . . assumptions and I couldn't bring myself to correct them.'

'What assumptions?' he said gently.

'That our marriage was a match made in heaven. How could I tell Dorothy and Harry the truth? They adored Scott. It would've caused too much unnecessary pain and hurt – and believe me, there was more than enough of that going about already. For a while they blamed themselves for his death because they encouraged him to get into cycling when he was a teenager. I felt it would be wrong to start discussing our marriage when Scott wasn't there any more to give his side of the story.'

Chris nodded gravely.

'People wanted me to be the grieving widow, so I was. I should've been honest but I could never bring myself to do it. Now, with the passage of time, I don't think I ever will.'

Chris shook his head. 'You did the right thing, Kirsty.'

'You think so?' She held her breath, waiting for his answer, realising how much she needed his approval.

He nodded. 'I do.'

Kirsty, choked with emotion, managed to say, 'I'm so glad I told you, Chris. You've no idea how guilty I've felt about it.'

'Oh, Kirsty, you have no reason to feel bad. You're a good person. *You* might have felt better if you'd been honest about your marriage, but the people that loved Scott would've felt a whole lot worse. In my book, that's an honourable thing to do.'

'Thank you.' She managed a smile.

She felt tears prick her eyes once more – this time tears of release. She had not understood how heavy the burden of the lie had been. 'I think,' she said bravely, feeling that she had nothing now to lose, 'I think that I might be in love with you.'

Chris's arms dropped suddenly to his sides. He took a step forwards, the glass crunching under his heavy boots. 'But you can't be. You're so beautiful and clever, Kirsty. Why would you want to be with me?'

She found that she was shaking. She put her arms around herself and held tight. She pulled her gaze away. Her voice, when she spoke, was croaky. 'I know you don't reciprocate my feelings, Chris. But I promise you that, after today, I won't mention them again.'

He took another step towards her and this time they were only inches apart. He put a work-roughened hand under her chin and raised her face up to his. His breath was warm on her face, his eyes felt like they were connected to hers in such a way that it was physically impossible to look away. When he spoke, his expression was grave and his eyes were full of tenderness.

'But that's where you're wrong, Kirsty.' His eyes, restless, searched her face all over, as if looking for something. 'In fact you couldn't be more wrong.'

Kirsty closed her eyes. The words crashed over her like the tide, washing away all the anguish and sadness of the last few months, and bringing with them healing and the feeling that this, right now, was the most perfect moment of her life.

'We've been good friends, Kirsty. But the more I got to know you, the more I realised that I couldn't stay here and see you, week out and week in, knowing I could never have you. That's why I took the job in Dubai, Kirsty. I wanted more than friendship. And when I saw you dating other guys, I knew I didn't stand a chance.'

'Oh, Chris, how could you think that? The only man I'm interested in is you.'

He smiled when she said that, and a single tear crept out of his right eye. She reached up and touched it with her hand. The tear was warm like blood and his face felt rough like fine sandpaper. He went on, his voice hoarse, 'I wanted to get as far away as possible. I thought I could forget you. But I know now I never could.'

'Ssshh,' she said and placed a forefinger over his mouth. He cupped her face in his hands and she wrapped her fingers around his forearms, hard and sinewy under the shirt. He bent and placed his lips on hers. They were softer than she'd expected, the kiss urgent and gentle. It lasted a long time and, when they pulled apart, still holding onto each other, Kirsty's legs were weak. Chris's chest rose and fell in shallow, rapid breaths.

He enveloped her suddenly in his arms and she pressed her face into his hard chest that smelt of grass and sweat and hard work. His hands were restless, touching her everywhere – on the back of the head, the shoulders, arms, all the way down her back, her buttocks – mapping out the contours of her body. She placed her hands gingerly on his back and pulled him to her, pressed her body against his. They lost their footing somehow and stumbled against the kitchen counter, glass screeching on tile, marking the floor. She did not care. She ran her hands through his short, wiry hair, across his broad shoulders, down the muscles of his upper arms. Then his lips were on her neck and he was pressing against her, hungry with lust.

'Oh, Kirsty,' he breathed into her ear, making her head spin with happiness. She stretched her head to the left, felt his lips on the thin, tender skin of her neck and closed her eyes in ecstasy.

And then she remembered who she was and where they were. She pulled away suddenly. 'We mustn't, Chris,' she said, wiping her mouth with the back of her hand. Her pulse was racing. She glanced anxiously at the door that led into the hall. 'The children might come in.'

He released her immediately, and both of them leant with their backs against the counter side by side, slightly out of breath.

When she'd composed herself, Kirsty said, 'What are we going to do?'

'Come with me, Kirsty,' he said, his voice like a lure. 'Come with me to Dubai. You and the boys.'

'I can't do that. You know I can't.' She was shaking her head, avoiding eye contact.

'Yes you can.' He stood in front of her once more, this time at a little distance, and brushed her right cheek lightly with the back of his hand. Her skin where he had touched her burned like a fever.

She struggled to think clearly but her brain was fogged and slow. She looked around her kitchen, and tried to break free of the spell he cast over her. 'But . . . but what about the house?'

He stepped closer, pressed his lips to her forehead. 'Rent it out.'

He moved his lips across her brow, down the bridge of her nose, his touch light like a feather. She closed her eyes. 'My job?'

'Resign.'

His lips were on her neck now – she fought against the pleasure, tried to think rationally. 'But what about the boys?'

'They'll adapt.'

'And Candy.'

He laughed into her neck, his breath like warm steam on her skin. 'Your friend Clare'll take her, you know that. She's always fussing over her when she comes here.'

Suddenly, Kirsty pulled away and buried her face in her hands. 'Oh, I don't know. It's such a big step, Chris. Uprooting the boys, leaving this house, my job, everything.' She removed her hands from her face and pleaded, 'Can't you just stay here?'

He shook his head solemnly and released her. 'It's too late for that. I've signed a contract. I've got tenants for the house. I've sold most of my equipment, or promised it to people.'

'But Dorothy and Harry would never get over it,' she blurted out, vocalising, at last, the stumbling block which she could not see a way around.

Chris sighed and stepped back a little. He took both her hands in his and regarded her severely. 'They might surprise you, Kirsty. I've noticed them slowing up of late. I saw Harry out walking with a stick the other day.' It was true. Harry had damaged a disc in his lower back and it was causing him terrible pain in his right leg. 'They're not going to be able to keep up with the boys for much longer, Kirsty. They'll not be able to mind them as much as they do.'

'I know,' said Kirsty with a heavy sigh. 'They are getting old. But they still want to see the boys, every day if they can. It seems . . . unfair to Dorothy and Harry to take the boys away from them now, after all they've done for us.'

He raised a hand and stroked her hair, tucked a stray lock behind her ear. She arched at his touch, like a cat. 'All Dorothy and Harry want is for the boys to be happy, Kirsty. And the boys can't be happy unless you are.'

Kirsty smiled sadly. 'Those boys are their life.'

'I know that,' he said. 'But you can't put your life on hold for them. And it's time for them to build a life that doesn't revolve entirely around you and the boys.'

She nodded, not entirely convinced, her heart which moments before had soared with happiness, now mired in anxiety.

Chris took her right hand. 'Please don't worry. We will find a way to be together, Kirsty. Because believe me, now that I've got you, I'm never letting you go.'

She smiled at him weakly, torn between elation and sorrow. Feeling that no matter what she did it would not be the right thing. That she could not win. 'Say it again.'

'Now that I've got you, I'm never letting you go.'

He pressed her palm into his cheek, his fingers over hers like a net. 'Kirsty, do you think I can make you happy?'

'I know so.'

'Then you have to believe. In us.'

She blinked. 'I do.'

'Things will work out, you'll see. When something's right, they always do.'

She closed her eyes. 'Promise me, Chris.'

'I promise.'

And though she could not see how, Kirsty tried very hard to believe that she could have what she wanted, without breaking the hearts of her in-laws.

Chapter Twenty-Two

Alone in the house on a wet and miserable October day, Janice stared at the pictures spread out on the table in her work room – snaps of her and Keith's August holiday on the Italian Riviera. One of them, a picture of her standing alone on the hotel balcony overlooking Portofino harbour, caught her eye. She picked it up.

She couldn't remember the photograph being taken but she recognised the strained smile, a reflection of how she'd felt the entire holiday, unable to shake off thoughts of Patsy, who had been constantly on her mind. Along with Pete.

After Keith told Pete he wasn't his biological father, Janice and Pete had hardly exchanged a word. Pete had started his new life at Manchester University a month after the holiday. And Janice had been filled with a sense of relief that made her feel all the more guilty.

She saw no reason to hope, in the foreseeable future anyway, that her relationship with Pete would improve. The thing he wanted from her – the identity of his father – she could never give him. He mistrusted her and could she blame him? She had lied to him for the first eighteen years of his life, and even now she would not give up the truth.

In keeping the adoption from Pete, Keith had been culpable too but only on her insistence. She was the architect of the deceit. All Keith had done, bless him, was to love Pete and be the best dad he could. Seen in this light, his actions were laudable, noble even. Thankfully Pete seemed to have divined that much. His weekly, or more often, fortnightly telephone calls home consisted of monosyllabic answers to her questions and long conversations with Keith. And Janice was glad that he and Keith had patched up their relationship.

Janice left the photographs where they were, strewn across the table, knowing that she would not scrapbook them today. She went down to the first floor and tiptoed along the landing, feeling like a trespasser in her own home. She stood outside Pete's closed bedroom door. The house was quiet now that he was gone. No loud music blaring from his room, no friends popping by to watch football or rugby on the big screen in the den. No arguments either.

She placed the flat of her palm on the bedroom door, her nails the colour of coral, and closed her eyes. She prayed to God that her son would be alright. That He would protect him and care for him and keep him on the path of goodness. God would have to, for left to his own devices, she feared that Pete was not innately capable of righteousness.

The doorbell chimed and Janice, startled, looked at her watch. It would be the man from Tesco – the highlight of her day. She went downstairs, stopping at the bottom of the stairs to check her appearance, then opened the front door.

When he had gone she stood in the kitchen, utterly forlorn, and stared at the mound of groceries on the island unit. Outside the rain pelted down relentlessly on the autumn garden and filled the gutters on the old house to overflowing. She sighed, and picked through the shopping, extracting perishables – milk, cheese, butter. She loaded these into the door of the fridge and tried to think of something to look forward to. She could think of nothing.

It wasn't that her diary was short on social engagements; it was just that her heart wasn't in any of them. She didn't care if she never went to another dinner party, or fundraiser ball or ladies' charity coffee morning again. The glitter of the social scene on which she and Keith played out much of their lives suddenly seemed tawdry, superficial, like cheap tinsel. As did the people in it – she wondered how many of them would stick around if they knew the truth about her. Would they judge her somehow culpable? Or worse, treat her like a victim, for ever tarnished, spoiled by what had happened?

She slammed the fridge door shut and separated out the tinned and dried goods. She filled the larder cupboard with these things and filled her head with the happy times before she and Patsy had fallen out. And, before that, a time when Pete was a little boy and Keith and she were newly married and she believed anything was possible.

She ripped open three green net bags of lemons and layered them in a tall, straight-sided glass vase with green foliage she'd collected earlier from the garden, before the rain. She set the vase in the middle of the table, stood back to observe the effect, and smiled – it wasn't quite the effortlessly artistic display she'd tried to copy from *Good Housekeeping* magazine. The lemons were a bit small and wizened, not the plump, unblemished yellow ovals she'd imagined. And the foliage looked like someone's hedge trimmings. Altogether, it was a bit of a disaster. What *was* she going to do with all those lemons?

For a fleeting moment she pictured herself describing the fiasco to Patsy. How she would laugh! And then Janice remembered that Patsy hated her, and her heart brimmed with despair. Only last month the girls' trip to London had to be cancelled. How could they celebrate fifteen years of friendship when Patsy wasn't there? How could they celebrate friendship at all when Patsy hated Janice so much?

Was this how things were to be from now on? It was unbearable. She no longer had a close girlfriend with whom to share the minutiae of her daily life, no-one to find humour in the mundane, to share the highs and lows of an ordinary, everyday existence. That was what best friends were for. But Clare and Kirsty, with young families, were too busy to spend the time with Janice that Patsy used to. And, much as she loved them, they could never fill Patsy's shoes.

There was something, of course, that would almost certainly make a difference to Patsy. Something that, if Janice told her, would make her understand why Pete was the way he was. And in her understanding maybe Patsy would find compassion and charity. But it would require so much of Janice. It would reveal her, and the respectable life she had so carefully hewn out of the misery of her past, to be a sham. She would have to strip herself bare, to recount the thing she had never told, to reveal so much of herself that she knew she could not do it. It was impossible.

And yet she couldn't go on like this.

It was not in Patsy's nature to relent. She was good at harbouring grudges and Janice knew that if she was going to back down, she would've done so by now. Janice could not stand by and watch the circle of friends that meant so much to her fall apart. She had known all along that she held the key to fixing this. She just never thought that she would have to use it. It would mean speaking of the thing she had never spoken of before, and had sworn to herself she would never reveal to anyone. The years of keeping her past under lock and key had been exhausting. The prospect of releasing that past, of giving it life and validity by talking about it, terrified her.

But it was the only way. She knew Patsy could be trusted with a confidence, even one as dreadful as this, and she knew also that Patsy was a hugely compassionate woman. She was quite certain that if Patsy knew the truth, she would forgive her. She would understand why Janice was such a bad mother and why Pete turned out the way he did.

She told herself all these things and still the fear haunted her like a stalker over the following days, silent and unseen but always present. She lived in fear during the day and at night, it crept into her dreams, disturbing her sleep and snapping her wide awake in the early hours. Drenched with sweat she would lie on the bed, with her stomach twisted like the bedsheets and her heart battering against her ribs. It was made all the worse because she could not share any of this with Keith, who lay asleep beside her, his chest rising and falling in peaceful oblivion.

It took her a full week to muster the courage to contact Patsy. And when she did, unable to trust herself to speak on the phone, she wrote her a letter in a spidery scrawl – she could not stop the pen from shaking. She begged her to come to the house when she knew Keith was away on business. And when it was written and sealed in a cream Manila envelope, Janice stood at the postbox for a full ten minutes with the letter in her hand, sweating, battling with her demons. It was only when Dr Jones from the house next door approached, hobbling on his walking stick and with his Jack Russell at his heels, that she let it slip from her fingers into the gaping red mouth of the postbox.

And then she waited.

By the time the allotted night came round, Janice had convinced herself that Patsy would not come and with that certain knowledge came relief – she would not have to go through with this after all. So, when the doorbell rang at five past eight, Janice was both astounded, and horrified, to find Patsy on her front doorstep, smartly dressed in a black coat and heels. She looked like she had just come from the gallery. She entered the house without being asked and went straight into the drawing room. Not a word passed between them.

Janice stood stupidly by the open door for some moments, staring out at the blackness and the fine, silent rain illuminated by the lamp suspended over the door. Then she closed it and immediately started to shake. Her entire body was a spasm of nervous impulses, utterly uncontrollable. She paused in the hall, leant on the table against the wall and took several deep breaths. The jerking in her muscles eased sufficiently for her to make her way into the drawing room. She found her friend perched on the edge of a sofa, her back ramrod straight.

Janice took a seat opposite Patsy and sat on her hands. Her head was full of a rushing sound like a fast-flowing stream. Patsy said, 'This had better be good.'

Janice blurted out, 'How's Laura getting on at uni?' It was a stupid question, born from her frazzled nerves and a desire to talk about anything but what she must.

'She's not at uni, Janice.'

'Sorry, college.'

Patsy carried on addressing the fireplace, as if Janice wasn't there. 'She's doing a HNC in Early Education and Childcare. An odd choice, don't you think, for a girl that aborted her own baby?'

Janice winced.

'I think she might be trying to atone for what she did. Maybe she thinks that helping other people's children will make up for what she – we – did. I don't know. It's not quite the psychology degree she'd hoped for. But she didn't get the grades, did she?' Patsy brought her gaze, hard and cold, to bear on Janice. 'And we both know why that was.'

Janice hung her head. 'I'm sorry.' She clasped her hands around her knees in an effort to hold her body together. She feared that if she let go she wouldn't be able to stop herself falling apart.

'Is that what you asked me here for? To say you're sorry?' The room bristled with Patsy's rage like a boxing ring with testosterone. She looked fierce and proud, a lioness. 'You said in your letter that you had something to say to me. Something,' she added, looking about the room, 'that you could only tell me in private.'

Janice nodded, and tried to form her lips into words but the muscles around her mouth were frozen with fear.

'Well, here we are. Just the two of us. I'm intrigued. What is it you want to say?'

'I . . . I . . .' Janice put her hand over her mouth. She felt the rise of nausea in her stomach and rose from the sofa. She bolted out of the room and into the loo, fell to her knees and brought up the contents of her stomach in the toilet. Embarrassed, she kicked the door shut behind her with the heel of her shoe. She knelt there for some moments, sobbing quietly, before wiping her mouth with a piece of toilet roll.

Outside the door she heard Patsy's voice, still hard-edged but tinged with concern now. 'Are you alright?'

Janice stood up and said loudly, 'Yes.' She got to her feet, flushed the toilet and washed her hands. She splashed her face with cold water and rinsed the metallic taste from her mouth. She dried her hands and face, leaving smudges of black mascara on the fluffy white towel. She could not bear to look at her face in the mirror.

Patsy was standing in the hall with her arms crossed when

Janice came out holding her stomach. She could not stop shaking – she felt so cold.

Patsy frowned, looking more annoyed than concerned. 'Are you unwell? Do you want me to call someone? Keith?'

Janice shook her head and looked at the floor. She concentrated on her breathing, taking long, slow breaths, pushing the air down deep into her lungs, holding it for three seconds, letting it go again.

'What is wrong with you, Janice? You've smeared make-up all over your face, you know.'

Janice stumbled past her to the stairs where she sat down on the bottom step and looked up. 'I don't think I can do this.'

'Do what, Janice?'

'Tell you . . . tell you what happened.'

'We all know what happened, Janice.'

'I don't mean between Pete and Laura.' Her mouth dried up, her throat constricted so that she could barely breathe, let alone talk.

'You're not making any sense at all, Janice.' Patsy looked at her watch and shook her head. 'I don't have time for this. I have to get home.' She started walking to the door, her high heels like hammers on the wooden floor.

'Please! Don't go!' cried Janice and she put her hands on either side of her head and squeezed hard. The pain helped her focus her thoughts and keep the fear at bay. It helped her differentiate between what was real physical pain and what was going on inside her head. 'Let me say it,' she breathed. 'I can only say it once.'

Patsy stopped and turned around slowly. Something in Janice's expression made her change her mind. Patsy's demeanour altered – her shoulders slumped, and she lowered her eyes as the anger leached out of her. With the fury gone, she looked tired and wretched. The make-up under her eyes did little to conceal the bags there and the deep laughter lines on her face made her look haggard. She walked tentatively over to the chair by the hall table, her heels clipping on the floor like castanets, and sat down. On the table was an old-fashioned white telephone that had belonged to Keith's mother, and which Janice had had restored for his fiftieth birthday. Patsy looked at the phone, looked at her hands, and then waited, her head bent as if in prayer.

The grandfather clock ticked away the seconds, the rain pitter-pattered on the arc of stained glass above the front door and the old house creaked as if it was a living thing. Janice raised her eyes to the light coming through the stained glass. It bore an image, not of the burning bush, the emblem of the Presbyterian Church, but the secular crest of the family who had owed the house before it became a manse. Janice closed her eyes.

She knew that she must act quickly. She must say the essentials before her body closed down and stopped working. Already her vision was blurred and she felt light-headed like she was about to faint.

Her throat felt tight and narrow like a straw. When she finally opened her mouth and formed the words that had lived inside her head for nearly twenty years it sounded like a stranger speaking.

'My father abused me for the first time on New Year's Eve when I was eleven.'

Patsy let out a little gasp and Janice opened her eyes but she did not look at her friend. She concentrated very hard on a dark brown knot, like a stain, on one of the old wooden floorboards. A pain, like a shard of glass, shot through her brain making her wince. But she was determined. She had lived in the shadow of fear and self-loathing all her life. She would not let him win – not this time.

She forced herself to go on, her voice flat and emotionless, like it was disconnected from her altogether. 'It went on for years. When I got away to university I thought I had finally escaped him. I went completely mad. By the age of twenty, I'd slept with forty different men, Patsy. I can't even remember their names, never mind their faces. And then one day, my father came up to visit me and when he found out I had a boyfriend, he raped me again.'

'Oh, my God, Janice. Oh, my God.'

'I never told my parents I was pregnant. I knew they wouldn't support me. I knew that if I told the truth, no-one would believe me. So I had Pete on my own, living on benefits. They've never seen him. I met Keith and moved away and told everyone they were dead. I hope they are dead, both of them.' Tears came now, silent and abundant, cascading down her cheeks like the rain on the windows. She had stopped shaking, but the knot in her stomach was as tight and hard as it had always been.

'Your father is . . .' Patsy gave a cry and then went quiet.

'That's right. Pete's grandfather, my father, is also his father.'

Patsy muttered something unintelligible like a whispered prayer and then there was silence for some moments before Janice spoke again.

'There's so much hurt inside me. My daddy betrayed me and so did my mammy.' Janice paused and swallowed a ball of grief that threatened to choke her, the way she did almost every day of her life. 'For years I didn't want to believe that she knew what was going on. But I think now she must've known. My father was a bully and she was afraid of him. I can never forgive her.'

She looked at Patsy then and was unable to summon up any expression at all. Patsy was crying silently. Her face was a mess of tears and snot. She fumbled in her pocket, pulled out a crumpled hankie and blew her nose loudly. When she was done Patsy said, 'Did you go to the police? Was he prosecuted?'

'No,' said Janice simply, too exhausted to offer an explanation. How could she explain to someone who had never been abused what it was to live in terror? To believe that you had somehow brought this terrible thing upon yourself? To be told that you had 'asked for it', that deep down you 'wanted it'? To be told these terrible lies often enough, and always under the shadow of fear, so that you came in the end to believe them to be true? It had taken Janice years of secret counselling to unravel these deceptions, to finally see herself as an innocent victim. And still she could not shake off the sense of shame, of worthlessness.

Patsy pressed the handkerchief to her lips. 'Why are you telling me this now, Janice? After all these years?'

'Because I want you to understand. From the moment I held Pete in my arms, Patsy, I could not love him – not wholly and completely. I remember the first time I had to . . . to . . . change his nappy.'

Her stomach heaved and she ran into the loo again. Nothing came up but her body retched and retched all the same. When she was done this time, Patsy was behind her, supporting her under the arm, guiding her back to her place at the bottom of the stairs. Janice slumped down, worn out – telling her story had taken almost every ounce of physical and mental strength.

'Wait here,' said Patsy and she went and got a glass of water from the kitchen. She knelt in front of Janice and pressed the cold glass into her hands and said, 'It's okay. You don't have to say any more.'

'No, I want to,' said Janice, summoning up the strength

to go on, determined to finish what she had begun. She took a sip of water and continued. 'When I had to change his nappy, I used to . . . I used to vomit.' The glass shook so much she thought the contents would spill out over her. She took a long drink to try and calm herself and, when she removed the glass from her lips, words came tumbling out, one on top of each other as though, imprisoned inside her for so long, they were now desperate for freedom.

'I couldn't bond with him. I couldn't love him no matter how much I tried, no matter how often I told myself that it wasn't his fault, that he was an innocent. It was so hard trying to raise him. Sometimes I used to leave him crying in his cot for hours because I couldn't bear to touch him.'

Patsy looked horrified. She put a hand to her mouth.

'I did. And I know it's awful. But I didn't know what else to do. I actually thought about ending it at times and killing Pete too. And then I met Keith and my life changed. He saved me, Patsy. He saved us both. Without him, I don't think I could've carried on.'

Patsy nodded.

'He never asked questions, you know. He just accepted me and Pete for what we were. And I'm so grateful to him for that. And for loving Pete unconditionally – the way I should've.'

Patsy's hand fell away from her face. She placed them on Janice's knees. 'Oh, Janice, you were a good mother. I was there. I saw you.'

Janice placed the glass of water on the floor. 'It's sweet of you to say that, it really is. But you're wrong, Patsy. It was always an act, an effort. I tried, I really did. But a part of my heart has always been closed to Pete. I went through the motions of being a loving mother, but Pete knew. He *knew*. He was always too clever.' She paused, wiped her nose with the back of her hand and sniffed. 'There's not a day goes by that I don't think about what happened. I can't look at Pete but I see my father. He has his mannerisms and his features, even his voice when it broke was my dad's.'

Patsy looked away from Janice and sniffed.

'You are right to blame me for what Pete did, Patsy, because I am responsible for what he is. Those early years scarred him badly and I could never make it up to him. The emotional damage was done, I couldn't undo it.'

Patsy shook her head vehemently. 'You're not responsible for Pete's character, Janice. And after all that's happened to you, I think you did a wonderful job. No-one could've done better.'

Janice let the praise wash over her, absorbing none of it. She deserved none. 'He won't speak to me now, you know,' she said quietly, staring at her hands. The shaking had stopped. 'We told him that Keith was his adoptive dad and of course he straight away wanted to know who his real dad was. I told him I didn't know.' She looked up into Patsy's face, blotchy from crying. 'How could I tell him the truth?'

Patsy shook her head in response.

'He called me an old tart, or something like that.' Janice forced out a croak of a laugh. Her throat felt dry and rough.

'That's awful,' said Patsy with feeling.

'It's okay,' said Janice with a weak smile. 'I don't care if he hates me. All that matters is that he never finds out.' She was filled with a sudden sense of unease. 'You understand that, don't you? How important it is that Pete never finds out?'

Patsy sighed, and made a tutting sound with her lips. She took Janice's hands in hers, pressed her palms together and held them the way you would if teaching a child how to pray. 'I understand why you feel like that, Janice. But would it be so terrible if he found out? Is it any worse than the alternative – believing you were promiscuous and don't even know the name of his father? It's not like you did anything wrong. You've nothing to be ashamed of.'

Janice shook her head incredulously. 'You don't understand. I *know* I'm not to blame. I spent years listening to a therapist telling me I wasn't to blame. And yet the shame never goes away. I don't want Pete to have to live with that shame. Can you imagine how he would feel if he knew that he was the result of . . .' She looked away from Patsy and took a few seconds to compose herself. 'The result of rape and incest?' She brought her gaze, hard and determined, back to Patsy. 'I want to spare him that, even if it means we'll never be close.'

'I don't know what to say. It's bad enough him knowing he's illegitimate. But this . . .' Patsy's voice trailed off.

'Illegitimacy doesn't carry the same stigma it used to, Patsy. No-one cares about that sort of thing any more. But this is too grotesque for him to ever find out. It could destroy him. This way I protect him. This way the shame is mine, not his.' Janice slipped her hands out from Patsy's grasp and folded them defensively across her chest. 'And anyway, he has a father. He has Keith.'

'But,' said Patsy gently, leaning back a little, 'if you let him go on believing this, he'll resent you.'

'Even if he knew the truth, he might still resent me. He might even be disgusted with me . . . blame me. Who knows? I can't bear him to know the truth.' She shivered and ran her hands up her arms. 'I just can't.'

'Don't you want to have a close relationship with Pete?'

Janice put her head in her hands. 'Of course I do. In an ideal world. But we didn't have a close relationship before this and I'm not sure anything would change that now.'

'Being honest with him might.'

Janice shook her head and rubbed her brow. 'No, it wouldn't. And I can't be honest with him. I won't. Not about this.'

Patsy let out a soft sigh and her shoulders dipped. She looked defeated.

'Promise me you won't ever tell anyone about this,' said Janice.

'You don't need to ask me that. But, yes, I promise. I take it Keith doesn't know, then?'

Janice shook her head. 'After I married Keith I wanted to start afresh. And I did. I put my past, and everything in it, behind me. I became the respectable wife of a lawyer. I changed the way I looked, the way I behaved, even the way I talked.' She tried to give a little laugh but it came out flat, like a wrong note. 'I didn't always talk like this,' she said, slipping into the down-to-earth Enniskillen accent she had worked so hard to eradicate. 'You're the only person, apart from a counsellor, that I've told. I don't want Clare or Kirsty or anyone else to find out.'

'They won't find out from me, Janice. You know that.'

'I'm terrified that Keith will find out what I was like before I met him. All the men . . . He would leave me – because he would, I know he would – and then the whole town would know what I was really like.' She was shaking. 'I couldn't bear that, Patsy. It would ruin Keith. He's chairman of the Rotary and the community council and an elder at the church. Can you imagine what the gossip would do to him?'

Patsy got up off her knees creakily and sat down beside Janice, elbow to elbow, on the stairs. 'Listen to me, Janice. He's not going to find out. Ever. You don't have to worry. It's in the past and that's where it's going to stay.' She pressed her hands between her legs and said in a voice that was cracking, 'I'm sorry that you had to endure all that, Janice. It must've been awful for you. It must still be awful.'

Janice bowed her head. Patsy was quiet for a little while. She cleared her throat and when she spoke again her voice was more assured. 'I owe you and Keith an apology. I'm ashamed of myself for carrying on with this ridiculous vendetta against you both. I . . . I just wanted someone to blame.' She paused, a sob escaped her lips and she immediately composed herself. 'I found out that Laura was as much to blame as Pete for what happened, but I didn't want to accept it. She's paid a high enough price for her foolishness, God help her. I chose to see her as a victim because it let me channel all my anger somewhere else. That was unjust of me.'

'That's alright,' said Janice.

There was a quiet rush of air as Patsy inhaled, held her breath and asked, 'Do you forgive me?'

'There's nothing to forgive.' Patsy breathed out and Janice went on, 'And if it's worth anything, I think Laura did the right thing having the abortion.'

'Oh, Janice, how can it be "right"? There is no "right" in that situation. No matter what she did it would've felt wrong – abortion, adoption, or keeping the baby and struggling to raise it as a single mum.'

'I guess what I mean is that it was the best thing to do under the circumstances. I would've had an abortion if I could.'

'No-one would blame you for that, Janice.'

'You couldn't get an abortion in Northern Ireland then and I didn't have the money to go to England.'

'Nothing's changed,' said Patsy bitterly. 'Laura was alright because she had our support and money to pay for the abortion, the flights and the hotel. We were made to feel like . . . like criminals, sneaking over the water to a private clinic.'

Patsy put her face in her hands. Janice put her arm around her friend and rubbed the small of her back in a circular motion.

Patsy sobbed quietly. 'I think of that baby, my first grandchild, every day, Janice. I imagine a little blond-haired boy – or girl – with rosy cheeks and blue eyes running into my arms, playing in my garden in the summer.'

'You'll have that one day, Patsy. When the girls are older and married and the time's right for having babies.'

Patsy sniffed and looked up. 'Yes, I hope so. But I'll never forget.' She wiped the tears from her face with the now-saturated handkerchief and said, 'Oh, look at me. Blubbering away like an idiot. I'm the one who should be comforting you – not the other way around.'

'That's okay. My hurt's an old one, Patsy, sealed if not healed by time. Yours is still raw.' She wanted to tell Patsy that her grief would ease eventually, but experience had taught her that was not the case. The pain didn't ease, it crystallised into something hard and cold, like stone. The hurt was always there.

Janice held onto Patsy's arm and rested her head on her friend's shoulder. They sat like that for some time, not speaking, listening to the creaks of the house and the rain outside. Exhaustion washed over Janice – her eyelids drooped like shutters and her limbs felt heavy as rocks. Yet she felt more at peace than she had done in a long, long while. Not just back to the time before she and Patsy had fallen out, but right back to her childhood when she was still innocent. Sharing her story had reduced the potency of its hold over her. It had not erased the horror of her past, but it had polished it until the rough edges were gone and it didn't chafe the way it used to. The thing she had feared most – telling her story – had, ironically, partly set her free.

Eventually Janice spoke. 'Do you think we can be friends again, Patsy?' She looked into the other woman's face.

Patsy smiled. 'Of course we're friends. As best as we ever were.'

'You will all be happy again, I promise.'

Patsy looked at the floor. 'I hope you will be too, Janice.'

Janice shrugged. 'I'm as happy now as I ever was, I think. I can't ask for more than that.'

'I'm sorry for banging on about my family's woes. Everyone,' said Patsy, turning her gaze on Janice, 'has problems.'

'There's nothing wrong with crying over someone you love, Patsy.'

Patsy sniffed. 'I've been uptight about Martin too.'

'Still no sign of a job, then?'

Patsy shook her head. 'We've used all our savings now. Martin sold his car and we used the money to pay off credit cards and loans. We've calculated that if we cut back on everything but absolute essentials, we can manage on what I make from the gallery, for a few months anyway. Martin's been a great help in getting the shop ready – you know we're going to open a coffee shop in the back, where the storeroom used to be?'

Janice nodded.

'He's worked like a Trojan. I'm very proud of him. If it takes off we might be able to save the gallery. But we're hoping it won't come to that.'

'I hope so too,' said Janice glumly. 'When are you opening?'

'In a fortnight.'

'Can I come?' asked Janice, smiling tentatively.

'Of course you can, you silly cow!' said Patsy, breaking into a smile and then she went on, serious again, 'You know, after what's happened to Laura and Martin, it's made us realise what's important in life. The holidays and the lifestyle never made us happy. It was each other and our family that brought us the greatest joy. Sometimes you can lose sight of that. And it's not like we're living in abject poverty. Yes, we'll have to tighten our belts but we're not going to starve.'

Janice brushed away the tears that had slid unnoticed from her eyes. She wished that she could have the same relationship with her son that Patsy had with her daughters. She would've traded every penny she possessed for a close relationship with Pete.

'What about you, Janice? What are you planning to do now Pete has gone? Have you ever thought about training to be a counsellor?'

'What, me?' Janice pressed her chest with the tips of her fingers.

'You're a survivor, Janice. You haven't let what happened to you destroy your life. Your experience could help other girls in the same situation.'

'Could it? You think so? I'd never considered that. I never thought I might have something to offer other people.' The idea was so alien to Janice that it left her almost breathless. But Patsy was right. It made sense of sorts. Now that Pete was gone, she had even more time on her hands and nothing to do. Maybe it was time to give something back – and to give her life some direction. She felt colour rise to her cheeks. 'Do you think I could actually make a difference?'

'You might do more than make a difference, Janice. You might save someone.'

Janice grasped Patsy's hands in hers. 'It would be good to do that, wouldn't it? And though it's not a reason for doing it and it sounds awful selfish, I think focusing on other people's problems would help me put mine in perspective.'

'Indeed it would,' said Patsy and she smiled and squeezed

Janice's hand, and Janice realised then that this was the reason Patsy had suggested it in the first place.

It was the end of November and autumn was gracefully giving way, day by day, to the icy grip of winter. A biting north wind had stripped the trees of the last of their curled brown leaves and people's thoughts were turning to all things Christmassy as an antidote to the long, dark winter ahead.

Four weeks had passed since the conversation with Janice, and Patsy couldn't get it out of her head. She stood in the empty gallery early on a Saturday morning filled with revulsion and hate for Janice's father. She couldn't stop thinking about the awful, graphic images and sometimes she wished Janice had not told her, it haunted her so. She put her palms over her ears and closed her eyes.

But in other ways, she was glad. Glad that her friend had been able to entrust her with such an unbearable secret. Glad that she had been able to help and that her friendship with Janice had been restored. And glad too because Janice's story had helped put Laura's into perspective.

She opened her eyes and lowered her hands. Unlike Janice, Laura had willingly engaged in intercourse – and not for the first time. Laura had been able to abort her unwanted child – an option not open to Janice. Of course Pete behaved reprehensibly but Laura, Patsy finally admitted to herself – the knowledge settling heavily in her stomach like an undigested Ulster Fry – had largely brought this tragedy upon herself.

This did not in any way diminish her grief at her daughter's suffering. And she couldn't get the notion out of her head that Laura had been somehow sullied, tainted in a way that could never be erased. Laura would be scarred by what had happened for the rest of her days in ways she was too young to understand now. Patsy bit her lip. If she married, would she, for example, tell her husband? Or would she keep her past a secret for ever, like Janice had chosen to do? Patsy's heart still ached for her unborn grandchild but she tried to console herself that they had done the right thing.

The door to the gallery burst open and Martin came in, carrying a black plastic bin bag in his arms. 'That's the rolls from the bakery,' he said cheerfully, as he kicked the door shut with his foot. 'You can't get much fresher than that.'

Martin dumped the bag on the floor and unzipped his ski jacket. He was wearing dark blue jeans and a rugby shirt – a far cry from the smart suits and stiff-collared shirts he used to wear to the bank. 'Bloody cold out there today.' He rubbed his hands together. 'Do you think we're ready, then?'

'As ready as we're ever going to be,' said Patsy and her stomach turned over. She put a hand on her belly, as nervous as a teenager at her first dance.

'What time's the photographer from the *Courier* coming?' asked Martin. It had been his idea to organise an official opening – and thereby gain free publicity in the local paper.

'Ten.'

Martin smiled at her, his face alive with excitement. 'Come on, Come and look.' He took her hand and led her over to the opening that led to what had once been the storeroom at the back of the shop. Except the door was gone and the room beyond wasn't a storeroom any more. They stood there at the threshold and Patsy stared in amazement at what they had achieved.

With sheer hard work, determination and a combination of ingenuity and imagination, the space had been transformed into a quirky, homely café. The mismatched china and the second-hand pictures on the walls had all come from charity shops, glad to be rid of unwanted boxes of tat. Patsy had sewn the tablecloths from roll ends of fabric purchased at the market and Martin had picked up the odd chairs at a second-hand auction.

There was a basket of dog-eared magazines on a sideboard under an old mirror in a chipped frame and tealights from IKEA on every table. Patsy's eye was drawn upwards to the cupola. Years of grime and dirt had been washed away, flooding the room with natural light. An old Christmas tree they'd found in the attic was erected in the corner by the loo and colourful paper chains – made by Laura and Sarah, bless them – served as Christmas decorations.

Patsy looked at Martin and said, 'It's fantastic. I can't believe what you've done.'

'What *we've* done, Patsy,' he said, putting his arm across her shoulder. 'Us. A team. Together we can do anything, you know.'

She looked up into her husband's face, and saw he was, like the sideboard he had rescued from a skip and painted cream, restored somehow. His face was just as lined and his hair still thinning on top, but in spirit he was a happier, more contented man.

An hour later the front room of the gallery was crammed to bursting. Patsy stood grinning at the camera, holding a big pair of orange-handled scissors with Martin at her side, his hands on her hands, their arms outstretched, the way they had once stood and pressed a blunt knife into their wedding cake. The camera flashed, the scissors sliced through the red ribbon tied across the doorway and everyone cheered.

'I declare the Devlin Gallery and Café open,' shouted Patsy with a flourish of the scissors above her head, and everyone cheered again.

'Who's ready for a cuppa?' called Martin and the small crowd cried, 'Yeah!' and surged into the room next door.

Janice, Kirsty and Clare, dressed to the nines, took a table right in the middle of the room. They were giggling and laughing and looking around excitedly, pointing out things to each other and examining the menu cards propped up between the salt and pepper shakers in the middle of the table.

Patsy went over with a little pad in one hand and a pen in the other, ready to take their order.

'Oh, look at you,' teased Janice, reaching out and touching the frilly hem of Patsy's old-fashioned apron. 'You look like Ma out of *Little House on the Prairie*.'

Patsy, laughing, put her hands on her hips and said, 'I'll take that as a compliment.'

'It is,' said Clare seriously. 'Ma was very pretty.'

'This is just wonderful,' said Kirsty, looking around. 'I love the paper chains and these tablecloths are so pretty.' She ran the flat of her palm over the seersucker checkered material. 'Everything's got a lovely homespun feel. There's a phrase for it, isn't there?'

'Shabby chic!' cried Janice.

'Well, we've done our best,' said Patsy modestly, delighted, and then turning to business said, 'To celebrate our opening we're offering every customer today a free cup of coffee. And the carrot cake's on special offer. It's to die for – I persuaded Mary Clark, Kirsty's neighbour, to bake for me.'

'Her baking's fabulous,' confirmed Kirsty. 'She made a lovely chocolate cake for me last week.'

'Was that because it was Scott's anniversary?' said Clare and the atmosphere shifted.

Kirsty nodded. 'She's so kind. She knew I was having Dorothy and Harry round. We had a nice meal and looked at photos and watched some old videos – and then we went up to the grave and left some flowers.'

No-one spoke and Patsy felt a lump in her throat.

'That must've been very upsetting,' observed Janice at last.

'Funny enough,' said Kirsty, quite matter-of-factly, 'I'd been dreading it. But it wasn't awful. Not like other years have been. There were tears, of course, and sadness, obviously.' She paused, fingered the salt shaker in the middle of the table and went on. 'But we laughed too and told funny stories about Scott and the boys loved it, talking about their dad.'

'You do a great job of keeping his memory alive,' Clare said and Kirsty gave her a small, almost secret smile.

'Hey, Patsy,' shouted Martin playfully across the heads of the customers. 'Are you going to stand there gabbing all day? There's people here dying of thirst!'

The crowd in the room roared with laughter and Patsy said, just as loudly as Martin, 'Sure, you know that's what I do best.'

And to her friends she said, her heart full of happiness, 'No rest for the wicked, is there? Now what are you lot having?'

'Just a coffee for me,' said Janice as the others picked up the menus and looked at them. 'I'll have to make it snappy.' She glanced at her watch.

'Why's that?' said Clare, looking up.

'I . . . eh . . . I have some business to attend to,' said Janice mysteriously and there was something about the way she said it that even Clare had the wit not to press her further.

'Well then, I'll get that coffee right away while the others choose,' said Patsy and she tottered off to the kitchen, beginning to wish she'd worn more sensible shoes and wondering what Janice was being so guarded about.

Chapter Twenty-Three

It was December, and Kirsty and David were waiting in the porch for Adam who had decided at the last moment, just before leaving the house, that he needed the toilet. Kirsty checked her watch – if he didn't hurry up they would be late for school. She noted the date on her watch and a wave of excitement rippled through her. Chris would be home in less than a week's time.

As if reading her mind, David said, 'When are we going to see Chris again?'

'Next week, darling. He's coming home for Christmas.'

David picked up an unopened Christmas card that was lying on top of the meter box and examined the stamp. 'You like him, don't you?'

'Yes. Do you?'

'He's okay,' said David, without much conviction. 'Do you miss him?'

'Yes.'

'As much as Daddy?'

Kirsty's heart skipped a beat. 'Yes,' she said.

David put the envelope back on the shelf. 'When can we go back to Dubai?'

They had all gone over for a week during the October half-term break. In spite of the scorching heat, Chris made sure they had a wonderful time. They went to water parks and wandered around the most amazing air-conditioned shopping malls Kirsty had ever seen. They went indoor skiing and rode camels at dawn to avoid the heat of the day. And one night they'd slept in Bedouin-style tents in the desert, staring up at the cloudless desert sky, studded with stars. And though neither of them vocalised it, they both knew Kirsty's visit was more than just a holiday. It was an opportunity for her to see if Dubai was somewhere she and the boys could call home.

'I don't know.' Kirsty took a deep breath. 'How would you like to live there for a while? You know, go to school and everything.'

David frowned. 'Are we going to?'

'No, I'm only asking if you would *like* to.'

'Okay.'

'Okay?' Kirsty was more than surprised by this reply. Perhaps he didn't fully understand the implications.

'Sure,' he said and shrugged, and what he said next demonstrated that he understood only too well. 'But when would I see my friends? And what about Grandma and Grandpa?'

'Well,' she said slowly, trying to make it sound as if she was making it up as she went along – and not something she had considered in every detail. 'We could come home during the summer holidays and you could see your friends then. Grandma and Grandpa could come out and visit us – as much as they liked. And it wouldn't be for ever, David. Only for a year or two. It would be a . . . a great adventure.'

David pulled a face, considering this, and Kirsty asked herself if she was mad, thinking of taking the boys away from everything they knew to start a new life in a foreign country – one where they didn't speak the language, temperatures reached over a hundred in the summer and the culture was completely alien. If the last three years had been about anything, they had been about providing stability for the boys. Yet, in one fell swoop she was proposing to obliterate everything she and Dorothy and Harry had worked for since Scott's death.

David picked up two stones from the windowsill where he had left them the day before, and weighed them in the palm of his right hand. 'But why can't Chris come and live here with us?'

Kirsty sighed. 'He has a job in Dubai. It's well paid and he . . . well, he just has to stick it out for a few years. And then he can come home again.'

Adam burst through the porch door just then bundled up in his coat, hat, gloves and rucksack. The handle of the door hit the wall with a thud. Normally she would've given off to him for marking the paintwork, but today she was glad of the diversion.

'We're going to be late for school if you don't hurry up,' said Adam, coming to a halt with his hand on his hip, mimicking both the voice and stance she adopted to chivvy them along when they were being tardy.

'You're the one that's kept us waiting, you cheeky wee monkey,' said Kirsty with an indulgent smile. 'Come on, let's get this show on the road.'

Later when was sitting at her desk in the deserted museum at lunchtime eating a sandwich, she reflected on the fact that she had what she wanted. Chris. It was what she had dreamt of – the chance to start a new life with the man she loved. But now that it was within her grasp, the dream had lost some of its allure. The well-worn phrase 'be careful what you wish for' rang in her ears. She thought of all the things she would miss – her home, Dorothy and Harry, her job and, most of all, her three dearest friends: Clare, Janice and

Patsy. They would always be her friends of course, but moving away from them was a bitter price to pay for being with Chris.

Why did it have to be Dubai? It was so far away, so *foreign*. Why couldn't he have got a job somewhere more ordinary like Manchester or London or Dublin? Somewhere in the same time zone and within easy travelling distance of Ballyfergus, the place she had learned to call home.

The alternative was to stay on in Ballyfergus – to live apart from him until he returned from Dubai. But that could be a long time. The knowledge that Chris loved her and their long, frequent telephone conversations had sustained her over the last four months. But she could not live like this, conducting a long-distance love affair, in the long term. And while she was happy that they were together at last, her heart ached for him. The separation was almost more than she could bear. Some nights she cried herself to sleep because she missed him so much, remembering the hot nights of love-making in Dubai while the boys slept in the room next door. She felt like her chest had been spliced with an axe, leaving an aching open wound.

She could and would make Dubai work. So long as she had her boys with her and she and Chris were together she told herself that was all that mattered. She would work hard at making sure the boys were happy. No relationship was plain sailing – like gardens, this one would require care and attention to blossom. The challenges in this one were just different to the ones she had faced with Scott. And one day they would come back here and live in Ballyfergus all the rest of their days.

And so with her mind made up, she resolved to do what she had put off these last four months – break the news to Dorothy and Harry.

It was the Sunday before Christmas and Kirsty and the boys had spent most of the day at Dorothy and Harry's house attending what had become something of an Elliott family tradition – a big get-together with Scott's extended family. Old aunts of Scott's, who hadn't seen the boys since last year, fussed over them like they were babies and elderly uncles pressed crisp twenty pound notes into their eager palms.

It was after five now and everyone but Kirsty and the boys had gone home. Kirsty sat in the high-ceilinged lounge while the boys watched a *Dr Who* DVD in the room next door. The logs hissed and crackled in the grate and the heavy gold damask curtains were drawn against the darkness outside. On the wall to the left of the fireplace hung a large gilt-framed photo of Scott in his graduation gown, holding a rolled-up red certificate in his hand. Kirsty tried not to look at it.

'That was nice of Chris to stop by and see us the other day,' said Harry, touching his neatly trimmed moustache with his fingers as if checking there wasn't something lurking in there that shouldn't be.

'Yes,' agreed Dorothy. 'He was telling us all about his job out in Dubai. It sounds like he's really enjoying it out there.'

'Still, it's a shame he couldn't make it today,' said Harry.

'Yes,' said Kirsty. 'Not enough time, I'm afraid. Today's the only day he could get up to Dungannon to visit his mother's family.'

Dorothy and Harry had accepted the news that Kirsty was seeing Chris with equanimity bordering on approval. Their reaction had surprised her. Perhaps knowing Chris personally had made the difference. She herself could not conceive of anyone disliking him. In any event, they treated him the easy way they always had and talked of him with fondness.

'Yes,' chimed in Dorothy. 'It would've been nice for him to meet some of the family.'

'Another time, perhaps,' said Kirsty, feeling slightly uncomfortable with the extent of the claim Dorothy and Harry made on her. It was so kind of them to include Kirsty in all the family gatherings and to talk of her as though she was one of their own. She realised with sudden insight that, at some point over the last three years, they had started to treat her like a daughter, rather than a daughter-in-law. And part of her liked that intimacy, that sense of belonging. But she also knew that if she didn't break free, it would suffocate her.

Dorothy started talking about Aunt Joan's recent hip-replacement operation and Kirsty tuned out. It was almost half past five. Nearly time to go home. But first she had to tell them that she was going to Dubai. She couldn't postpone it any longer. That was why Chris was absent today – not because he'd had to go to Dungannon, but because Kirsty thought it wise that she break the news to her in-laws alone. The food she had eaten earlier sat in her stomach like a brick and her hands twisted nervously in her lap.

Dorothy stopped talking and said, 'What did you think, Kirsty?'

'I thought she looked very well.'

'Who?'

'Aunt Joan.'

'No,' said Dorothy with a tut. She gave Kirsty a peculiar look and said, 'I was talking about the ham. You didn't think it too dry, did you?'

Kirsty forced her muscles into a smile. 'Sorry. I thought it was just lovely. I could taste the honey.'

'You're tired, love,' interjected Harry, always quick to protect her from Dorothy's tongue, which could be unintentionally sharp at times. 'My mind drifts like that too when I'm tired.'

The talk of tiredness brought a yawn to Kirsty's lips.

'See. I said she was tired,' said Harry.

Kirsty covered her hand with her mouth and the yawn turned into a weary smile. 'I really should be thinking of taking the boys home. They've school in the morning and I've work.' But she made no move to go and fidgeted with the folds of her pleated silk skirt.

'Roll on the holidays,' said Harry and he gave her a big smile, revealing his perfect white dentures.

Kirsty took a deep breath. 'But, before I go, there's something I need to . . .' Nerves made her voice high-pitched and squeaky. She stopped, cleared her throat and began again. 'I've something important to tell both of you.'

'What's that?' said Harry genially, but his fingers were working nervously at the tassles on his chair. He returned his gaze to Kirsty, a pained smile on his lips as though he knew already it would be bad news.

Dorothy looked sharply at Kirsty over the paper she had been half-heartedly reading. She folded it and placed it carefully on the coffee table. Then she took off her glasses and set them on top of the paper. She smoothed her skirt over her knees, folded her hands on her lap and waited.

Kirsty said, 'I'm going to move out to Dubai with the boys.'

Kirsty's heart pounded against her chest. Dorothy simply froze exactly as she was and Harry's face fell. There was a long, stunned silence. This news would change everything between them. Her happiness could only come at the expense of Harry and Dorothy's.

At last Harry, glancing at his wife's crestfallen face, cleared his throat and said, 'I . . . well . . . I imagine you've given this a lot of thought, Kirsty.'

Kirsty lowered her head and fought the urge to cry. 'I have.'

'I hope you don't mind me asking,' he said, frowning so hard he looked like he was in pain, 'but are you and Chris planning on getting married at some point?'

'No.'

Harry sat back in his chair and ran his index finger over his moustache. 'I see,' he said, thinking, and then he went on, 'You'd be taking quite a gamble going out there as a unmarried woman. These cultures aren't as tolerant as the West. If things go wrong, you'd be on your own.'

'Nothing's going to go wrong, Harry,' said Kirsty firmly, slightly irritated by the personal nature of his questions and the implication that Chris would abandon her. She knew that would never happen. And marriage, as she well knew, was no guarantee of anything.

'Well, it's ah . . . it's come as a bit of a shock, hasn't it, Dorothy?' said Harry, mustering up a rigid smile, trying, bless him, to pretend to be if not exactly happy for her, then at least accepting.

When he got no response from a shell-shocked Dorothy, he carried on bravely, only his wavering voice betraying his true emotion. 'Chris is a good man, Kirsty. Shall I tell you what I like most about him?'

'What's that?' said Kirsty, her voice little more than a whisper.

Harry was rheumy-eyed and it looked like it required a great deal of effort to keep in place the small smile on his face. 'What I like most about Chris is the way he is with those boys. It puts my mind at ease, so it does, watching him with them. I know he'll be good to them.' The smile slipped at last and his features settled into a picture of misery. 'Dorothy and I are fond of Chris and we can see how happy you are with him. Happier than you've been in a long time.' He paused and stared hard at her, his eyes bright with knowing. 'A very long time.'

Kirsty blushed and looked at the floor. Was it possible that he *knew*? Had Scott spoken to his father before he died about how sterile their marriage had become? Or had Harry simply guessed? She had been so careful not to betray her true emotions regarding Scott. But had she fooled only herself? She felt like a fraud. She could not bear to look at Harry and glanced at Dorothy instead.

She was sitting ramrod straight like a statue, tight-lipped, tense. It was hard to tell from her expression what her thoughts were. Kirsty thought she might be angry and her stomach tightened into a ball. 'You haven't said anything, Dorothy.'

Dorothy started as though snapped out of a daydream. She let out a long, audible sigh, and Kirsty saw then that her hands, in her lap, were shaking. 'It's just so sudden. So unexpected. You've only been seeing him for a few months and he's been in Dubai for most of that.'

Kirsty realised that Dorothy was in shock. Unlike Harry, she had not seen this coming. Maybe she hadn't wanted to. Kirsty leant forwards, clasped her hands together and said very gently, 'I've known Chris for three years, Dorothy. I know everything I need to know about him.' Dorothy just stared at Kirsty in response and there was a long, anguished pause.

'Please,' said Kirsty, her voice closing up on her as she realised how much Dorothy and Harry's approval meant to her. 'Please say you're happy for me.'

Dorothy sighed again and she was shaking all over. When she spoke, her voice was brittle, and she would not look at Kirsty. 'I'm glad that you've found happiness again, I really am. But I can't say I'm pleased that you're proposing to live together – what kind of an example is that for the boys?'

Kirsty had anticipated this reaction from both her

conservative in-laws, and she did not take offence at it. They were from a different generation that lived by different values, that was all. 'I know you're concerned about the stability of the home to which I'm taking David and Adam. But you don't need to be.'

'But,' went on Dorothy, not listening to her answer, 'that's not what . . . it's . . .' She shook her head and her lined face crumpled. 'The boys. You'll be taking my boys away.'

She cried unreservedly then, great heart-wrenching sobs that tore at Kirsty's heart. Dorothy, so strong and proud and capable, who had borne her son's death so bravely, rarely cried and this made her heartbreak all the harder to bear. Immediately Harry was at his wife's side, his arm around her ample waist, consoling her.

'There, there now, love. I know. I know,' he whispered softly like a prayer and smoothed the lines on her brow with the tips of his fingers. Kirsty, embarrassed at being a witness to such an intimate moment, looked away.

Taking the boys away from their grandparents seemed like unspeakable cruelty. How could she do this to Dorothy and Harry? And yet, how could she not? What alternative did she have? Stay here and wait for Chris to come back? It could be years. She did not think she could endure it.

'We knew things couldn't stay the same for ever, Dot,' said Harry. 'And if we had chosen a replacement for Scott, we'd be hard-pressed to find anyone better than Chris Carmichael, wouldn't we?'

Dorothy sniffed and wiped the tears from her eyes with her hand. 'Yes, I know,' she said sadly. 'I know all that. And I know you're right. But it doesn't make it any easier to bear. Does it, Harry?'

Harry took her hand in his and squeezed it. 'No,' he said quietly and shook his head, seemingly lost for further words.

They may have only a few years to live, thought Kirsty. How could she leave them now when they were at their most vulnerable? How could she do that to them? Chris was right – the boys would adapt, but not Dorothy and Harry.

'Why Dubai?' said Dorothy through her tears, speaking to Harry as though Kirsty was not there. 'Why so far away, Harry?'

Harry raised his shoulders and lowered them and Kirsty could see then that he too had succumbed to tears.

'I won't go,' she blurted out suddenly, her face burning with shame. Shame that she had so thoughtlessly, so selfishly put her desires above everyone else's in this family.

Dorothy and Harry looked at her then, with mirrored expressions of astonishment on their faces. They glanced at each other and Harry briskly wiped away the tears from his creased cheek. Dorothy sniffed and pulled a handkerchief from the sleeve of her cardigan.

'Kirsty, you mustn't pay too much attention to Dorothy and I. Of course it's a blow for us,' said Harry and he tried to smile. 'And we'll be devastated to see you and the boys go.'

Kirsty was crying now, not really listening to what Harry was saying. She put her face in her hands. 'I haven't thought this through, have I? What moving to Dubai would mean to you and the boys. I've thought only of myself. Only of what I wanted. I love Chris. But if he loves me he can wait for me.'

'And spend the next few years of your life being miserable?' It was Dorothy's voice, firm and directive, back in control. 'Don't you think you've been miserable long enough?'

The loneliness would be hard to bear, Kirsty thought, but she would console herself with the knowledge that she had done the right thing, the honourable thing – paying back what she owed.

But what if Chris wasn't prepared to wait? What if he met someone else? She couldn't bear it. No, she mustn't think like that. She would *have* to bear it. She gritted her teeth, pressed them together so hard they hurt. She had tried so hard to do the right thing by the boys, by Scott, by her in-laws. She would just have to keep on trying.

'Kirsty, listen to me.' This time Harry's voice was firm and more assured than ever as if, having allowed himself a brief moment of weakness, he had emerged stronger than before. 'Look at me, Kirsty. Look at me.' He snapped his fingers.

Kirsty raised her head, the act itself an effort, and squinted through her tears. Her head had begun to throb and she felt so weary, so worn out. She could not fight any more. 'It's okay. You don't have to worry. I'll not take the boys to Dubai.'

'Yes, you damn well will.'

Kirsty opened her eyes fully and blinked, brought to by the unfamiliar sound of Harry swearing. He was red in the face and his eyes burned with an intensity she had never seen before.

She opened her mouth and managed to form the word, 'What?'

'You are going to go to Dubai with Chris Carmichael to make a life there for all of you. Of course we're upset at the prospect, but do you think we'd have it any other way?' Harry looked at Dorothy, his face returning to its normal hue, and she nodded sadly in agreement.

'I don't understand,' said Kirsty feeling foggy-headed, foolish. Was she hearing things? Imagining what she wanted so desperately to be true, rather than what actually was?

'Do you think we would stand in the way of your happiness, Kirsty?' asked Dorothy. 'We would never allow that to happen. We couldn't live with that on our conscience.'

Confused, Kirsty shook her head. 'But I thought . . . you said . . .'

'Never mind what we said,' said Dorothy sharply and then her voice softened, the way it did when she talked to the boys. 'You're happier now than you've been in years, Kirsty. We can see that. And it makes our hearts glad. And we know that Scott would want to see you happy too.' She glanced at Harry then and nodded, affirming to herself, as much as her husband, the truth of this statement.

At the mention of Scott's name, Kirsty briefly averted her eyes.

'Are you giving me your blessing?' she said incredulously, hope rising like sap.

Dorothy and Harry both nodded, though there was little trace of joy in their faces.

The tears flowed silently and freely down Kirsty's face then. This, she understood, was love in its purest form. To give freely and seek nothing in return. Kirsty was no church-goer but a verse from the Bible came to mind, one that she and Scott had chosen for their wedding. How did it go? *Love is patient and kind . . . Love does not insist on its own way . . . it is . . . not resentful . . . Love endures . . . love bears all things.* And Dorothy and Harry would endure. They would bear their hurt and pain because they put Kirsty and the boys' happiness above their own. And this they did because they loved them so much.

'Thank you for this. And for . . . for everything,' said Kirsty simply, unable to articulate these thoughts in words. 'As long as I live I will never forget what you have done for me and the boys.'

A pleased smile passed between the older couple and some of the tension in the room dissipated. A wave of relief washed over Kirsty and the muscles across her shoulders relaxed.

And now she was desperate to cheer them up, to give something back to them. She leant forwards in the chair, wrung her hands together, and said, 'It'll only be for a year or two, at the most. You can visit whenever you like. And I'll bring the kids back here for the whole of the summer holidays – and Christmas too.'

Dorothy's face brightened. 'Would you?'

'Of course I will. I promise.'

'And I'll get the boys to phone you at least once a week and you can email David as often as you like, Harry. You'll see them at least four times a year – you will come out and stay with us, won't you?'

'Try keeping us away,' said Dorothy.

Harry fingered his moustache once more as if searching for something tangible and dependable when so much around him was shifting and changing. 'The boys aren't so young any more – and neither are we. Lately, I've been finding it difficult to keep up with them. Especially with this old leg.' He tapped his shin with the stick he always kept by him now and smiled bravely. 'I know Dorothy has too. We've had the very great joy and privilege of being involved in their lives on a daily basis when they were young. But the truth is, they don't need us as much now as they used to.'

Kirsty could see at once what he was trying to do – make her feel less guilty and Dorothy better. 'Of course they need you. They love you,' interjected Kirsty quickly.

Harry cocked his head a little to one side and looked at the fire, acknowledging this. 'Aye, and we love them too. But it's time for things to change.'

'I love you both,' whispered Kirsty, choked with gratitude. 'I will never forget the kindness you have shown me. And I know I can never repay you.'

'Oh, yes you can,' said Dorothy and when she lifted her face to look at Kirsty, her eyes were bright with tears and her cheeks flamed red. 'You give those boys the best life possible. And love them, Kirsty, love them as much and as hard as you can. That's all we ask. If you and Chris can do that, then we will be content.'

Content but not, Kirsty noted, happy. The loss of their only son was too great a blow – she saw then that they would never recover from it. They had moments of great pleasure, joy even, and anyone meeting them for the first time would never suspect the burden of sorrow they carried between them. But they would never be truly and completely happy again. In the maelstrom of their grief, they had clung to the boys, the living embodiment of the son they had loved and so cruelly lost. And who could blame them? Who could judge them for that? Not her.

Now, though, it was time for them to let go of David and Adam. Kirsty too. To give them the freedom and space to grow into new lives in another place, like transplanted seedlings reaching for the sun, while their lives contracted through age and inevitable ill-health. And even in their sorrow, Kirsty believed they understood that only too well.

It was New Year's Eve and Janice stood in her kitchen opening boxes of canapés from Marks & Spencer and arranging them on square white china plates. She wore a black silk-trimmed jersey dress and smart animal-print platform heels.

The pleasant hum of good conversation and background music drifted from the drawing room into the kitchen. The pelting rain on the windows made the inside feel all the more homely and cosy. For this year's party, if you could call it that, was a much more restrained affair than last year's with a smaller guest list and a nicer, more intimate feel. Only twenty or so people were there – people Janice regarded as true friends.

She was relieved when Keith said they hadn't the cash to spend on a lavish party that anyway would appear vulgar in the current climate of redundancies and austerity – Keith's firm had recently had to let one of the conveyancing lawyers go. Janice smiled at the memory of last year's party when she and the others had locked themselves in the en-suite, a tribe apart, away from the rest of the guests. They'd acted like silly teenagers – but it had been fun. She remembered too the resolutions she and her friends had made last year and suddenly that party seemed like a very long time ago.

So much had happened since then. Clare and Kirsty had seen their resolutions realised, but not without heartache, and Patsy's life had been turned upside-down in ways she never could've foreseen. Janice tried to recall her wishy-washy resolution – what was it she had said back then? Something about *starting a new project*? She was always starting projects, a fact that served to highlight her lack of direction and goal-less existence. But not any more. She had found the courage, with Patsy's support, to finally do something meaningful with her life.

'We've come to help,' announced Patsy, teetering into the kitchen in high-heeled patent leather boots. She looked well and relaxed in a red floaty dress, though that might have had more to do with the glass in her hand than her outfit. Behind her was Clare in flats, black velvet evening trousers and a simple sleeveless top that showed off her well-defined shoulders. She'd lost nearly two stone in the last six months and looked fabulous. Kirsty was last, looking radiant and pretty in a printed wrap dress.

'Shall I get rid of these?' asked Patsy and, without waiting for an answer, swiped the M&S boxes into the bin and climbed onto one of the breakfast bar chairs. Janice smiled and placed a sprig of parsley on top of a mound of cocktail sausages.

'Let me do something,' said Clare, and Janice set her to work making crudités.

'What can I do?' said Kirsty.

'Would you mind making up a platter of cold meats? They're in the fridge. Over there on the top shelf. Yes, just there.'

Patsy put her elbows on the granite surface, held her head in her hands like it was too heavy to remain unsupported and surveyed the proceedings. 'So when are you going to get me a couple more paintings for the gallery, Clare?' Addressing the wider company, she added, 'I sold all of them over Christmas, you know. People were fighting over them to buy as presents.'

Clare cut a red pepper in half and started poking out the seeds with the point of the knife. 'Soon. I promise. It's just been a bit manic over Christmas. Did I tell you I heard from the Director of Arts Development for the Arts Council?'

'Really!' cried Patsy, her interest aroused.

'Yeah, she phoned me between Christmas and the New Year.'

'What'd she want?' Patsy put her glass to her lips without taking her eyes off Clare.

'She's putting together a showcase of new Northern Irish artists for a touring exhibition of the UK and she wants me to contribute two paintings.'

'Why, that's fabulous!' exclaimed Patsy, almost spitting a mouthful of wine over Janice's carefully arranged canapés.

'That's amazing!' squealed Janice and Kirsty said, 'Well done!'

'Do you realise how big this is? She wouldn't be doing

that if she didn't think you were good, Clare,' went on Patsy, clearly dumbfounded by Clare's apparently laid-back attitude to this development. 'You do know that, don't you?'

Clare smiled contentedly and sliced half a pepper into lengthwise strips.

'This is really important, Clare,' said Patsy. 'It could be the kick-start your career needs.'

'Well, let's see what happens, shall we? If success is meant for me, it won't go past me.'

Kirsty eyed Clare curiously. 'You mean like serendipity?'

'That's right. I'm delighted to be asked to contribute of course, don't get me wrong,' said Clare, piercing Patsy with her intense stare, the knife frozen in mid-air. 'And I'd be thrilled if it led to exhibitions and commissions. But if it doesn't, there'll be other opportunities.'

'You sound a lot more relaxed about your career,' observed Kirsty.

'I guess I am,' said Clare, bringing the knife down onto a hard carrot. 'And yet, I'm just as productive as when I was worrying about it all the time. In fact, my recent pictures are better than the ones I did for Patsy's exhibition.'

'Well, you know what they say,' said Janice and everyone looked at her. 'You can't force creativity.'

'And yet without discipline, creativity can be squandered,' said Clare and everyone nodded. 'Like everything in life, it's about getting the balance right.'

'And have you?' said Patsy.

'I think so. It's a real juggling act most days, but Liam's getting better. He's helping around the house more.'

'And how are things between you and Liam?' said Janice. 'Are you still going for counselling?'

'Oh, yes, it's helped enormously. We're much happier now, both of us. I'm not saying it's perfect, but we're getting there.

We book a babysitter and go out – just the two of us – twice a month. And Izzy's a lot better than she was. The malice towards me has gone. We're quite good friends now and it's absolutely lovely.'

Janice observed, 'Maybe with less tension in the house between you and Liam, Izzy feels more secure. That might partly account for her improved behaviour.'

'Mmm,' said Clare. 'I think you might be right.'

There was a short silence and Patsy said, 'Well, things are looking up in the Devlin household too.' She set her glass down on the smooth granite of the island unit and helped herself to a sliver of crumbed ham. Kirsty smacked her hand playfully and they both laughed.

'How do you mean?' said Kirsty.

'The café and gallery did really well over Christmas. Far better than we'd thought. We're never going to get rich from it, but it's bringing in enough to live on.'

'And is Martin enjoying it?' asked Clare, peeling a carrot with rapid flicks of the peeler.

'He absolutely loves it. Honestly. Ask him yourself. He's like a new man. He loves working with people and all the old ladies that come in just adore him.'

'Your Martin's lovely,' said Kirsty, rolling a slice of ham up into a tube. 'He's so sweet-natured.'

Patsy nodded, gracefully accepting the compliment on behalf of her big, gentle husband. 'It was his idea to introduce the breakfast menu, you know. It means we're busy all day, from when the doors open until we close at night. And when people come in for lunch, or whatever, they often buy a small gift or one of those handmade cards we introduced.'

'Doesn't Martin miss the bank?' asked Clare.

Patsy threw her head back and chuckled. 'Like a hole in the head. He's happier now than I've seen him in a long time. And I'm really proud of him. He's not afraid of rolling his sleeves up and getting stuck in.'

'So has he given up looking for another job in banking?' persisted Clare.

Patsy paused and adopted a thoughtful expression. 'Yes. Even if we had the choice, we wouldn't go back to the way we were living. Sure, we don't have as much money as we used to but there are more important things in life than money, aren't there?'

The others were silent then. Janice wondered how much of this statement was Patsy putting on a brave face. And yet there was an undeniable, essential truthfulness in her words too.

They worked companionably, Patsy chatting on, entertaining them with indiscreet, funny stories about her customers at the gallery. Janice smiled. It was good to see Patsy back to her old self – upbeat and cheerful – though she knew that her friend would always carry within her a deep and hidden well of sorrow for Laura and her unborn child.

Janice had always enjoyed a comfortable life with Keith, but the things that made a life happy were beyond price – love, inner contentment, a sense of contribution and personal fulfilment. So too were the things that made her unhappy and which she could not change – pain, sorrow, grief for her lost innocence and a close relationship with her son. Pete had come home, mellowed a little, for the holidays and Christmas had passed off tolerably enough, but the barrier that prevented true intimacy between them would be for ever impenetrable.

When there was a lull in the conversation, Janice said, 'Patsy, I have something for you.' She wiped her hands on a towel and went over to a drawer and pulled out a fat, plain white business envelope.

'I thought we weren't giving each other gifts this year,' said Patsy, eyeing the envelope suspiciously.

'Well, it's not a gift exactly. In fact, it cost me nothing at all. Here. Take it.'

Patsy took the envelope, pulled back the flap and stared at the thick wad of banknotes inside.

Janice beamed. 'There's one thousand pounds in there. Exactly.'

'I don't understand,' said Patsy, her face falling. 'What is it?'

'It's your deposit. For the holiday.'

Patsy set the envelope down on the counter and pushed it away. 'I can't accept that, Janice. You know I can't. It's very generous but . . .'

'You don't understand, Patsy. It's not my money. It's yours. I got it from McCurdy Dobbin, the travel agents. They agreed to return your deposit.'

Patsy opened her mouth, and formed her lips into a shape. No sound came out. She re-shaped them and said, at last, 'But how?'

'Let's just say I pulled a few strings. There's no point having a well-connected husband if you can't do that now and again, is there? Keith and Jimmy McCurdy are both in the Rotary. I went to see Jimmy first – in fact I went to see him on the day of the café opening – and explained the situation. And, after a little bit of gentle persuasion from Keith, Jimmy agreed to refund the deposit in full.'

'Oh, Janice,' cried Patsy, holding the envelope to her breast. 'I can't believe you did that for me.'

'It was the least I could do,' said Janice quietly. Her heart skipped with happiness – the joy in helping her friend was far greater than any pleasure money could buy. 'I thought you might be able to have that second honeymoon after all. Maybe not to Botswana but . . .'

'That's exactly what we'll do,' said Patsy and she opened the envelope and looked at the money again as though she had not quite believed her eyes first time round. 'We'll have a lovely romantic break somewhere, just the two of us. Do you know, neither of us have ever done the Ring of Kerry. Isn't that awful? Maybe we'll go there.'

'I have something else to tell you,' interrupted Janice, before the conversation drifted too far away.

'What's that?' said Clare, arranging the cut-up vegetables artistically on a plate.

'I've been accepted to do a one-year foundation degree course in counselling at the University of Ulster.' Pleased with herself and finding she was suddenly, inexplicably shy, Janice blushed.

'Counselling!' exclaimed Kirsty, looking at Clare in astonishment.

'But why counselling?' said a perplexed Clare. 'Is it something you've always wanted to do?'

'Not exactly.' Janice wiped her hands on a cloth. She glanced at Patsy and said, 'I think it's something I might be good at. I'd like to help people. And I've far too much time on my hands these days,' she added briskly. 'I might as well do something useful with it.'

'Good for you,' said Patsy, still clutching the envelope to her breast.

'I think that's absolutely wonderful,' said Kirsty quietly. 'I really do.'

'It's going to be tough going back to studying at my age. But I always regretted not finishing my degree.' Janice shifted her gaze away from her friends and fussed with a plate of mini vol-au-vents. 'I've always felt a little . . . inferior in the company of educated people.'

'Well, this'll change all that!' said Patsy brightly.

'It's the most exciting thing I've done in years,' said Janice. 'And the most scary.'

But she wasn't daunted by the fear – she understood now that fear was something to be tackled, overcome, faced up to. Because once you broke through the fear, there were multiple rewards to be reaped, not least of which was self-confidence. She would never again let fear hold her back in life. She had learned so much from her experiences; she felt she had so much wisdom to share. It would be a sin to let it go to waste.

'You'll be absolutely fine,' said Clare, in that serious way of hers. 'I'm sure of it.'

'Thanks,' said Janice, buoyed by the vote of confidence. 'And meantime I'm going to train as a Samaritan.'

'You mean on the helpline?' said Kirsty, incredulously.

'That's right.'

Patsy, who already knew of this development, let the others do the talking.

'That's amazing,' said Kirsty. 'They do an awful lot of good.'

'They save lives,' said Janice simply.

A short, reverent pause followed this comment and then Janice said, 'It's quite a big commitment. You have to do a three-to-four hour weekly shift and one overnight stint a month.'

'And what does Keith think about it?' asked Kirsty, aligning the last slice of roast beef on the plate and going over to the sink to wash her hands.

'He's amazingly supportive. You know Keith,' Janice said and half-laughed. 'So long as I'm happy, he's happy.'

'You're a lucky woman, Janice,' said Patsy with feeling.

'I know.'

Clare nodded. 'But why the Samaritans? Why not volunteer

in the local Oxfam shop? Or help with the Thursday lunch club for the elderly at the church?'

Janice shrugged again. 'I could do, I suppose. If truth be told, there's need everywhere you look. But I'm drawn to the idea of helping people on a one-to-one basis. People in really desperate situations that have no-one to turn to.' She fixed her gaze on Patsy. 'If I can make a difference to just one person's life – if I can save someone from . . . from a terrible situation, it'll be worthwhile.'

'Well, I think it's absolutely wonderful,' interrupted Patsy.

'Now, you mustn't tell anyone about this, all of you. I'm not really supposed to tell anyone in my local community but I know you can keep a secret.' Janice waited for the murmurs of assent to die down and then she added, 'I'm going to be doing some fundraising for them though, and I'll be expecting you all to dig deep!'

The tension was broken and Janice, riding on the ripple of gentle laughter, steered the conversation into happier waters. 'What's the latest on you and Chris?' she said to Kirsty and, finding her mouth parched, took a drink of wine.

Kirsty finished wiping her hands on a towel, threw it on the counter and said, 'I thought you'd never ask.'

She beamed happily at them each in turn and Janice, the suspense killing her, let out an exasperated sigh and said, 'Well, go on. Tell us.'

Kirsty, still beaming like someone demented, said, 'Chris asked me to marry him.'

'He has not?' gasped Clare, stunned.

Kirsty nodded girlishly. 'He has. And I've accepted. We're getting married at February half term in the registrar's office on Victoria Road.'

'Oh, my God!' cried Patsy and she ran over to Kirsty and embraced her. Janice followed suit and Clare, the least demonstrative, even managed a reserved sort of hug and a peck on the cheek for her friend.

'Congratulations!' cried Clare.

'Oh, I love a wedding,' said Patsy, sniffing back tears. She fumbled for a hankie in her handbag, which lay discarded on one of the kitchen chairs.

Kirsty laughed heartily, her eyes sparkling with happiness. 'It's going to be quite a low-key affair but I couldn't do it without you three! And Liam, Keith and Martin are all invited too.'

'Great!' said Patsy. 'Now tell us what we really want to know – what are you going to wear?'

'I don't know! I haven't had time to think about that.'

Patsy frowned and exchanged a concerned look with Janice.

'You're going to have to buy a wedding dress,' said Patsy.

Kirsty screwed up her face. 'I don't know if I want to wear a dress. I might have a suit that'll do.'

'We'll have to take her shopping,' said Janice with finality, rolling her eyes at Patsy and Clare. 'Or God knows what she'll end up wearing. Some old mothballed creation from the back of the wardrobe, no doubt, that hasn't seen the light of day in years.'

Kirsty put her hand on her hip, and said in mock indignation, 'I'll have you know I don't have any moths in my wardrobe.'

'I didn't say you had,' said Janice, and she found herself laughing so hard her stomach ached.

'Alright. Stop taking the piss,' smiled Kirsty. 'You can take me shopping and help me pick an outfit.'

'When?' said Clare with a grin.

'How about next Saturday?' said Kirsty, sobering. 'Dorothy and Harry would take the boys. And if Liam's playing golf,

Clare, just drop Josh and Rachel off there too. The boys would love to see them. And Dorothy and Harry wouldn't mind. You know that.'

It occurred to Janice then just how much Kirsty was giving up in following Chris to Dubai. She hoped her friend hadn't underestimated how much she relied on the support network around her. Life would be tough in a foreign land, even with Chris to help. And yet, when she looked at her glowing face, happiness radiating from her like an aura, and when she thought of how honourable Chris was, she knew she had no reason to worry for her.

'Is Chris coming over again before the wedding?' said Janice.

'No, that's him until the weekend before. Oh God, I can't wait to see him!' Kirsty made no attempt to hide her sheer joy at the mention of his name. 'After the wedding we're going to have lunch at The Marine,' she said, referring to the smartest local hotel. 'And Chris and I are going down to the Slieve Donard in Newcastle for a couple of nights for our honeymoon. Chris can't afford to take more than a week off work. So as soon as we come back to Ballyfergus, he'll fly out to Dubai. And then in April, all being well, we'll join him.'

The weight of this statement sunk in and the rest of them were suddenly silent and glum-faced. 'We'll miss you terribly,' said Janice.

Kirsty sighed. 'I know. I'll miss you too. But I'll be home in the summer and other holidays too and it'll only be for a couple of years.' She paused then and her eyes were teary. 'Promise you won't forget me?'

'You know we won't,' said Clare. She stretched out her hand and touched Kirsty on the knee. 'Sure we won't, girls?' she said, without taking her eyes off her friend. The others voiced their agreement and Janice forced a smile.

'Is your dad going to give you away?' asked Clare brightly, removing her hand and trying, Janice guessed, to generate an upbeat mood.

The corners of Kirsty's mouth turned up. 'Yes. And I'm going to have three bridesmaids.'

'Chris's granddaughters?' said Janice. 'I thought you said there were only two of them.'

Kirsty's smile was secretive. 'No, they're going to be flower-girls. And I won't be having bridesmaids exactly.' She paused and looked at each of them in turn. 'More like Matrons of Honour.'

Janice caught her breath with sudden understanding and looked at the others. Clare was smiling and realisation spread across Patsy's features like sunlight from behind a cloud. 'You don't mean . . . us?'

Kirsty clapped her hands and rocked with laughter, her rich red hair around her face like a veil. She was crying now, silvery streaks running down her cheeks.

'Of course I mean you! Who else in the world would I have than my three best friends?'

They clinked glasses, each woman beaming with joy while the rain pelted the windows and the wind whistled round the chimneys of the old house. It was the start of a new chapter for them all. And whatever storms this new year might bring, they were ready for them – safe and secure in a friendship that had been tested, and proven as enduring as time itself.

Reading Group Guide for
The Art of Friendship

1. How does the theme of redemption function within the book?

2. Compare and contrast the various ways that abortion is addressed within the novel.

3. Motherhood is a prevalent issue throughout the novel. How do the women's various approaches to motherhood impact our empathy for them?

4. How important are the men throughout the book? Does this portrayal impact the importance of fatherhood?

5. What significance is there in the fact that two of the lead characters end up with significantly older men?

6. Did Janice make the right decision in not telling her son who fathered him? Would Pete have benefited from the opportunity to understand his mother's unnatural behaviour towards him?

7. The women in the novel are the best of friends, and yet they keep important secrets from each other. What role do secrets play within the novel? Are they a necessary part of every friendship?

8. How does Pete's reaction to Laura's pregnancy characterise him? Is he destined to be a representation of Janice's worst fears?

9. Consider the stories of the four women. Who is the most relatable and sympathetic of the four?

10. The novel showcases two very different ways of raising children. Janice and Keith are strict, whereas Patsy and Martin are more lenient. However, both of their children get into trouble. Consider what this comparison suggests about a parent's role.

11. What role do the women's friendships play in their lives? How important are these friendships?

Win a Luxury Food and Wine Gift Box with

LEWIS & COOPER

• PURVEYORS OF FINE FOOD AND WINE SINCE 1899 •

Lewis & Cooper – award-winning purveyors of fine food and wine since 1899 – is offering *The Art of Friendship* by Erin Kaye readers a chance to win one of three delicious Chairman's Choice food and wine gift boxes (worth £115!) containing some of their favourite food and wine treats.

The gift box is specially filled with L&C Rouge and Blanc wine, single malt whisky, chocolate truffles, Mrs Bell's Blue cheese and a selection of special nibbles and savouries. It's great for sharing with (or hiding from) your friends! There are even rashers of Yorkshire dry-cured bacon, complemented by Hot and Nutty Chairman's sauce – perfect for a late night snack.

Take a look at www.lewisandcooper.co.uk/friendship for a complete list of sumptuous contents, and details of their full range of hampers.

To enter this free prize draw, simply visit www.harpercollins.co.uk/avon and answer the question below. The closing date for this competition is May 31st May 2010.

In *The Art of Friendship*, what is the name of the village where the drama takes place?

A) Ballyfergus
B) Cork
C) Dublin

Lewis & Cooper is also offering all readers 7.5% off any telephone shopping order over £50 (excluding special offers) from February 1st – March 30th 2010. Why not create your own gourmet gift hamper packed with delicious foods and wines you'd be hard pushed to find in most high street stores. Alternatively, stock up on some fine foodie treats for a great night in.

To claim you're *The Art of Friendship* discount, please order through the **freephone** line 0808 108 0309 quote 'Art Of Friendship 2010'.

Competition Terms and Conditions:

1. This competition is promoted by HarperCollins Publishers, 77-85 Fulham Palace Road, London, W6 8JB ("HarperCollins").
2. This promotion is open to all UK residents aged 18 years or over except employees of HarperCollins, and Lewis & Cooper (or their parent, subsidiaries or any affiliated companies) and their immediate families, who are not allowed to enter the competition.
3. No purchase necessary. Only one entry per household. To enter, go to www.harpercollins.co.uk/avon and enter your details. Responsibility cannot be taken for lost entries. Proof of sending is not proof of receipt.
4. All entries must be received by midday on 31st May 2010. No entries received after this date will be valid.
5. The prize is a Chairman's Choice food and wine gift box for each winner.
6. The prize is non-refundable, non-transferable and subject to availability. No guarantee is given as to the quality of the prize.
7. No cash or prize alternatives are available.

HarperCollins Publishers reserve their reasonable discretion to substitute any prize with a prize of equal or greater value.

8. Winners of the competition will be drawn at random from all correct competition entries by an independent adjudicator and notified by no later than 1st July 2010 by telephone.
9. Any application containing incorrect, false or unreadable information will be rejected. Any applications made on behalf of or for another person or multiple entries will not be included in the competition.
10. HarperCollins decision as to who has won the competition shall be final.
11. To obtain the name of the prize winner after the closing date, please write to AVON/The Art of Friendship, HarperCollins Publishers, 77–85 Fulham Palace Road, Hammersmith, London, W6 8JB.
12. Entry instructions are deemed to form part of the Terms and Conditions for this competition.
13. By entering the competition you are agreeing to accept these Terms and Conditions. Any breach of these Terms and Conditions by you will mean that your entry will not be valid, and you will not be allowed to enter this competition.
14. By entering, you are agreeing that if you win your name and image may be used for the purpose of announcing the winner in any related publicity with AVON, without additional payment or permission.
15. Any personal information you give us will be used solely for this competition and will not be passed on to any other parties without your agreement. HarperCollins' privacy policy can be found at:

http://www.harpercollins.co.uk/legal/Pages/privacy-policy.aspx

16. Under no circumstances will the promoter be liable for any loss, damages, costs and expenses arising from or in any way connected with any errors, defects, interruptions, malfunctions or delays in the promotion of the prize.
17. HarperCollins will not be responsible unless required by law, for any loss, changes, costs or expenses, which may arise in connection with this competition and HarperCollins can cancel or alter the competition at any stage.
18. Any dispute relating to the competition shall be governed by the laws of England and Wales and will be subject to the exclusive jurisdiction of the English courts.

<u>7.5% Discount Terms and Conditions:</u>

1. You must spend over £50 to be applicable for the 7.5% discount.
2. To claim the discount, you must order by telephone on 0808 108 0309, quoting 'The Art Of Friendship 2010'.
3. This discount is applicable from February 1st – March 30th 2010.
4. The discount is only available for UK mainland deliveries.